Honeytrap

Aster Glenn Gray

Copyright © 2020 Aster Glenn Gray

All rights reserved.

ISBN: 9798662662612

Honeytrap

Part One
1959

CHAPTER 1

"It's natural," Mr. Gilman said – "Well, not *natural*, exactly. But certainly not unusual for two young men thrown constantly into one another's company, facing peril together, perhaps saving each other's lives, to become, hmm. Attached to each other."

Mr. Gilman stood in front of his office window, gazing at a golden tree shedding its leaves on the wide lawn. From the corner of his eye, he watched the young man who sat on the other side of his desk: Special Agent Daniel Hawthorne, dark-haired and handsome and, at this moment, possessed of a perfect poker face.

"I was in England during the war," Mr. Gilman mused, "and this sort of David and Jonathan friendship is very common there. It can be a beautiful thing, such a friendship, as long as it doesn't begin to shade into something... well, a little *Brideshead Revisited*, if you know what I mean."

"I'm afraid I don't, sir," Hawthorne said mildly.

Mr. Gilman raised his eyebrows. Hawthorne was the literary type.

Still, it was good of him to pretend he didn't understand the allusion. It would be far easier to sweep this all under the rug if

Hawthorne kept up his end by denying everything.

"I mean," Mr. Gilman said, "that an ordinary young man, like yourself, with powerful, ah, passions, which normally he channels toward young women – your file suggests you've got a bit of a reputation in that regard…"

Hawthorne's eyes flickered toward the file on Mr. Gilman's desk.

"Well, when a young man like that finds that his work keeps him on the road so constantly that it's impossible to meet nice girls, and throws him instead into the companionship of another man for months on end…"

Hawthorne's face took on an expression of puzzled innocence.

Mr. Gilman coughed. "Well," he said. "Circumstances have made it necessary to move both you and Agent Preston to new assignments."

He feared an outburst, but Hawthorne said nothing for a long moment. At last he replied, "I'll go where the Bureau needs me."

"Good man," Mr. Gilman said. He gazed out at the golden tree, his hands in his pockets. Then he returned to sit in the leather chair behind the desk. "Have you been following the coverage of Mr. Khrushchev's visit to America?"

"I might've seen it mentioned in the newspapers," Hawthorne allowed.

"The reporters have been enjoying themselves, haven't they? It isn't every day a Soviet Premier visits the United States. But one thing they missed," Mr. Gilman said, "is that someone attempted to assassinate Mr. Khrushchev in Iowa."

"Sir?"

Mr. Gilman removed a folder from his top drawer. "On September 23rd, Chairman Khrushchev passed through Iowa on a train. On the way, the train paused for a couple of whistle-stops, so Chairman Khrushchev could shake hands and kiss babies, rather like an American presidential candidate. Shortly after one of these whistle-stops, in the town of Honeygold, county seat of Honeygold County, some of the guards heard a thump against the side of the train. When they examined the train at the next stop, they found a bullet embedded in the siding."

Mr. Gilman flipped open the folder to show a photograph of the damage. As Hawthorne leaned forward to look at it, Mr.

Gilman continued, "Naturally, we immediately dispatched agents to the place where they heard the original thump. The shooter was long gone, but they found what they believe to be the shooter's blind."

Mr. Gilman flipped to the next photograph: a small trampled area in the tall grass, littered with cigarette butts. Next, a close-up photograph showing the faint outline of two boot prints in the dirt. "Marlboro cigarettes," he said. "Size 14 men's boots. Unfortunately the ground was too hard to get a clearer impression of the tread. The agents followed the trail as best they could, but it ended in a nearby creek bed."

"The shooter knew the area, then."

"Most likely." Mr. Gilman moved to the next picture: a bullet casing. "They found this among the cigarette butts. From a Mauser pistol – World War II era, they say. Probably someone's war trophy."

"A pistol?" Hawthorne said. "For a long-range shot?"

"An odd choice for an assassination attempt, isn't it? Frankly," Mr. Gilman said, "I'm inclined to think it was a farmboy amusing himself by taking a few potshots, never dreaming that the train carried such an important personage, but…" He shrugged. "Naturally the Soviets have been in a tizzy. And, unfortunately, there's one more piece of evidence that suggests it could have been planned. When our shooter ran out of cigarettes, he rolled his own cigarette using a page torn from a magazine."

He flipped to the next photograph: a close-up of a ragged square of paper with a burnt edge, the name of the magazine in the lower corner.

"*The Good Shepherd*," Hawthorne read.

"We've looked into it, of course. A one-man crackpot operation in Indiana. Mr. Thomas Salt sends mimeographed copies of his rants to his subscribers every other month. America has wandered from its roots as an agrarian nation, industrialization will destroy us all, et cetera. He doesn't actually say that a spot of thermonuclear war would do us all some good, but it's certainly implied."

"And what better way to start a thermonuclear war than assassinating the leader of the Soviet Union?" Hawthorne said. "Where was Thomas Salt on September 23?"

"Our agents have ascertained that he was at a church meeting all day," Mr. Gilman said. "They also managed to persuade him to part with a list of his subscribers. Normally they would have continued the investigation from there, but unfortunately..."

He paused long enough that Hawthorne prompted him. "Unfortunately, sir?"

"The Soviets threw a fit. Well, they had been throwing a fit all along, of course: they wanted to investigate themselves, which naturally we had to refuse, and... Well, discussions deteriorated to the point where they accused us of using the excuse of an investigation to try to cover something up. As if we couldn't have done a perfectly competent job assassinating Mr. Khrushchev if we had a mind to."

"Naturally," Hawthorne said wryly.

"Well. During their talks at Camp David, Mr. Khrushchev – who seems to be quite taken with the idea of Soviet-American friendship at the moment – suggested to President Eisenhower that we might cooperate to investigate the problem. A Soviet agent and an American agent might, as it were, work together."

"Sir?" Hawthorne sounded like a child who had expected coal in his Christmas stocking and found a present instead.

Mr. Gilman smiled. "I expected the lower-level Soviet bureaucrats to drag their feet for months. But Khrushchev must have given them a kick in the pants, because they've coughed up an agent." Mr. Gilman slid a slim dossier across the desk. "Lieutenant Gennady Ilyich Matskevich. Supposedly he's an officer in the Soviet military, but between you and me and the gatepost it's almost certain he's KGB."

Hawthorne flipped the dossier open. "Not a lot of information."

"He only arrived in the United States two months ago. I suspect they're tossing him to us as a sacrificial lamb because he's their most junior agent. Of course they may be taking the opportunity to send us a drunkard or an idiot. A problem agent they want to get off their hands." Mr. Gilman paused, just for a moment, and then went on, "Naturally I thought of you. As I recall, you speak a little Russian."

"A very little. When I was a kid we lived next door to some White Russian émigrés. They used to babysit my sister and me, and we picked up some of the lingo. But of course that was a long time ago."

"It's more important to us that you studied it quite off the record," Mr. Gilman said. "The KGB may not be aware that you have any grasp of the language at all. Better not let Lieutenant Matskevich know either. And, frankly, while that may prove useful, it's more important to me that you've got a reputation for working well with difficult agents. I want you to befriend Lieutenant Matskevich. Show him that Americans aren't the bogeymen that *Pravda* makes us out to be."

"Yes, sir."

"Show him America in the best possible light. No trips to the slums, no forays below the Mason-Dixon line. I don't want to give him the opportunity to gather propaganda."

Hawthorne raised his eyebrows. "By propaganda you mean true reports about race relations in the south?"

Mr. Gilman looked at him.

Hawthorne subsided. "Sir."

"Of course," Mr. Gilman said, "it's likely to be a challenge. The last thing we want is for news of the assassination attempt to leak out, so you can't let anyone know that's what you're investigating: you'll need some sort of cover. And then, of course, the Russians can be difficult to work with. Unfriendly, obstructive, all business. Enormous prudes, too."

He paused, just for a moment, watching Hawthorne from the corner of his eye. A muscle jumped in Hawthorne's cheek.

Yes. For all that pretense of innocence, he knew very well what this was all about.

"I suggest that you take this Gennady Ilyich Matskevich to a strip club to get acquainted," Mr. Gilman suggested with a smile. "I imagine the sight of all those beautiful American girls would do you both a lot of good."

CHAPTER 2

Gennady Ilyich Matskevich indicated the mini golf course with a sweep of his mini golf club. "This is what Americans do for fun?"

"Mini golf," Daniel informed him solemnly, "is *thrilling*."

He was hoping to startle a grin out of Matskevich, but Matskevich maintained his deadpan. "More thrilling than last a corn maze?"

"At least up there with a drive-in movie theater," Daniel told him. Matskevich's mouth twitched infinitesimally, and Daniel added, with a sigh, "It's too bad all the drive-ins are closed for the season. There's nothing like watching a movie through a bug-flecked windshield while listening to a tinny little speaker that's out of sync with the screen."

"Hollywood movies are all so much alike," Matskevich returned, "they are probably more enjoyable when you can't hear the dialogues, anyway."

Daniel attempted to fake indignation, but a grin broke through. He cleared his throat and suggested, in his most patronizing tone, "If mini golf's too hard for you, we can go to a bar instead."

Matskevich shook his head. "There are bars everywhere, all around the world. When we colonize the moon, a bar is the first thing we will set up. Whereas this minigolf..." Matskevich spread his arms. "This is really American." A pause. Daniel folded his arms, waiting for the punchline, and Matskevich did not disappoint. "Boring and flat."

"There's a windmill," Daniel protested. "How can you possibly call that boring?"

"Is this what you do for fun here? Watch the blades of a windmill turn round and round? In Moscow," Matskevich said, "we have the Bolshoi."

"Mmm. Where you watch dancers turn round and round?" Daniel scoffed.

Matskevich lifted his chin. "At least the windmill," he said, "is probably less predictable than your Hollywood movies."

"Hey now," protested Daniel. He lifted his golf club as if it were a sword. "How dare you cast aspersions on the honor of Hollywood?"

He jabbed the golf club at Matskevich like a fencing foil. Matskevich parried the blow and jabbed at Daniel, forcing him backward. Daniel attempted a sweeping slash. The weight of the golf club head pulled him off balance, and as he stumbled, Matskevich scoffed, "Even an American can't believe Hollywood has *honor*."

Daniel forfeited the duel by laughing too hard to continue. "At least give mini golf a try," he urged.

"Of course," Matskevich said. "We have already paid to play this game, so we should not waste it. But I will not enjoy it."

He approached the first hole with a look of intense concentration, like a cat stalking a sunbeam, and Daniel suppressed a grin. He figured that Matskevich had orders a mirror image to his own: if Daniel was supposed to show America in the best possible light, Matskevich doubtless was supposed to appear unimpressed by everything.

Daniel had been nervous about this assignment. Oh, immensely relieved to get it, of course. He'd walked into Mr. Gilman's office fully expecting to be fired, so getting any second chance at all was a stunning piece of luck, and a second chance that gave him the opportunity to work with a real live Soviet agent…

Daniel had been fascinated by the Soviet Union ever since he was a child, listening to the Polyakovs' bloodcurdling stories about escaping Leningrad by the skin of their teeth in the early days of the Revolution. Not that they called their lost city Leningrad. "How dare *that man* stain our darling Piter with his name!"

Piter: short for St. Petersburg.

And here finally was a chance to learn more about the Soviet Union: to get to know a Soviet agent, see if the brainwashing and dictatorship had squashed all the individuality right out of him or if there was still a real person under there, with thoughts and opinions and maybe even a sense of humor...

Well. The sense of humor, at least, definitely existed.

But relieved and thrilled as Daniel had been, he had also felt very nervous. As Mr. Gilman had pointed out with his exquisite Phillips Exeter tact, this was the kind of assignment you gave a problem agent. A drunk, an idiot. A Communist so doctrinaire that he could be counted on to loathe his American partner on principle.

An FBI agent stupid enough to sleep with his partner.

Not that Daniel and Paul been sleeping together anymore by the time that Mr. Gilman summoned Daniel to his office. That had ended a month before, after yet another argument about yet another waitress. Maybe Daniel really *had* been flirting with that one, but only because Paul would think Daniel was flirting whether he flirted or not, and Daniel figured he might as well be hung for a sheep as a lamb.

"None of this is really real to you," Paul had said. He leaned across the booth as he spoke, his voice barely more than a whisper, but so intense that it felt like a shout. "You're fucking around with me because it's convenient."

"*Convenient*," Daniel choked. *Convenient* was jerking off in the shower, hiring a prostitute, maybe – if you wanted to stretch it – jerking off with a frat brother while dead drunk. It was not a six-month-long relationship that could get him fired, ruin his reputation, estrange him from his family, and lose him every friend he ever had.

"Yes, convenient!" Paul snapped. "You don't know a damn thing about the manly love of comrades. You're going to go back home and marry a nice girl and leave me flat. You can't even stop ogling waitresses."

Christ.

Even if Matskevich had been a drunken fool, it would have

been a relief to have a new partner.

And he wasn't a drunk or an idiot – and he wasn't good-looking, which was a different kind of relief. Matskevich was two or three inches shorter than Daniel (no giant himself at 5'10"), with light brown hair and a round Slavic face: high cheekbones, heavy eyebrows. Dark gray eyes, quick and observant.

Not that it would've mattered if he'd looked like Marlon Brando in *A Streetcar Named Desire*. Daniel was done with men, after the debacle with Paul. But still, this made it easier.

"Hawthorne?" Matskevich's Russian accent, light though it was, mangled Daniel's last name. "Your turn."

"Oh, right." Daniel hurriedly moved to put his golf ball on the tee. "You can call me Daniel, if you want."

Matskevich tipped his head to the side. "No," he said. "I think I should not."

"Oh." Daniel was surprised; almost hurt. But then he shrugged. "Last names are more professional, I guess." He positioned the golf ball and gave it a putt. "We'll hit Des Moines tomorrow. We'll finally be able to start investigating the case."

***

The agent in charge of the Des Moines field office was a man named Mackenzie or MacDonald or something like that, but Daniel had never heard him called by his full name: he was always Mack.

Mack eyed Daniel and Matskevich wearily when they arrived. If Daniel hadn't met him before, he might have thought Mack was annoyed that they had arrived only a few minutes before the office closed up, but in fact Mack always looked tired. The deep pouches under his eyes gave him a certain resemblance to a bulldog.

"Oh, it's *you*," Mack said. "Shut the door." Daniel shut the office door behind them, and Mack fell back in his desk chair and rubbed his hands over his stubbly face. "I can't believe Gilman saddled me with a KGB agent."

"I am not a KGB agent," Matskevich said.

Mack gave him a long look. He let out a rattling smoker's cough, then stabbed a finger at Daniel. "Listen, Hawthorne. It's going to be a big fucking international incident if anything happens to that guy, so you treat him like he's the president and you're the whole goddamn Secret Service, all right? I don't want to deal with the press, and I especially don't want to deal with the paperwork."

"Yes, sir," Daniel said.

Mack sighed and rolled out a drawer. He slapped a file down on the desk. "Here's what I got for you."

Daniel flipped it open. "A missing Mauser!"

Mack drank the last two inches of coffee from a mug on his desk, and winced. "I hope to God it doesn't come to anything."

"What? Oh..." Daniel had continued reading. "Stolen from the office of State Congressman James Abbott." He sat back in his chair. "Well, that's... fun. Who is he?"

"Commie-baiter," Mack said. "Always in the papers. Decorated World War II veteran." He removed a newspaper clipping from his desk and shoved it to them. "I did a little digging. He was part of the delegation that met Khrushchev at Garst's farm on the day of the shooting, so he can't be the shooter, thank God. Just imagine the press."

"He didn't have the gun to shoot with, anyway," Daniel pointed out. "It was stolen..."

Matskevich was already checking the date. "In April. Before the Chairman's visit was announced."

"You mean the theft might be entirely unconnected?" Mack sounded like he had been given a Christmas present.

"Might be. We'd better check it out, anyway."

"*You'd* better check it out," Mack corrected Daniel. "I'm sure as shit not sending a Russian spy to a congressman's office, even if he is only a state congressman." He attempted another drink from his coffee mug, and frowned at finding it empty. "Guess who visited the Congressman's office the day of the theft?"

Daniel scanned the police report till he found the list. "The entire state of Iowa," he cracked.

Mack gave him a withering look. "Funny guy."

"All of his staffers," Daniel said. "His wife and kids. A delegation of constituents from... Where's Appaloosa?"

"Wrong side of the state," Mack said.

"People have cars, Mack."

Mack grunted.

"Plenty of fellow state congressman... Any anticommunists?" Daniel said.

"All of them. This is Iowa, kid." Mack ran a hand over his balding head, and added, "Most of them were at Garst's farm, too."

"Fine. There was a class field trip from a local elementary school. A Boy Scout troupe..."

Daniel looked up, and found Matskevich looking over at him. "There is a Boy Scout camp near Honeygold," Matskevich said. "Camp Dubois."

(The very first night they had set out on the road, they had spread a topo map of Honeygold County on the floor of the motel room and spent some time studying it.

"Camp Dubois would've been a good place to stash a getaway car," Daniel had commented, tapping his finger on the spot on the map. "A Boy Scout camp would've been closed for the season in September."

"Closed? Hard to get into?"

"No, probably just a wooden barrier on the gate. Easy to move aside.")

"You can't harass a whole troupe of Boy Scouts just because there's a Boy Scout camp in Honeygold County," Mack said.

"No, of course not," Daniel agreed. "But we might just drop by to have a chat with... who wrote this police report? Daniel Jones," he said, answering his own question, and grinned. He always tried to find a commonality with anyone he needed to interview: that made it easier to get chummy, make them want to talk. The shared first name was an easy in. "We'll drop by the police station and have a chat with him."

"So he can tell you in person that the Iowa PD doesn't have any leads on the theft?" Mack asked.

"Sometimes people have a feeling," Daniel said. "Maybe not enough evidence to put into the official report. But that's something, anyway."

Mack shrugged, as if to say, *Suit yourself*. He looked at them both for a long moment, and suddenly smiled at Matskevich. It made his worn hangdog face oddly beautiful. "My unit met up with some Soviets at the end of the war," Mack said. "Nice fellas. 'Course, we didn't have a single word in common, but we just handed cigarettes and pictures of pin-up girls back and forth, and everyone got along swell. Always thought it was too bad our two countries couldn't remain on good terms after the war."

Matskevich looked startled. "Yes, sir."

"Doubt it'll last long now," Mack said. "But I hope you have a good time while you're here."

***

"I wish I could help you." Officer Daniel Jones was a pudgy young man, and his round moon face looked genuinely distressed. "But stolen property – if you don't find it fast, it's usually gone. Unless it's something rare and valuable. Then sometimes it shows up years after on an auction block. Just last month, Daniel Green..."

"Another Daniel!" Daniel joked. "Is he here? We'd have a quorum."

"Naw. He's retired now, practically. But last month he was at an estate sale, and he recognized some pearls that went missing about thirty-five years ago – Roaring Twenties, those big long necklaces? – well, he found them at the sale, and that got him looking at the other jewelry, and it turned out that little old lady who died must've been the biggest klepto west of the Mississippi, because she had three whole jewelry boxes of stolen property."

"Gosh!" Daniel said, heartily admiring.

Officer Jones grinned, as pleased as if it were his own case Daniel had admired. "But we never got any leads on the Mauser. And believe me, we tried. Congressman Abbott's a personal friend of the Chief's."

"And there's no way to narrow down who might have taken it? Who had access to the key, or anything like that?"

Officer Jones shook his head. "He had it in a display case, you know, not locked or anything. Chief chewed him out for that, but of course it was too late to do anything."

Matskevich looked up from the wanted posters on the wall. He had obligingly effaced himself for most of the interview, but now he said, "Is this normal? An unlocked gun in a government office?"

Officer Jones looked abashed. "Well, it wasn't loaded or anything," he protested. He rubbed the back of his neck, and added semi-belligerently, "Why are you asking about the gun, anyway? It's been missing six months."

"We believe it was used in the commission of a murder," Daniel said. That was the cover story he and Matskevich had agreed on when asking questions about the Mauser.

"Gosh!"

"Of course, it's not definitive," Daniel said, leaning forward conspiratorially. "We'd have to have the gun to match ballistics. That's why we dropped by to talk to you, actually," he said, and slipped a business card from his wallet. "If any leads turn up, can you contact me? I'm not likely to be in town long, but a message to the Des Moines field office will find me."

"Of course!" said Officer Jones. His shoulders straightened, then slumped slightly: "But it's not likely, you understand. After it's been so long, and everything."

"Of course," Daniel told him. "I know it's a long shot. We've just got to explore all avenues, that's all."

It was trending on toward dusk when they left the police station. "Let's leave for Honeygold tomorrow," Daniel suggested. "Hit the town tonight. Want a tour of Des Moines?"

Matskevich made a dismissive gesture. "All American cities are the same."

Daniel smiled and let that ride. "At least let's do something this evening," he said. "Catch a movie, maybe. Go to a strip club."

"A strip club!" Matskevich sounded appalled. "We have known each other for three days, and already you are trying to gather blackmail?"

"No!" Damn Mr. Gilman, anyway. Naturally a Soviet agent would take it that way. "No. I just thought it would be a good way to relax, blow off steam..." He was digging himself in deeper. "Or we could go duckpin bowling," he suggested. "I saw a sign for it just a couple blocks away."

"Duckpin bowling. What is this?"

"It's a game..." Daniel wasn't sure how to explain bowling. "It's fun," he said. "C'mon. Aren't KGB agents allowed to have a good time?"

Matskevich's eyes narrowed. "I am not a KGB agent," he said, and for a horrible moment Daniel thought that his careless strip club suggestion had destroyed the friendliness that had grown up between them, and they would spend the duration of the investigation in stony professional silence.

But then Matskevich added, "So there are no rules that say I cannot have a good time. If that's what duckpin bowling is," he added, in a tone of skepticism.

Daniel gave a shout of laughter. "Well, we'll go to the bowling alley, and you can decide for yourself."

***

After duckpin bowling, Matskevich insisted on trying the pinball machines in the bowling alley, and then getting a beer at the bowling alley bar. "We could have been drinking all this time as we bowled?" he asked Daniel.

"If you wanted to drop a bowling ball on your toes, sure," Daniel returned.

"Well, so, perhaps it is better we waited." Matskevich drained his beer, and gestured at Daniel's half-full glass. "Drink up!"

"No, no, one'll do me," Daniel said, laughing, but firm, and Matskevich shook his head and sighed and drank two more beers on his own.

He seemed none the worse for it in the morning, when they drove off early into the crisp clear autumn day. Farm equipment clogged the narrow county roads: the corn harvest was underway. "It'll be nice if they ever build that interstate highway system," Daniel said sourly, as they crept along County Road K22 behind a combine. Daniel had agreed to do most of the driving if Matskevich wouldn't smoke in the car. "Oh well. I guess this'll give you a good look at America, huh?"

Matskevich didn't reply, just peered thoughtfully at a scarecrow wearing a battered Dodgers hat. He had rolled down his window earlier, and sometimes leaned out of the car to take in the sights as they passed through little country towns with jack-o-lanterns on the porches and American flags flapping in front of the post offices.

"You remember our cover?" Daniel asked.

Matskevich turned away from a farm stand piled with pumpkins. "We are pollsters. We have come to investigate how Khrushchev's visit affected American views about Communism and the Soviet Union." He paused. "People will believe this?"

"Oh yes," Daniel said. "Americans are very gullible." Possibly not the best tidbit to share with a Soviet agent. Oh well. "We'll stop by the minister's house first," he added. "Methodist, if they've got one. If he takes to us, that will clear the way for us with everyone else in town."

***

"I've always thought," Daniel said, "that the ministers are the beating heart of any American town, so of course I wanted to talk to you before we began to poll more widely, Reverend Johnson."

Daniel had headed for the Methodist minister's house directly upon arriving in Honeygold, and now he and Matskevich sat ensconced in Reverend Johnson's pleasantly cluttered front room, drinking cups of coffee provided by Mrs. Johnson.

Matskevich sat with a steno pad on his knee, poised to take notes once Reverend Johnson started sharing useful information, but right now he was looking at Daniel incredulously, as if he thought Daniel were laying it on far too thick. Daniel ignored him. He had grown up in the Midwest. There was no such thing as too thick here.

"We're looking to interview a broad cross-section of the town," Daniel went on. "We're particularly interested in people who opposed the visit, to see if seeing Khrushchev changed their views... If they went down to the whistle-stop at all, that is."

"Oh, just about everyone went," Reverend Johnson said. "Even most of the Baptists, never mind their preacher told them they shouldn't go see a godless Communist." He smiled just a little.

Daniel matched his smile. "I'm guessing you didn't tell your congregation the same thing?"

"No, no. I thought it might be asking just a little bit too much of human nature to tell them not to attend the most exciting event that's ever happened in Honeygold. In any case, it seemed to me that the right thing to do was to show Mr. Khrushchev a warm welcome. Maybe he'll be less inclined to shoot missiles at us if he remembers friendly crowds."

"That's exactly the sort of thing we're looking for," Daniel said warmly, and Matskevich's pen began to scratch. "If you could just help us reconstruct who all went to the whistle-stop...?"

"Oh, well, it truly was most of the town," Reverend Johnson said. He thought for a moment, then proceeded to list a who's who of Honeygold: the mayor, the sheriff, the newspaper editor ("Milly Douglas, she took it over after her husband died; you'll want to talk to her"), the librarian, the high school principal. "The whole high school went, in fact. I guess he figured he'd have an epidemic of truancy on his hands otherwise, so he gave the whole school a field trip. The marching band played the Marseillaise when the train came in. I suppose it *should* have been the Internationale, but somehow no one could bear to order the sheet music..."

At last Reverend Johnson wrapped up: "Even Eddy Wright and his cronies went, and they were violently opposed to the visit." (Daniel noticed Matskevich's pen pause at the word *violent*.) "I suppose curiosity won out in the end. They all fought in Korea and I suppose they saw the Communists do some pretty nasty things..."

"It was the Chinese who fought in Korea," Matskevich said. "Not the Soviets."

It was the first time he had spoken, beyond the first exchange of greetings, and Reverend Johnson looked at him in some surprise. "Is that a Polish accent, son?"

Now Matskevich looked surprised, just for a second. "Yes," he said, with a razor smile. "So you see, I know my Communists."

Reverend Johnson smiled too, with genuine sympathetic warmth. "Of course you're right," he said. "It was the Chinese in Korea, not the Soviets. But I imagine Eddy and his friends were thinking that a Communist is a Communist, at the end of the day. Maybe it was good for them that they came and saw that Khrushchev was just a man, in the end."

"When you say they were opposed," Daniel said, "what sort of things were they saying?"

"Oh, well. They were talking big in the roadhouse, so naturally I didn't hear it myself. But it would be easy to arrange an interview with Eddy," Reverend Johnson added. "If you need a place to stay, his mother rents out rooms to travelers. Edna

Wright. She hasn't had an easy time of it. First her husband died in World War II, and then Eddy... well, like I said, he had a bad time in the war."

"We are looking for a place to stay, thank you," Daniel said, instantly recalibrating his plans. "Is there anyone who didn't go?" he added. "A sort of control group, if you will."

"Oh, well, Mr. Purcell, of course," Reverend Johnson said, and again he gave that small smile. "He was leading a prayer meeting down at the Baptist Church. He'd be a good one to interview. Naturally I don't accord with his views on everything, but he's got quite a lot to say." The indulgent smile briefly grew wider, and Reverend Johnson hid it by taking a sip from his coffee cup. Then he looked at his cup in surprise. "My goodness, it's gone cold. Have we been talking for so long?"

He sounded dismayed. Daniel stood up, and Matskevich followed his lead. "I think we've taken too much of your time," Daniel said.

"Oh, not at all, not at all. It's been a pleasure. It's just that, well, there's a church supper tonight – you're invited, by the way; please come – and I haven't finished my part of the preparations..."

Matskevich's eyes lit at the words *church supper*. "We will come," he said, and then glanced at Daniel. "Won't we?"

He looked as eager as a child who had just been invited to a circus. "Well, I don't know," Daniel hedged, mostly to tease him; but when Matskevich's eyes widened, Daniel couldn't help grinning. "Of course we will. I expect much of the community will be there, won't they, Reverend Johnson?"

"Oh yes," Reverend Johnson said. "And I'd be happy to introduce you to anyone you'd like to talk to."

"Wonderful. Then if you could just give us directions to Mrs. Wright's house...?"

"Head on south to Pear Street, then four blocks down to the left. Church supper starts at five. I'll have my eye out for you."

They crunched through the fallen leaves on Reverend Johnson's front walk, back out to their car. Once they were in the car, Matskevich said, "If we stay at Mrs. Wright's, we will have to pretend to be pollsters even in our sleep."

"I know," Daniel said. "But think how much information we could gather this way! I'm hoping she'll be an incorrigible gossip."

"Yes," Matskevich allowed. "It's a good idea. Only you must remember to remain in character."

"Well, same to you, partner," Daniel reminded him. "You're not just a pollster; you've got to remember that you're Polish as long as we're in Honeygold." He turned to look at Matskevich. "*Are* you Polish? Matskevich doesn't sound like a Russian name."

"It's Belarusian." Matskevich sounded faintly belligerent. "From my father's side. On my mother's – mostly Russian; a Polish grandmother. But now we are all Soviet."

Daniel had known that there were a lot of different ethnicities in the Soviet Union, and yet somehow he had simultaneously considered it an ethnically homogeneous mass of Russians. "A Soviet melting pot," he mused. "Your country is like America that way."

"Yes," Matskevich agreed. "That is something our countries have in common."

***

The folding tables lining the walls of the church basement fairly bowed under heaping bowls of coleslaw and potato salad, pans of baked beans, meatloaves slathered in ketchup, baskets of biscuits and plates topped with wiggling Jell-Os – and that was just the dinner. Dessert covered two tables of its own: pies of all kinds, a layer cake decorated in a pattern of wheat sheaves, chocolate chip cookies and caramel popcorn balls.

Matskevich stared, wide-eyed. "It's all free." Daniel told him.

"Free?"

"These church suppers are meant to promote good fellowship. Anyone can come and eat."

They worked their way around the tables together. Daniel, who had been to about a thousand of these things in his life, partook sparingly, but Matskevich loaded up, his face alight.

At least till they reached the Jell-Os. These he eyed doubtfully, finally lifting a serving spoon to prod a carrot- and cabbage-flecked lump of yellow Jell-O. "What is this?"

"Perfection salad," Daniel said. "I've never seen it with

cabbage before."

"But what *is* it?" Matskevich persisted. "What is the..." He prodded it with his fork. "The wiggly part."

Daniel's mouth twitched. "Lemon Jell-O," he answered gravely. But he couldn't resist asking: "What did you think it was?"

"*Zalivnoye* – how do you say – meat jelly."

"Aspic," Daniel said, and muffled a guffaw behind his hand so the good church ladies wouldn't see him laughing. Matskevich looked disapproving enough on his own.

But he took a small spoonful of perfection salad. Daniel looked at him in surprise, and Matskevich shrugged. "Well, why not? Try everything. You never know what is good."

"I can tell you right now that perfection salad is not," Daniel told him. "My aunt Rebecca likes to make it, and it's terrible."

"Perhaps it is better with cabbage," Matskevich said, and levered it into his mouth. He didn't spit it back, but after chewing it for about two seconds, he grimaced and swallowed it whole, like a python. "When do they bring out the beer?"

"I don't think they do," Daniel said. "They're Methodists." Matskevich looked incredulous, and Daniel couldn't resist expanding, "In fact, I think the whole county may be dry."

The incredulous look morphed into an expression of fascinated pity. Daniel almost laughed. "How do they live?" Matskevich asked.

"Probably they drive to the next county over and tote back beer in secret."

"Ah!" Matskevich smiled. "People are the same everywhere."

Daniel felt that he had misrepresented the good teetotalers of Honeygold. "Not everyone," he said. "Just the reprobates."

Matskevich mouthed the word *reprobates*, and then said, "I will go in search of these reprobates, then. And you will talk to the upstanding citizens?"

"Fair enough." The reprobates were more likely to know if someone had sneaked off on the day of Khrushchev's visit – and far more likely to share that knowledge with someone who joined in as they passed around a bottle of whiskey.

Daniel ambled in the general direction of Reverend Johnson, and soon enough found himself introduced to at least half of the worthy citizens the reverend had mentioned that afternoon. He was chatting with Milly Douglas, the editor of the *Honeygold Courier* ("What would be a good time to drop by and look at your photographs from Khrushchev's visit? Tomorrow? Excellent."), when he saw, to his horror, that Matskevich had drawn a crowd.

Had he blown his cover? Daniel felt a chill down his back: God knew what these good Iowans would do if they discovered a genuine Soviet agent in their midst. A lynching wasn't out of the question.

But as Daniel edged in that general direction, he saw that it wasn't that kind of crowd. These people weren't angry: they were listening, almost literally with baited breath, as Matskevich told a story.

"I had come all this way from Poland," Matskevich was saying. "Deep in East Germany, without the proper papers, without a word of German, trapped in the glare of this German policeman's flashlight – this light that was so blinding that I could not even see the man who held it. He shouted something in German, and I thought in the next moment they would have me, and then it would be a beating and a slow train to Siberia."

Matskevich paused. Daniel found himself holding his breath with everyone else, even though he knew perfectly well that this story had to be made up. Then Matskevich went on: "But instead – they left. He must have told them he found no one."

There was a collective exhale. "But why?" asked Mrs. Wright.

"Who can say? I never even saw his face." Matskevich took a bite of meatloaf and chewed thoughtfully. "Perhaps it was mercy; perhaps he did not want to do the paperwork. People say that the motives of evil are inscrutable, but it seems to me that goodness is more mysterious. Why should he do this thing that brought him no benefit, indeed put him in danger?"

The crowd began drift away at the edges, now that the exciting part was over, and Daniel slipped closer. Matskevich's voice dropped to a normal volume as his audience left: Daniel saw that he was speaking to Reverend Johnson. "That is the end of the story, really," Matskevich said. "I reached West Berlin the next night, and found a job washing dishes not long after. And after some time I managed to contact my aunt who had emigrated before the war, and she sent me the money to come to America..."

Daniel listened, fascinated. The whole story was poppycock, of course, but still, it was...

Well, it was interesting that Matskevich could tell such a vivid story about someone escaping the USSR. Daniel would mention it in his weekly report.

***

Matskevich must have found his reprobates, because Daniel lost track of him after that. Once the crowd dwindled to a few scattered groups, Daniel went in search of him.

When Daniel was growing up, the reprobates tended to congregate out back under the lilac bushes. (Daniel, a goody-two-shoes, had been genuinely shocked when he stumbled upon them passing around a bottle of gin and a pornographic blue-bible). He figured it would be about the same at the Honeygold Methodist Church.

And indeed, he found Matskevich sitting on the back steps with a pie tin on his lap, watching the dusk creep over the cornfields. "Hawthorne," Matskevich greeted him.

The faint scent of peppermint schnapps on his breath made Daniel flinch. "I can smell that you found the reprobates. Was the famous Eddy Wright there?"

Matskevich had taken a bite of pie, but he swallowed it almost unchewed and answered, "Yes. They all teased him very much when I asked about Khrushchev's visit: he had sworn he would not see Khrushchev when he came, but at the last minute he got in the car and went along with everyone else. They thought all the other young people went, except, oh, not Mary Lou; but they did not remember this for a long time, although she was sitting right there."

"Maybe Mary Lou tried to assassinate Khrushchev," Daniel joked.

"Why not? Women assassinated tsarist officials. And in the war, we had women fighter pilots, women bombers, women snipers..."

"Yes, yes. All right. It's certainly possible. So let's say... Mary Lou walks out to the blind by the railroad tracks – which we ought to do ourselves, by the way."

"Yes, certainly."

"She smokes of pack of Marlboros. Those are usually a men's cigarette brand..."

"There are different cigarettes for men and women?"

"Oh yeah. Market diversification. It makes it easier to sell more product. So Mary Lou is on the hillock, smoking a whole pack of men's cigarettes, reading a pamphlet about God's blessings on the agrarian way of life and holding her Mauser pistol in her lap – do you think she just didn't realize a pistol isn't a good long-range weapon?"

"Hmm."

"All while wearing her size 14 men's boots," Daniel finished.

"Some women have large feet," Matskevich said. He stubbed his cigarette on the concrete step. "But not Mary Lou. Tiny fairy feet." He held out his hands to show the size, then took up his fork again and poked at the last sliver of pie.

"Did you steal someone's pie pan?" Daniel asked. "Did you eat an *entire* pie?"

"There was only half of it left, and Mrs. Land gave it to me." Matskevich widened his eyes and sucked in his cheeks in an exaggerated starving waif look. "I am supposed to return the tin tomorrow. She has promised that her husband will show me his war memorabilia. He has a gun he brought back from the war, she thinks perhaps a Mauser, but she is not sure."

"Oh, good thinking. Do you want to take point on the Mausers? It'd look odd if we're both asking about them, but if it's just you..."

"Yes. Then they will just think I am fascinated by war trophies." Matskevich shrugged. "I do not think much will come of this one: Mr. Land fought in Italy. Still, there were Germans there, so perhaps." He held out the pie tin. "Do you want a bite?"

"Sure." Daniel was stuffed, but he could fit in another bite or two. "Oh, you got the rest of the chocolate pie. It's good."

Matskevich lit another cigarette. He leaned back on the steps and blew a stream of smoke toward the darkening sky, then lifted his flask. "Drink?"

Daniel shook his head. "Can't stand schnapps. Sorry."

Matskevich looked up at him, his face indecipherable, and Daniel wondered if he shouldn't have tried to choke the schnapps down in the name of friendship between nations, after all.

But then Matskevich shrugged and took a swig himself. "A very bad habit, drinking."

The sharp peppermint scent of the schnapps filled the air. Daniel heaved himself to his feet. "I'm going to head on back to Mrs. Wright's. Are you coming?"

Matskevich lifted his cigarette. "I will finish my cigarette first," he said. "You go ahead. I want to sit and think."

CHAPTER 3

As a matter of fact, Hawthorne's drinking habits – or non-drinking habits, more precisely – seemed liable to undermine Gennady's mission, and he contemplated this fact with concern as he watched the dusk sink toward darkness.

Oh, not his official mission: not the investigation into the assassination attempt on Khrushchev. No one expected that to be successful anyway. "Now listen, Gennady, it's obvious what actually happened," Stepan Pavlovich had said. "Clearly the Americans tried to assassinate our Nikita Sergeyevich but failed through poor marksmanship, and now they're trying to cover it up."

Gennady did not think this was at all the obvious explanation. Surely the Americans weren't so sanguine about their chances of winning a thermonuclear war? But he said, "Of course, sir."

"Really," Stepan Pavlovich said, exasperated, "this whole investigation, one of our agents working with an American, is just..." His jaw clenched. He let out a slow breath, and went on, "Well, it's the Chairman's idea, so of course it's brilliant. As I'm sure he foresaw, it's an opportunity for us to gather more intelligence about the Americans' investigative methods. Keep a good eye on your American partner."

"My American partner," echoed Gennady. "Yes, of course, sir."

He tried to sound serious, professional, but inside he bubbled with glee. Such a trip had been the dream of Gennady's life since he first read Ilf and Petrov's book about their American road trip, *One-Storied America*. Driving for days on beautiful smooth American highways, listening to American radio, stopping at diners for coffee and doughnuts – and with an American partner, to boot. Gennady could get to know a real American, see what they were really like, once you got past the fake smiles.

"And if you *do* find the monster who tried to kill our Nikita Sergeyevich," Stepan Pavlovich added, "certainly there will be a place for you in my department."

Gennady's cup of happiness ran over. An American road trip, an escape from Arkady's office: what more could the day offer?

But these dreams lasted only until Gennady reported back to Arkady, who was pacing the floor in fury. "Stepan Pavlovich is trying to undermine me again," Arkady fumed. "Putting you on a joint Soviet-American investigation? He's trying to frame us all as American spies, I know it. Well, fuck him, I'll turn this to my advantage. Honeytrap the American agent for me, Gennady."

Gennady's hopes for the trip collapsed. He did not want to go from being pawed by Arkady to being pawed (and probably worse) by an American agent.

But. But. "Wouldn't it be better to send a woman to seduce him?" Gennady asked.

Arkady waved an impatient hand. "It will be fine. Any man will fuck a younger man if he can't find a girl."

Gennady supposed Arkady was speaking from experience, yet he felt he ought to temper Arkady's expectations somehow. "I'm not sure..."

"Listen," Arkady interrupted. "I can see why you're worried, Gennady, it would be better if you were younger and prettier. But after all, you don't look nearly as old as you are – that baby face."

He reached across the desk to clasp Gennady's chin, and turned his face from side to side. "Make sure you shave. And get an American suit. As for the rest, you're a naturally seductive person, Gennady, it will be all right."

He gave Gennady's cheek a quick double pat, hard enough that it was almost a slap.

So Gennady went home and got drunk and sulked, because in

the first place you couldn't imagine Ilf blackmailing Petrov, theirs was one of the great friendships of literary history and they would never betray each other. And in the second place, if the American behaved like Arkady, it would spoil his beautiful trip.

He could just see it, driving down a black tarmac highway, with the sunlight dappling through the trees arched overhead, just like in Ilf's photograph – and the American would grope him over the gear shaft. He would drag Gennady into bizarre perverted capitalist sex practices. He would probably sodomize him with a Coke bottle. Unfair, unfair.

But as Gennady began to sober up, he realized that it was all more likely to go wrong in the opposite direction: it might be impossible to seduce the American. How did you seduce a man, anyway? All Gennady had ever done was exist in Arkady's general vicinity. And in any case Arkady had shifted his attentions instantly when Nikolai (younger and prettier) got assigned to the department.

Gennady stumbled into the bathroom to vomit. Then he opened the window to stick his head out into the early October air. By Moscow standards, October in DC was hardly cool, but it cleared his head, at which point the obvious solution presented itself.

Drunkenness.

Get a man drunk enough and he would do anything. Piss icicles into snow banks in negative forty degree weather; brawl with traffic cops. Kiss other men.

Just look at Alyosha, who was married to Gennady's cousin Oksana, although they were always fighting and breaking up and then Alyosha would wander Moscow looking for her. He would show up at Gennady's door dead drunk, crying about Oksana, Oksana, how could he live without Oksana? Falling on Gennady's neck and sobbing into his shoulder and kissing the side of his face, as Gennady explained that Oksana was not there, and no, he didn't know where she was, and "Get off me, you oaf, I don't even look like her."

"You taste like her," Alyosha said once.

"Everyone tastes like eau de cologne when that's what you've been drinking!"

When Grandfather was home, Gennady would pin Alyosha down and sit on him till he went to sleep. If Grandfather was elsewhere, and Alyosha had brought something drinkable ("I draw the line at furniture polish, Alyoshka"), Gennady would drink with him and they would jerk each other off, because why not? After all, Gennady didn't get to see his girlfriend Galya often, and a hand was a hand was a hand; and it kept Alyosha from wandering back out into the night and maybe drowning in two inches of filthy water in the gutter.

So, anyway, although Arkady had probably overstated the case with *all men want to fuck other men*, most men would at least fuck around with other men if they were drunk enough. All Gennady had to do was wait for this Special Agent Daniel Hawthorne to get bombed, then sit on his lap and let nature take care of the rest.

And now Gennady was on the American highway, enjoying the silly roadside attractions (the World's Largest Catsup Bottle!) and Burma Shave signs and friendly attendants at all the gas stations, who were happy to give you road maps and discuss directions to any place nearby. (You could tell this was a nation that had not suffered a land war in nearly a hundred years.)

And Hawthorne wasn't a bad traveling companion. Certainly not to Arkady type. Oh, of course he had his faults: the attempt to gather blackmail with the strip club suggestion had been laughable, although in a way Gennady was glad that the American was trying to collect blackmail on him as well. It evened things up somehow.

And really Hawthorne wasn't as stupid as the strip club ploy would suggest. In fact, Gennady suspected the strip club was only an opening gambit designed to put Gennady's guard down in its incompetence, and really Hawthorne meant to talk him into slandering the Soviet Union. Devious, but clever, you had to admit. The strategy played to Hawthorne's strengths: he was likeable, good-looking, funny. Easy to talk to, if you let yourself talk.

Gennady didn't really want to blackmail him.

Not that he was likely to have the chance, given that Agent Hawthorne didn't drink. Oh, a beer with dinner sometimes, but beer was barely even alcohol, it didn't count. No true drinker would turn down a flask just because he didn't happen to like the drink, when it was schnapps, which was meant for human consumption, no furniture polish!

Well, after all, that solved the Ilf-and-Petrov problem, didn't it? If Hawthorne never got drunk enough to honeytrap, then Gennady would never be in any position to betray him. Unfortunate, of course (Gennady lit another cigarette as he imagined explaining this to Arkady), but after all, it would blow the whole mission to push the seduction angle too hard, and the most important thing was to find out who tried to shoot our dear Nikita Sergeyevich, wasn't that true, Arkady Anatolyevich?

That would be altogether the best solution. Except it didn't seem likely that they would solve the case, and if they didn't, there would be no promotion out of Arkady's department. So, so, so.

Well, no matter what happened, Gennady would have this American road trip. And for the honeytrap – well, he would just wait and see.

CHAPTER 4

On their last day in Honeygold, Daniel and Matskevich hiked out to the shooter's blind. They started at the station where Khrushchev's train had stopped, which was really just a platform at the edge of town, and followed the tracks eastward. "The shooter can't have walked out this way on the day," Daniel commented, when they'd gone about a mile. He turned back, gesturing at the platform, still in sight. "There were people waiting at the platform all day. He would've been visible."

"The investigators thought he came in along the creek," Matskevich reminded him.

"Yes, of course. I'm just... double-checking their work, I suppose."

The original investigators had marked the blind with a little red flag on a pole. Without the flag, it would have been difficult to find: just a slight hollow hidden in the tall grass about halfway up a rise that wouldn't have been called a hill anywhere but Iowa.

They canvassed the area, just in case the earlier investigators had missed anything, but they found nothing. The earlier investigators had boxed up the cigarette butts and the bullet casing; time and rain had done for the boot prints.

At length they both sat down in the blind, and watched and listened for a while. Daniel retrieved a pair of soda bottles from his jacket pockets. "Orange or grape?"

"I have never had grape soda." Matskevich popped the lid and took a drink. He winced.

"Here, take the orange," Daniel said, and switched out the sodas.

Matskevich looked at him. "Do you like the grape?"

Daniel shrugged. "It's all right." He took a drink, rubbed the back of his hand across his mouth, and gestured at the train tracks with the neck of the bottle. "You feel that rumble in the ground? Train's coming."

Soon they could hear the vibration as well as feel it. "He would have plenty of time to prepare," Matskevich observed.

"Yeah. And of course he must have been able to hear the noise from the whistle-stop from here. They had the marching band going and everything. He would have heard it get louder when the train pulled in, and quiet down again when it pulled out."

A freight train rattled past, obscured by the long dry grass.

"A poor sightline," Matskevich observed.

"It would've been worse in September," Daniel added. "The grass would be thicker." He looked around. "It'd be hard to find this place if you didn't know it was here."

"So a local, then. Except it seems they all have alibis."

Daniel made a face. "*Everyone* went to the whistle-stop," he agreed. "Or to Mr. Purcell's anti-Communist meeting."

"Perhaps Mr. Purcell sent an assassin." Matskevich raised his eyebrows. "Did he seem like this sort of person? A man who can convince others to kill?"

Daniel considered the possibility. "He met me at the door with a gun," he began.

"A gun!" Matskevich sounded startled. Daniel supposed Soviet citizens were too cowed to try that sort of thing on KGB agents.

"Oh, sure. He wanted me to know that he wasn't going to talk to a government shill of a pollster, and he thought Khrushchev's whole trip was a disaster from start to finish and Eisenhower ought to be ashamed of himself for ever letting the man set foot on American soil. I told him that was exactly the sort of thing I wanted to hear, that I was looking for people who weren't afraid to speak truth to power, and he invited me in for coffee. We talked for two hours. He gave me a pamphlet about how fluoridation is a Communist plot and showed me his gun collection."

"Mmm. You enjoyed yourself immensely."

Daniel grinned ruefully. "The crackpots are always entertaining."

"And the gun collection?"

"No Mauser. He fought in the Pacific, anyway. But he *does* have his great-uncle's Enfield rifle from the Civil War. And a whole lot of knowledge about guns, in general. He would've known better than to send an assassin with a pistol."

"Ah, but a Mauser... perhaps he wanted to make it look like Nazis were involved." But after a moment of considering this wild theory, Matskevich shook his head. "Only if he ever had a Mauser, the whole town would know, and someone would have told me. He does not sound like a man to keep things to himself."

"No. He's a big talker," Daniel agreed. "Did Jon Land let you look at his pistol that might be a Mauser?"

"Well," Matskevich said. "It was in an upstairs drawer, and that would be difficult for him to get to." He tapped his legs at the knee. "His legs are missing below here."

"Why the hell does he keep his war trophy *upstairs* if he lost his legs in Europe?"

Matskevich shook his head. "He lost them here. Combine accident."

They considered this grisly fact in silence. Matskevich lay back on the trampled grass and looked at the sky. "So he told me all about the battle where he won his prize," he said, "and all about his comrades in arms, who were jealous, because he was the only man in his unit to lay hands on such a fine gun. He's quite certain of this. The best war prize in the county. Of course Sheriff Woodley has his Mauser, but it was already broken when the Sheriff got it, it can't fire... I checked this too, later, and it's true. The gun is so safe that the Sheriff's children took it to school for..." His brow knit.

"Show-and-tell?"

"Yes. This. The Sheriff's Mauser was crushed somehow, a tank perhaps. Whereas Mr. Land's pistol is perfect, it could still fire if he had the ammunition. And then Mr. Land sent his son upstairs to fetch it."

"And?"

"It's one of ours. A Tokarev. Lost, far from home. I think it was glad to be back in Soviet hands, if only for a moment."

His face took on a wistful look. Daniel looked at him, then away, and took a notebook and ballpoint pen from his pocket. "As I see it," he said, "There are three possible explanations for this shooter. Option one: it was an accident."

Matskevich sat up again. He lit a cigarette. "This is the outcome your boss wants."

Daniel hesitated just for a moment. "Yes," he admitted.

Matskevich swept his cigarette from his lips and blew out a stream of smoke. "All right," he said. "An accident. A man or perhaps a teenage boy brings his Mauser pistol, a prize war trophy, up on this hillside to... oh, shoot some rabbits, perhaps. He sits here and smokes a pack of cigarettes and shoots just one shot – only one bullet casing left, after all..."

"Or he cleans up his other bullet casings," Daniel interjected.

"And leaves the cigarette butts?"

A fair point. And also: "The Iowa State Police would have found the spent bullets if he had discharged his gun more than once. They checked the site pretty carefully before they got called off."

"Yes. So. He sits waiting for rabbits long enough to smoke a whole pack, but the only time he shoots, his shot goes so far wide that he hits the side of a train instead."

"Yes," Daniel sighed. "The accident theory does sound a little far-fetched when you put it that way. All right. Option two: This was an assassin sent by an organized group. Which I suspect is what *your* bosses believe."

In fact, Daniel suspected Mr. Gilman was right in thinking that the Soviets believed the US government was behind the assassination attempt, but it seemed impolitic to say so straight out.

Matskevich shrugged.

"But if it was an organized group," Daniel said, "why did they pick a rank amateur? Look at the amount of evidence he left behind. The cigarette butts, the bullet casing. Footprints so clear that we know his shoe size. And why a pistol? That's a terrible weapon for a long-range shot. He's lucky he hit the side of the train."

Matskevich lit a cigarette. "Maybe he isn't supposed to shoot from the hill," he suggested. "Maybe the assassin is supposed to go to this whistle-stop and get close enough to shake hands and shoot the Chairman at close range. A pistol is the right weapon for this. But on his way, he chickened."

"Chickened out," Daniel corrected.

"Chickened out. Yes. He stops to have a smoke to steady his nerves. He smokes the whole pack, and he misses his time at the stop, and then the train is passing and he must try to make the shot from here..."

Daniel considered the possibility. He jotted a note in his notebook. "You'd think that an organization with any reach could find an assassin with steadier nerves."

"Perhaps they are a small organization. Small but fanatical. They see their chance to strike a blow against Communism and they take it." He stubbed out his cigarette. "But no, I think this does not work. This place would not be on anybody's route to the platform. He did not chicken out and stop. He came here on purpose."

Daniel nodded.

"In any case, looking for an anti-Communist organization does not narrow our list of suspects very much," Matskevich added.

"I'm afraid not," Daniel said. "But the list of anti-Communist wing-nuts who either don't realize or don't care that assassinating Chairman Khrushchev would lead to thermonuclear war, or even consider that desirable, has to be at least a little shorter."

"Are there such people? Who would consider nuclear war desirable?"

"A very conservative Christian sect that wants to jumpstart the apocalypse, maybe. But most of those groups are very apolitical: render unto Caesar what is Caesar's and God what is God's." Daniel stopped, and then added. "Of course, most religious people aren't gunning for the apocalypse."

"Of course. Even a godless Communist does not believe that *most* religious people want the world to end in a mushroom cloud."

"I expect your people would be pleased if the shooter turns out to be a religious fanatic."

Matskevich nodded. "Yes, of course. It's always nice to have a prejudice confirmed."

"But even if he is a religious fanatic – and his choice of reading material suggests it – that doesn't mean he's part of any kind of organization," Daniel said. "And that leads us to the third option: this was the action of a lone fanatic."

"Which is what you believe," Matskevich said.

Daniel hesitated, then nodded. "Yes," he admitted. "The sloppiness in leaving evidence behind, the poor choice of weapon: it suggests that he's an amateur with no military training. Maybe the pistol was the only gun he had access to. Maybe he didn't even know that it's the wrong kind of gun to fire a long-range shot. He tried to shoot Khrushchev because… oh, who knows. He hates Communists. Or he wants fame, notoriety. Maybe we're looking for a Raskolnikov."

Matskevich looked surprised. "You know our Dostoevsky?"

"I've read *Crime and Punishment*," Daniel said. "In translation," he added hastily. "I think it probably loses something in the process."

"Oh, maybe not. Sentence by sentence, you know, Dostoevsky is not such a good writer. But still the force of the book builds up, it doesn't matter about the sentences, and after all he had a great knowledge of the human soul " He pointed at Daniel. "You should read *Brothers Karamazovy*. Very useful for a man in your position. It will give you a new understanding of the darkness of the human heart."

Daniel brightened. "I'll read *The Brothers Karamazov* if you'll read, oh – let me think of an American novel."

"Some capitalist propaganda," Matskevich scoffed.

"*The Grapes of Wrath*," Daniel suggested triumphantly. "I defy you to read that and call it capitalist propaganda."

"What is it about?"

"A family loses its farm in Oklahoma during the Great Depression, and they drive out to California to look for a better life."

"Ah! No, I've read this," Matskevich said. "By your John Steinbeck?"

"You've read Steinbeck?" Daniel was astonished. But of course if the Politburo was going to allow any American literature into the Soviet Union, it *would* be Steinbeck.

"Yes, of course!" Matskevich said. "Very popular in the Soviet Union. I liked it almost as much as Ilf and Petrov."

"Who?"

"You don't know Ilf and Petrov?" Matskevich mimed astonishment. "They are two Soviet writers, very funny. They visited America in 1935, and wrote a book about their trip."

"All about how America is a land of capitalist misery, I bet."

"No, no. Those are the kinds of books you in America write about the Soviet Union – "

"Now wait. Steinbeck also wrote a book about his visit to the Soviet Union, and his *Russian Journal* isn't like that at all!"

" – but we are more fair-minded. A wonderful book." A slight nostalgic smile touched Matskevich's lips. Then he gave his head a shake, and said, "But we have wandered very far afield from our shooter. And I think we must hope he is not a Raskolnikov," he added, "because Raskolnikov was only caught because he turned himself in. And this I think does not happen often in real life."

Daniel nodded grimly. He stood up. "Let's go check out the creek bed," he said. "Maybe the shooter dropped something."

"Like what? Drivers license?" But Matskevich was on his feet as well, dusting bits of grass off his pants.

They climbed to the top of the ridge and followed a line of poplars – "A windbreak," Daniel told Matskevich. "The settlers planted them to slow down the winds across the prairie."

"Good cover for the shooter," Matskevich observed. "Probably he could not have been seen from the houses."

They clambered down a ravine into the creek bed. It was dry at this time of year, only a little water here and there, floating thick with leaves. Daniel walked on the sandy bank, while Matskevich picked his way from rock to rock. He held his arms out for balance, a look of pleased concentration on his face, like a schoolboy out for a lark. He was, Daniel remembered from the dossier, only twenty-four.

"Don't twist your ankle," Daniel told him. "Unless we find something big at Camp Dubois, we're hitting the road tomorrow to talk to *Good Shepherd* subscribers."

"Yes, good," Matskevich said. He balanced precariously on a jutting rock, and took a long awkward step onto a lower flat stone. "We should interview Mr. Don Westmark in California."

"No!" But Daniel laughed as he said it. "Why the hell is some guy in California subscribing to a regional Midwestern rag anyway?" Daniel asked, and then answered himself: "Probably he moved there and took the subscription with him. No, we'd better start with the subscribers in Iowa. It *had* to be someone who had some familiarity with this area. They'd never have been able to find that spot on the hillside otherwise. I don't suppose it could be Mary Lou after all?"

Matskevich shook his head. "When Khrushchev came, she was looking after her sick grandmother. This old lady," he said, and he sounded aggrieved, "accused me of being a Communist spy."

Daniel attempted not to laugh, then giggled uncontrollably.

"Yes, yes, very funny. She is like this with everyone, Mary Lou said, traveling salesman too, including that nice boy who came by last summer selling subscriptions to that magazine, what was it?"

Daniel stopped walking. "Matskevich!"

"*The Saturday Evening Post*," Matskevich said, with a studied carelessness that showed that he knew that Daniel had hoped he would say *The Good Shepherd*.

Daniel shook his head. "So it's not Mary Lou. If it's not someone in town, then maybe it's someone who used to live here. Or a Boy Scout who liked to sneak away from camp to watch the trains. It'd make sense for the shooter to be someone young and dumb enough not to think about the possibility of kicking off a nuclear war."

One of the rocks tipped. Matskevich's arms pinwheeled. He caught his balance just in time to hop down on the sandy creek bed, then stepped aside and peered down at his tracks in the sand.

Daniel turned to look back at his own tracks along the sandy bank. He had left a clear trail. "If the shooter came this way, he must have stayed on the rocks," Daniel said. "Or he would have left tracks for the first investigators to find."

"Could he climb out of the creek bed without leaving tracks?" Matskevich asked.

But when they reached Camp Dubois, it was instantly clear that he could have. The Boy Scouts had built a rock dam on the creek, which an agile person could easily clamber up without leaving a trace.

They looked through the camp. Matskevich paused to swing the wooden arm of the gate on the access road, just to see that it could easily be done. But they found nothing. If there had been tire tracks or footprints, the October wind and rain had long since washed them away.

"If they had investigated this right afterward," Matskevich said, "perhaps they would have found something. But now – " He cut his hand through the air in a wrathful gesture.

"Maybe *that's* what they want," Daniel suggested. "If we never find anything, then everyone can believe what they want to believe. That's convenient for everyone on both sides."

"Everyone except us," Matskevich pointed out. "Even if nothing is what they want us to find, they will not promote us for finding it."

Daniel sighed. "Everyone except us," he agreed.

CHAPTER 5

They did not get an early start the next morning. Their departure was delayed by Mrs. Wright, who was scandalized that they intended to leave before church.

"Of course we must go to church," Gennady said, with a reproving look at Hawthorne, who made a face at him over the toast.

Secretly, Gennady was delighted. His apartment in DC had been across from a church, and every Sunday he had seen the churchgoers arriving: women in big hats that looked like flowers from above, small children twisting in uncomfortable shoes. It fascinated him that so many showed up, when no one was making them go – or at least not the government; it occurred to him now that perhaps the Mrs. Wrights of the world had a hand in it.

He would have liked to attend a service in DC, just to see what it was like, but that would have suggested an interest in religion unbecoming in a Soviet citizen. But now, he had an excuse: the *Good Shepherd* magazine suggested a religious component to the shooting, an important clue in the case...

Perhaps his glee was not so secret. When Mrs. Wright left to fetch her hat, Hawthorne told Gennady, "Don't look so thrilled. It's church, not the stripper's tent at the county fair."

"You and your strippers," Gennady said, and cast upon

Hawthorne a sorrowful look that made Hawthorne snort.

Gennady had expected that they would slip quietly into church, that he could observe without being observed. Of course he should have known better: in a small town outsiders can do nothing unobserved.

A greeter caught them at the door and pumped their hands effusively, and in moments they were surrounded on all sides by manically beaming Americans. "I guess you don't have much opportunity to go to church in Poland, do you?" one woman said, her voice simultaneously sympathetic and avid, as if she hoped to hear that this lack of church-going had blighted his childhood.

Fortunately, Hawthorne somehow managed to extricate them, and steered them to safe harbor in a pew near the back. Gennady glanced around to assure himself that others were sitting, and sat with relief once he had ascertained this would not mark him as an outsider.

He continued this surreptitious surveillance of the congregation as the service progressed, to ensure that he stood when they stood, knelt when they knelt, took out a book when they retrieved their books from the pockets built into the back of the pews. He had to glance over at Hawthorne's book to make sure of the page, and caught Hawthorne looking at him, a smile flickering at the corner of his mouth, as if it amused him to see a godless Communist so earnestly aping these Methodist ways.

"Glad I entertain you," Gennady said, very softly, under cover of the rustle as everyone flipped to the right page. Hawthorne's grin broadened, and he looked like he might reply, but the church was quieting down, and he bent over his book instead.

The only difficult moment came near the end of the service. Everyone rose, so Gennady rose too – after all, he had followed the congregation in everything else – but Hawthorne pushed him back down.

"Communion is only for members," Hawthorne explained softly.

Gennady felt brutally conspicuous: caught out somewhere that he had no business to be. "So? And we want everyone to know I am not a member?"

"Are you kidding? You heard Milly Douglas. They'll be thrilled to have a potential convert in the house."

But Gennady's heartbeat did not even out until they were on the road out of town. He wanted a cigarette; he cursed himself for agreeing to Hawthorne's promise to drive if Gennady did not smoke in the car. So what if he barely knew how to drive, the only way to get better was practice.

"We shouldn't have gone," he told Hawthorne.

"I didn't want to go," Hawthorne protested. "You're the one who insisted."

That was true, which only annoyed Gennady more. "It could be important for the case! If the shooter is motivated by religion..." He drew in a deep breath. "I don't see why you couldn't let me go up with everyone else."

"It's disrespectful. Would you let me pretend to be a Komsomol member?"

"That's not the same. It's difficult to become a Komsomol member."

"It is? I thought everyone had to join. Like Hitler Youth."

"Komsomol is not like Hitler Youth!" Gennady shouted. Hawthorne fell silent, abashed, and Gennady continued, more quietly, "You are thinking of the Young Pioneers, maybe. Everyone joins that in school. But it's *not* like Hitler Youth. We camp, we sing songs, we learn skills – like your Boy Scouts. Only for girls, too."

"It's not mandatory to join Scouts."

"Well, so. I'm sure many people are left out because of the expense. Capitalism," Gennady scoffed.

Hawthorne did not reply. Gennady cranked down the window, then cranked it back up, mostly to keep his hand occupied so it did not stray to his cigarettes.

At last Gennady said, "Do you really think we are like Nazis?"

Hawthorne glanced over at him. He looked troubled. "No," he said, but Gennady felt he said it only to keep the peace. Hawthorne would not have compared Young Pioneers to Hitler Youth if he didn't see a similarity in his mind.

But, after all, it was probably not his fault: American newspapers and magazines painted such a misleading picture of the Soviet Union, always obsessing about nuclear war, as if the USSR was just salivating for a chance to destroy all life on earth, when it was the United States that had death cults who wanted nothing more than an apocalypse. And Hawthorne talked about these cults so casually, as if this was a normal thing to exist in the life of any country.

"Hawthorne," Gennady said.

Hawthorne winced. "Please," he said. "Call me Daniel."

Gennady was silent. "I am saying your name incorrectly," he said, after a long pause.

"It's pretty well tailor-made to be hard for a Russian-speaker to pronounce."

Gennady did not really want to call Hawthorne by his first name. Of course it was good that they had a friendly working relationship, but still, with their countries at loggerheads (even if temporarily they were pretending not to hate each other), they could not really be friends, no matter how much they liked each other.

"Daniel," Gennady said. He looked out the window when Hawthorne grinned. "Stop at the next town. I want to have a cigarette."

***

They drove to Omaha that day. Hawthorne wanted to stop at the FBI field office before they hit the road. "Of course it won't be open on a Sunday," he said. "I'm sorry for the delay, but I need to send in a report before we head on."

"Yes, all right." Gennady ought to write a report, too. Stepan Pavlovich had engaged a secret PO Box for this purpose, although even so he cautioned Gennady not to write anything too juicy, because of course the Americans would start reading all his reports as soon as they found the PO Box.

And of course for this reason it was impossible to report to Arkady on the progress of the honeytrap, which was just as well, because on this topic Gennady had nothing to say except, "Have you considered insinuating Soviet spies into strip clubs? These are very popular with American agents."

And he didn't feel like writing this. It was not just that he did not want to honeytrap Hawthorne himself, although he ought to make some attempt, or else what would he say to Arkady when at last the case was closed?

No. He did not really want to see Hawthorne honeytrapped at

all.

But fortunately he was not writing to Arkady, but to Stepan Pavlovich, and to him Gennady could write about the alibis of the people of Honeygold, and the church supper (now that was something Ilf and Petrov had missed!), the Boy Scout camp ("Not as well maintained as a Pioneer camp"), the layout of the terrain around the shooter's blind.

He must try to make it sound like they had made good progress, although in his heart Gennady did not think they would ever catch their shooter, barring a great stroke of luck. Too much time had been allowed to elapse while the American and Soviet agencies squabbled, too much evidence lost to wind and weather and the lapse of memory, and anyway even in the best of circumstances a lone shooter was a difficult creature to find.

The thing to do now, therefore, was to stretch out the trip and experience as much of America as possible. Although it had to be admitted that Omaha was not an exciting place on a Sunday. When they stopped for a late lunch, even the diner seemed sleepy.

"We could find a bookshop," Hawthorne suggested. "See if they have *The Brothers Karamazov*?"

He really meant to read it? Gennady was startled, then pleased. "Yes, all right," he said, and added amiably, "And I will read an American book. If there is one you would like to recommend?"

"Maybe one of Steinbeck's other books? If you're looking to avoid capitalist propaganda," Daniel said, with a smile. "Have you read *East of Eden*?"

"No." In truth, Gennady had not really cared for Steinbeck: his anti-capitalism felt too familiar, not as deliciously foreign as other American books. But it did not seem quite right to say that really he didn't care if Daniel gave him capitalist propaganda, as long as it was new and interesting.

Daniel chatted up the waitress, who gave them directions to a small bookstore nearby: a narrow storefront, its front window cluttered with books and globes and an old chess set. It reminded Gennady of Dickens' *Old Curiosity Shop*.

A little bell rang above the door as they entered. The shop smelled of dust and coffee and old paper, a good comforting smell, and the tall shelves flanking the door created almost a tunnel as they entered, as if they were walking into another world.

A black cat appeared at the end of the tunnel, claws clicking daintily on the scarred hardwood floor. "*Koshka*," Gennady said, and bent hopefully with his hand outstretched. The cat meowed and rubbed her soft head against his hand.

"You like cats?" There was a hint of laughter in Daniel's voice. Gennady ignored him and stroked the cat's back with one hand as he scratched her behind the ear with the other.

"She'll let you pick her up," a gravelly disembodied voice said.

Indeed, the cat snuggled in against Gennady's chest, and gazed up at him with winning golden eyes. Gennady rounded the bookshelf to discover a woman of – perhaps sixty? Hard to tell; Americans did not seem to age like normal people – sitting behind a cash register.

One side of her mouth curved up; the other corner remained turned down, that whole side of her face immobile, remnant of a stroke, perhaps. "That cat loves everybody," she said, with the raspy voice of a lifelong smoker. "We have a kid who comes in to shoplift every week and all she ever does is make love to him with her eyes."

Gennady stroked the cat. She purred. "You let him steal from you every week?"

"Ah, well. Usually he brings back the book from the week before, so he's borrowing, really. If he'd just ask..." she said, and let out a husky laugh. "You boys lookin' for anything in particular?"

"*Eden*..." Damn. He had forgotten the title.

"*East of Eden*," Daniel supplied. "And *The Brothers Karamazov*."

"Fiction's thataway."

Thataway was the far back corner. They passed the rest of the aisles in the store as they went, and Gennady glimpsed other browsers there: an elderly man dabbing his nose with a handkerchief, a child building a book city while her mother browsed, a pretty girl in a black turtleneck sitting on the floor of the poetry section.

The bell above the door chimed again, and the cat leapt out of Gennady's arms and streaked toward the sound. "Fickle creature," Daniel said, and Gennady laughed, although he felt a trifle bereft.

"Fickle," he repeated, cheering himself with the new word.

Daniel moved with confidence along the crowded aisle. "Here we go," he said, after an impossibly short time, and pried *East of Eden* from a packed shelf.

It was a hefty tome, and Gennady sighed inwardly. It was only fair, after all, *The Brothers Karamazov* was even longer; but he would have preferred something shorter, something that was not about the misery of capitalism, because he could read about that in translation back home.

"You don't have to read it." Daniel sounded almost apologetic. "It was just the first book that came to mind."

"Yes," Gennady said, and added, apologetic himself, "I read English slowly."

"I can find you a shorter book," Daniel said, cheerful again. "What kind of books do you like, anyway?"

Gennady considered. "Mysteries, ghost stories, adventures. Creepy books," he said, and paused. He could not think of the English word he wanted. "Books with dark houses and bloody knives," he said, after some thought.

"Well, I'll see what I can find."

While Daniel searched the shelves, Gennady looked at the crowded aisle rather helplessly, *East of Eden* still in his hands. He had thought he knew American literature well, albeit in translation. He read all the authors he could find in Moscow: not only Steinbeck but Twain, Hemingway, Jack London, Poe. But of course there were a thousand other American authors, thousands upon thousands he had never even heard of, so many books that they overspilled the shelves to stand in precarious stacks in the aisles.

But of course, English editions of Twain and Hemingway would be wonderful presents, even for friends who did not speak English. And like lightning the thought struck him that this bookstore might have that Holy Grail, *For Whom the Bell Tolls*, pined for by Soviet readers but not yet published in the Soviet Union.

Gennady found three copies, and nearly sat down in the aisle to read it at once. But no: he could read later. Now, he must search the shelves for more treasures.

He took all three copies, and six other books of Hemingway. Then Dumas' *The Three Musketeers* for his cousin Oksana: they used to play at being musketeers together when they were children. For his girlfriend Galya – who was probably not his girlfriend anymore, but was not her fault he had not answered her letters, after all, and only a monster could fail to buy her an American copy of her very favorite book, Robert Louis Stevenson's *Kidnapped!*, especially when this copy had such wonderfully dramatic illustrations. For Grandfather, who was old-fashioned in his tastes, a selection of Mark Twain...

He was debating the *Complete Works of Edgar Allen Poe* when Daniel returned. "What about – my God, what do you need all those books for?"

"Presents," Gennady explained indignantly.

"Are they all going to fit in your suitcase?"

Gennady looked sorrowfully at his beautiful stack, and then began the bitter task of dividing it into two piles: one that he absolutely must buy now, and another of books that could be left behind in deference to that limited suitcase space. America had other bookstores. He could buy *A Farewell to Arms* later.

"Is Moscow full of Hemingway fiends?" Daniel asked.

"Oh, yes. We all love Hemingway. I will be greeted as a conquering hero when I bring this home," Gennady said, hefting *For Whom the Bell Tolls*. "It has not been published in Moscow yet."

"All these others have?" Daniel sounded surprised, like he thought the USSR was a floating island where they read nothing but Marx.

"Yes! Do you think we are philistines? Hemingway is one of us, almost Russian, so brave and stoic and sad: even under Stalin, we read him." Only then did Gennady notice the book in Daniel's hand, and remembered that he had asked Daniel to pick out a book for him. He set aside his sorting. "Ah! What have you chosen for me?"

Daniel held it up. *"The Haunting of Hill House."*

The cover looked promising: the gable of a house peeking out from behind a tangle of plants in unnatural colors, violent gold and turquoise. "A ghost story?"

"Not exactly," Daniel said. "There isn't a ghost, I mean, the house itself is evil. But it's not really about the house. It's like

Dostoevsky," he added. "It's about the darkness of the human heart, the little deadly ways that people are unkind to each other."

Gennady doubted an American author was capable of writing a book the least bit like Dostoevsky, but he nodded indulgently. "Yes, all right," he said, and added the book to his depleted stack. He had kept all three copies of *For Whom the Bell Tolls* (he had visions already of the wonderful trades he would make with these books: the latest issues of *Foreign Literature*, tickets to French movies at the Moscow House of Cinema), but otherwise he had set aside everything but the Dumas, the Stevenson, a single illustrated *Adventures of Tom Sawyer* for Grandfather, who after all did not read English. "I will read *For Whom the Bell Tolls* first, I am sorry, but then I will read *The Haunting of Hill House*."

"No, of course. You've been waiting for this Hemingway for years, after all."

Gennady's heart warmed at this evidence of understanding. "Yes," he said, and added impulsively, "I will buy your *Bratya Karamozovy* too."

"You don't have to," Daniel protested.

"No, no. I will put it on my expense account. After all, it is spreading Russian culture," Gennady said. He scanned the shelves until he found Dostoevsky, and added, "But I can exchange for a shorter book if you like. *Notes from Underground*?"

"No, I read that in college. And I've always meant to read *The Brothers Karamazov*, anyway."

Gennady plucked the book from the shelf and added it to his pile. He paid for the books, an absurdly small sum it seemed to him, and returned to the sleepy streets of Omaha with a swagger in his step.

"Want to hit a bar?" Daniel asked.

"No!" Gennady said, and realized only after he said it that Daniel was only teasing: he knew very well that Gennady wanted nothing more than to sit down and read.

"Let's get takeout," Daniel suggested. "That way you won't even have to stop reading for dinner."

"Yes," Gennady agreed. He added, with an attempt at American overstatement, "That sounds perfect."

CHAPTER 6

"So what we've found," Daniel said, slumping in the vinyl diner booth, "is diddlysquat."

He had spent the day writing his report in the FBI field office, which made him painfully aware of how little they had discovered in Honeygold. Even Matskevich's spirited story about escaping Poland seemed stupid when Daniel wrote it down: of course a KGB agent would be able to lie with gusto. It meant nothing about his deeper feelings about the USSR.

"Diddlysquat," Matskevich echoed, pronouncing the word carefully, as if he were tasting it. Then he added, "What was it your Thomas Edison said? We have now found nine hundred and ninety-nine ways not to make a light bulb?"

"I bet even Thomas Edison got frustrated along about the 950th attempt," Daniel said, and then made a face. "We haven't been working on the case nearly that long. It's just…"

He wanted to solve the case – to prove himself worthy of this second chance that Mr. Gilman had given him. But he could hardly discuss that with Matskevich, so instead he took up his menu and began looking over its offerings as if it might not have the same thing as every other damn diner in the entire Midwest. He was so tired of diner food.

"Hey fellows. My name's Angeline, and I'll be your waitress. Do you know what you'll be having, or do you want my recommendations?"

Daniel looked up, and the sight of Angeline blew his troubles out of the water. She was gorgeous, with long red ringlets and a shirt just tight enough to make a peek-a-boo gap between the buttons just above her breasts. Her perfume wafted over them: Shalimar, floral and citrus and musk.

"I always like to hear a lady's recommendations," Daniel said, casually resting one arm along the back of the booth to show off the breadth of his chest.

"Well, generally I say the veal," she said, "although our burgers are real good too, and sometimes a burger is the only thing that'll hit the spot, you know? And of course you've *got* to try the milkshakes."

"What flavors of milkshake?" Matskevich asked.

Angeline's gaze, hitherto friendly and polite, lit up about a thousand watts. "Oh my gosh! What a *cute* accent!" she cried, and then blushed red and hid the lower half of her face behind her ordering pad.

Daniel promptly fell a little bit in love, and simultaneously accepted defeat. When a girl looked at your buddy like that, it was useless to try to compete.

"Um, I mean we have chocolate and vanilla like everyone," Angeline said, "but Peggy, that's my boss, she owns this place and she's the cook too – she's always trying new flavors. We had a cherry one last summer which was to *die* for. Right now it's cranberry, which – " she lowered her voice – "I don't think is *quite* as good, but it's sure better than the pumpkin we had *last* Halloween."

"I'll try it," Matskevich declared. "And the veal, please."

"The same," Daniel said. Angeline left, and Daniel leaned across the table and punched Matskevich's shoulder. "I think she likes you, champ."

Matskevich shook his head. "American girls are always so friendly."

"Really? American girls are always coming up to you and crying 'Your accent is so *cute*'?"

A smirk briefly escaped Matskevich's control. "Better luck tomorrow, my friend." He glanced after Angeline, whose red hair was visible above the swinging door into the kitchen, then leaned across the table and asked, "What is cranberry?"

"Cranberry! Oh, you've had it before. It's the fruit they use in *mors*," Daniel said. The Polyakovs used to make the Russian fruit drink for Daniel and Anna.

But Matskevich looked at him strangely: it was an odd thing for an American to know. "I used to take my girlfriend Janet to a little Russian place in DC," Daniel explained, which was true, although the place hadn't served *mors*. "Got fond of the food."

"It's better than American food."

"Hey now," Daniel protested. "Don't judge us based on the diners."

"Take me to a nicer restaurant, then. What else do we have an expense account for?"

"Not to waste taxpayers' money on caviar," Daniel sputtered.

Fortunately, Angeline forestalled further argument by returning with their milkshakes. "Here you go," she said. "I put extra maraschino cherries on," (she had, politely, adorned both milkshakes, although she addressed her remarks to Matskevich), "except I know not everyone likes them so I won't be offended if you take them off."

"I love cherries," Matskevich assured her. He stirred the milkshake with its long spoon, and looked up at her, not smiling exactly, but with a warmth and intensity in his gaze that was almost more beguiling than an actual smile.

She bit her lip. "If you don't mind me asking," she said, "where are you from? I've never heard an accent like that before."

The brightness went out of Matskevich's gaze, as if a candle had been doused. "Poland."

"Oh! Gosh, I shouldn't have asked, should I?" Angeline cried. "It probably brought up bad memories. I'm so sorry. My mom is *always* telling me not to pry, and here I am – "

"Angeline!" a woman shouted from the kitchen.

Angeline gave a little hop. "And that's Peggy. Be right back with your veal!" She fled, her red curls bouncing against the back of her green checkered uniform.

They both watched her go till she disappeared through the saloon doors into the kitchen. Daniel raised his brows at Matskevich. "What? No 'There I was, trapped in the glare of this German policeman's flashlight like a deer in the headlights'?"

Matskevich scowled at him. "No, of course not. This is not a story to tell a pretty girl who has nothing to do with the case – no."

Daniel, abashed, twisted a maraschino cherry on its stem. "Of course," he said, and set the cherry aside. He had always thought maraschinos were too sweet, anyway.

***

Angeline dropped off their veal without a word, her cheeks crimson with mortification. But at the end of the meal, she brought them two slices of chocolate pie they hadn't ordered: "I really am so sorry," she told Matskevich. "It must be an unhappy memory, how you escaped, right? I mean, getting past the Iron Curtain, and all that."

"Don't worry about it," Matskevich told her. "It was not so bad, really, only I don't like to talk about it." He pressed a hand over his heart. "The family left behind…"

"Oh," she gasped, a hand over her heart too. "I didn't even think of that. I was just thinking about the difficulty getting across the wall."

"No, no, don't worry about it," Matskevich told her, and now he really did smile. "I'm here now, and this is the important thing."

"Yes," Angeline agreed, and for a moment they gazed at each other. Daniel sighed inwardly and began to eat his pie.

Angeline gathered up her full skirts and slid in the booth next to Matskevich. "Let me make it up to you. I'm off shift in fifteen minutes, and I've got to go to this Halloween party at Sigma Phi tonight, so… would you like to come?"

Matskevich's face lit. "A Halloween party?"

"You've never been to one?" Angeline clasped her hands. "Oh please, then you've *got* to come, then. It will be so much fun!"

"Yes, of course," Matskevich said.

A shout from the kitchen: "Angeline!"

She darted a kiss on Matskevich's cheek. "Fifteen minutes," she said, and dashed away, leaving Matskevich to gaze after her, his face still lit from within like a jack-o-lantern.

Daniel abandoned his chocolate pie. He slid out of the booth. "I'll just leave you to take care of the check, then," he said, and left with all due haste.

***

Daniel went back to the motel room, and tried to settle down with *The Brothers Karamazov*. He couldn't concentrate, and went for a long walk instead. The motel room was still empty when he returned, and he tried to read *The Brothers Karamazov* again. At last he gave up and turned on the television to immerse himself in the soothingly anodyne world of *Ozzie and Harriet*, all old married couples and boy-girl love affairs.

He jumped up to turn off the television when he heard the key in the lock, then hastily turned off the light, just in case Matskevich had Angeline in tow.

But Matskevich was alone. Daniel switched the light back on as Matskevich toed off his shoes by the door. "Did you have a good night, *Poland*?"

Matskevich ran his hand over his hair, as though to smooth it, although this only rumpled it more. "Very fine."

"It must've been pretty good," Daniel said. "You're – are you *smiling*?" He lifted a hand over his eyes. "Stop, stop. I'll be blinded."

Matskevich tossed his suit coat over the back of a chair. He sat cross-legged on the foot of Daniel's bed, wafting before him a faint whiff of Shalimar. "We went to her Halloween party," Matskevich said. "Have you ever been to a Halloween party? Of course you have," he answered himself. "It was in a fraternity," he added, pronouncing the word with relish, "carved pumpkins lit with candles all along the rail of the porch, and apples floating in a barrel, and everyone all dressed in bright costumes. They asked what my costume was, and I told them I was dressed as a Russian spy."

"*Matskevich!*"

Matskevich grinned. He looked like an imp, with his rumpled hair kicked up like little devil horns. "It's best to hide in plain sight. Like 'The Purloined Letter.'"

"You've read – ? Of course you've read Edgar Allan Poe. Did you read every American author you could get your hands on?"

Matskevich ignored this. "So we stayed a long while," he

said, "and ate brownies and popcorn balls, which are popped corn covered in caramel. But at last it became clear her old boyfriend wasn't coming – this is why she needed a date this evening, so he could see she has moved on. What is wrong with this man, that he lets a girl like that slip through his fingers? And so I walked her home, and I put my arm around her because it was so cold..."

"Oooh."

"I thought it was only American men who wore stupid coats because you think it looks manly, but her coat was too thin, too," Matskevich mused. "But even so, we stood a long time talking on her porch. She lives in a little house with three other girls. Is this common among American college students? And then..." Matskevich's toes curled. There was a hole in the toe of his right sock. "She kissed me."

"You're supposed to kiss *her*, you lummox."

"I was going to," said Matskevich, unperturbed. "She kissed me first, that's all. And then..." He paused, savoring Daniel's impatience, and finally saying, "and then she went inside to go to bed, and so here I am."

"*Matskevich*," Daniel moaned.

"She's a nice girl," Matskevich said. "She didn't want to wake her roommates."

"You could've brought her back here. I would've pretended not to wake up."

"Oh no," Matskevich said, and wagged a finger at Daniel. "I've heard about your reputation."

Daniel's heart stopped. "My reputation?" he echoed, and felt like a slug under an upturned rock, a filthy slimy voyeur who wanted his partner to bring a girl to the room so he could listen in. The creaking bed, the squeaking bedsprings, heavy breathing, giggly half-stifled moans.

He felt a painful awareness of how good Matskevich looked like this, sitting on the bed in his shirtsleeves, his hair rumpled, his eyes bright with the excitement of kissing a pretty girl.

Jolie-laide. Ugly-pretty, a term Daniel had learned in high school French: a person who seems plain till their features are lit by emotion, animation. The other boys in his class had trouble understanding the term, and Daniel had pretended he didn't get it either, although like the girls in the class he got it at once. It gave him a queer uncomfortable feeling that there was something wrong with him, a streak of girlishness that shouldn't have been there.

Matskevich didn't notice Daniel's guilty silence. "Oh yes," he said. "That Daniel Hawthorne is a terrible womanizer, they told me. If you do manage to seduce any women," he added, in a tone that suggested he doubted any woman could have taste so poor, "you will have to get a second motel room. I need my rest."

Daniel's blood had begun to flow again. He sounded creditably snide when he said, "And I suppose you want me to put it on my expense account?"

"Of course. This is what an expense account is for."

Daniel shoved Matskevich's shoulder. "Go get a shower," Daniel told him. "You smell like her perfume."

Matskevich grinned like a Cheshire cat, and left. But the scent of Shalimar, bergamot and rose, lingered after he had gone.

CHAPTER 7

The next day, Gennady and Daniel hit the road to talk to the *Good Shepherd* subscribers.

They started with the western Iowa subscribers, following Daniel's theory that the shooter must be a local. But nowhere did they find the magic confluence of *Good Shepherd* and Mauser and person without an alibi for September 23.

The interviews struck Gennady as useless, and he settled comfortably into the assurance that they would be on the road for two or three months. It was pleasant, anyway, this chance to stop in such a wide variety of American homes, and hear the inhabitants tell their life stories, which they generally proved happy to spill in return for Daniel's sympathetic nods.

Gennady could have scoffed at them for talking so eagerly, but he felt that ease himself, and often ended the day sitting on the foot of Daniel's bed, or even lying beside him if the bed was a double. This was partly a sop to Arkady's honeytrap assignment: he could easily work it up to sound much more seductive than it was. *I was lying on his bed, Arkady Anatolyevich! I can't imagine why it didn't work.*

But mostly it was pleasant to bother Daniel. It was nice to take off his suit coat in the overheated American motel rooms, and lie on his stomach and kick up his feet and pester Daniel till he put down *The Brothers Karamazov* and began to talk.

Gennady liked particularly to hear Daniel talk about his childhood: reading the crime magazine *True Story* on the sly ("we weren't supposed to read it, but everyone did"), taking a paper delivery route to earn money to buy a proper baseball glove, buying an orange Ne-Hi cola (never grape, he noticed) and going down to the creek to fish...

Gennady sighed with contentment. This was the America of Ilf and Petrov. "Did you live out in the country?"

"No, Shinocqua's a small town. If you went a couple blocks north of my house you'd hit countryside, but if you walked a few blocks in the other direction you'd strike the downtown. A gas station and a drugstore and a movie theater... The theater's closed now; television's killing the small town theaters. I used to head downtown after school sometimes to the newspaper office where my mother worked."

"I thought American women didn't work."

"It's more common than you'd think from the magazines," Daniel said. "I suppose your mother worked."

"Oh, yes," said Gennady, momentarily eager. He would have liked to brag about his mother, who had been posted as security to Yalta near the end of the war, during the great conference between the Big Three powers.

But of course this was impossible: he could hardly say that his mother and his father and his grandfather had all worked at the GRU, given that he was supposedly not a Soviet intelligence agent at all, although the Americans would have to be dim to believe it.

Gennady fell back on generalizations. "Most women in the Soviet Union work. But they are very good mothers, too," he added. "My mother recited poetry for me." And in the interest of setting the conversation firmly on another path, he sat up and recited Pushkin's "Ya vas lyubil."

It worked: Daniel looked fascinated. "That's beautiful," he said. "I have no idea what it's about, but even so."

Gennady could not resist bragging. "When I was in school, I won a volume of Pushkin's poetry in a recitation competition. Our poets," he added, "are the best in the world."

"Oh? Have you read any American poets?" Daniel asked.

"Are there any American poets?"

Daniel hit him with a pillow. "I'll lend you my copy of Walt

Whitman," he said, then looked aghast. "No, wait. I don't think Whitman is a good place to start."

"He isn't very good?" Gennady teased.

"Um... He's a little obscure. It would be better to start with Emily Dickinson or Longfellow. I can still do 'Paul Revere's Ride,' though not as well as you do Pushkin."

"Let's hear it, then."

So Daniel stood and recited, and Gennady lay down again and listened with his head on his crossed arms. "There's a galloping rhythm to it," he said, enchanted. "That's very American, isn't it? A poetry of movement."

"Yes," said Daniel.

But he looked at Gennady so strangely that Gennady said, "What?"

"I don't know. Most people aren't interested in poetry, I guess," Daniel said, and then clarified, "Most men, at least."

"Poetry isn't manly?" Gennady scoffed. "Like wearing a coat that is actually warm enough isn't manly? Poetry is..." How to explain? "When there is nothing else, when all the world has gone mad, you recite poetry to hold things together, to give life order and meaning. The world is shaking, but poetry is steady."

Daniel was nodding. "I was in a rear unit in Korea," he said, "and we only got bombarded a few times. But it was still terrifying, and I recited 'Invictus' over and over in my head. 'I am the master of my fate, I am the captain of my soul.'" He grinned. "Strong words for a man who might get blotted out by a bomb at any moment."

"Well, of course. In such times you need strong words."

One evening, in one particularly warm motel room, Gennady rolled up his sleeves to his elbows. They had been chatting for some time when Daniel put his hand on Gennady's bare forearm, emphasizing some point that he made, which Gennady couldn't remember afterward because when Daniel touched him, he froze, mentally even more so than physically.

It was a brief touch, just a second perhaps or even shorter, and after Daniel took his hand away Gennady wanted it back. If that was all he was going to do, after all, that was pleasant, and it had been a long time since someone touched him – since someone he wanted to touch him had touched him.

He had once heard a rumor that Stalin used to make his

Politburo members waltz with each other. He wondered about it afterwards: if it was purely terrible, to waltz with another man while Stalin laughed at you, or if they found a kind of comfort in it, if it was good to be close to another person even if it was only for Stalin's amusement, and even though you knew that your dancing partner would denounce you the next day as a counterrevolutionary spy if the Party demanded it, and you would do the same to him.

Perhaps under those circumstances you could only be close to someone if Stalin made you do it.

Gennady tucked his elbows under his body and lay down on his arms like a Sphinx.

"Tell me," said Daniel. "Did you leave a girl behind in Moscow?"

"Yes," said Gennady.

But he didn't want to talk about Galya. Once Arkady had started bothering him, it had become impossible somehow to answer her letters, and eventually she had stopped writing him. His stomach clenched at the memory.

But it was getting better now: time heals everything, it would be all right. Things had gone well, had gone beautifully with Angeline.

But none of this could be explained to Daniel, so Gennady said only, "She's moved on by now."

"You don't think she's waiting for you?" Daniel sounded startled.

"No, no. All this waiting around for people is a waste of time," Gennady said. "We're all basically replaceable people, after all, she should find someone close by." Daniel regarded him curiously, and so Gennady went on the attack: "What about you? Do you have a girl?"

"Not right now. The job has kept me on the road so much..."

"A girl in every port, then," Gennady teased.

"No, no." To Gennady's surprise, Daniel flushed. "What the hell kind of picture does that Soviet dossier paint of me?" Gennady widened his eyes with false innocence – *what dossier?* – and Daniel said, "Come off it, Matskevitch. I saw a dossier on you, so I'm sure you saw one about me."

There was no safe answer to this statement, so Gennady didn't say anything. At length Daniel let it go with a sigh. "My last steady girlfriend was Janet," he said. "We started dating while I was at the FBI Academy a couple of years ago."

"And then?"

"And then I got sent into the field, and she wanted a boyfriend who was home more than once every six months, so we broke up."

"Ah," said Gennady, triumphant, and Daniel hit him with a pillow.

"That doesn't mean people are replaceable," Daniel said. "It's just that Janet and I weren't really in love, that's all. We liked each other a lot and had a good time together, but when it got tough, we didn't care enough to make it work. If we had loved each other, it would have been different."

"Do you believe such a love exists?"

Daniel looked at him strangely. "That's what love is. The will to be together despite obstacles."

Gennady shook his head. "Bourgeois romanticism."

"How would you define love, then?"

"A pretty word for the sexual instinct. A way to deflect the masses' attention from the misery of their lives by feeding them heightened emotions and focusing their hopes of future happiness on sexual passion."

Daniel laughed.

"What? Why is that funny?"

"You sound like the movie parody of a Communist," Daniel said.

Gennady sat up, furious. "Well, you sound like a typical brainwashed capitalist," he said. "How can you believe in love at your age? A teenager can believe it perhaps, but once first love is past then you know that these things never last forever, and all those heightened feelings were just a sandcastle built on the fact that you wanted to fuck."

Daniel twitched like a prudish maiden aunt at the word *fuck*.

"I have noticed that Americans are obsessed with the idea of Communist brainwashing," Gennady added, "but I think this obsession is because you know in your hearts that your own Hollywood is brainwashing you. How else could you believe that love is all you need for happiness?"

Daniel didn't reply. Deprived of fuel, Gennady's anger lapsed. He lay down again on his stomach.

"Well, I don't agree," Daniel said at last. "But that just shows the brainwashing is working, doesn't it?"

"Yes, I suppose," Gennady said. He rolled over onto his back. "You shouldn't listen to me too much," he advised. "You'll be happier if you stay brainwashed."

"Well, thanks," Daniel said, and now he laughed. "That's the key to happiness, is it?"

"Delusion?" Gennady said. "Yes."

"You don't believe that 'The truth shall set ye free'?"

"We are talking about happiness, not freedom," Gennady objected.

Another pause. "I suppose I always thought they went together," Daniel admitted.

"That's also very American. Like your Declaration of Independence: life, liberty, and the pursuit of happiness..." But this seemed like a dangerous subject, so Gennady shifted the topic. "Did you have Fourth of July celebrations in your town?"

Gennady had arrived in the United States too late for the Fourth. His colleague Sergeyich had described the fireworks and the parades: "Not as good as we have in Moscow for May Day, of course. But worth seeing! Very different!"

"Of course," Daniel said. "Every town has them. I played the trumpet with the high school marching band and we marched in the parade every year. Boy, did it get hot in those band uniforms..."

Daniel talked on for a while. Gennady relaxed, and listened contentedly, his eyes drifting shut as the sleepy heat of the radiator suffused the room. He roused from his doze when Daniel poked his shoulder. "Matskevitch," he said, "don't you think you'd better sleep in your own bed?"

"No," Gennady mumbled sleepily.

"I think you'd better," Daniel said. He gave Gennady's shoulder a shove. Gennady crawled over him, on the grounds that this was the most direct route to the other bed. Daniel shoved him again, and Gennady catapulted over the space between the two beds, and landed with a bounce. He sat up, newly exhilarated, and Daniel laughed at him again. "Go to sleep!" he ordered.

***

So the campaign to get Daniel to trust him, to place confidence in him, was going well. This was fortunate, because their attempt to find the would-be assassin was not going well at all.

In early December, they reached the last Iowa subscriber, who lived in a little town called Dresden, which Gennady privately hoped would yield the shooter. It would please everyone, Soviets and Americans alike, if the fellow turned out to be German. An escaped Nazi, preferably. The perfect scapegoat.

But unfortunately the subscriber, Miss Cora Nelson, was a gentle old spinster with a brace on one leg, barely visible under her long old-fashioned skirts. Polio, she told them. "And I had been the star of the girls' basketball team at my high school before. Have some more springerle?"

Gennady obligingly took a fourth Christmas cookie. Each cookie had a little scene imprinted on it: this one had a picture of Christ on the cross. "Tell me," Gennady asked. "How did you come to subscribe to *The Good Shepherd*?"

Despite the cookie decoration, Miss Nelson did not seem like a religious fanatic. Through their visits to subscribers, Gennady had come to recognize the signs: massive Bibles on the side table, embroidered Bible verses and tacky paintings of glowing golden Jesus on the walls. Certainly Miss Nelson had nothing like that life-size Christ on the cross, splashed with scarlet blood, that had dominated a living room in Sioux Falls.

"Oh, a nice young man was selling subscriptions door to door," Miss Nelson said. "He was trying to raise money for his tuition at Durrell College, poor thing, and he seemed so disheartened that I bought a subscription just to cheer him up. More coffee, dear?"

"Yes, please," Gennady said.

Miss Nelson made to fill his cup. "Oh, dear. I'll just make another pot. It won't be a minute..."

"No, no," Daniel interposed hastily. "We've got to be moving on. We've eaten far too many of your cookies already."

Gennady shamelessly pocketed a final springerle. "Is there a German restaurant in town?"

Miss Nelson brightened. "Oh, yes! You'll want to go to the

Gasthoff. Minnie and her husband own it. She was point guard, you know, on the team."

At the Gasthoff that night, Gennady nearly ate his weight in sauerkraut and sausages, enjoying Daniel's growing incredulity as he watched Gennady transfer the mound of sauerkraut into his mouth. "This is like a taste of home," Gennady told him.

"Lots of sauerkraut in Russia?"

"Oh yes. We love sauerkraut," Gennady assured him. "Maybe it's the German influence. Russia is like America in this," he mused, "both of our countries had many German immigrants. Catherine the Great brought them into the Volga region." He began to slice up another sausage. "And then Stalin moved them all to Kazakhstan during the war. Like your Japanese internment camps," Gennady added.

"Those were closed when the war ended," Daniel shot back.

"Yes, well. When was Little Bighorn? And yet your Indians are still on reservations."

"Do you really want to play *whose country is more terrible* chicken, Matskevich? I think we both know that I'm going to win."

"Why? You are so sure your country is less terrible?"

"No," Daniel said. "But I'm going to win because I can say that it's awful and no one is going to throw me in jail for it. Whereas you'll be up a creek if I put you in a situation where you'd have to criticize Khrushchev, won't you?"

Gennady eyed Daniel with new respect. This showed a new willingness to fight – well, not dirty exactly, you could not call the tactic anything but fair – but with all weapons at his disposal.

Gennady bowed to inevitable defeat. "Our Nikita Sergeyevich has never done anything wrong in his life," he announced. "Of course if you criticize him I must defend him from slander and lies."

Daniel cracked out a laugh, and then looked at Gennady sharply, as if to see if Gennady was joking or not. Gennady sipped his root beer (he had been horribly misled by the name: it was not alcoholic *at all*) and maintained his poker face.

"Are you serious?" Daniel asked.

Gennady widened his eyes ingenuously. Of course he wasn't going to answer that: he had no doubt that this conversation would go directly into Daniel's next report to the FBI.

Gennady didn't hold it against Daniel. Naturally he would be under orders to scare up blackmail material. It was frankly unfair, though, that all Daniel needed to do was trick Gennady into telling a couple of Khrushchev jokes, whereas Gennady would have to work this stupid honeytrap in order to blackmail Daniel. And it was never going to work, because Daniel never drank. They were at a German restaurant and he was drinking a non-alcoholic soda *on purpose*.

Daniel had been eyeing Gennady this whole time, as if he thought Gennady might break down and tell him *yes, yes that was a joke, Khrushchev has done all sorts of horrible things, he worked for Stalin you dunce*. But finally Daniel looked away and pulled a map out of his briefcase. "I think we ought to head north," he said. "Get northern Minnesota and Wisconsin out of the way before the winter really takes hold."

"Yes, all right." Gennady didn't care particularly where they went as long as they kept going. He had heard good things about the beer in Wisconsin: lots of German influence there, too. Bratwurst, Friday night fish fries.

"Probably we should have started there earlier," Daniel said, "but I really hoped we'd hit a lead in Iowa. It just doesn't make a lot of sense for the suspect to come from out of state."

This line of thought sounded likely to lead them back to Honeygold County, which was much less exciting than driving up to Wisconsin. "Perhaps we ought to go to California to interview Mr. Don Westmark," Gennady suggested slyly.

Daniel replied, as Gennady knew he would, "No. Why would he drive all the way to Iowa to take a pop at Khrushchev when Khrushchev had just been to California?"

Of course it was a reasonable point. Really Gennady had suggested it mostly because the prospect of California might make Minnesota and Wisconsin sound more palatable to Daniel.

It seemed to work, because Daniel sighed, "We'll head north. Southern Minnesota is closer to Honeygold than eastern Iowa, anyway."

Gennady shoved the final bite of sauerkraut into his mouth. "To the land of ten thousand lakes." Gennady had seen this on Minnesota license plates. "It sounds like a fairy tale kingdom."

"Yes." Daniel sounded surprised. "I suppose it does."

CHAPTER 8

They really ought to have started in Minnesota back in October and worked southward.

That was what Daniel was thinking as he drove through an increasingly heavy snowstorm in mid-December. The temperature hovered around thirty-two degrees, and the huge wet snowflakes clumped together on his windshield, despite the action of the windshield wipers.

"We're looking at the possibility of an ice storm tonight. Hope your wood boxes are full, folks. Stay warm out there!" the radio announcer said.

"I really thought we'd find a lead in Iowa," Daniel muttered.

He was talking to himself: Matskevich had fallen asleep when the storm started to get bad, to Daniel's baffled amazement. Apparently he was not concerned that they were going to slide off the road to an icy death. But at the sound of Daniel's muttering he blinked awake and peered at the thickening snowfall, and observed, "We ought to stop somewhere."

"Thanks, genius," Daniel snapped. "I'm planning to next time I see a motel."

"Daniel." Matskevich's hand touched Daniel's shoulder. "Thank you for driving."

Daniel's shoulders relaxed at the brief touch. His face heated.

He cleared his throat, and said, "I'm sure we'll find a place eventually."

"Yes, of course," Matskevich said. "It will be all right. This snow looks worse than it is."

"It's not the snow I'm worried about," Daniel said. "It's the ice."

But just around the next curve, a sign rose up out of the darkness. *Bluegill Motel*, it said, and in blessed red letters beneath: *Vacancy.*

The freckled young girl at the desk in the Bluegill Motel greeted them with a sunny, "You got in right ahead of the storm."

"So we did," Daniel agreed, although now he felt concerned on her behalf: she looked so young, possibly even a high school student. "Will you be able to get home before the snow hits?"

"Oh, I live here. My mom and pop own this place. They're out checking on the generator; it's going to be a lousy night. So I'm holding down the desk right now." She pushed aside an algebra textbook and heaved a logbook into its place. "Let's see. Right now we've got…" A pause. Her merry freckled face grew worried. "We've only got one room left," she said, "and there's only one bed. Is that all right?"

Daniel hesitated. Paul certainly would not have taken it. A room with one bed would look bad to Mr. Gilman if he heard about it.

But Matskevich said, "It must be all right. If we press on in this snow, probably we will crash the car and die."

"All right," Daniel conceded, and nodded at the girl. "We'll take it."

At least the bed was a double. But Daniel felt uneasy, an uneasiness that thickened and fill the room like cigarette smoke as he showered and shaved. He wondered if Matskevich felt it too, or if it was all in his own head and Matskevich was thinking of nothing but a good night's sleep.

By the time Daniel emerged from the bathroom, Matskevich had already stripped down to his shorts and undershirt. The well-worn undershirt clung to his chest. Daniel cleared his throat, and cracked, "Are pajamas a decadent capitalist invention?"

Matskevich didn't look up from *The Haunting of Hill House.* "Yes."

Daniel slipped between the covers on the other side of the bed, sliding down till the blankets reached his chin. There must be at least a foot of bed between them. It would be fine.

Matskevich tugged the lamp's pull chain. The light snapped off. "Good night."

***

When Daniel awoke, the room was cold.

It was still dark, but lighter than he expected. He sat up, shivering as the cold air seeped through his pajamas, and saw the moonlight reflecting off the snow through the window. The needles on the pines hung like wind chimes, clumped together by the ice.

"The power has gone out."

Matskevich's muffed voice came from across the room. He was pulling a sweater over his head.

"It's an ice storm," Daniel realized. "Damn. We may be stuck for days."

He made a move to get out of bed, but Matskevich said, "Stay. Keep the bed warm."

It was just as well that the room had achieved such a boner-killing chill, because that authoritative voice caught Daniel somewhere low in his gut. Matskevich disappeared into the bathroom, and reappeared with the dry towels thrown over his shoulder and an ice bucket full of water in his hands. "In case the pipes freeze," he told Daniel.

He settled the bucket of water on the bedside table and tossed the towels over the bed as extra blankets. Their coats followed, and Daniel scrounged his gloves and his scarf from his coat pockets. "Can you bring me a pair of socks?" Daniel asked. "They're on the left side of my suitcase."

"Yes, yes. A sweater too," Matskevich said, and soon after he deposited these things on Daniel's head.

At last Matskevich slipped back into bed. Daniel expected him to keep to his own side, or at most to lie down back to back. But Matskevich nestled in against him, his arm sliding around Daniel's chest. "Aren't you going to buy me dinner first?" Daniel cracked.

"What?"

"Oh..." Daniel considered explaining the joke, then decided that it would only make things awkward. More awkward.

Besides, he really didn't want Matskevich rolling over. It was warmer this way, with Matskevich's chest against his back, and his arm around Daniel's stomach, and even the tip of his cold nose tucked into Daniel's neck.

He couldn't resist complaining about this last. "Your nose is like ice, Matskevich."

"It will warm up." Matskevich's lips brushed Daniel's neck as he spoke. Goddammit. And his hand was – was he stroking Daniel's stomach?

Daniel smacked Matskevich's hand. "Cut it out."

Matskevich stopped. He began to withdraw his arm, but Daniel grabbed it and held it in place.

"It's warmer this way," Daniel said, excusing his action to himself as much as Matskevich. His face flushed with nerves and the first stirrings of arousal.

He plunged his hand into the icy sheets, which cooled him down. Christ, he needed to get laid. By someone *other* than Matskevich, who was a Soviet agent, for God's sake, and probably not interested anyway, no matter how seductive that hand had felt. It was probably just... the Russians were touchy-feely people. He'd seen those photos in *Life* after World War II, the Soviet soldiers kissing American GIs on the lips. The socialist kiss of brotherhood.

God, he'd loved those photos. He had clipped them out and kept them secretly, guiltily, without really understanding either his compulsion to look at them or his guilt.

Matskevich's hand remained still now. Possibly he hadn't been stroking Daniel's stomach, after all, just wriggling into a comfortable position. And it didn't mean anything that Daniel had reacted to that touch, just a physiological reaction. Perhaps he felt a certain attraction to Matskevich but, after all, attractions were as common as houseflies. He didn't fall in love with every attractive waitress who brought them milkshakes and he was not going to fall in love with Matskevich.

The blankets warmed into a soporific cocoon, and Daniel began to relax. Matskevich had forgotten to close the curtains, and the moonlight filled the room with a sweet silvery light. The soft heavy snow clung to the ice-covered spruces, picturesque as a Christmas card.

"This reminds me of when I was a kid," said Daniel, "sleeping on the sleeping porch at my grandparents' house at Christmas."

"The sleeping porch?"

"Yeah. Do you have them in Russia? It's just a screened-in porch so you can sleep cool in the summertime. But at Christmas Grandma and Grandpa didn't have enough room for all their guests, and I was the oldest boy, so they put me out on the porch."

In his mind's eye, the view out the motel window blurred with the view from the sleeping porch, years ago.

"They'd pile the blankets on till I could hardly move," Daniel said. "It was warm if you stayed still, but if you so much as twitched your pinkie finger, the sheets were like liquid nitrogen. So I'd lie like a baby in swaddling clothes and look out over the fields. Grandma and Grandpa's house was at the edge of town, and there was a long view across the fields. You could see the lights of the next town over, miles away, shining against the darkness of the night..."

"That sounds nice." Matskevich's Russian accent had grown thick with sleepiness.

"Yeah."

Silence followed – the perfect silence of a night after a snowstorm. Daniel was drifting drowsily when Matskevich said, "Tell me more about these Christmases."

"We always had an enormous feast," Daniel murmured. "There'd be cranberry sauce – real cranberry sauce made with cranberries and orange peel, not that stuff you get out of cans nowadays. And a great big meatloaf. Grandma never liked turkey so we always had meatloaf with her homemade tomato sauce on top. And all the aunts would bring different kinds of pie... cherry and apple and sweet potato..."

"You make a pie out of potatoes?"

"Sweet potatoes. It's a different plant. You've never had sweet potatoes?" Daniel asked, and he almost rolled over to look at Matskevich, except that the first slight movement brought him in contact with the icy sheets.

And it wasn't a good idea to roll over so they were face-to-face, anyway.

"Are they good?" Matskevich asked.

"What? Oh, sweet potatoes. Delicious. Better than regular potatoes."

"This I don't believe."

"You'll have to try them and see," Daniel said.

The moonlight cast blue shadows on the soft white snow. Daniel's eyelids were drooping again when Matskevich asked, "Did you eat like this at all the holidays?"

"Hmm? No. I mean yes," Daniel said, his voice confused with sleep. "There was always a lot of food, but not always meatloaf and pies. At Easter we had ham like everybody else. Do you celebrate Easter in Russia?" he asked. His eyelids felt too heavy to hold up. "I guess probably the Communist Party doesn't approve…"

"Approve, no. But, after all, in Russia you have to have Easter. You've waited so long for the spring…"

His breath, still warm against Daniel's neck, grew slow and even. Daniel's eyelids drifted shut again, and he fell asleep.

***

"Do you have plans for Christmas?"

It was the next morning. They had hiked into the nearest town (Matskevich looked immensely smug in his thick Russian coat and tall boots) and had the good fortune to stumble on a diner with its own generator, where they were greeted with steaming cups of coffee and an apologetic warning that "The kitchen's *really* busy – it may be ages before your food comes out – but after all, it's not like there's anywhere else you can go today!"

Which was true, of course, so they settled in at a corner table.

"Plans for Christmas?" Matskevich echoed. "No."

"Do you want to come to Christmas with my family? Drink some eggnog, sing some carols. Try a sweet potato pie."

The idea had come to Daniel as they hiked through the snow that morning, past houses bedecked with Christmas wreaths. Why shouldn't Matskevich experience a real American Christmas? He had been so interested in Daniel's ramblings the night before, and after all, it would certainly fulfill Mr. Gilman's instructions to show America in the best possible light. What better light could there be than the glow of a Christmas tree?

But Matskevich looked doubtful. "What will you tell your family about me?"

Of course Daniel couldn't tell them that Matskevich was a KGB agent. "That you're my FBI partner. A defector from Russia."

Matskevich frowned. "I think your family will not like an outsider at Christmas.

"Oh, they won't mind. Mom loves to have the house full of guests. She'll be pleased as punch to have you. And so will I."

A look of surprised, almost shy pleasure crossed Matskevich's face. "Then yes. Of course I will come."

CHAPTER 9

Daniel's childhood home was a palace.

Actually, it was a two-story house with a wide front porch: a comfortable American professional's home. Gennady and Daniel had visited a number of such places on the *Good Shepherd* subscriber list (surprising how many professional men thought the world would be better off if the society that underpinned their wealth disappeared), and if this had been merely another interview Gennady would not have been intimidated.

As it was, however, he sat in the car, clutching the bottle of brandy he had brought as a hostess gift.

His own people were professionals too: his mother and his father and his grandfather had all worked in Soviet intelligence. And what had it gotten them? A single room in a *kommunalka* apartment where Gennady still lived with his grandfather and intermittently his cousin Oksana, whenever Aunt Lilya got tired of Oksana's husband Alyosha and kicked the whole family out.

"It's better here anyway," Oksana once told Gennady dispiritedly, sitting on the sagging cot that she schlepped from apartment to apartment. "Not so many people in the room. And it gets us away from the *shpionka*."

The *shpionka* was a Young Pioneer who spied on Oksana and Alyosha when they had sex. This was a hazard in any *kommunalka*; Gennady and Galya always used to go to the park, because the bushes were more private than any place in the apartment, and talked wistfully of someday, perhaps, if they were lucky and got on the right list, getting one of those apartments Khrushchev was building. Two whole rooms of their very own.

This house had at least eight.

"Gennady?" Daniel said.

Gennady swiftly got out of the car. "I wish I could have brought *Sovetskoye Shampanskoye*," he said.

"The brandy will be all right."

"Anyone could bring brandy." He wanted something impressive and Soviet, something to smooth his crumpled pride.

Daniel's mother received the brandy with that rapturous American enthusiasm that Gennady had difficulty believing was real. "Brandy! This will be perfect to fire the Christmas pudding."

"Haven't you charred enough holes in the ceiling?" Daniel joked.

"Now Daniel, that was only the one year," Mrs. Hawthorne scolded. She told Gennady, "I put a little too much brandy on the Christmas pudding the first year I made it and it did leave a mark on the ceiling, but I've refined the technique since then... Do come in, do come in. It's too cold to stand outside on the porch here. Oh! I should have presented this to you first thing, shouldn't I?"

And as Gennady came in the door, stomping snow off his boots, she fetched a small plate, which held a white bread roll with a sprinkling of salt on top. "I don't know if people in the Soviet Union still do this," she said apologetically, "and it's probably the wrong kind of bread. It's really impossible to get good black bread here, I'm afraid, or I would have bought some, but..."

Gennady was smitten. "You're so kind," he said, and ventured an American exaggeration of his own: "It's perfect."

She beamed. "What nice manners you have."

"He's a good influence on me," Daniel announced.

"Yes, well, you probably need it, Danny boy. Now, Gennady – is it all right if I call you Gennady?"

Gennady nodded.

"Oh, good. It will feel much friendlier than calling you Mr.

Matskevich all weekend. Now, I'll give you a quick tour of the house and drop you off in Daniel's room to get settled. You don't mind sharing, do you? Anna will be in her old room with her family, and Aunt Rebecca and Uncle Oscar will have the guest room..."

"That will be fine, Mom," Daniel said. "We're grateful just to be indoors. I was just telling Gennady how they used to stick me on the sleeping porch at Grandma and Grandpa's house."

"Oh, weren't those Christmases wonderful!" Mrs. Hawthorne paused as she hung Daniel's coat. "It's just as well we don't have quite as many guests, the house wouldn't hold them – not that Mom and Dad's house held them then, either! But I do miss having the whole family together... Let me take your coat, Gennady. Do you want a pair of slippers? I remember the Polyakovs always kept slippers for their guests. *Tapochki*, I think they called them. So much cleaner than tracking slush through the house..."

"All right, all right," Daniel laughed, "I'll take my shoes off. You go ahead and show Gennady around, Ma, I'm familiar with the house."

"Oh, all right. Come on, Gennady. The library's just to your left, you can borrow any books you like while you're here..."

The library was a light airy room lined on two sides with crowded bookshelves. Gennady thought of his own home again. *This is our library – that stack of books over in the corner. We had a bookshelf once, Czech, you won't believe how long we stood in line for it, and then Alyosha sold it for beer money, that bastard...*

"And here's the dining room," Mrs. Hawthorne said. Gennady followed her mechanically. This room held a dark handsome wooden table and a matching sideboard, which contained a set of blue dinner plates.

And here's the table where we eat, I used to sleep under it when I was a child...

"I don't use the dining room very much, I'm afraid. Of course we'll be using it for Christmas dinner, but if you don't mind we may eat in the kitchen tonight? I'm planning to make blini – oh, Daniel, how do you feel about blini for dinner?"

For Daniel, shoeless now, had caught up with them. "I love blini."

"Not *real* blini," Mrs. Hawthorne said apologetically, "with buckwheat and so on – but just little pancakes, almost like crepes. Oh, I don't know if they're really what you eat in Moscow…"

"My mother likes to try cooking new cuisines," Daniel told Gennady. "Ma, are you still cooking out of *How to Cook and Eat in Chinese*?"

"Occasionally. It's difficult when there's no one to tell you if the dish tastes like it's supposed to…"

They followed her into the kitchen. Here there was no stink of spoiled cabbage, no burn rings on kitchen table, just a clean cluttered welcoming room with red checked curtains and a shining refrigerator almost as fancy as the ones at the American Exhibition in Moscow.

And here's our kitchen. We only share it with six other families, really lucky, Oksana's mother shares with eighteen. And we've got a refrigerator! Till just a few years ago we kept things cold in a box outside the window.

"Well, at least the Polyakovs liked these blini. They gave me the recipe, and it's the only Russian food I ever made to their satisfaction."

"Who are these Polyakovs?" Gennady asked.

"Oh, they used to be our neighbors – White Russian émigrés, you know. They watched Daniel and Anna when they were little," Mrs. Hawthorne said.

Gennady flashed a look at Daniel. Daniel avoided his gaze by taking the lid off a china jar shaped like a Dutch girl and peered intently inside. "I suppose Daniel and Anna picked up a little Russian?" Gennady asked Mrs. Hawthorne.

"Oh yes. They used to chatter away like it was their own secret language," Mrs. Hawthorne said blithely.

"And yet his accent is still so poor," Gennady murmured, with a meaningful look at Daniel.

Daniel avoided his eyes and turned a beaming smile on his mother. "New fridge, Ma?"

"Oh yes. I thought I had better replace the appliances before I retire from the newspaper. Get the house spic and span while there's still money coming in. Look at the freezer space!"

They dutifully admired the packets of frozen peas and tub of vanilla ice cream. Then Mrs. Hawthorne led them through the living room ("Daniel, you and Anna will get the tree as usual tomorrow, won't you? I still like the old custom of trimming it the night before Christmas") and up the stairs to the second floor. "And here's Daniel's old bedroom."

My childhood bedroom – oops, we already did that part of the tour, didn't we? Under the table. Now I sleep on a trunk with a chair pulled up at the end to make it long enough. Hope you're comfortable hanging from the ceiling like a vampire bat, because that's how you'll be sleeping!

"I already set up the cot for you, Gennady, I hope you'll be comfortable."

The cot was a flat padded plank, you could sleep on it for years in perfect comfort. Much nicer than the collapsible canvas cot that Oksana used, which was already ruining her back.

Maybe he could buy one of these and take it home as a present.

"Oh yes," said Gennady. "Thank you for all your kindness."

"Oh, it's nothing. I'm just glad we could give you a real festive Christmas. Now I've got to go finish packing the Christmas cookies. You boys come down and help me taste-test them once you're settled, all right? Daniel, I hope you'll make the eggnog again, somehow it always comes out chunky when I do it."

"Of course, Ma," Daniel said.

After she left, Gennady prowled the room, peering at the strange triangular felt flags on the walls, the half-finished model RAF fighter on the desk, the bookcase underneath the window seat. The books had fallen at a diagonal, terrible for their spines, and Gennady bent to straighten them. *The Boy Scouts in the Blue Ridge. The Boy Scouts in the Maine Woods. Don Strong of the Wolf Patrol.*

"This room is a shrine to your childhood," Gennady said.

"Those scout books were my dad's when he was a kid," Daniel said.

At the end of the scouting books stood a photograph album. Gennady snatched it up and sat on the window seat to leaf through it.

"My dad gave me his old Brownie camera when he left to work in the hospitals during World War II," Daniel said.

When Gennady's father left for the war, he just disappeared.

Probably he had died in one of the early battles, when the Nazis slaughtered whole Soviet armies, but they never found a body, he was still officially just *missing*.

"Dad told me to take pictures so he could see what we'd been up to when he came back," Daniel was saying. "That's Anna's seventh birthday," he added, gesturing at a blurry photograph of a little girl blowing out the candles on a chocolate cake. The date in the top left corner read *Sept. 1942*, the year badly blotted as if a child had written it. "We saved our sugar rations for weeks to make that cake."

Halfway through February of 1943, their ration cards had been stolen. They had lived off shchi made of spoiled cabbage leaves stolen from the neighbors' trash till the ration cards came through for March, and Gennady had taken to haunting the trash cans behind the officers' club, where they sometimes threw out – actually *threw out* crusts of bread, which the feral children of Moscow fought over like wild dogs.

That was how he broke his arm. He spent the next month recuperating under the table, and that was when he first read Ilf and Petrov's *One-Storied America*, over and over, as if it were a fairy tale.

"Your sister is almost my age," Gennady said.

Daniel shifted uneasily. "I suppose this all seems extravagant to you."

Gennady clenched his jaw. He said in clear deliberate Russian, "Thank you, Stalin, for our happy childhoods."

And yes: Mrs. Hawthorne was right, Daniel understood Russian, he rocked back on his feet as the words landed. Gennady closed the photo album. "Well, so, I should have guessed you'd speak Russian. Were they hoping I'd talk in my sleep?"

"I guess so." Daniel looked intensely uncomfortable.

"No, don't worry about it; it's what we would have done," Gennady replied. He felt better now, as if the scales had balanced between them: it was possible even to be magnanimous. "I want to try your mother's Christmas cookies. Are these also springerle?"

The look of relief on Daniel's face was almost comic. "She's never made those before. There are always sugar cookies, and I bet she'll make gingerbread men now that Toby – that's my nephew – is old enough to bite off their heads. And Mrs. Gottwald down at the *Journal* has probably sent lebkuchen..."

***

Of course, Gennady knew that not all Americans lived like this. He and Daniel had visited *Good Shepherd* subscribers who lived in squalid apartments, listing trailers, little farmhouses that still lacked indoor plumbing. This house, these decorative tins that Daniel and Gennady were helping Mrs. Hawthorne fill with five different kinds of cookies, this was the life of the haute bourgeoisie – and if in the Soviet Union people of a similar professional stratum lived the squalid apartment life, well, wasn't that equality? Just because one followed a profession, why should one live better than the proletariat?

In Moscow, this reasoning would not have held water for three seconds: just look how the high Party officials lived! But in America, with no Party officials in sight, it offered a fragile thread of comfort or at least moral superiority.

"I don't suppose we could mail one of these tins to your folks in Russia?" Mrs. Hawthorne asked.

"Oh..." Gennady stared at the linzer cookies packed on top of the boxes, their jam filling winking like jewels. "The customs officials would eat it."

He was suddenly afraid that she would ask about his folks, and hastened to change the subject. "Who will receive these cookies?"

Mrs. Hawthorne rattled off a list: relations, coworkers at the *Journal*, neighbors, friends from church. "I hope you'll take these over to the Greens, Daniel. You know Helen's living at home again since her husband died, God rest his soul."

"*Ma*," Daniel groaned, and then swallowed his exasperation and said, "Of course, Ma."

Gennady perked up. "Helen?"

"She was my girlfriend in high school," Daniel said. "But she broke up with me after I left for college because she'd fallen in love with someone else, and just because he's dead now doesn't mean she wants to get back together with me, *Ma*."

"She might," Mrs. Hawthorne said. "How can you know if you never see her? They were inseparable in high school," she added, as an aside to Gennady. "They started going steady junior year. Daniel gave her his class ring – "

"Which she mailed to me during my second semester at college! Because she fell in love with Reggie!"

"Because she didn't want to wait four years for Daniel to graduate to get started with her life," Mrs. Hawthorne said. "Which is fair enough, of course. Half the girls in her class married right out of high school; she didn't want to be left out. And I'm sure she loved Reggie. But she loved Daniel, too, and I don't think anyone ever totally gets over someone they truly loved. What do you think, Gennady?"

Gennady nibbled a linzer cookie thoughtfully. "Perhaps you are right," he said, "that if you have really loved a person then there will always be a sort of tie between you. But that tie isn't the same thing as love, it's just an echo of it, you couldn't base a marriage on it all on its own. But," he added, because the opportunity to tease Daniel was irresistible, "after all, maybe it could grow again into love. Daniel should take the cookies to the Greens and see."

Daniel cast his eyes at the ceiling. "*Et tu, Brute?*"

But he gained a reprieve for that night: it was already dark by the time they finished packing the tins. "You can go to the Greens tomorrow, Daniel," Mrs. Hawthorne declared. "Tonight, we'll move right into the kitchen for the blini. I got smoked fish down at LeClair's, Gennady – I expect it's not quite like the smoked fish you get in Russia, but we're pretty proud of it here in Wisconsin…"

There was a smoked trout, still in its speckled skin, and a creamy white fish that Mrs. Hawthorne identified as Menominee, and three golden fish no larger than Gennady's hand. "Chubs," Mrs. Hawthorne said. "They're my favorite: so tender. And we've got a bowl of sour cream, and a crock of butter, and…"

"You got caviar?" Daniel peered at a blue bowl full of orange fish eggs.

"Only salmon roe." Mrs. Hawthorne was apologetic, as if at home Gennady might be used to gray beluga.

"Very good," Gennady assured her.

"We have jam, too," Mrs. Hawthorne said. "The Polyakovs always said that in Russia you don't eat your blini with jam, but my children always liked it that way. And of course…"

She opened the freezer and removed a bottle of Stolichnaya.

Gennady pressed a hand over his heart. "You are the tsaritsa of all the Russias."

"I hope not," Mrs. Hawthorne laughed. "That didn't work out well for her, did it? We don't have proper vodka glasses, but Alexandra Kropotkin's cookbook says cordial glasses are just about the right size."

The handsome cut glass cordial glasses looked much smaller than the twelve-sided tumblers Gennady was used to, but perhaps there had been smaller vodka glasses before the Revolution. Anyone who could afford special vodka glasses probably had less sorrow to drink for, anyway. "Yes, yes," Gennady said. "Very good."

"Are there any other drinking customs we should follow?"

"Take a bite right after you drink," Gennady told her. "You should always eat when you drink, always. And never drink alone." In Russia, it would also have been proper to match each other drink for drink and toast for toast, but he suspected both Hawthornes would keel over and die if they tried to keep up with him.

They had a jolly evening anyway, taking shots when they wanted and eating blin after blin. "How are you still so sober when you've had six shots already?" Daniel marveled.

"Practice," Gennady told him. "But here, give me a seventh and perhaps I will dance a *gopak* on the table."

"Do you even know how to dance that?" Daniel scoffed.

"Anyone can dance anything when they are drunk enough, my friend! Give me ten shots and I can do a tango."

"And who will be your partner?"

"Your lovely mother, of course. Do you waltz, madam?" Gennady asked, and they did a turn around the kitchen before the scent of burning blini prompted Daniel to snatch the turner from Mrs. Hawthorne's hand.

"I haven't drunk like this since I was a college girl," Mrs. Hawthorne confessed, flushed and laughing, as she threw herself into a chair. She had downed all of two shots.

"During Prohibition?" Daniel asked, grinning at her over his shoulder.

"Oh yes, during Prohibition. None of this moonshine business, though. Mamie's family used to vacation in Canada during the summers, and she would come back with a box of the good stuff for us – brandy and rum and I don't know what – of course I stopped after I met your father. He was a teetotaler," she added for Gennady's benefit.

Gennady nodded gravely. "You have many years of drinking to catch up, then?"

"Well, I wouldn't put it quite like that! But certainly I can't take a shot as neatly as you. How do you do it?"

"You just tip your head back – back – and pour it right down your throat." Gennady suspected this technique of shot consumption had developed to cope with liquids considerably less palatable than Stolichnaya. "Here, I will show you how we drink *na brudershaft* – to brotherhood."

"Oh, wonderful! How?"

"You interlace your arms, like so – yes, just like that. And then you drink from your partner's cup. And then…" He planted a swift kiss on Mrs. Hawthorne's cheek.

She yelped with laughter. "Oh, you bad boy! You should have warned me." She kissed his cheek in return. She smelled like vanilla and sugar. "I used to be a terrible flirt when I was drunk," Mrs. Hawthorne reminisced. "Clearly you're just as bad."

"It's not that kind of kiss," Gennady protested.

"It's like the kiss of peace, I suppose," Mrs. Hawthorne said. "Oh, I suppose you're not familiar…"

"But I am. Daniel has taken me to church."

"Daniel! You went to church? On *purpose*?"

"For the case, Ma."

"It is a kiss of brotherhood," Gennady explained. "It means now we are proper drinking brothers."

"Drinking buddies," Daniel corrected.

"Drinking buddies. Yes. Now we can call each other by the *ty* form, if only you had it in English. Or if Daniel would like to practice his Russian?"

Daniel menaced him with the pancake turner. Gennady filled two of the cordial glasses with vodka and lifted one to Daniel in mock salute. "*Davai na brudershaft, Daniil.*"

Mrs. Hawthorne, laughing, snatched the pancake turner from Daniel's hand. "Oh, all right," Daniel said. He took his cordial glass too. "*Davai na brudershaft.*" They interlaced arms, and drank, and Gennady kissed Daniel's cheek, then poked Daniel in the ribs when he didn't return the kiss: "You too. Unless you want to be drinking enemies?"

Daniel gave Gennady a smacking kiss of such force that his stubble scraped Gennady's face. Mrs. Hawthorne clapped her hands together, laughing. Gennady said, "Now you must call me Gennady. No more of this Matskevich."

"You could have just said that anytime," Daniel said, wiping his lips with exaggerated care. "No kissing necessary, *tovarisch*."

"The Polyakovs did not teach you how to say *tovarisch* correctly?"

"The Polyakovs did not speak Bolshevik!"

Gennady laughed.

Then Mrs. Hawthorne said more seriously: "This is a beautiful ritual, Gennady, but please don't do it with Anna tomorrow. Her husband's a very jealous man."

"Of course, of course," Gennady said. "When she is here, I won't drink at all."

"Like that's going to help," Daniel scoffed. "You're a terrible flirt even when you're sober." His eyes caught on Gennady's, the glance just a little too meaningful to seem teasing. Gennady felt something like a bee sting in his chest, and remembered quite suddenly, *the honeytrap.*

He was a guest in Daniel's house; he had met Daniel's mother, and eaten her bread and salt. How could he pursue the honeytrap after that?

And the comforting thought came to him that the honeytrap had already failed. He had given it a good college try, as the Americans said, even to the point of cuddling close to Daniel and holding him all night in the Bluegill Motel, and Daniel hadn't taken the bait. What more could Gennady do? Of course if Daniel threw himself at Gennady's head he would fulfill his mission, but otherwise, enough was enough. *Finis.*

Arkady would be furious. Gennady took another shot.

"Gennady's cut quite a swathe through the waitresses of the Midwest," Daniel was telling his mother.

"Of course he has. Girls love the accent, don't they? And he looks like trouble."

"With a capital T and that rhymes with P and that stands for pool," Daniel said. He smacked his palms together. "Have you heard *The Music Man,* Gennady?"

Gennady took another shot. "No."

"Oh, we'll have to play the record then. This is great. All of American culture encapsulated in one musical." Daniel disappeared, and a record began to play in the living room.

Mrs. Hawthorne slid a fresh hot blin under Gennady's nose. "Remember to eat something when you take a shot," she said, smiling, and Gennady smiled back at her hazily. "Daniel's just teasing. I know you won't make trouble for Anna."

"Of course not," Gennady assured her. "I would never hurt your children."

She kissed his forehead, and he felt momentarily close to tears at the motherly gesture. "You're a wonderful person," he told her earnestly.

"I think you've had enough to drink," she said, and kissed his forehead again.

In fact he had a few more shots during *The Music Man*; not a lot, just enough to cheer him up again. By the time the record finished, he had reached a state of such euphoric sleepiness that Daniel had to shake him awake.

"Why don't you go on up, Matskevich?"

"Gennady."

Daniel smiled. "Gennady. You're falling asleep on the table. Go to bed."

The upstairs was cold, which relieved Gennady in a strange way: at least they didn't keep the whole house warm. And the cot was very comfortable. Mrs. Hawthorne had made it up with a soft down pillow and flannel sheets and a thick handsome quilt that Gennady pulled up over his nose. He felt pleasantly light-headed from the vodka (he must have lost some of his tolerance in these months in America) and cozy as a mouse in its hole.

When Daniel came up a little later, he didn't turn on the lights, but undressed in the moonlight that trickled in through the Venetian blinds. He had a very fine chest, well-muscled, smooth, with just a thin line of hair down the center, and in the dusky light his skin looked softly blue. "You look like an ancient British warrior," Gennady muttered.

Daniel clutched his discarded shirt to his chest. "You're awake."

Gennady propped himself up on an elbow. "They dyed

themselves blue and ran into battle naked," Gennady said, nodding at Daniel's bare chest. "I suppose they looked like that."

"They also spiked their hair with lime," Daniel said. He grabbed a pajama top and put it on so hastily that he got the buttons in the wrong buttonholes. Gennady pulled the blanket up over his mouth to hide his smile.

"Pull that up over your eyes, why don't you?" Daniel suggested. "Stop watching me undress."

Gennady lowered the quilt again. "Why? Are you deformed?"

Daniel threw his shirt at Gennady's head. By the time Gennady had disentangled himself (perhaps he was more inebriated than he thought; the shirt seemed to have enough arms for an octopus), Daniel had already changed into his pajama pants, and was slipping into his bed on the other side of the room.

"Go to sleep," Daniel said sharply.

Suddenly Gennady felt ashamed of himself. He had behaved like Oksana's *shpionka*; behaved like Arkady, leering at Daniel's chest. And for what, when he had just decided not to pursue the honeytrap?

Habit, perhaps.

Daniel's voice came through the darkness, gentler now. "Good night, Gennady."

Daniel had forgiven him, it seemed. Gennady pulled the quilt back over his nose. "Good night, Daniel."

CHAPTER 10

The next morning, Daniel took a tin of cookies over to the Green's house. It was partly to please his mother, partly curiosity to see Helen – but mostly self-defense.

Matskevich undoubtedly wasn't *trying* to flirt with him. The Soviets had different ideas about how men should behave toward each other: the "fraternal kiss of socialism," after all.

But all the same, the way that Matskevich orchestrated that exchange of cheek kisses, and told Daniel to call him Gennady from now on... and then compared Daniel to a naked British warrior daubed in woad...

Well, when Daniel got into bed after that, it wasn't hard at all to imagine Matskevich (no, Gennady; *Gennady*) sliding into bed with him, just as he had when the power went out at the Bluegill Motel – only this time he wouldn't be driven by the cold. Gennady kissing Daniel's neck, murmuring teasing things into Daniel's ear, sliding his hand under Daniel's pajama top, under his waistband...

Daniel had thrown back all the covers and walked down the cold hall to the bathroom. Mr. Gilman had given him a second chance, and Daniel wasn't going to blow it – *blow it*, he thought, and had to bite his sleeve to keep from giggling like a nasty-minded schoolboy.

Paul had been shocked by that nasty-mindedness. He had

slapped Daniel across the face once for trying to blow him: "That's filthy and I won't have you doing it." Then, more gently: "The ancient Greeks thought that was a degrading act for freeborn men."

As if it mattered at all what the ancient Greeks would have thought of what they did, when right-thinking people would be horrified that they did anything at all.

And undoubtedly the Soviets thought the same way. If he made a pass at Matskevich, if Matskevich even saw him *thinking* about it, it'd probably cause an international incident, Jesus H. Christ.

Even after he went back to bed, Daniel hadn't slept very well. But the cold walk through the snow to the Greens' woke him up, and he felt tolerably alert by the time he rang the doorbell.

Through the door Daniel could hear Bing Crosby's Christmas carols, laughter, a boy's shout of "I'll get it!" and the sound of pelting feet – and then the door flew open, and a boy of about seven or eight looked up at him.

He looked almost startlingly like Helen: brown hair and round cheeks and a light smattering of freckles. The resemblance only strengthened when Helen herself appeared behind him, and Daniel had the abrupt disorienting feeling that he had slipped somehow into another life, where he and Helen had gotten married and this little boy was their son.

Helen's welcoming smile turned into a look of surprise. "Daniel!"

Daniel summoned his most charming smile and held out the tin of cookies. "My mother sent these over for you," he said. "She conscripted me as her delivery boy as soon as I got home for Christmas."

"Well isn't that sweet! I've always thought your mother was just the sweetest woman in Shinocqua," Helen said. She took the cookies with a smile and put a hand on her son's head. "Have you met Jimmy before?"

"Jim," the boy corrected, almost in a whisper, and his mother smiled at him.

"Jim," she corrected herself.

"Jim," Daniel said, and stuck out his hand to shake. "It's nice to meet you, son." The boy ducked his head and shook Daniel's hand, and then he was off like a shot, retreating toward the sound of laughter and Christmas music.

Daniel and Helen smiled at each other. "Kids," she said, the one word an explanation. "Do you have any of your own yet?"

"Not yet. The job keeps me on the road too much to meet any nice girls," he said, and became aware too late that the comment sounded like an invitation.

"You'll find someone," she told him. "A nice boy like you? There have to be a dozen girls who would be happy to follow their G-man around the country."

And she wasn't one of them: she had never wanted to leave Shinocqua. Daniel smiled too, to show that he understood. "I'd stay and chat, but I've got other cookie deliveries to make."

"Of course," Helen said. "Give my love to your mother. Merry Christmas, Daniel!"

"Merry Christmas!"

The snow crunched beneath his boots as he walked home. He was remembering that final summer before he left for college. God, how tragic they thought they were, their young love sundered by fate; or rather by the fact that Daniel wasn't sure he wanted to go to college already married, and Helen was quite sure that she did not want to leave Shinocqua for four years in married student housing.

But neither of them admitted any of that until Christmas break. That summer, they clung to each other and cried and swore that they would do anything to stay together, and drove out to the Point to make love in the moonlight on the shores of Lake Michigan. Helen wore a red checked dress with big red buttons down the front, easily undone.

They meant to do it on the beach, but it began to spit rain, so they retreated to the car and lost their virginity together in the backseat. Helen gave him one of the buttons from her dress, and Daniel placed it solemnly in his treasure box (a shoebox really) with all the other sentimental detritus of young love: notes, ticket stubs, the boutonnière (carefully dried) that she had pinned to his tuxedo for prom.

After the Point, Daniel had asked his mother for Grandma's engagement ring, which was meant to go to Daniel's fiancée. "Danny," his mother said, "listen to me. You know we think Helen is a wonderful girl. But you're so young, and you're going to learn so much about yourself in college, and you need to give yourself room to grow."

He wondered if she might have said something different if she had known exactly what he would discover about himself at college.

Would he have ever realized he was queer if he had married Helen? Maybe not; and in that moment, as he crunched through the hard icy snow, the possibility seemed seductive, a vision of simple, wholesome life, with no secrets to keep.

They could have gotten married the summer after graduation, as so many of their classmates had. Four years in married student housing while Daniel was in college, then back to Shinocqua, where they would have settled down, a respectable married couple with two or three kids. Growing old together, hand in hand on the porch swing.

Paul had been right when he complained that Daniel wasn't serious. Even in his romantic daydreams, Daniel had never been able to imagine their relationship lasting more than a year or two. Maybe he could have invited Paul home for Christmas, once or twice, but the welcome would have definitely chilled after that, the questions grow more pointed. Shouldn't Daniel be looking for a nice girl to marry?

And perhaps they could have gotten an apartment together, for a while. But if they kept it too long, people would start to talk. Promotions would slow down, and then stop. Perhaps dismissal from the Bureau, in the end.

Hadn't he been relieved, after all, when he and Paul broke up? Not just because he was tired of Paul's obsession with the ancient Greeks, Paul's jealousy whenever Daniel noticed a pretty waitress. Daniel hadn't wanted it to end on such a sour note, but he had wanted it to end.

He had never had the courage – or the cruelty? – well, the single-minded devotion to Paul to sacrifice his job and his family for him.

Daniel had reached the house now, and he practiced a smile until it felt natural before he went inside. If visiting Helen made him look sad, it would only make his mother think more seriously about her half-joking plan to get them back together.

But when he came inside, his mother was distracted. "Anna called while you were gone," she said. "She and Joseph won't be getting in till dinner. He's got some things to catch up on down at his office..."

Typical Joseph. "But Anna and I have been cutting down the Christmas tree together since Anna was five," Daniel objected.

His mother sighed. "She'll be here in time to help decorate the tree, at least. I was hoping you and Gennady could chop it down this year? Gennady, it's a Christmas tradition for Daniel and Anna to cut down our Christmas tree at the old Hawthorne place."

Gennady was midway through a piece of cinnamon toast, but he pushed back his chair obligingly. "Yes, yes. I wish to see this old Hawthorne place."

"Ha! Yes, come see our country estate," Daniel scoffed.

"It's just a woodlot, Gennady," his mother said. "Daniel's father sold off the farmland for money to buy his practice, but no one wanted this section. It's too hilly even to pasture cows." She clasped her hands together. "I'll have hot chocolate ready for you when you get back. I usually make it with a little cinnamon, Gennady. Anna read somewhere that they make it like that in Mexico, and when we tried it we liked it so much that we started to make it like that every Christmas. But I can make plain hot chocolate for you if you like."

"No, no," Gennady assured her. "I'm happy to try this Mexican hot chocolate."

***

"What is your sister like?" Gennady asked.

They were driving through the countryside toward the woodlot, and the sun shown so brightly that even the tired snow sparkled. "Well, let's see," Daniel said. "Anna's very bright, very creative – you should have seen the Christmas cookie decoration schemes she used to come up with. One year she modeled the cookies after Dala horses – she made her own cookie cutter and everything... She painted a bunch of ornaments in that style, too."

That was the year John had beaten Daniel up, right before college broke up for Christmas vacation. Daniel rubbed his right ear.

"That was Anna's senior year. There were so many cookies she had to rope me in to help decorate." Daniel had complained long and loudly. Everything had irritated him that Christmas: everyone kept joshing him about his black eye, and it was a strain keeping up the pretense that he'd gotten it in a fair fight. "Anna made boxes for all her friends and all her beaux, and boy, did she have a lot of both."

"What does she look like?"

"A lot like me, if I were a girl."

"Ah. She must be very beautiful, then."

Daniel stared straight ahead through the windshield. Then he said, still not looking at Gennady, "People are going to misunderstand if you say things like that."

"Is Joseph very jealous?"

Daniel was embarrassed. That was not the kind of misunderstanding he had in mind. But it was also true, so Daniel said, "Yes. I think the reason they're coming so late is that Joseph isn't happy there's going to be a man who isn't a relative in the house."

"I'm sorry," Gennady said.

"No, it's not your fault. He's just like that. Honestly, I don't think he likes coming to our family Christmases in the first place. He'd rather have her to himself."

"Well." Gennady sounded disapproving. "Maybe she should divorce him."

Daniel had entertained this thought himself. But it startled him to hear Gennady suggest divorce so forthrightly, without even lowering his voice, and he did not know how to respond.

Fortunately, they had reached the woodlot, so Daniel busied himself in parking the car by the side of the road. The air stung Daniel's face as they got out. It was colder here than in town. "Here we are. Chateau Hawthorne. The footmen will take your bags."

"Is there a house here?" Gennady asked.

"On the woodlot, no. There was a farmhouse on the land Dad sold."

"The farmhouse where you slept on the sleeping porch?"

Daniel was rooting around in the trunk for his father's old hacksaw. "No. That belonged to my mom's parents." He found the hacksaw and slammed the trunk shut. "C'mon. We saw a few good spruces this way last year. We'll probably find one just the right size if the deer haven't gotten them. I'd better talk to Ma about leasing the hunting rights before the deer overrun the place... Dad always used to take care of that sort of thing."

The voracious deer had eaten most of the underbrush, so they walked through the snowy forest almost as easily as if it were a park. Daniel led the way uphill toward the spruce grove where he and Anna usually got the tree, but he paused when Gennady said, "Is this the sort of tree we want?"

Daniel considered the spruce with an expert eye. "That's a little too tall for the living room ceiling. We want room for the star on top."

Gennady considered the tree gravely. "And the branches are crooked. It must have straight limbs to hold the ornaments," Gennady said, and smiled when Daniel looked surprised. "We have holiday trees too. For New Year's. I suppose it is the German influence again."

They hiked through snow dotted with deer tracks. Daniel's thighs burned from the steep slope. "You and your sister have been getting the tree since you were five years old?" Gennady asked.

"Yes. Well, since Anna was five. We always went out with my dad, except when he was away for the war, of course. But after that, he took us every year until he died." Daniel paused, momentarily lost in memory. "That was a couple of years ago. Just before Christmas. Anna and I almost didn't go get the tree that year..."

"I didn't know your father died so recently."

"Yes. A heart attack. It was very sudden," Daniel said. A lump rose in his throat. "We used to spend a lot of time out here," he said, excusing his emotion to himself as much as explaining to Gennady. "Not just for the Christmas tree. Dad was my Boy Scout troop leader, and always brought the troop out here to camp. He meant to donate the land to the Boy Scouts when he died, but Pete Gardner gave them a camp first, the rascal."

"You must miss him."

"Yes," said Daniel, although the words caught him on the raw. He did miss his father, and he had been devastated when he died. But at the same time...

At the same time, a part of him had been relieved, because this meant that his father would never *know*. No matter what happened, he would be spared the knowledge that his son was a deviant.

Daniel cleared his throat, and said roughly, "Here's the spruce grove."

They considered trees in silence for a while. Then Gennady said, "We think my father died in the war. He was in one of the early armies, one of the ones that was encircled and wiped out."

"I'm sorry," Daniel said.

"It's all right. This was very common, many of my classmates lost their fathers too. And, after all, we all had Comrade Stalin."

Daniel stared at him. Gennady looked back, bland and serious. But the look on Daniel's face must have proved too much for him, because Gennady burst into laughter.

Daniel laughed too, almost wild with relief. "That was a *joke?*"

"Your face! I'm sorry." Gennady laughed some more. "A joke and not a joke. Oh, I don't know. It's hard to explain. Americans can't understand about Stalin."

"Try me," Daniel suggested.

But Gennady looked grave again, and didn't answer. "What about this one?" he said instead, gesturing at a tree. "Good straight branches for ornaments.

"Oh! Yes, that's just about the right height. If you'll hold it steady, I'll saw."

Daniel knelt to saw through the trunk. The branches made a screen between them, so that Daniel could barely see Gennady, only the tips of his boots. He was about halfway through the trunk when Gennady's voice filtered through the branches. "Did you have any friends whose fathers beat them? Really, really beat them."

Daniel heard an echo of Paul's voice, after Daniel noticed the tiny scars on his back left behind by the thin metal tongue of a belt. *He was trying to beat the devil out of me*, Paul said, flat and distant, as Daniel touched the marks; and Daniel had put his arms around Paul, and held him, and for once Paul had let himself be held.

"Why do you ask?" Daniel asked.

"Perhaps that will help you understand about Stalin. How we all loved Stalin," Gennady said, "because we were so afraid of him. No, you can't understand this," he answered himself. "You're an American, you always think it should be possible to stand and fight."

This was an awkward conversation to have on his knees while sawing through a tree trunk. "I know you can't always fight," Daniel said, and thought of John again. Daniel had been too stunned to fight back. He had just let John hit him.

"Or at least to flee," Gennady said. "You think that if you are afraid it should be possible to do something, to fight back or get away. But sometimes it isn't, sometimes there is nothing to do but endure, and then people fall in love with the thing that they fear because there is no other way to protect themselves. They hope that if they love perhaps they will be loved in return. Do you see?"

But Daniel couldn't answer: the saw was about to break through. "Brace yourself, Gennady, the tree's about to go."

The saw jerked through the last bit of trunk. The tree fell into Gennady's arms, and Gennady held it upright as Daniel clambered to his feet to help steady it.

They were looking at each other through the tree branches. Gennady searched Daniel's face, his gray eyes serious, almost worried.

"But you don't love Stalin now," Daniel said.

Gennady's expression shifted into mockery. "Oh, I don't know. Can you ever stop loving someone you really loved?"

Daniel was aghast. "My mother was talking about romantic love," he protested. "And also, I think that yes, sometimes people *do* stop loving someone that they used to really love. And I don't believe," he added stoutly, "that a love compelled by fear is real love anyway."

"Of course it's real. You just don't want to believe it because you Americans have made love your god and you believe God must be perfect. No, you can't understand," Gennady said, and shifted the tree so the branches obscured his face again. "You've watched too many Hollywood movies, you don't live in reality anymore. You think love is the most powerful thing in the world. But really it's fear, because fear can compel love. Come on, Daniel," he said, and hefted the tree. "Let's get this tree back to the car."

***

Aunt Rebecca and Uncle Oscar had already arrived when Daniel and Gennady got back with the tree. But Anna did not arrive in time for dinner, although the roast got dry in the oven as they waited for her.

It wasn't till they were drinking after dinner coffees that Anna swept in with her son Toby. "Joseph had to take care of some things at the office," she explained, her voice bright and brittle as an icicle. "So we agreed he'd follow along when he could."

"That's fine. We're just so glad you're here," Ma said. "Do you want a cup of coffee, dear? You're just in time to decorate the tree, too."

"Oh, you've already gotten the tree!" said Anna, and looked for a moment like she might cry. But then she forced a smile, and accepted a cup of coffee, and chattered away with a bright hard pretense at gaiety.

It hurt Daniel to watch, so he excused himself to begin untangling the Christmas tree lights. He and Anna could have a real talk while they decorated the Christmas tree.

But when Anna joined him not long after, she had Gennady in tow. "Mom's taken Toby up to bed," Anna said. "I asked Gennady to help decorate the tree. You don't mind, do you, Daniel?"

"Of course not," he said, although he was annoyed: he suspected she had brought Gennady along specifically to avoid talking to Daniel alone. "Why don't you two sort out the ornaments while I finish these blasted lights? Gennady, you don't *have* to let Anna tell you the history of every single ornament if you don't want to."

"But of course I want to," said Gennady, with a bright impish smile at Anna.

She looked very pretty that night, with her cheeks flushed and a sprig of holly in her dark hair. As she unpacked the Christmas ornaments, Gennady kept glancing at her admiringly, and Daniel watched Gennady watch Anna.

Then Gennady caught Daniel looking, and smiled at him. Daniel looked away and busied himself in twisting the lights around the tree.

Anna opened box after box of ornaments: delicate glass icicles, cut-paper snowflakes, little wooden horses. Gennady galloped one of the horses across the rag rug, which made Anna laugh. "I painted these myself," she said. "So they'd look like those Swedish horses, you know, Dala horses. My best friend when I was ten came from a Swedish family and they had the most beautiful painted wooden horses."

"You are very talented," Gennady told her.

"Oh! Well, I was, I guess, before I got married." She gave an abrupt awkward laugh, and opened the next box of ornaments. "Oh Daniel! Do you remember the year we made these beaded Christmas tree balls?"

Daniel stood atop a stool wrapping the Christmas lights to the very pinnacle of the tree, but he looked over to see Anna holding up a scarlet ball worked in patterns of gold beads. "You mean the year that you forced me to make ornaments and then redid the ones I made because they weren't good enough?" Daniel said.

"Only one of them!" Anna protested.

"It's good that you kept him in line," Gennady said with false gravity. "Otherwise he would be insufferable."

"You're both insufferable," Daniel said. He got off his stool and plugged in the Christmas lights.

A minor Christmas miracle occurred: all the lights came on, no bulbs blown out. The soft white lights gleamed on the Christmas tree.

Anna clasped her hands. "Oh, it's so elegant. It's almost a shame to put up the ornaments."

"Anna!" Daniel protested. "How can you say that after all those years you forced me to pin beads to Christmas balls and cut out snowflakes?"

Anna laughed. "Of course we're putting up the ornaments," she said. "Christmas isn't about elegance. Christmas is for excess!"

***

Very early the next morning, Anna's son Toby woke them all running down the hall shrieking, "It's Christmas! It's Christmas!"

Daniel threw off his covers, on the theory that if you had to get up you had better do it at once. Gennady, on his cot, dragged his blanket over his head. "What is happening?"

"It's a time honored tradition for children to wake up the whole house before dawn on Christmas morning," Daniel said, rapidly exchanging his pajama bottoms for a pair of thick corduroy pants. He wished that his mother would embrace the idea of central heating. "Toby wants to open his presents."

"At home," Gennady said, voice muffled by blankets, "we give the children presents on New Year's Eve, so there is no occasion for this…"

"*Christmas, Christmas, Christmas!*" Toby howled.

"This hullaballoo?" Daniel suggested, pulling on the Christmas sweater Aunt Rebecca had knit for him years earlier.

"Hullaballoo? Yes. Hullaballoo. The sun is not even up."

Daniel dumped another one of Aunt Rebecca's sweaters on Gennady's head and smacked his bottom through the covers. "Get up and put the sweater on. No tie today. We're all very informal on Christmas morning."

Gennady groaned in protest. That smack on the bottom had been a mistake: it made Daniel want to drag him out of bed, to mock wrestle on the floor and then…

Well, obviously in imagination this ended with Gennady making a very different kind of groan.

Daniel hastily headed for the door. "It's also a Christmas tradition for Ma to make French toast," he said as a parting shot.

Toby was still trying to wake Uncle Oscar with a loud rendition of "Jingle Bells" when Gennady came downstairs. The sweater was a little too large, but the dark green color suited him. "You know I'll feed you even if you don't look like a starved waif," Daniel's mother laughed.

Gennady sucked in his cheeks and pulled the sweater sleeves down till they nearly covered his hands. "But you might feed me more if I do."

But then Uncle Oscar appeared, affecting loud yawns and grinning as Toby dragged on his hand, and then there was nothing for it but to gather around to Christmas tree to open presents.

Since Dad had died, Daniel had taken his chair at Christmas, but now he installed Gennady there and stood leaning against the back of the chair. Toby capered with impatience as Anna doled out presents. Uncle Oscar and Aunt Rebecca sat on the couch, Aunt Rebecca's knitting needles clacking. Daniel's mother didn't sit at all, but floated through the room filling coffee cups and taking photographs with Dad's old decrepit Brownie camera.

Suddenly Daniel's mother came over to Gennady, a tin of cookies in her hands. "Gennady dear," she said, "I've got a present for you."

Gennady's eyes widened. "But I don't have anything for you."

"Oh, don't worry about it! You brought that lovely brandy that I'll be using to flame the Christmas pudding. That's a present for us all."

Gennady took the tin with both hands. He removed the lid and gazed down at the linzer cookies arranged on top, and smiled with such pleasure that he looked shy when he lifted his eyes to Mrs. Hawthorne. "Thank you."

"Oh, it's not much," said Mrs. Hawthorne, pleased as punch. "If Daniel had only let me know you were coming a bit sooner," this with a mock glare at Daniel, "I would have gotten you something nicer, but as it is..."

"It's good," Gennady assured her, "It's perfect."

"If I'd known I would have gotten you something too," Anna added. "Why don't you take one of the Dala horses? Whichever one you like best."

"And do keep that sweater," Aunt Rebecca told Gennady. "It's one of mine, dear, I knit it."

"Aunt Rebecca," Daniel protested laughingly, "you gave that sweater to me."

"And I can tell it's barely been worn!" she said, and shook her knitting needles at him.

"RAWR," said Toby, attacking one of Uncle Oscar's bunny slippers with his new stuffed T. Rex.

"Thank you," Gennady said. "Thank you."

He was smiling down at the Christmas cookies like he didn't know where to look. Daniel ruffled his hair roughly. "I got you a present too," he said. "Anna, can you grab it under the tree there? The one under the purple Dala horse."

Anna tossed the present to Gennady. Daniel leaned against the back of the chair to watch Gennady open it. The tips of Gennady's ears flushed as they all watched him slit the tape with his fingernail, unwrapping the present without ripping the wrapping paper. The Brownie camera clicked.

At last Gennady removed the wrapping paper to reveal a slim volume of Emily Dickinson, the cover illustrated with a simple spray of pressed flowers. He smiled up at Daniel. "I should buy you a volume of Pushkin."

"It's not like I could read it in Russian," Daniel pointed out, and Gennady's eyebrows quirked.

"The Polyakovs didn't teach you that?"

"Oh, hush, you," Daniel said, and smacked his shoulder. But he couldn't help grinning. "Merry Christmas, Gennady."

CHAPTER 11

After Christmas they hit the road again, and for a long time they made no progress in the case. They interviewed *Good Shepherd* subscribers, they tracked down Mausers, they diligently checked alibis for September 23, 1959. But nothing came of it.

Gennady's suspicion that they wouldn't find their shooter had settled down to a near certainty, although of course he didn't mention that in his reports to Stepan Pavlovich. His goal had shifted: now he intended to waste as much time and money as possible, so Stepan Pavlovich would get fed up and send him straight back to Moscow when they finally recalled him. That would keep him out of Arkady's office.

Besides, he was enjoying the trip. It was winter in earnest now, not a very cold one by Gennady's standards, but snowy.

Late one night, as they crossed a park on their way back from a bar, they stumbled on a makeshift ice rink, a sheet of ice surrounded by walls built of snow.

"We used to make ice rinks just like this in the park in Shinocqua," Daniel said, his breath puffing like smoke in the moonlight. "We, my Scout troop I mean, we'd set up a booth and sell hot chocolate to raise money to pay our scout camp expenses."

Gennady was enchanted. "These ice rinks are common?" he asked, and when Daniel nodded, Gennady said, "I'll buy ice skates. For both of us." That would discharge his debt for the Christmas gift of Emily Dickinson. "I'll put it on my expense account."

"Gennady," Daniel protested.

Gennady widened his eyes in false innocence. A well-fattened expense account could only aid in his quest for demotion, after all. Not that a couple of pairs of ice skates would be much compared to some of the shenanigans Sergeyich got up to.

A more pressing concern occurred to Gennady. "Can you skate?"

"Can I skate?" Daniel scoffed. "I'm from Wisconsin."

"Oh, yes. You think that's very cold," Gennady said, patronizingly, and ducked when Daniel threw a handful of snow at him. He packed a snowball himself and hurled it at Daniel, and the two of them chased each other around the deserted park in the moonlight, hurling snowballs and insults until Daniel caught Gennady in a headlock. Gennady swung Daniel on his back in the snow, and fell on him to rub snow in his face as Daniel, laughing, tried to shove him off.

At last he succeeded, and Gennady fell beside him in the snow, panting for breath. Daniel smiled at him, his teeth very bright in the moonlight and his eyes dark. One ice-encrusted glove moved to touch Gennady's cheek, and the thought struck Gennady that Daniel was going to kiss him.

Gennady sat up. His breath burst out of him in white clouds.

Daniel sat up too, and began beating snow off his coat. Gennady staggered to his feet and went to sit on a playground swing. "What is the time?"

Daniel checked his watch by moonlight. "Getting on toward one."

Gennady felt disquieted. He must have been wrong, they had not drunk so very much after all, Daniel probably had not been going to kiss him. It was just that Gennady had kissing on his mind because of the honeytrap, it made him see things that weren't there.

If Daniel actually threw himself at Gennady, it would be wrong not to report it; a betrayal of his country not to turn over this prime piece of blackmail material on an enemy agent. Or... Gennady twisted on the swing's chains. Perhaps it was not a betrayal of the USSR, but only Arkady, and who cared very much about that?

Well, but he could tell Stepan Pavlovich instead of Arkady. If Daniel ever threw himself at Gennady.

Which Daniel would not do. Everything would be fine.

The swing set shivered under the weight as Daniel settled in the swing next to Gennady's. "You okay?"

"The beer is catching up with me. We should go to the motel."

But as they trudged through the snow, he was remembering another snowy day, last winter in Moscow, the first time he had taken Galya out. Such a beautiful girl, he had felt so lucky that he was nearly too shy to kiss her – had not kissed her until they parted in the Moscow subway, until he was riding the escalator away from her, and she shouted after him, "You've dropped a mitten, Gosha!"

And he ran back down the escalator, and took the mitten from her hand, and kissed her just as naturally as if they had kissed a thousand times. But it had been the first, and he had bounded up the escalator and burst out in the bright cold city with the feeling that he was emerging into a new world.

When Galya stopped writing to him, the cessation of letters had felt distant, like something that was happening to somebody else. Now it broke upon him close and near and almost choked him.

"Are you all right?" Daniel was peering into his face.

"Yes," Gennady said. He rubbed a mitten (the selfsame mitten he had dropped in the Moscow subway) over his eyes. "I was thinking about Galya."

Daniel's face softened. He was pleased, Gennady thought, to see that Gennady was not such a cynic about love after all. "Why don't you try to win her back, Gennady? Bring her a big present from America. Tell her you were thinking about her. Sweep her off her feet."

"Did you try this with your Helen when she mailed you your ring?"

Daniel groaned. "I can't believe my mother told you about that. No." He grew pensive. The snow that had seemed so light and airy when they were chasing each other now clung heavily to their boots. "I was sad when she mailed me the ring," he said, "but I had fallen in love with – " A slight hitch in his voice, and his stride as well. "Well, with someone else. But you haven't," he added, to Gennady, his tone hovering halfway between a statement and a question.

"No," said Gennady. "But, after all, it's possible to fall out of love with someone, without being in love with someone new." He wrinkled his nose. "At least, I can. *You* it seems are always in love with someone."

Daniel swept up another handful of snow and tossed it into Gennady's face.

It wasn't all snowball fights and ice-skating, of course. But even the work itself was pleasant. Most people would spill their hearts for a few kind words, it seemed, and so Daniel would sympathize *Good Shepherd* subscribers into telling their whole life stories, and work his way around to find out where they had been during Khrushchev's visit. If someone proved recalcitrant, Gennady would wind them up with a few brusque comments – sometimes his foreign accent was enough to get them going by itself – and once Daniel smoothed their ruffled feathers, then they would tell everything to spite Gennady.

And it was interesting to hear about their lives. Gennady had known of course that American banks were evil, but he learned a good deal more about it, and worked up a good report about the history of farm foreclosures for Stepan Pavlovich. Quite a lot of the *Good Shepherd* subscribers had lives right out of *The Grapes of Wrath*, driven off their farms when they fell behind on the mortgage.

"It's funny that they are so happy to tell an officer of the Federal Bureau of Investigation how much they hate the federal government," Gennady mused one snowy evening, as he shot billiards in the corner of a bar. Daniel refused to play pool with him. He wasn't even drinking beer, but a ginger ale.

Daniel rolled his shoulders in a shrug. "There's a fine American tradition of loathing the federal government. It's practically patriotic." He sipped his ginger ale. "I suppose Soviet citizens wouldn't tell a KGB officer how much they hated the Party over tea and cookies?"

The image was so irresistibly funny that Gennady's next shot went wild. He leaned against the pool table to laugh.

"Doesn't that bother you?" Daniel asked. His brown eyes

were bright and kind, his head tilted forward in the very attitude of a sympathetic listener, and Gennady actually opened his mouth, on the cusp of answering, as if he could just say, *of course it bothers me, naturally I hate the KGB*, as if he could criticize his country to an American agent who would undoubtedly report it right back to the FBI.

Gennady swallowed the words as they were rising in his throat, and nearly choked on them.

Well, so this was why the *Good Shepherd* subscribers all spilled their guts to Daniel. Gennady had seen that the sympathetic listener trick was effective, but it was different to feel its lure himself, like the pull of a rip tide.

Gennady began to dispose of the pool balls with neat tense shots. "Still trying to gather blackmail material?" he asked lightly.

Daniel looked dismayed. "It would get you into trouble if you said anything bad about the KGB, wouldn't it?" he said.

Gennady wanted to strike him with the pool cue. "Why should I say anything bad about the KGB?" he asked. "The KGB is heroically protecting the USSR from capitalist spies and western imperialist provocation."

He didn't sound quite sincere enough: there was a little bit of a schoolboy singsong, like a child reciting a lesson. But Daniel nonetheless looked taken aback. "I'm sorry."

And that apology bothered Gennady more than anything. As if this were something personal, rather than part of Daniel's job.

CHAPTER 12

In the middle of March, just when Daniel thought he might die of the horrible combination of professional boredom and unrequited love – almost certainly unrequited? Probably unrequited? Oh, it had to be unrequited. As if the Russians would ever hire a queer agent.

Unless they didn't know, of course.

Unless Gennady didn't know, himself. Didn't let himself know, the way Daniel had tried not to let himself know for years, until he met Paul.

Gennady bought them both ice skates, as he'd promised. One night in late February they found another makeshift outdoor ice rink, and skated until there was no one else left on the rink, just the two of them skating in the moonlight. Gennady linked his arm through Daniel's, and spun him in a do-si-do till they both fell on the ice, where they sat and warmed themselves with shots from Gennady's flask.

"Brandy?" Daniel teased.

"I wanted to try it. It always sounds so good and warming in English stories." Gennady lay down on the ice, arms stretched above his head.

"And has it displaced vodka in your heart?"

"Of course not. But it isn't bad," Gennady said, and took another swig. His lips looked wet and shiny in the moonlight, and Daniel nearly leaned in to kiss him.

But then Gennady wiped his lips and sat up again.

Maybe, probably, almost certainly it was entirely one-sided on Daniel's part. Maybe he was just incapable of going very long without falling in love with *someone*, and Gennady was there to be loved.

And then in the middle of March, they had a breakthrough in the case.

***

They had stopped at a field office in Cincinnati so Daniel could send in a report. He ought to state it baldly, he thought – "No new leads in months" – and then perhaps Mr. Gilman would shut down the case, and end their partnership, and Daniel would no longer have the opportunity to stare longingly at Gennady's mouth.

Instead, he was trying to think how to gussy up his report so the case still sounded promising. Eke out a few more weeks of partnership with Gennady. Torture himself a little more.

"Agent Daniel Hawthorne?" the secretary said. "We've got a message for you."

"For me?" Daniel said.

He felt sick. It had to be a message from Mr. Gilman, closing the case for lack of progress.

The secretary handed over a slip of paper. "From a Daniel Jones of the Des Moines Police Department."

Daniel managed to draw in a breath. Then he read the message.

Found stolen Mauser in glove compartment of Congressman Abbott's son.

***

"I pulled Peter Abbott over for reckless driving," Officer Jones explained. Daniel and Gennady had driven back to Des Moines and met Jones, at his insistence, in a diner rather than the police department. "I asked to see license and registration, and when he leans over to open the glove compartment, there's the gun. Scared me half to death. So I ask, 'Have you got a permit for that?' And then he got real squirrely, and started babbling away about how it's his father's gun, and that's when I connected the last name to our conversation..."

"Thank God you did," Daniel said warmly. "This is the first good lead that we've had in months."

Jones expanded with pride. "So I took him and the gun back to the station," he explained. "And sure enough, it's the missing gun. I told my chief, 'That's wanted in an ongoing FBI investigation,' and he says to me, 'Shit, son.' Because he'd contacted Congressman Abbott the moment that I radioed in that I had arrested Peter Abbott, and the congressman wanted his gun back."

"Did he get it?"

Jones' eyes flickered away from them. "He plays poker with the chief."

All right. They wouldn't be able to match ballistics.

"The congressman asked to meet me. He thanked me particular for looking after his son." He swallowed. "Said he'd remember my name."

Gennady looked at Daniel. His eyebrows rose very slightly, as if to say, *Do we pursue this?*

"Even a congressman is subject to the law," Daniel said. He turned his attention back to Jones. "What kind of car does Peter Abbott drive?"

Jones relaxed, just a little. "1958 Thunderbird," he said. "Turquoise." He managed a weak smile. "*Sweet* car."

Daniel hoped Peter had been stupid enough to drive it on the day of the assassination attempt. People might remember such a flashy car.

"I don't suppose," Daniel said, "that you got a mugshot."

Jones slid a photograph across the table, and Daniel and Gennady both leaned in to look. Peter Abbott was a fair-haired young man, good-looking in a nondescript way.

"Is he a big man?" Gennady asked. "Big feet?" And then Daniel remembered the size fourteen boots.

"Oh, gosh. Six-four maybe? I didn't look at his feet, sorry."

"Did he smoke?" Gennady asked.

"Chain-smoked Marlboros the whole time we had him in custody. Real nervous," Jones said, and sighed. "I wish you'd been here. He would've spilled the beans if I'd just known the right questions to ask."

Goddammit. Daniel understood why they had to keep the assassination attempt hush-hush, but it was maddening to know that Peter Abbott could have been cooling in his heels in a cell right then, and instead... "I hope his daddy didn't spirit him out of the country."

"Gosh!" Jones looked startled. "What'd he *do*?"

"I wish I could tell you," Daniel said, with real chagrin. "But it's classified."

"Oh, well..." Jones looked disappointed, but accepting. "Well, I don't know. In the station the congressman was mostly just scolding Peter. You know. Peter ought to spend more time studying and less hot-rodding. Typical old-man stuff."

"Studying?" Gennady said. "He is a student?"

Jones nodded. "Durrell College. Little liberal arts college on the edge of town. He told me, 'cause he was on his way there when I pulled him over. Gotta get back in time for curfew, that's why he was going forty miles over the speed limit."

Daniel and Gennady looked at each other. Daniel looked back at Jones. "I don't suppose," Daniel said, "that you know if Peter Abbott has any priors?"

"Just some speeding tickets," Jones said, and then, rather bashfully, took out a notebook and pushed it across the table. "I wrote them down..."

"God bless you," Daniel said, and Jones blushed red.

"I just thought it might be useful."

"Here," Gennady said, and jabbed his finger at the third speeding ticket.

September 23, 1959. Stopped going 85 miles an hour, heading east on County Road K22, just inside the limits of Honeygold County.

Gennady and Daniel looked at each other again, and Daniel just about kissed Gennady right there, in front of Jones and God and everybody. "We've got him."

***

"You suspect *who* now?" Mack said, in a tone that suggested he hoped against hope that he had heard them wrong.

"Peter Abbott," Daniel said.

"Son of Congressman James Abbott," Gennady said. He added, with perhaps an unnecessary level of zest, "The Congressman plays poker with the Des Moines chief of police."

Mack groaned.

"We're Feds, Mack," Daniel reminded him. "We can take on a member of the poky old Iowa State Legislature."

"Christ." Mack rubbed both hands over his face, then drank some coffee out of a near-empty cup. "Get your suit pressed," he told Daniel. "You'd better start dressing like an FBI agent again if you want to take on the goddamn Abbotts."

***

Daniel had been dressing down for the last few months while they were undercover, and it felt strange to put on his crisp FBI suit again. Pants with creases so sharp they could probably cut butter. His best tie: a present from his father, the last Christmas before Dad died. He had been so proud of Daniel. His son, the FBI agent.

Thinking about that gave Daniel a funny feeling in his stomach as he adjusted his tie. He met Gennady's eyes in the mirror. "Very pretty," Gennady told him.

Daniel laughed and turned sharply away from the mirror, as if that would make Gennady less likely to notice he was blushing. "You don't call men pretty," he told Gennady. "Men look handsome. Or dapper. If you have to comment on their appearance at all," he added, rather desperately.

"Dapper," Gennady said, as if tasting the word.

Daniel's desire to kiss him surged. He rubbed the back of his hand over his mouth instead, and said roughly, "*You* look like something the cat dragged in." Gennady looked down at his rumpled Soviet suit, and Daniel added, "We should get you a new suit."

Daniel was appalled as soon as he said it. It was a terrible idea to take Gennady to a clothing store, and watch him try on suit after suit, clothes that actually fit him for once, until they found one that looked especially good...

"An American suit?" Gennady said. "No. It will cost too much."

"Really? All of a sudden you don't want to use your expense

account?"

"I am not going to waste the money of the Soviet working people," Gennady responded indignantly.

Daniel nearly laughed at him. Where had that indignation been when Gennady insisted they had to eat dinner at King Cole, the swankiest restaurant in Indianapolis?

("I will put it on my expense account if you can't explain it to your FBI," Gennady had informed him grandly. He ordered with such munificence – frog legs, escargot, cherrystone oysters, two bottles of wine, a filet mignon and a rack of lamb – that the chef sent out crepes Suzette for free, and as they walked back to the hotel, Gennady could speak of nothing but his delight at seeing the dessert set alight at tableside. "Whoosh!" he cried, miming the upward rush of flames. He tripped over an uneven place on the sidewalk and laughed when Daniel caught him, and Daniel felt a mad urge to push him into the nearest alley and press him against the brick wall and kiss him, wanted Gennady to kiss him back, as greedy for Daniel's mouth as he had been for the oysters and wine.)

But now Gennady's face was tense. His indignation, for once, was not an act. Daniel remembered then that Khrushchev had refused to wear evening clothes when he visited the US: he had appeared at swanky dinners in a regular suit and tie, and forced everyone else in his entourage to do the same. Perhaps this suit had more symbolic value than Daniel appreciated.

Or possibly Gennady had noticed Daniel salivating over the prospect of seeing Gennady all dressed up in a fancy suit. That might well make him wary, too.

"You're not going to look like an FBI agent if you're dressed like that," Daniel said, trying to explain.

Gennady lifted his chin. "Mack dresses like this."

"Mack can get away with it because he's been with the Bureau for decades," Daniel protested. But then he sighed. "Oh, fine. Wear your horrible suit if you want. Maybe it's just as well if Peter Abbott hears there's a man with a bad suit and a Russian accent after him. It might scare him into talking."

***

"We'll hit up the registrar first," Daniel said, as they drove across town to Durrell College. "I gave her a call from the field office; she'll have Peter Abbott's transcripts ready for us." At least he hoped she would. She hadn't sounded too happy about it on the phone. "His attendance records, his schedule. It's another brick in our case if he wasn't in class September 23rd. Then we'll hit up the yearbook office..."

"Yearbook?" Gennady interrupted.

"It's a book that colleges print every year. High schools, too. Photos of all the students, which clubs they belonged to, things like that. We can find out which frat Peter's in – which fraternity," Daniel clarified, and then clarified again: "Fraternities are social clubs for men. They're a big deal on most campuses. Lots of frats have a house that their members can live in..."

All of a sudden, quite stupidly, he could feel his face getting hot. He hoped it wasn't turning red.

But Gennady seemed focused on assimilating this new information about the American fraternity system. "So these fraternity members – "

"Brothers," Daniel corrected. "The members of a frat are called brothers."

"Brothers."

"Yes. We'll want to interview the brothers in Peter's frat."

"They will mention these interviews to Peter, I think."

They were driving through campus now: handsome red brick buildings, stately trees just beginning to bud. "I sure hope so."

"Ah." Gennady's eyes narrowed. "You want him to hear? So he will know that we are closing in on him, like wolves circling. Perhaps if he is frightened enough, he will..." He paused, just for a moment, and then smiled as he remembered the phrase. "'Spill the beans'?"

Daniel nodded. "Now that we've lost the Mauser, all we're ever going to have is circumstantial evidence," he said. "We'll never be able to touch him if he doesn't confess. But he may break down and tell us everything if he gets nervous."

He pulled into a parking space in front of the registrar's office, located in a gracious white house with white and purple crocuses sprinkled over the lawn. "Very pretty," Gennady said.

"Liberal arts colleges usually are. I went to one," Daniel added, quite unnecessarily, "before I went to fight in Korea.

Transferred to a state university after I got back."

"Why did you change schools?"

It was a perfectly reasonable question, but Daniel's face got hot again. "Oh... Well... My class had already graduated. It just seemed easier to start over fresh..."

Gennady, thank God, was not fully paying attention. He was already getting out of the car, intent on the registrar's office. Daniel followed hurriedly up the porch steps.

The registrar was a motherly woman: portly, prematurely gray, with a pair of glasses on a chain that she slid onto her nose to study Daniel's badge. "You really are FBI," she said, and sighed. "I'm sorry I was so abrupt on the phone, but frankly I suspected it was a prank call. I mean, the FBI calling about Peter Abbott..."

"It seemed unlikely?" Daniel asked.

"Well, yes, honestly. He always seemed like a sweet boy... Of course I know people can hide all kinds of perfidy behind a well-mannered mask, but still."

"Do you know him?" Daniel asked.

"Oh, just a little bit. He's in here just about every semester – always signs up for a heavy course load, then needs to drop one of the classes. Always so apologetic and polite." She slid a folder across the table. "Here you go. Everything you asked for. He's had some problems with his grades, of course, but no disciplinary issues."

Daniel glanced over the transcript. The Bs and Cs of Peter's freshman year deteriorated into Cs and Ds, with an increasing number of Fs beginning in his junior year. "Is he on academic probation?"

"Well..." The registrar shrugged. "His father's on the Board of Trustees."

"Ah," Gennady breathed, a soft satisfied sound, as if pleased by this evidence of American venality.

"He wants Peter to be a doctor," the registrar said. "I had a good chat with Peter about it once, back in his sophomore year. 'Peter,' I said, 'why don't you major in English? Every time we talk, you're telling me how much you're enjoying the English course that you're just about to drop, because you need that time to study for biology.' But he told me his dad thought English was a waste of time." She shook her head. "You said on the phone that you wanted his attendance records for last September, too, didn't you? Here they are. He went to class every day except..."

"September 23rd." Daniel's gaze had already jumped down the page.

He tried to check his excitement, but some of it must have leaked into his voice, because the registrar's forehead crinkled with worry. "A lot of students skipped that day," she said. "They wanted to go see Khrushchev, and who can blame them? It's not often you get to witness a piece of history like that."

"It may not mean anything," Daniel agreed, and flashed her a smile. "I don't suppose you could direct us to the yearbook office?"

***

Sylvia Winfield, the yearbook editor, wore a black turtleneck that gave her a vibe about as beatnik as you were likely to find in Des Moines. "Peter *Abbott*?" she asked. "What'd he do to get the FBI interested in him?"

"It surprises you that the FBI would be interested in Peter Abbott?" Gennady asked.

She tucked a strand of her unfashionably long blond hair behind her ear. "I'm surprised that *anyone* would be interested in Peter Abbott," she said, and laughed, a sudden booming laugh that filled the room. "I went on a date with him," she explained, "after he got the Thunderbird..." Another laugh burst out of her. "Don't look at me like that!" she told Gennady.

"I was admiring your enterprise," Gennady assured her. He had his hands in his pockets, a tilt to his head, a bright intent look in his eyes that made Daniel's heart squeeze with jealousy.

"You were thinking nice girls don't admit they go out with men for their cars." Sylvia was grinning. "Well, it wasn't *just* for his car, I assure you. He's not bad-looking. Here, let me show you a picture. That's probably what you're here for, anyway. Mug shot?"

"Something like that," said Daniel, with a smile.

She pulled a 1959 yearbook off the shelf. Within ten seconds, she'd located the page with Peter's picture, and pushed the yearbook across the table to them. "There. Not bad-looking, right? And he seemed so nervous when he asked me out that I couldn't bring myself to turn him down. But he turned out to be a bit of an egghead," she said, "an egghead without actually being smart, which is a bad combination."

"An egghead," said Gennady. "I'm sorry, what is this?"

"Oh, an intellectual. A fake intellectual, in Peter's case. I told him my major was psychology and he started explaining psychology to me – I *know*," she said, grinning at Gennady when he laughed. "According to Peter, the root of all psychological problems lies in man's disconnection from nature. He tried to quote Wordsworth, and he got muddled before he even reached the 'host of golden daffodils.' Unfortunately for Peter, I learned the poem by heart back when I was a little pigtailed schoolgirl in a one-room schoolhouse. 'I wandered lonely as a cloud that floats on high over dales and hills...'"

Gennady's eyes brightened as if this quotation were a piece of buried treasure.

"Of course I didn't say anything," Sylvia added, "it was so hard to get him talking in the first place that I wasn't going to stop him. But he must have seen I wasn't impressed, because that's when he started driving like a maniac. We'd driven out to a drive-in movie theater, see, way out in the country – he parked way in the back so we could barely even see the picture – and on the way back to campus he started going a hundred miles an hour on one of those little gravel back roads."

"Jesus," Daniel said.

"Oh yeah. I screamed at him to stop, and when he finally pulled over I yanked the keys out of the ignition and told him that either I was driving us home or I'd throw his keys into the cornfield. His choice."

"Which did he choose?" Gennady asked.

"Oh, I drove us home. That made it all worth it, getting to drive the Thunderbird, but..." She shook her head. "Dead silence the whole drive. And then when we got back – " She huffed out a sigh. "He asked if I'd like to go out again. Honestly!"

A little silence followed. Daniel inspected the yearbook photos; not just Peter's, but the other photos on the page. The quotes they had picked, the listings of clubs and fraternity affiliations, the in-jokes. He slid the yearbook halfway across the table toward Sylvia and tapped the blank space below Peter's name. "Did Peter just forget to turn in his club affiliations?"

Most of the other names had clubs listed in that space: French club, basketball, glee club, whatever. At least 75% had a Greek affiliation: fraternities and sororities clearly ran the social life at Durrell.

"No. He's not a fraternity member," Sylvia said. "He wouldn't have asked me out if he was, because I'm not in a sorority. But there's a difference between not doing Greek life because you don't want to..."

"Like you?" Daniel said.

Sylvia grinned. "...and not doing Greek life because they don't want *you*."

"Yes," Daniel agreed. "He looks like a composite of a thousand fraternity portraits."

Laughter bubbled out of Sylvia. "He does, doesn't he? Poor kid." But then she looked concerned. "He's not dangerous, is he? Like Ed Gein? I know you can't tell me exactly what you're looking into, but if we're in danger then we ought to know."

"No, nothing like Ed Gein," Daniel assured her.

She looked into his eyes, as if trying to read the truth there. Then she shrugged. "Oh, well. Maybe he's smuggling dope across state lines or something."

"How did you guess?" Gennady asked, with comic fake dismay. Sylvia laughed and flipped her hair over her shoulder.

Daniel cleared his throat. "Do you mind if we keep the yearbook?"

"Go ahead. We've got spares. Is there anything else you need? I've got Abnormal Psychology starting in..." She checked her wristwatch. "Fifteen minutes."

"No, no, you've been a lot of help," Daniel said. "Is there anywhere on campus to eat? Snack bar or something like that?"

"They do good burgers at the Grill in the Union. It's just across the quad – the building with the turrets. You can't miss it."

***

"She liked you," Daniel said.

They were sitting at a corner table at the Union Grill. Gennady was carefully rearranging the onions on his burger for maximum coverage, and did not look up at Daniel. "She is young, she is bored, she is just passing the time. Flirting is a pleasant way to do that," he said.

"She would've gone out with you if you asked," Daniel said, feeling rather as if he were picking at a scab.

"Or with you," Gennady shot back. "Go ask her. A date will be good for you." He waved a hand, as if shooing Daniel away to go get laid.

Daniel slouched. "It's not a good idea to ask witnesses out of dates."

Gennady huffed out a sigh and took a pointedly enormous bite of his burger. Daniel toyed with a fry, hating himself. He felt like a bizarre funhouse reflection of Paul and he did not know how to stop.

Gennady swallowed. He took a swig of soda. "Hurry up and eat. How can you be so slow when we are finally making progress?" Gennady tried to steal a few of Daniel's fries. Daniel smacked his hand, and Gennady withdrew with an exaggerated show of pain. Daniel snorted and started to eat his fries himself.

After all, Gennady had a point. Not about Sylvia Winfield, of course, it really was a bad idea to date a witness, but in general. It had simply been too long since Daniel had gotten laid. His own fault for mooning over Gennady, of course. He should have spent those endless winter evenings in bars scoping out the available ladies, instead of watching Gennady's hands on the pool cue, with his sleeves rolled up to his elbows, displaying his lean muscled forearms...

Ah, fuck.

"Who is Ed Gein?" Gennady asked.

"A murderer," Daniel said. He shifted uncomfortably in his seat. Gein came from Wisconsin, and Daniel could not help feeling that this was a point of shame for his home state. "Everyone in his hometown thought he was just this harmless ineffectual loner until they found out that he had killed some people pretty gruesomely."

"Mmm. A Peter Abbott type."

"You can see why he came into Sylvia Winfield's mind." Daniel took a bite of his club sandwich. "When's Peter Abbott's next class?"

Gennady opened the registrar's folder to check. He made a face. "Tomorrow morning. Well, so we will have time to prepare. Or perhaps he will come in for a snack?"

He looked up hopefully, as if Peter Abbott might magically materialize. Peter Abbott did not, so Gennady stole another one of Daniel's fries (Daniel let him this time), and bent the study the transcript. The sunlight slanted down through the high window to light his hair, his hands.

Daniel caught himself looking, and tore his gaze away, fixing it instead on the door to the Union Grill, just in case Peter did appear. The place was quiet at this hour, and only a few people came in: a young couple holding hands, a knot of girls in plaid skirts, a professorial type who looked around as if baffled to find himself in this place, and walked back out.

"How do these grades work?" Gennady asked.

Daniel looked back over at him. "The highest is A. The lowest is F."

A pause. Gennady tapped one finger on the table, as if counting up. "Is there an E?"

"No. I guess E slept in the day that they were inventing letter grades."

Gennady made a face at him. "So Peter's grades," he said, pushing them across the table to Daniel. "They are bad, and getting worse. Last spring, about the time he took the Mauser – two Fs. Do you think he planned to shoot himself?"

"Maybe." Khrushchev's visit to America hadn't even been planned yet, let alone announced, so Peter could not have planned to shoot him when he first took the gun.

"But then he chickened?"

Daniel looked away. "Or he thought better of it once he actually had the gun. That might have made it feel more… real, I guess."

Daniel had thought about killing himself after John beat him it. It was not the injuries that drove him to it, his bruises had almost healed by then, but the prospective shame if John told everyone that Daniel had kissed him. Rumors flying across campus, whispers everywhere he went, expulsion from the frat, expulsion from the college maybe, and if his parents found out…

He had crept down the stairs and slipped into the library to open the top left-hand drawer on his father's desk, and take out his father's service revolver. But the shock of the cold gun against his skin, the weight of it, had jolted Daniel back to reality. If he shot himself that was it, the end, his life burning out like a reel halfway through a picture, so you never did find out how the story ended; and he did not want his story to be over. There had to be another way out.

And three days later, an army recruitment poster suggested a solution. He could enlist to fight in the Korean War. A good, solid, patriotic escape.

Peter Abbott, on the other hand, had gone back to college. Of course it was not exactly a parallel situation, but nonetheless...

"I feel kind of sorry for him," Daniel admitted.

"Do you?" Gennady sounded disdainful.

Daniel felt startled – almost hurt. "Don't you? He's sort of pathetic."

"If his bullet had hit our Nikita Sergeyevich," Gennady said, "there would have been war. Nuclear war, probably, perhaps an end to all life on earth. And for what? Because a rich boy is sad he is too stupid to follow the path his father set out for him? If he had shot himself for that reason – that would be pitiable. This..." Gennady shook his head. "He is sad, so the whole world should end? No. This is evil, and it will be good when we catch him."

CHAPTER 13

In truth, Gennady felt that he had better nip this talk about feeling sorry for Peter Abbott in the bud: he did not need any such thing to find its way into his dossier. *You felt sorry for the dog who tried to shoot our Nikita Sergeyevich? Traitor! Scum! Ten years in the camps!*

It didn't matter anyway how Daniel and Gennady felt about him. Peter Abbott had to be caught, so it was better to feel nothing at all.

After they finished their late lunch, they meandered toward Peter's dorm, and wandered through the parking lot behind it, where they found the Thunderbird. Daniel took the precaution of letting the air out of Peter's tires. "A terrible thing to do to such a fine car," Gennady said.

"All's fair in love and war," Daniel told him.

They knocked on Peter's door, but no one answered. Daniel chatted for a very long time with the housemother, who complained at length about the hoodlums on the fourth floor while Daniel nodded and made small sympathetic noises.

"Was this a good use of our time?" Gennady complained afterward when they went to try Peter's door again.

"She told us he's still on campus," Daniel said. "His daddy hasn't spirited him out of the country to Montenegro. That's something."

"If we ever manage to meet him face to face." Gennady knocked sharply on Peter's door.

But once again, no one answered. "Why don't we hit the campus bar?" Daniel suggested. "It's a Friday night. Maybe Peter's out drowning his sorrows."

Peter was not in the campus bar, but Daniel and Gennady got beers anyway, and settled down in a wooden booth scarred with carved hearts and initials. They had not eaten since their lunch at the Union Grill – the housemother had not offered so much as a cracker – and by the end of his first beer Gennady felt mellow. "I'm getting another."

"You wanna slow down on the drinking?"

"No." Gennady slipped out of the booth and patted Daniel's head clumsily.

He did buy a snack to go along with his beer: a basket of fries, the only food that the bar served. It disappointed him slightly. He had hoped for something exotic, like the pickled pig's trotters they found in a southern Indiana bar. He had not particularly liked those, but still it was something to have tried them. And now his time for trying American foods was running out, because they were closing in on Peter Abbott, and their trip was almost over…

The fries were hot and crisp and salty, very pleasant with the beer. Gennady ate a handful and asked Daniel, "What is a drive-in movie theater like?"

"What?"

"Sylvia Winfield said that Peter took her to one. Way out in the country. What is the point of driving so far when you could see the movie in a regular theater close by?"

"The movie isn't the point," Daniel said. "The point is to climb into the backseat and make out."

Gennady stared at him. Then he started to laugh.

"What?" Daniel snapped.

"Was this your plan?" Gennady asked. "Last fall, when we drove from DC to Des Moines, and you were sad the drive-in theaters were closed? Were you going to – ?"

"Shut up!" Daniel hissed. He lunged across the table, as if to put his hands over Gennady's mouth, but Gennady batted his hands away easily.

"Were you? Were you? Did the FBI tell you to honeytrap

me? And when this did not work, you shrugged your shoulders and said, ah well, better try a strip club, he is more likely to respond to a woman anyway?"

Daniel fell back in his seat. "No, you moron," he said. "Not everything's about blackmail, you know. And making out isn't the only reason people go to drive-ins. Haven't you ever heard of an exaggeration? That's just why couples go there on dates. Helen and I used to go to the drive-in outside of Shinocqua to make out in the backseat." His eyes grew far away. "That's where I lost my virginity."

"At a drive-in?" Gennady was scandalized – it sounded so public! – and yet oddly delighted.

"Not at the drive-in. In the backseat. We drove out to the Point – it's a lookout over Lake Michigan, so you could see the water and the stars and the lighthouse way off on the rocks..."

Gennady balled up a napkin and tossed it at him. "You're a romantic."

Daniel grinned sheepishly. "We wanted to do it on the beach," he admitted. "But it was too cold, so we went back to the car."

"Too cold? Did you take your girl to the beach in January?"

"It was July," Daniel protested.

"And you thought it was too cold? Americans!" Gennady stabbed a French fry at Daniel. "It is too cold to go to a drive-in now, though. You've lost your chance."

Daniel buried his head in his arms. "Gennady..."

Gennady did not for a moment believe that Daniel had been sent to honeytrap him, but the idea gave him an unholy glee, and he could not resist needling Daniel about it. "You should have gotten me drunk. I would not have minded."

Daniel lifted his head to stare. "Really?"

"Didn't I tell you that you are very pretty?"

"Gennady – " exasperated.

Gennady laughed. "Of course the blackmail – that part would have been unpleasant."

"Gennady! Do you really think that I'm out to blackmail you any way I can?"

Daniel sounded so genuinely pained that Gennady grew serious. "No," Gennady assured him. "No, my friend, I'm only teasing. It was just funny, the way you said – about the drive-in theaters – " He started giggling again.

Daniel groaned.

Gennady smacked his back. "No, no. I don't believe you are plotting evil against me. Even in the beginning, when you suggested the strip club, it was just exuberance of spirits, wasn't it? But I didn't know you yet, it would have been wrong to be too trusting. Don't look so sad," he added, because Daniel still looked truly pained. "After all, you would only be doing what you are told to do. What is that saying? About love and war?"

"'All's fair in love and war,'" Daniel said, and then added, "But our countries aren't at war."

"No. This would be a bad place for me if we were: in the middle of the United States, with no way out."

They fell silent. The noise of the bar rose up around them: the clink of pool balls, the clatter of glasses, a collective whoop from a group of young men.

Gennady's light-hearted mood fell away from him. He drained his beer. "I do not think Peter will come here tonight."

"No," Daniel agreed. "That would be too easy."

On their way out, they passed a countertop littered with flyers and magazines. They had passed it on their way in, too, but this time Daniel paused, and after a moment's puzzlement, Gennady saw why: half-buried amid the welter of magazines lay half a dozen copies of *The Good Shepherd*.

"The Durrell student," Gennady remembered. "Selling the magazine door to door to pay his tuition. He must have left his extras here."

Daniel plucked one from the pile. "Well," he said. "Guess that explains how Peter Abbott got a copy."

***

The next morning, Gennady and Daniel took up a position perhaps twenty yards from Peter Abbott's Applied Mathematics classroom. Gennady leaned against the wall below the windows and watched the students as they came: mostly young men, but a few girls too, all too intent on their own conversations to do more than glance incuriously at Daniel and Gennady.

Except for Peter. If Peter had kept moving, Gennady might not have been able to pick him out from the crowd; but when

Peter saw Daniel in his snappy FBI suit, he stopped stock still, and his blandly handsome face paled.

Then Peter turned tail and bolted, disappearing down the stairs the way he had come. Gennady made a move to go after him, but Daniel put a hand on his shoulder.

Gennady subsided against the wall, but he objected, "What if he tries to run away?"

"He's not going to get very far in the Thunderbird. And you'd be surprised how few people try to run, anyway," Daniel said. He folded his arms over his chest. Only a few last straggling students were hurrying into class. The classroom door closed, and the hall was silent. "Paul and I caught more than a few guys just by hanging out till they confessed. They knew why we were there and eventually their nerves cracked."

"With Peter Abbott this might take one interview." Any doubts Gennady had harbored about Peter's guilt had evaporated: not just because he ran, but because unlike all the other students he had noticed them, and knew at once why they were there.

***

Peter did not show up for his next class that afternoon. "I do not think he can afford to skip class, with his grades," Gennady said, disapproving.

"I bet he's too nervous to study, too," Daniel said. "Probably quaking in his boots somewhere."

"Quaking...?"

"Hiding. Shivering in fright. Peter Rabbit," Daniel said, and his mouth flipped up in a half-smile. "I bet he's been saddled with that nickname more than once. Did Beatrix Potter ever make it to the Soviet Union? Children's stories about naughty rabbits getting shot at by gardeners?"

"No, I don't think so," Gennady said, and he felt a sort of relief as he said it. It was odd, he had always been so eager to devour the pieces of American culture that made it to the Soviet Union, and yet now that he was in America, it distressed him a little to see how little Soviet culture had come to America in return.

They went back to Peter's dorm, and knocked on his door

again. This time someone answered, but only Peter's roommate, Kenneth Price, as the nametag taped to the door proclaimed. "Peter's gone to class," Kenneth Price said, in response to Daniel's question. Then he added, as if he couldn't quite believe it, "You want to see Peter?"

"Is that unusual?" Daniel asked.

"Well..." Kenneth eyed Daniel's suit doubtfully. "What do you want him for?"

"Just to chat," Daniel said, with a smile.

Gennady peered past Kenneth into the room, hoping to see a photograph of Khrushchev with a target drawn on it, or perhaps a bulletin board headed "Assassination Plans." Sadly, Peter was not so careless. "Was Peter a Boy Scout?"

Kenneth looked startled by Gennady's accent. "Um, I don't really know. We're not exactly friends, I just got assigned to room with him because my previous roommate graduated early... What's all this about?" Kenneth half-closed the door, shutting off the view of the room.

"We just need to ask him a few questions, that's all," Daniel said, flashing another all-American smile. He removed a card from his breast pocket. "In connection with..."

"Classified matters," Gennady rapped out, unsmiling.

Kenneth looked between them, and then slowly, as if Daniel might bite, plucked the card from his hand. "I'll let him know."

"And if he tries to run for it," Daniel said, smiling even more widely, "you'll give me a call, won't you, Kenneth?"

Kenneth's voice rose slightly. "What's all this about?"

"Don't worry," Gennady told him, still unsmiling. "He's no danger to you."

Kenneth looked not at all reassured. He nodded slowly and shut the door.

***

Their web of circumstantial evidence grew. They discovered that Peter had indeed been a Boy Scout, and attended Camp DuBois five years in a row. They found a filling station owner on Peter's route from Honeygold who remembered the turquoise Thunderbird on the fateful day. "Just the car, though," Daniel complained as they drove away. "Didn't even look at the driver.

That's filling station operators for you. A defense attorney could rip that apart in court."

"We still have the speeding ticket," Gennady reminded him.

He felt that it was not so much frustration with the filling station owner that made Daniel grumpy, anyway, but a more general frustration because they could not get an interview with Peter Abbott. He was never in his dorm room ("I think Kenneth kicked him out," Daniel opined. "Doesn't want to be murdered in his sleep"), and he turned tail and ran whenever he saw them.

Yet they continued to see him: he did not leave campus. "You'd think that he would run home to his powerful father," Gennady mused.

"He must not think Dad will come through for him this time," Daniel said. "Maybe stealing Dad's war trophy was the last straw." He thought about it for a moment. "Or he's afraid of his father's disapproval."

Of course all of this boded well for getting a confession eventually: Peter Abbott behaved like a guilty man who was likely to crack under pressure. But nonetheless Gennady felt a frenzy of impatience. What if they were recalled before they caught him? To be demoted and sent back to Moscow had been good enough when it seemed to be his only option, but now that they had found Peter Abbott, when they only needed to get a confession from him, and they simply could not get two words with him...

It was maddening.

"We need to take a more aggressive approach," Gennady told Daniel.

"What? Beat him up?"

"Very funny. How will we beat him up if we cannot even get close enough to speak to him? No," said Gennady. "We need to trap him. I am thinking, we will position you so that he will see your FBI suit and turn to run in the opposite direction. But we will pick a point where there is only one route of escape, and I will stand at the other end, and catch him there."

"Oh." Daniel nodded. "That's a good plan. Do you have a place in mind?"

"I am thinking his applied mathematics class," Gennady said. "We have not been there since the first day, and we know he has been attending it" (Daniel had become quite chummy with the registrar), "and there are only two staircases down from that floor. If you stand at the end of the hall by the classroom, you will block the east staircase."

"And you'll catch him at the bottom of the west stairs?"

Gennady nodded.

"And you *won't* beat him up," Daniel said, almost reluctantly, as if he hated saying it but couldn't help himself.

"Of course not," said Gennady, and added, just to appall Daniel, "After all, he is the son of an important man."

"*Gennady* – "

"No, no. Honestly," Gennady said, a little peeved, "we do not beat people up nearly as often as you Americans think."

***

The plan went like clockwork – at first. Gennady secreted himself in a doorway where he had a view of the stairs without being easily visible to the students, and waited till he saw Peter Abbott go up. Then Gennady positioned himself at the bottom of the stairs.

Gennady just had time to light a cigarette before Peter Abbott came rocketing back. "Peter Abbott?" Gennady said pleasantly.

Peter flailed to a stop at the landing halfway down the stairs. His face blanched. "They've sent a KGB assassin," he gasped.

Gennady flicked his cigarette aside with an insouciance that he felt befitted a KGB assassin. "What did you expect," he asked, with his heaviest Russian accent, "when you tried to assassinate our dear Khrushchev?"

"I didn't kill him!" Peter cried. "I didn't even hit the train car!"

"But you confess you tried?"

Gennady took one step up the stairs as he spoke. Peter let out a frightened animal squeak. He turned to go back up the stairs – just as Daniel appeared at the top.

Peter froze in terror. Then he plunged down the stairs.

Gennady moved just in time to block Peter's escape. Peter crashed into him, knocking out his breath, and Gennady did not see it when Peter pulled a knife from his pocket.

He felt it, though, when the knife slashed across his side. No pain at first, but a streak along his skin like something very hot or very cold, a feeling of skin sagging open like torn cloth.

He shoved Peter away. The knife skittered across the floor, and Peter did not stop to pick it up, but cannoned through the door.

Gennady followed. But he couldn't seem to run, and by the time he had pushed through the front door, Peter's long legs had already carried him halfway across the lawn. Gennady went down the steps, puzzled that he could not move faster; then missed the last step, and his foot came down hard on the sidewalk and sent a jolt all through his body so that he stumbled against the rail.

Then the pain hit Gennady. He looked down at his side, and saw the whole side of his shirt red with blood.

"Gennady!" Daniel caught him by the shoulders. "You're bleeding – Gennady – "

"Go after him!" Gennady shouted.

"Gennady..."

"*Go!*" Gennady shouted.

And only then – far too late – Daniel took up the chase. Peter Abbott was already out of sight.

CHAPTER 14

"Idiot!" Gennady shouted.

Daniel felt weak with relief at the sound of his voice. He had come right back after he'd lost Peter Abbott, and when he caught sight of Gennady sitting on the steps of the mathematics building, his side bloody, his head hanging low...

Daniel had thought he might be dead.

"Idiot!" Gennady snapped again. "You lost him?"

"He got a head start," Daniel said.

"Only because you did not give chase at once!" Gennady lurched to his feet, and swayed, and batted Daniel away when Daniel moved forward to catch him. "Stupid!"

"You got stabbed!" Daniel protested.

"So? As you see, it's not fatal. You should not have stopped, you should have gone right after him. Not one step back!"

Daniel got the chance to steady Gennady, after all, because Gennady nearly fell when he came down the steps. Daniel could smell his blood and sweat.

"We should get you to a hospital," Daniel said.

"Wonderful," Gennady gritted out. "Take me to a hospital and tell them *my Russian friend got stabbed as he tried to assassinate a Congressman's son.*"

"You weren't trying to assassinate a Congressman's son."

"But who will they believe? The Russian spy, or the

Congressman's son? No," said Gennady. He had steadied himself again, and removed his arm from Daniel's hand. "No hospital. We have to go talk to Mack."

"Gennady – "

"We have to tell him that Peter Abbott confessed!"

***

As far as Daniel could tell, Gennady stayed upright on their way to the car mostly by force of will. He looked terrible when he finally sank down in the passenger seat: pale and sweaty, his face so tense that it looked like a mask.

"Are you still bleeding?" Daniel asked.

Gennady gave him a withering look. "It is the nature of wounds to bleed." His Russian accent sounded thicker than normal.

"You realize it's not going to do anyone any good if you bleed to death. Especially when you're the only one who heard Peter's confession. What did he say?"

"That he did not even hit the train." Gennady's face sagged. All of a sudden the ginger went out of him, and he glanced over at Daniel, young and hurt and lost. "It is not a very good confession, is it?"

Daniel smacked a hand against the rim of the steering wheel. "Christ, it's good enough. Now that he's gotten started, he'll tell us everything if only we can get out hands on him again."

"Yes," said Gennady, and the acerbity was back in his voice. "If only."

Daniel stopped at a stoplight, and closed his eyes, just for a moment. He should have pursued Peter immediately. It was only…

He had forgotten everything else when he saw Gennady bleeding.

"Daniel."

Daniel opened his eyes to find that the light had turned green. He gunned the engine.

"I thought you were going to die," Daniel said, trying to excuse himself.

"Yes, well, so. He missed the vital organs. A slice across the side, that will heal. And I got a confession," Gennady repeated, as if that were the most important thing. "So everything is fine."

***

"What the hell is wrong with you?" Mack shouted.

Gennady's face was very pale. His lips looked badly chapped. He moistened them, but didn't answer, so Daniel had to say, "Peter Abbott stabbed him."

Mack stubbed out his cigar in the ashtray. Daniel found himself straightening to attention: a private about to receive a well-deserved dressing down. "Hawthorne," Mack said, "do you understand what a fucking problem it will be if a Soviet agent dies on American soil? Do you realize the magnitude of the international incident that could cause? Next time one of you gets stabbed I want it to be *you*. Do you understand me?"

"Yes, sir. I'm sorry, sir."

"Didn't I tell you this before? The very first time you came into my office? Protect him like you're a Secret Service agent and he's the president. Does a Secret Service agent let the president get stabbed?"

"No," Daniel said.

"Then why the hell is Agent Matskevich *bleeding in my office*?"

"No excuses, sir."

"Sir." Gennady's voice was hoarse. He cleared his throat, and continued, "It was my fault. I insisted that we had to catch Peter Abbott. He heard the accent and thought, a KGB assassin, and he began to cry out that he didn't shoot Khrushchev, he only hit the train car."

"He said that? He confessed?"

Gennady nodded. Mack smiled like a jowly cherub. He threw open the office door and shouted, "Sanders! Esposito! Washington! Drop what you're doing and – "

He was telling them to go after Peter Abbott, oh, and someone grab a First Aid kit, and do you have any idea where the kid might try to hide out, Hawthorne?

Daniel did his best to answer Mack's questions, but he kept glancing at Gennady. Spots of blood showed on his suit coat where he had his hand pressed to his side. "Why don't you sit down?" Daniel suggested, and tried to herd Gennady toward the couch.

It ought to have been easy to move him when he was having trouble even standing, but Gennady planted his feet. "I'll bleed on it."

Mack, orders handed down, closed the door. "It's all right, kid," he said, his voice gruff, and when Gennady didn't move, Mack grabbed up his newspaper and spread it over the couch. "There you go. Siddown."

Gennady sat gingerly. Mack crouched down beside him. "Jesus," he said. "You've wrecked that suit. Hawthorne, you'll have to take him to the department store tomorrow and get him a new one."

Daniel's mouth went dry. So he'd have to watch Gennady try on new clothes, after all. "Yes, sir."

"Now we'd better get a look at that wound," Mack told Gennady.

Gennady's face lost what little color it had. He clutched his suit coat around him. "*No.*"

Mack frowned. "Kid – "

Gennady shrank into the couch like a kicked dog. Daniel moved to Gennady's side and put a hand on his shoulder. "I've got a first aid kit in the car," Daniel told Mack. "Gennady and I could clean the wound up at the motel. I'll put a tarp over the bed to keep the blood off. You know that newspaper's not going to protect your couch for long."

The newspaper rustled as Gennady shifted. Mack looked skeptical. "You think a first aid kit's gonna cover it, Hawthorne?"

"If it won't, the motel's close to a hospital."

"I'm not going to a hospital," Gennady insisted.

Mack heaved himself to his feet. "Take him to the hospital if you gotta," he told Daniel.

"I'm not – " Gennady's voice rose uncontrollably. He shut his mouth so tightly that his jaw jumped.

"Sorry, kid," Mack said, and he rested a hand lightly on Gennady's hair, just for a moment. "If Hawthorne thinks you'd better go to the hospital, you're going. I can't have you dying on us."

"No one would care much," Gennady said

"Oh, they'll care if it gives them the chance to write

headlines about American treachery," Mack told him. "Trust me. Now go."

***

"I would care," Daniel said.

"What?"

They were driving back to the motel. It had gotten dark while they were talking to Mack, and Daniel was driving very carefully to give Gennady the smoothest possible ride. The car smelled like blood.

"If you died," Daniel clarified. "I would care."

"Oh, well. You would care, my grandfather would care, and my aunt Lilya and my cousin Oksana and even her jackass husband Alyosha. My friend Sergeyich, even Galya, maybe, although I'm sure she has a new boyfriend now, perhaps married already, who knows? Many people would care, but no one important, no one with power. Why do you think they chose me for this mission? If I die, it is easy to forget me."

Sweat broke out on Daniel's upper lip. Somehow that felt worse than when he had taken Gennady's *No one would care* literally.

"You're not going to die," Daniel said, and hoped his voice was steady.

"No. Worse luck." Gennady's voice was taut.

They went over a pothole. Gennady gasped painfully. Daniel blurted, "Why don't you have a cigarette?"

In his peripheral vision, he saw Gennady glance at him. "Really? In your car?"

He sounded so relieved, so hopeful, that Daniel felt like a monster for not thinking of it before. "Yes, absolutely."

The window crank squeaked. Daniel came to a stop sign and glanced over to see Gennady biting his lip with pain as he rolled down the window. "Here, let me do that," Daniel said, and leaned over Gennady to do it. He could feel the heat of his body, smell the blood, the scent so thick that he could taste it at the back of his throat.

He was careful not to touch him – he would have given anything not to hurt him – but Gennady made a little noise anyway, a sort of grunt, and Daniel's face grew painfully hot. It wasn't sexual, exactly. He wanted to take Gennady in his arms and hold him and keep him safe from everything.

God, if only he'd grabbed Peter Abbott. But no, he'd stopped at the top of the steps to savor the moment, and Peter Abbott bolted like a cornered rat and stabbed Gennady, and if he'd stabbed just a little to the left Gennady would have bled to death on the tiles in the lobby of the mathematics building...

Gennady was fumbling with his lighter. Daniel took the lighter and lit the cigarette for him, and Gennady took a long drag and relaxed against the seat. "Feel better?" Daniel asked.

"The worst is yet to come," Gennady said. His voice had taken on a distant, rather hazy quality, as if the cigarette had affected him like a narcotic. "We'll have to clean the wound."

***

Daniel left Gennady in the car as he set up the motel room as a meatball surgery: draped his tarp over one of the beds, arranged the contents of his first aid kit on the bedside table. A roll of bandages, a pair of tweezers, a big bottle of iodine. The radiator coughed anemically when he turned up the heat.

He'd wrap Gennady up in blankets after the wound was cleaned. That's what you were supposed to do for an injured person, wasn't it? Keep them warm and hydrated.

He filled a glass of water and set it on the bedside table, too, and set his flask of brandy beside it.

Then he took off his suit coat, rolled his sleeves to his elbows, and went out to fetch Gennady.

Gennady was leaning against the car window, eyes closed. In the harsh lights of the motel parking lot he looked bone white, and Daniel jerked open the car door with a sudden surge of dread.

Gennady got out of the car neatly enough, but then his legs nearly gave out under him: he practically fell into Daniel's arms. "Oh," Gennady muttered, and Daniel held him, just for a moment longer than necessary, and breathed in the scent of his hair.

"All right," Daniel said. His voice sounded gruff. "Come on."

Gennady leaned on Daniel as they walked into the motel room. He sat heavily on the tarp, which rattled beneath him, and awkwardly removed his suit coat.

The thick dark fabric of the suit had shown little blood, but the right side of his shirt was sodden. Daniel gagged. Gennady started to giggle, a jagged sound that rasped on Daniel's nerves.

"You are like my boss Arkady," Gennady said. "Such a horror of blood. Perhaps it is wrong that we laugh at him for it, we ought to respect a Stalingrad soldier…"

"I'll be all right," Daniel insisted. Already the wooziness was passing. "I'll just go get some hot water. Okay?"

It took the bathroom tap some time to warm up. By the time Daniel had returned with an ice bucket full of hot (well, lukewarm) water, Gennady had removed his button-down shirt. Goosebumps riddled his bare arms. His blood-stained undershirt clung to his skin. "The undershirt…" Gennady said, with a feeble gesture toward it.

"We'd better cut that off," Daniel decided.

Gennady stirred. "Wasteful."

"Do you really think you can salvage this?" Daniel asked him, and Gennady blinked and looked down at the blood-soaked undershirt, with one side torn where the knife had sliced through.

"Maybe not," he conceded.

"It'll just reopen the wound if you try to pull it over your head, anyway," Daniel said. He slit the t-shirt from hem to neck with his pocketknife and slid it off Gennady's shoulders. It stuck to the dried blood on his side, and Daniel sacrificed a handkerchief to soak the stuck parts in warm water, softening the blood until the shirt came off.

Now Daniel could finally see the wound: a long slice, just deep enough to bleed like hell, although the bleeding seemed to have slowed, thank God. It was hard to tell with Gennady's side still such a mess of blood.

Daniel took a deep breath, which filled his mouth with the taste of blood and made him feel woozy all over again. He let the breath out slowly, then continued to clean the wound gently with his handkerchief.

At least the knife hadn't gotten close to any vital organs. Gennady's ribs had protected him. "Thank God you moved so fast."

Gennady shook his head. "He aimed badly. I think he has never stabbed someone before, he could not do it."

It took a while, and two changes of water, but at last Gennady's side was clean again. The wound still oozed blood, but the bandages in the first aid kit would be enough to handle it. "You're a lucky stiff," Daniel said. "We won't need to go to the hospital."

Gennady huffed out a breath.

Daniel was feeling sick again. He had put this next part out of his mind, but now he'd have to face it. "We're going to need to disinfect the wound," he said, and hoped that his voice sounded calm and steady. "I've got the iodine ready. It's going to hurt, but it has to be done."

Gennady closed his eyes. "Make it quick."

"I'll give you one of my belts to bite. They used to do that in the Revolutionary War when the doctors had to saw a soldier's limb off."

"Yes," said Gennady. "They did this during the war, once the anesthesia ran out."

"Oh." The syllable turned into a hurt animal sound as Daniel said it. He swallowed again, although there was no spit left in his mouth.

"I won't scream," Gennady promised. Sweat glistened on his face. "Someone might call the police if they heard."

"Gennady, we really can go to the hospital..."

"*No.*"

Daniel fetched the belt. Gennady shoved it in between his teeth and bit down. The eye-stinging scent of iodine filled the room as Daniel poured it onto a handkerchief.

"Now," Daniel said, and pressed the handkerchief to the wound.

Gennady did not scream. His whole body arched, and his breath came in short fast pants, like an injured animal's. Daniel could hear his molars grinding behind the belt.

"It's all right, it's all right," Daniel said, as much for himself as Gennady. "Almost done, almost done. I'm so sorry. All right – all right. All done."

There was only a little blood on the iodine-soaked handkerchief. "It's all right," Daniel said again, and tossed the handkerchief aside. He taped a bandage over Gennady's wound, and sat back to look up at him.

Gennady brushed tears roughly from the corners of his eyes.

"Did I scream?"

"No."

Gennady cleared his throat. He sounded hoarse. "Are you sure?"

"I'm sure," Daniel told him. "Let's get you a glass of water."

Gennady insisted on holding the glass for himself. Water sluiced out of the sides of his mouth, dribbling down his chin, but he got most of it down, and then settled the empty glass on his knee, holding it steady with both hands.

"Vodka?" he asked.

"I've got brandy."

"Give it to me."

Daniel measured two fingers of brandy into the glass, and Gennady kicked them back without batting an eyelash at the burn.

"All right," Daniel said. "I'm going to get this cleaned up, and then... No. first I'm going to get you a shirt. I don't want you catching a cold on top of everything else." He had felt hot while he cleaned the wound, an effect of nerves perhaps, but now he could feel the ambient chill of the room. The damn heater hadn't warmed it up at all. "I'll lend you one of my flannel pajama tops. It's warm and it's old, so it doesn't matter if you bleed on it."

Gennady lifted his arms so Daniel could slide them into the pajama sleeves, and sat passively as Daniel did up the buttons. "Funny," Gennady murmured. "They told me you had a lot of experience undressing people, but they said nothing about dressing them back up."

"Oh, shut up," Daniel said, smiling up at Gennady. Gennady smiled wanly back, and Daniel felt a powerful rush of tenderness for him, intense and unnerving, the desire to cup Gennady's face in both hands and kiss his lips till there was warmth and color in his cheeks again, as if he were Sleeping Beauty and Daniel the destined prince.

The image was so powerfully urgent in his mind that for a dizzying horrible moment he thought he had actually done it. But then he thumped back to reality, and found that his hands had nearly finished buttoning the pajama top, and Gennady was still smiling, a sleepy distant smile as if he were imagining something nice.

"Do you want me to set up the pillows so you can sleep propped up?" Daniel asked.

Gennady looked startled to be recalled to the present. "I don't know."

Daniel bit his lip. "If I got the pajama bottoms out for you," he ventured, "do you think you could put them on yourself?"

Gennady's face took on a look that Daniel could only interpret as *please don't make me*. "It's just that your pants will get blood on the sheets," Daniel said apologetically. "We'll have to throw that suit out, Gennady."

"Throw the suit out?"

"I'll buy you a new one tomorrow, just like Mack said."

Gennady's brow furrowed. At last he nodded. "We can't get blood on the sheets," he said. "If you'll help me with my shoes. And the belt."

Daniel took off Gennady's shoes, and his socks for good measure. The belt was more of a struggle, and he could feel his face flushing, and hated himself for his awareness of their proximity even under these circumstances.

Fortunately, Gennady managed to effect the change into pajamas while Daniel took the bloodied clothes out to the dumpster. He had moved to the clean bed, and sat atop the covers as if he'd run out of energy to pull back the blankets. Daniel's pajamas were too big for him, and he looked small and startled and wary as Daniel came into the room.

"It's just me," Daniel said softly. Gennady nodded, and Daniel added, "Don't you think you'd be more comfortable under the blankets?"

Gennady's brow crinkled thoughtfully.

"Here," said Daniel, more gently. He folded back the blanket on the other side of the bed. "Why don't you get under the covers, Gennady?"

Gennady understood the gesture, if not the words. He gingerly moved himself over onto the sheet, and began to say something in Russian, *Ty budyesh* – then stopped, and mumbled, "You will be here?"

He had used the *ty* form – the informal form. Daniel touched Gennady's hair lightly. "Of course," Daniel said. "Go to sleep, *tovarisch*. Did I say it right that time?"

"No."

"Too bad." Daniel pulled the blanket up, tucking it gently under Gennady's chin, and barely restrained himself from kissing his forehead. "You can teach me the proper way to say it in the morning."

Gennady's eyelids flickered shut. Daniel wanted to lie down beside him, to cradle Gennady in the curve of his body and kiss the tender places behind his ears and murmur soft things into his neck; to take care of him and protect him from the world.

"*Prostitye*," Gennady murmured. *Forgive me.*

"It's okay," Daniel assured him.

Daniel tossed a pillow and a blanket in the narrow space between Gennady's bed and the wall. Then he settled down alongside the bed, like a faithful dog, to keep watch during the night.

CHAPTER 15

Gennady woke up the next morning dizzy and disoriented and in pain. His side throbbed; his throat hurt; his mouth felt dry as toast.

He couldn't do anything about the rest of it, but a glass of water might help his throat. He sat up, and stayed still for a long moment till spots stopped dancing before his eyes, and then very gingerly swung his legs over the edge of the bed.

His feet connected with something soft, which grunted at the contact. "Daniel," said Gennady. "Why are you on the floor?"

Daniel was wiping sleep out of his eyes. "I wanted to be close by in case you needed anything. Do you need something? I don't think you ought to be getting up."

"Water," Gennady said.

Daniel disappeared. Gennady rubbed his face, and noticed with surprise that he was wearing Daniel's pajamas. Oh, Daniel; and Gennady felt a sentimental softness toward him, and a sort of horror at the thought of the honeytrap, a horrible thing to do to someone so good and kind and trusting who deserved only good things in this world. How could he have ever considered it?

But of course it had not been his own idea, but Arkady's.

That moment in Mack's office yesterday – that was the sort of excuse Arkady always came up with, "I'd better get a look at that wound," when really he did not care at all, he just wanted

Gennady to sit on his desk with his shirt off.

Of course Gennady knew really that Mack was not like that, he really had just wanted to make sure that Gennady would not bleed to death in his office. But all the same he had been so grateful when Daniel stepped in, and wished that he could thank him, except it was impossible without explaining about Arkady, which he could not do. Give the Americans a piece of blackmail material against an important Soviet intelligence asset like Arkady Anatolyevich? No.

"Are you all right?" Daniel asked.

Gennady looked up, startled, and held out his hands for the glass of water, although lifting his left arm hurt his wound. Still, he managed to drink the water on his own, and only spilled a little.

"How are you feeling?" Daniel asked.

"Terrible."

Daniel looked startled, then smiled ruefully. "Well, you did just get stabbed. Christ! I'm sorry. Do you want some aspirin?"

"Yes. Aspirin," Gennady said, and took three. "It's not your fault," he added. "Peter Abbott..." He could not think how to finish that sentence, either in English or Russian. He would have liked to drink a big glass of vodka and crawl back under the covers, but no. They had to go out again, redeem themselves for yesterday's failures. He stood, and was pleased that he swayed on slightly. "We should get going."

"Gennady?" Daniel's hands were on his shoulders. The touch was very light, but in Gennady's current state immobilizing. "I think you should lie down again. Take it easy today."

"No," Gennady said, although his head was swimming. "Breakfast. Meat will put iron in my blood."

***

"Toast and scrambled eggs and sausage," Gennady told the waitress. "And orange juice."

He wished for good strong Russian tea, or at least coffee and a cigarette. But any one of those things would go to his head in this state, and if he weakened even slightly Daniel would bundle him back into bed.

Daniel looked unhappy enough as it was. "Gennady," he

began, once the waitress had gone.

"You let Peter Abbott get away," Gennady reminded him sternly. "We have to find him."

Daniel rubbed his hands over his face. He looked tired. Well, that was his own fault for sleeping on the floor. "We have to stop at the department store first," Daniel said. "You can't just walk around in shirt sleeves all day."

Gennady couldn't face a department store. The crowds, the queues, the hours on his feet as they waited. "My other suit..."

"Is at the dry cleaners."

Gennady sagged. Suddenly everything seemed too loud and bright: the plates clattering in the back of the diner, the gurgle of the coffee maker, the hot burned scent of the coffee. He pressed his palms against the sticky table. His side hurt.

"Gennady?" Daniel said. "You okay?"

Gennady was so tired he wanted to crawl into Daniel's half of the booth and lie down with his head in Daniel's lap.

But then the waitress arrived with the orange juice, and the tart citrus taste cleared his head and awakened his stomach. When the food arrived, he gingerly nibbled his toast.

The toast went down easy, and even most of the scrambled eggs, but the greasy sausage defeated him. The third time he gagged on a bite, Daniel said, "Just leave it, Gennady."

"That's wasteful."

Daniel transferred the sausage from Gennady's plate to his own. "Then I'll eat it," he said. "Waitress? Another orange juice, please?"

Another orange juice appeared: that magical American service again. It was good, freshly squeezed, and between the juice and the food Gennady felt more alert already. He would probably not faint in the department store queues.

"So," said Gennady. "This department store."

"Have you been to a department store?"

Gennady bristled. "We have department stores," he said. "Our GUM is very famous, very beautiful."

"But not an American department store." A smile spread across Daniel's face. "I'll take you to Younkers. You're in for a treat."

***

Moscow's flagship department store, GUM, was a vast arcaded architectural masterpiece built in the days of Catherine the Great, probably before the United States had even become a nation.

Gennady clutched this fact to his heart as Daniel led him into Younkers, a seven-story behemoth that bustled with shoppers. It was busy, but not crowded – no queues at all, of course not, this was America, here you did not see people waiting in line for hours.

If Gennady had been feeling better, he could have viewed Younkers with detached scorn: capitalistic excess, all of it, rows upon rows of unnecessary clothes, probably too expensive for the working people to buy anyway.

But he was too tired to summon detachment and instead only felt sad. Galya would have loved to shop here; she so loved pretty clothes and bright colors. "You look like a stilyaga," he once teased her, and she smacked his shoulder but looked pleased, all the same. The stilyagi wore loud ludicrous clothes and listened to American jazz, hooligans, bums, and yet – well, they living their lives, at least, you could not say that about everybody.

Oksana would have loved this department store, too. She hated waiting in lines, and here she would not have to, she could have just walked in and chosen from racks and racks of clothes in every size and style and color, so many choices that Gennady felt overwhelmed. Daniel waylaid a helpful saleswoman – "This chump ironed a hole in his own suit, can you believe it?" Daniel said, big American smile, and the saleswoman smiled back. A pretty girl, soft dark hair, Jewish perhaps, like Galya. "Could you round up a half dozen suits for us?"

In Moscow this would have earned nothing but scoffs, but the American saleswoman did it with a smile. "This one's thirty percent off," she said, and so Gennady took that suit and fled into the dressing room, where he lit a cigarette to calm his nerves.

It really was too much. Just one style of suits, or maybe two, in all the different sizes – that would have been enough.

It took him some time to get dressed: he had to move carefully for fear of reopening the wound. But he managed it, and looked at himself in the mirror, and surprised himself into a smile: and as long as he was smiling, he thought, he really might pass for an American, as long as he did not speak. The accent would give him away.

"You okay in there?" Daniel asked.

Gennady started, and winced: the movement pulled at his injured side. "Yes. The suit fits."

"Come out and let me see it."

"I can tell if a suit fits," Gennady complained.

But he came out anyway. Daniel sat on a bench across from the dressing rooms, his legs stretched out in front of him, but when Gennady emerged he straightened up and looked him over.

It was a light gaze, almost clinical, but nonetheless it made Gennady uncomfortable. "Well?"

Daniel rummaged through the suits. "You ought to try on some of the others."

"Why? This fits."

"All of these suits will fit," Daniel said. "You ought to get one that looks good on you. Here." He thrust forward a charcoal gray suit with a narrower waist. "Try this one."

"Do I have to try it on? If you are so sure it will fit?"

"Gennady."

Gennady retreated into the dressing room. He had never thought much about clothes, but once he had changed, even he could tell this suit looked better, trimmer. More attractive.

Get an American suit, Arkady had said.

"I like the other one better," Gennady said.

"Really?" Daniel sounded disbelieving.

"More comfortable."

"Really? Is this one too tight in the waist?"

Gennady came out of the dressing room. Daniel looked at him, and his gaze grew suddenly bright and warm, and Gennady nearly turned around and went right back inside the dressing room.

He set his jaw instead and sat down beside Daniel, slouching and crossing his arms over his chest. Daniel started to laugh. "What?" Gennady snapped.

"You just remind me of my sister. She *hated* shopping when we were kids. Every time Mom made her try on a particularly darling dress, she'd slouch just like that."

Pretty Anna, with holly in her hair. Gennady found it hard to picture her slouching and sulking, and then not hard at all: he could see it as if there had been a snapshot of the scene in Daniel's photo album, and his heart went out to her.

"Probably she felt ridiculous," Gennady said.

"Do you feel ridiculous?" Daniel asked. "You look good, you know."

Gennady looked up. Their eyes met, Daniel's eyes a warm soft brown, and Gennady wanted quite suddenly to kiss him, and no alcohol to blame it on this time, although of course everyone knew that blood loss left you muddled, not enough blood in the brain.

"Gennady?" Daniel said softly, and Gennady bit his lip and looked away.

That was when he saw Peter Abbott, standing in the aisle just across the way, looking at the hats. Come to buy his disguise at the department store.

Gennady nudged Daniel, just a light rib in the elbows, and Daniel followed his eyes and snapped to attention like a hunting dog. They exchanged glances, a few small hand motions, and then Daniel was up – that hunting dog tension gone – ambling as if he hadn't a care in the world to cut Peter Abbott off from the far end of his aisle.

Gennady slid, very slowly, to the end of the bench, watching Peter Abbott from the corner of his eye. The boy remained totally absorbed in the process of choosing the right hat, like a child playing dress-up.

At last Daniel appeared at the far end of the aisle. "Peter Abbott?" he said pleasantly.

Peter Abbott dropped the hat. Gennady rose just as Peter Abbott turned to flee, and Peter stopped dead at the sight of him.

Then he sagged like a pricked balloon. He didn't even try to run as Daniel closed in on him, although Gennady moved to block the end of the aisle of hats (a whole aisle of hats!) just in case. "I'll come quietly, I promise," Peter Abbott said. "Please don't make a scene. If this gets into the papers…"

"We don't have any intention of making a scene," Daniel assured him, taking one of Peter's elbows in a death grip that might look friendly to an untrained eye. He checked Peter's pocket, and removed the pocketknife. "Just come on out to the parking lot."

Peter Abbott let out a little gasp, almost a cry, as Gennady came up beside him.

"No one's going to assassinate you," Gennady scolded him. He took Peter's other elbow. "If the KGB wanted you dead, you never would have seen them coming."

***

Gennady rather expected Peter to try to escape once they left the department store, but he came quietly as promised, even to the point of holding out his wrists to be cuffed after Daniel put him in the backseat. Gennady slid into the seat beside him and glared, just in case Peter had any ideas about trying anything, but Peter just stared at his big wrists in their handcuffs and looked about ready to cry.

He stirred only when Daniel piloted the car out of its parking space. "Couldn't you just kill me, after all? Maybe we could make it look like a hit-and-run accident."

"Are you serious?" Daniel asked.

Peter's leg jiggled. "Dad's going to be *so* mad at me. It's going to look so bad for his campaign when news of my arrest gets out. Whereas if I died, it might bring out the sympathy vote."

"Why should we help your father?" Gennady asked. "Probably he put you up to kill Khrushchev."

He did not really believe this: he just wanted to see if Peter denied it. Sure enough, Peter cried, "No! No! He had nothing to do with it! It was my idea. I acted on my own. I thought it would make Dad proud, but then when Khrushchev came to town Dad went and – and shook his hand, so I guess I got it wrong, as usual. Dad always says I can't do anything right. You'd think he'd be used to it by now, but he always gets so mad... And this will be all over the papers." Peter sounded like he might suffocate. "He's going to be so *mad*."

"Peter," Daniel said, his voice oddly gentle, "You've got bigger problems right now than what your dad thinks, you know that, right? You've just been arrested for attempting to assassinate a world leader."

"But I didn't hit him!" Peter cried.

"But you still shot at him," Daniel said, more gently still.

"But I didn't *hit* him," Peter insisted, like that made everything all right.

"How did you expect to hit anything," Gennady asked, exasperated, "when you took a long-range shot with a pistol?"

"I *knew* a pistol wasn't the right gun for a long-range shot," Peter replied sullenly. "I'm not *stupid*. No matter what Dad thinks." He bit his lip, then turned to Gennady with a new wild light in his eyes. "Couldn't you take me to the KGB?" he asked. "They probably want to send me to a labor camp or something, right? Couldn't we do that?"

Gennady stared at him. "Peter. Your first idea is better. Let's run you over with the car, that would be a quick death."

"Gennady!" Daniel protested.

"He stabbed me! And I can't tell one murder joke?" Gennady protested. Then he added to Peter: "I'm sorry. I would give you your request if I could, throw you off a cliff, but Agent Hawthorne – he believes in the rule of law. Arrests, trials. The free press. Though we have been trying very hard to keep all this out of the press," he added.

Peter gazed at Gennady as if Gennady were his hope of heaven. "You have?"

"Yes, yes. Assassination attempts are very bad for relations between countries. But," Gennady said, "still, even if this stays out of the papers, your father will hear of it. And, I think, he will come running to see what has happened, just as he did when you were arrested for the possession of his Mauser."

Peter moaned.

"What can your father say to you that is so bad, Peter?" Gennady asked. Then he answered himself: "What Stalin said, probably, when he heard that his son tried to shoot himself, and failed: 'Ha! You missed!'"

"*Gennady*," Daniel protested.

"I wanted to go in for a closer shot," Peter insisted. "Only there were so many police there that I couldn't, and… How did you find me, anyway? I didn't even hit the train."

"Well," said Daniel. "Actually, you did."

There was a slight pause. Then Peter said, almost dazed: "I hit the train? But I can't hit the broad side of a barn."

"Well, a train's longer than a barn, I suppose," Daniel said.

"It just keeps going."

"And I hit it? You'll tell my dad I hit it?" Peter said.

Gennady looked at him in some exasperation. "This is what you care about?" he demanded. "You could have started a war. If you had hit Chairman Khrushchev, we would all be dead right now, the whole earth just a radioactive rock."

Peter twisted his big hands together so tightly that his knuckles showed white against his skin. "I didn't think of that," he muttered, and then, louder: "I didn't mean for that to happen."

"That," Gennady told him, "would not have stopped the war. We are all very lucky that you are such a bad shot."

CHAPTER 16

Daniel and Gennady got roaring drunk that night, more or less on the orders of Daniel's boss Mr. Gilman. They called him from the FBI field office to tell him the good news. "Wonderful! Wonderful!" Mr. Gilman said, his elation coming through despite the tinny quality of the long-distance line. "You caught him? A confession you say?"

"Naturally we'll want him executed," Gennady said, leaning over the phone. He tried to sound serious, but the happiness bubbled out in his voice: it was thrilling to be young and alive and to have solved an impossible case. Stepan Pavlovich would be pleased. It meant a promotion for sure, no more Arkady ever.

Mr. Gilman laughed good-naturedly. "A congressman's son? You'll be lucky if he sees the inside of a prison."

Gennady had expected this. His comment about execution had been merely for form.

"Report back to DC to tell me the details, Hawthorne," Mr. Gilman said. "No reason to hurry. You boys hit the town and have a good time tonight."

Of course they could not go at once. Peter's arrest had to be processed, Mack informed in detail of all that had happened ("Did you pay for the suit?" Mack asked, when they reached the part about finding Peter in the department store. Daniel smacked his forehead, so aghast that Mack let out a rasping belly laugh.

"I'll send someone down to Younkers to take care of it. Sanders! Get over here!"). Much paperwork to be completed, which Daniel took care of while Gennady slept on Mack's couch.

He felt much better by the time they hit the bar that evening: sleep and happiness were both great healers. But his blood still felt thin, so he drank only sparingly, and laughed a great deal as Daniel got rip-roaring drunk.

"Do you know," Daniel told him, peering somberly into Gennady's face, "I wasn't even sure you'd have a personality?"

Gennady laughed at him.

"No, really," Daniel insisted. "After all the brainwashing, and dictatorship, and…" A roar over by the dartboard drowned out the rest of his sentence.

"This is your Hollywood brainwashing," Gennady told him. "They've made you think we are all faceless drones."

"I know." Daniel's gaze was unnervingly intense. "You have more personality than just about anyone I've ever met."

Gennady knocked Daniel's hat playfully over his eyes. "You're drunk, *tovarisch*."

Daniel tried to straighten his hat, and left it more crooked than before, and smiled with such pleasure that it hurt Gennady in a funny way. The word *tovarisch* was so overused in his own country that it meant nothing, you called people comrade even if you wished they were dead, and it was strange to see Daniel take it as an affectionate nickname.

Although it was, in a way. Gennady would not have called any other American *comrade*.

"Gennady," Daniel said.

"What?"

Daniel opened his mouth, then shook his head. "Nothing."

Gennady put an arm around his shoulders and gave him a shake. "Well, what? What is it you want to tell me, my friend?"

Another roar from the dartboard.

"Let's get out of here," Daniel said.

"All right." Gennady was still sober enough to drive.

Daniel, on the other hand, nearly fell off his barstool when he tried to stand up. He burst into the immoderate laughter of a drunken man, and Gennady put his hand on his elbow to steer him out of the bar.

When they reached the parking lot, Gennady removed the

keys from Daniel's pocket. "I'm going to drive," he said.

Daniel made a feeble grab for the shiny keys. But he let Gennady bundle him into the passenger seat, and did not complain when Gennady got in on the driver's side and started the engine.

Gennady drove slowly through the quiet streets. In the silvery moonlight it all looked very beautiful, even the Coca-Cola ad chipping off the brick wall of a hardware store, and tears came into his eyes. Now that they had caught Peter Abbott, this trip would end. They wouldn't want him traipsing around the United States to no purpose.

He stopped at a stoplight and brushed the back of his hand over his eyes, and glanced at Daniel just in case he had seen. But Daniel was gazing in drunken fascination at the shining red traffic light. "It's so beautiful."

"Red is the most beautiful color," Gennady agreed.

"*Krasnii* and *prikrasnii*," Daniel said. The car behind them honked – the light had turned green – and Gennady hit the gas without properly engaging the clutch, and flooded the engine.

The other car went around him. Gennady swore and restarted the car and drove on. They passed the edge of town, the last of the streetlights, and drove out into broad dark open country.

"You're not a very good driver," Daniel confided.

"It's not too late to leave you by the roadside," Gennady told him, but despite himself he was smiling again. His throat hurt with sadness. "I'm going to miss you, my friend."

"You don't *have* to leave me by the roadside," Daniel said.

Gennady opened his mouth, and then decided not to correct Daniel's misconception. Daniel was drunk enough that he might cry when Gennady pointed out their partnership was almost over, and Gennady wanted to enjoy this happiness while it lasted.

Suddenly, much too close, another pair of headlights plunged out of the blackness. Gennady jerked the wheel to the right. The car lurched as it left the pavement for the grassy shoulder, and lurched again when Gennady hit the brakes. Daniel slipped off his seat into the seat well.

The other car flashed past. Gennady clutched the wheel, panting. The wound in his side throbbed.

"We'll get out and rest," Gennady decided. "We'll look at the stars."

The cool night air felt good on his face when he got out of the car. Out here, so far from electric lights, a hundred thousand stars dappled the sky: not just the bright ones that you saw in towns, but so many others fainter and smaller. It gave the night sky a look of depth, as if you could fall upward into it and keep on falling forever.

Gennady felt for a moment that he *was* falling, and grabbed the handle of the car to steady himself. *Oh, Gennady, you're drunk, drunk.*

"I bet you can't see stars like this in Moscow," Daniel said, as if the Milky Way was an American invention.

Gennady looked over at Daniel. He looked pale and handsome in the moonlight, like a movie star in black-and-white. "In Moscow, no," Gennady said. "Out at the dacha, the sky is just like this, and very beautiful."

Daniel was looking at him with a peculiar intensity. Gennady pressed his palms flat against the car door and did not look away.

That was when Daniel kissed him.

It was unexpected and yet not surprising. After all, they were both very drunk, and when you were drunk lips were lips and hands were hands and it felt good, the warmth of Daniel's mouth after the cool night air, the warmth of his hands touching Gennady's jaw, Gennady's hair, the soft spaces behind Gennady's ears. Gennady's hands rose to Daniel's chest, fingers bunching in his shirt, holding him at bay without pushing him away. Thinking: *by the roadside, in the open? Careless, careless...*

But the thought seemed small and distant, and Daniel's lips warm and close. Gennady made a tiny noise in his throat.

Daniel broke the kiss. He rested his forehead against Gennady's, laughing a little, his breath soft on Gennady's face as he murmured, "*Tovarisch.*"

Reality crashed over Gennady like ice water. Daniel was an American FBI agent. Could he truly be so careless as to fling himself at a Soviet agent's head?

Perhaps he really had been assigned to honeytrap Gennady.

Gennady swung Daniel around and slammed him against the car. "Idiot!" he yelled. "Idiot! What are you doing?"

Daniel's hands rose to protect his face. "I'm sorry," he gasped. "I'm sorry!"

Gennady smacked his hand against the car frame. "How could you be so careless? Kissing an enemy agent! Why do you think I was assigned to work with you?"

"To... to investigate the assassination attempt on Khrushchev..."

"No!" Gennady smacked his palm against the car again. "That's only part of it. I'm supposed to gather intelligence on the United States and blackmail material on you." Daniel blinked at him, his face crumpling with confusion, and Gennady yelled, "Idiot! I've been sent to honeytrap you!"

Gennady gave him a final shove, and Daniel slid to the ground. Gennady stood over him for a moment, then walked a few paces to the edge of the cornfield. His side ached abominably. He felt he might be sick.

How could he have confessed his secret mission to Daniel? That was a shooting offense, surely, telling official secrets to an enemy agent. Stupid, stupid, unnecessary and stupid. He had not needed to tell Daniel about the honeytrap. He could have just pushed him away.

"Are you going to blackmail me, then?" Daniel's voice was painfully steady.

"No," Gennady snapped. "I would have let you incriminate yourself further if I were."

"Oh." Daniel laughed a little wildly. "Yes, I suppose fucking in the backseat would be better blackmail material than a kiss."

Gennady swung back toward Daniel. The movement tugged at his injured side, and tears rose in his eyes, from pain and unhappiness and a sense of the bitter unfairness of the world. It occurred to him only now that he could have let Daniel kiss him and then just *not told*.

Well, but he hadn't been sure that Daniel wasn't trying to honeytrap him. No. It had been necessary to put a stop to things.

Daniel sat on the ground, his knees drawn up to his chest. "Do you hate me now?"

"Why would I hate you?"

"Oh, you know." Daniel let out a trembling sigh. "Most decent people are disgusted by deviancy and..." A sickly smile touched his mouth. "Perversion."

Gennady's heart melted. He went back over to Daniel and put a hand on his head. Daniel's hair was very soft, and Gennady ruffled it gently. "You've never been this drunk before in your life, have you?" Gennady asked. Poor Daniel with his teetotal upbringing. "When you're very drunk, this sort of thing just happens sometimes. It doesn't mean anything."

Daniel gave another brief wild laugh. He knocked Gennady's hand away. "Do you know why I got assigned to work with you? Mr. Gilman reassigned me after he discovered Paul and I were lovers. Can't have two FBI agents fucking around the countryside." Daniel laughed again. "The Soviets are e-*nor*-mous prudes, he said. I guess he thought even I couldn't fuck this up. Pun intended. Christ!" He buried his face in his hands.

Gennady looked at him, baffled, uncertain. Getting drunk and fucking around, that was normal, it was just a thing that happened. But calling a man your *lover*...

Well, so, so, so? So what if Daniel wasn't quite normal. Lots of normal people were terrible. They were two separate axes entirely, goodness and normality, and goodness was more important even if most people didn't believe that.

Daniel lifted his head. The tears on his eyelashes gleamed in the moonlight. "I thought it was just Mr. Gilman who knew," he said. "But if the KGB knows, then the whole FBI has to know too."

"No, no," Gennady said. "No one knows. This honeytrap, it was..." He paused. His mouth tasted sour. "It was just my boss's idea, not a directive from on high. A long shot, as you Americans say. Arkady wanted his own source in the FBI. Your dossier describes you as a womanizer, not..."

A homosexual? Gennady shied away from the word. It was too insulting to apply to a friend, even if it might be technically accurate.

Could it be accurate if Daniel slept with that many women, anyway?

Gennady shouldn't be divulging the contents of a secret GRU dossier to an American agent anyway. Fuck.

"Paul used to get mad about it." Daniel sounded weary. "The manly love of comrades ought to be enough for me, et cetera, I shouldn't even look at women. Maybe you're right and love is just a pretty word for fucking."

"Daniel!" Gennady said. He knelt down beside Daniel and grabbed both his hands, which startled Daniel into silence.

"Listen to me. If things were different, Daniel, if we could be friends – "

Daniel's eyes widened. "Can't we still be friends? I'm sorry I kissed you, Gennady. I won't do it again."

"I'm not talking about that at all. We can't be friends because our countries are enemies. Oh, they are getting along right now, but it won't last. The interests of the USSR and the USA are inherently opposed."

"But don't you like me?"

"Yes, of course. But that doesn't mean we're friends."

"But that's what being friends means." Daniel looked baffled.

"That's only the beginning of friendship," Gennady told him. "Friendship means trust and loyalty and…" How to explain the difference between friendliness and friendship to such a promiscuously friendly people as the Americans?

Gennady gave it up as impossible. "Listen, Daniel. If we could be friends, then I would want you to tell me all of these things, to pour your heart out to me. But as it is, you should keep your mouth shut and think whether you want the Soviet Union to know all of this about you."

That, at least, Daniel understood. His eyes widened again. "You won't…"

"No, *I* won't, but I am not the only Soviet agent in the world, Daniel. You can't be so careless about who you kiss, you can't go around spilling your heart out to just anyone, and especially not to me, when you already know that I am an agent of an enemy state."

"But that doesn't mean we're enemies."

"Daniel." Gennady was exasperated. "Just because we are enemies doesn't mean we have to hate each other. We can like each other very much even, but at the end of the day we are still enemies. We will *always* be enemies."

"Always?"

"Unless you become a communist, I suppose," Gennady said.

Daniel released a long shaky breath. "So – always," he said. His face crumpled abruptly; he shut his eyes tight. "You must despise me. A pervert *and* an idiot."

Gennady cupped Daniel's cheek and turned Daniel's face up toward him. "Of course I don't despise you, Daniil, don't be silly. It was very foolish, but after all, you are very drunk; and Soviet agents are not so prudish as your Mr. Gilman thinks, I know these things happen."

Daniel blinked up at him. His eyelashes brushed Gennady's palm like butterfly wings. Gennady kissed his cheeks soundly, then pulled him to his feet. "Come on," Gennady said. "Let's find a motel. Perhaps you won't even remember this in the morning."

CHAPTER 17

Daniel woke up lying on top of a bedspread, fully clothed but shoeless, with a dull headache and a cottony mouth and only the vaguest idea where he was. A motel room, clearly, although he couldn't remember how he'd gotten there. The last thing he remembered...

He buried his face in the pillow as mortification broke over him in waves.

Kissing Gennady. And Gennady had been so pliant at first, his lips parting, questioning, his hands gentle against Daniel's chest...

Until he slammed Daniel against the car. *You idiot!*

He had really thought Gennady was going to beat him up. The way he flung Daniel against the car – God, he was *strong*; slung Daniel like a sack of potatoes.

Gennady's hands on his shoulders, the furious glitter of his eyes. Daniel's heart pounding in his chest, the struggle to breathe. Like John all over again...

How the hell could Daniel have been so stupid?

The alcohol had blotted most of their conversation out of Daniel's memory, but he remembered about the honeytrap. God, Gennady would be in a load of trouble if the KGB ever found out he had betrayed his secret mission to an American agent. Did they still shoot people in the Soviet Union for that sort of thing?

Not that they would ever find out. Only Daniel knew, and even if he could have told without incriminating himself, he wouldn't.

Gennady must hate him now.

Except... Daniel remembered the affectionate way Gennady had said *Daniil*, the Russian form of his name. And those kisses at the end of the conversation, one on each cheek. Just kisses of friendship. Daniel had seen the Polyakovs kiss their émigré friends just like that.

In fact old Mrs. Polyakov used to finish off the cheek kissing with a kiss on the lips with her lady friends, which always made Daniel and his sister Anna giggle (a lady kissing another lady!). But of course Gennady must have known how easily this could be misinterpreted, given the context.

Daniel sat up slowly. He swung his legs out of bed, and had to grip the mattress to steady himself.

Gennady had left him a glass of water on the bedside table. A note, too, held down by the corner of the ashtray. *Having breakfast at the café across the street. G. I. Matskevich.*

Daniel tucked the note in his breast pocket and smoothed it. Then he drank the water and slowly stood. The movement set his head spinning. All right: no shaving this morning.

In fact, even changing out of yesterday night's rumpled clothes seemed too much to contemplate without the aid of coffee. In any case it was already... He checked the clock. 9:58. Shit. Would Gennady even still be at the café?

Of course he would. Gennady was probably on his third muffin and his fifth cup of coffee, reveling in the chance to linger over a three-hour breakfast.

Daniel stuck his feet in his shoes and shuffled out of the room. He was, he discovered, in room six at the Sunrise Motel, in the town of... Well, some town in Iowa, probably. Unless they'd made it to Illinois the night before.

There was indeed a café right across the street: the Westport Diner. Gennady sat reading in a booth by the window, visible from the motel room, and Daniel stood for a long moment and stared at him, mortified all over again. He did not know how to face him.

Then Gennady looked up and saw him, and smiled, and Daniel melted with relief. He hurried to cross the street.

When Daniel approached the booth, Gennady pushed a plate bearing a half-eaten cinnamon roll toward him. "Daniel," Gennady said. "Have you had one of these?"

It was so characteristic and normal and utterly unchanged from yesterday that Daniel could have cried. "A cinnamon roll? Sure."

Gennady gave him a look of deepest betrayal: Daniel had let the side down by not telling him about cinnamon rolls long ago. "They're very good here. You should get one."

Daniel lowered himself into the other side of the booth with a groan that was only partly faked. "I'll see if I can survive coffee and toast."

Gennady's eyes half-closed, in that look that made him look like a contented cat. "Overhang?" he taunted.

"Hungover?" Daniel taunted back. He expropriated Gennady's coffee cup. Gennady snagged it back before Daniel could get a sip.

"Remember anything from last night?" Gennady asked, his tone slightly mocking.

But Daniel could see the real question in Gennady's eyes. Gennady remembered, and he knew Daniel remembered, and he was giving Daniel a chance not to speak of it ever again.

Daniel, to his surprise, felt disappointed. But it had to be better this way.

"I don't even remember leaving the bar," Daniel said, with his most hangdog expression. "I didn't sing, did I?"

"There were bluebirds over the white cliffs of Dover all the way to the motel," Gennady said with relish.

"Oh *no*," said Daniel, and hid his face in his hands, the mortification genuine even though the cause was spurious.

"Coffee," he heard Gennady saying to the waitress. "Toast. A cinnamon roll..." Daniel shook his head and groaned, and Gennady told him, "I will eat it if you can't."

Once it seemed likely the waitress was gone, Daniel lifted his head. "We ought to get a move on," he pointed out. "We've got a long drive ahead."

"Why hurry?" Gennady said. "It's Thursday today. We could not get back before the offices are closed on Friday. And no one will be in the office over the weekend, so there is no reason to reach DC before Monday."

Daniel stared. "I just thought…"

He had figured Gennady would want to dispense with his company as soon as possible after last night.

Gennady stretched expansively. "We should take our time. Now that we've wrapped up the case, they'll reassign us both when we get back."

Of course. They had been assigned to work together on the assassination attempt, and now that they had solved it, their partnership would end.

The waitress returned with coffee and toast and cinnamon roll. Daniel stared at the dark surface of the coffee.

"Ilf and Petrov had only ten weeks on the highways of America," Gennady mused. "We've had three months. We're lucky, my friend."

"We'll aim to get into DC on Monday, then," Daniel conceded. "Is there anywhere in particular that you would like to see?"

Gennady's eyes brightened. "Well…"

Daniel settled in with his coffee and listened as Gennady laid out an itinerary that included the Grand Canyon, the sequoias, and a visit to Key West to meet Ernest Hemingway. "You realize, of course," Daniel said, "absolutely none of that is on our route."

"It's true," Gennady admitted, with a sigh. "Your country is too big, my friend. But still let's see as much as we can. You have to grab happiness when you can find it."

CHAPTER 18

As it happened, they didn't drive far at all the first day. Gennady fell asleep about five miles down the road, and when he woke up hours later, he found that Daniel had pulled over in the shade, opened the car windows, and fallen asleep himself.

Daniel's cheeks were faintly flushed, his lips parted; the soft breeze ruffled his hair. There was a sweetness to his expression as he slept, and Gennady felt a painful tenderness toward him. He would have liked to touch his face.

It had been brave in a way – yes, truly brave – for him to kiss Gennady at all.

And Daniel had been gentle, had been asking. And had good reason to believe that Gennady might say yes: Gennady had led him on for the honeytrap, and anyway Gennady had been drunk and happy enough that he *would* have said yes, if it wasn't for the honeytrap. Because people did do these things when they were drunk...

Daniel woke, and stretched, and yawned. Gennady looked away. Daniel commented ruefully, "Neither of us are going to sleep a wink tonight."

"Probably we will."

"Probably you need it. Are you feeling all right?" Daniel made a slight movement, as if to touch Gennady's shoulder, but pulled back with sudden embarrassment.

Gennady felt bereft. He would have liked Daniel to put an arm around his shoulders in his old friendly way. "I'm fine," Gennady said, in the approved American style. "Only tired. And hungry," he added.

"Let's find a place to eat...lunch? Dinner?" Daniel checked his watch. "Three o'clock snack. Some chicken soup would be good for both of us. And then I guess we'll check into a motel and see if we can drive farther tomorrow."

The second day was better. They purchased a picnic lunch, and ate it by a stream below one of those enchanting American covered bridges. Gennady had the supreme pleasure of watching a horse pull a shiny black wagon over the rumbling boards. "Do people still drive wagons in America?"

"Not usually. That was an Amish buggy."

"Amish?" And Gennady listened with fascination as Daniel described the Amish, who used very little modern machinery, but lived their lives almost the same as they had a hundred years ago.

But once Daniel explained the Amish, he lapsed into silence again, and sat tugging at the short spring grass. He seemed downcast now, and Gennady wondered if Daniel's friendliness before had simply been flirtation – except that Daniel was friendly to everyone, and it couldn't be that he was *always* flirting.

No. Probably he was quiet because he was brooding on the honeytrap.

Daniel roused himself to smile. "I got a box of cracker jack. You want some?"

"Cracker jack?"

"I thought maybe you wouldn't have had it." Daniel tossed a small bright-colored box in Gennady's lap. "Try it. There's always a prize at the bottom."

Cracker jack was like the popcorn balls at Angeline's Halloween party, popped corn covered in caramel, good and sweet and crunchy. At the bottom of the box, Gennady found a little metal stagecoach. "That's good," Daniel commented. "You don't find the metal prizes much anymore. Mostly it's plastic these days."

Gennady turned the little stagecoach over in his hand. "Do you want it?"

"Nah. You keep it. Souvenir of your trip to the States."

Gennady kept it in his hand as they drove on down the road, holding it tightly enough that the little wheels dug red marks into his palm.

Early in the war, when Gennady was perhaps six or seven, his mother had made a joke about Stalin without realizing that Gennady was under the table. He still remembered her face when she caught sight of him: his mother who adored him, who recited poems to him when he couldn't sleep, even though she was so tired herself after her long hours at work that she would fall asleep mid-line. Then, spoiled child that he was, he tugged her sleeve and demanded she go on, and she woke up and smiled at him, and continued as if she didn't need to sleep.

But when his mother realized he had heard her dismissive words about Stalin, for a moment she had looked at him with something like hate in her eyes. As if he were a little Pavlik Morozov. They all learned his story in school: Pavlik Morozov, the Young Pionner murdered by his uncles for informing on his grain-hoarding father. Hero and martyr. An example for all Soviet children.

And the next day, through God knew what black market connections, Gennady's mother brought Gennady a chocolate bar. A bribe, although at the time he didn't understand it as such. Because it was not safe for her to say to her own child, *Don't tell anyone what I said, don't have me sent to the camps.*

It was terrible, terrible, when parents had to be afraid of their own children, when a worm of terror in every human heart ate away at every good thing. It had found its way even into his friendship with Daniel, who was an American and ought to be exempt – except that now he had the honeytrap hanging over his head.

If only there was some way to show someone your soul – not with words, which so easily became lies, but some way to let a person know that they could truly trust you not to hurt them.

But there was no way to show that except time, and Daniel might worry for quite a long time before he would believe that Gennady truly would not tell. No matter how much you loved and trusted a person, even as much as a mother loves her only child, it was impossible to feel safe if that person knew something that could destroy you, when you had no possible means of retaliation, no blackmail to hold over their head in return.

Well, that at least could be fixed.

"You know," Gennady said, "I've admired some of the things that Khrushchev has done. Stopping Beria after Stalin died, the Secret Speech, his trip to America. But at the end of the day, really he's been an ineffective fool."

The car swerved. "*What*?" Daniel said.

Gennady's heart roared in his ears. He could taste something sour in the back of his throat. "When he gave the Secret Speech..." Gennady added doggedly. "Did you ever read it?"

"Yes, it was published in the *New York Times*. Gennady..."

"It wasn't secret really. It was read across the country, everyone was talking about it. And I thought, maybe now things will really change, maybe we will become a normal country. But then less than a year later the tanks rolled into Budapest and crushed the Hungarians and it was like the tanks rolled over any hopes of freedom in Russia, too."

Daniel pulled over on the grassy verge. For a moment they sat amid the buzzing insects. Gennady contemplated his imminent demise once the GRU heard about this.

Well, perhaps not demise. He might be sent to the camps, or simply fired, certainly never allowed out of the country again. The exact punishment really depended on the political climate when they heard.

Daniel was staring at him. "Gennady, why are you saying this?"

Gennady felt like a beetle pinned to a card, a stupid beetle who had walked up and stuck himself on the pin because he felt sorry for the man who was having such trouble pinning him. "I thought you might worry less about the honeytrap if you knew something just as damaging about me."

Daniel continued to stare. "That's probably the bravest, stupidest, kindest thing anyone has ever done for me."

Gennady gasped in a breath. He took his flask from his pocket. "Very stupid, yes."

"No, I mean all of it, Gennady," Daniel said. "That was incredibly brave. And it was sweet of you to do it just because... well, of course I have been a little worried. It's not that I don't trust you, it's just..."

Daniel hesitated. Gennady took a swig. "It's just impossible to trust anyone," he filled in.

Daniel looked taken aback. "Well, I wouldn't say that exactly. It's just... well..." He was silent for a long moment, and then burst out, "I hope you trust me enough to believe me when I say that I won't tell anyone what you just said about Khrushchev."

Gennady was beginning to feel a little better. "Yes, well, so. You'd be very foolish to do it. The point is that now we both have the power to destroy each other's lives, so neither of us can use it."

"It sounds less sweet when you put it that way," Daniel said wryly.

Well, maybe it did, but you couldn't depend on sweetness. Mutual fear was a more reliable deterrent.

The little metal stagecoach had fallen into Gennady's lap. He retrieved it, and took Daniel's hand, and put the Cracker Jack prize on his palm. "You'll keep it?" he said.

Daniel's mouth curved up at the corner. "Of course," he said. "Thank you."

CHAPTER 19

On Monday morning they split up outside of a subway station in DC. "I guess this is goodbye," Daniel said, trying to sound jaunty.

"Yes, I suppose so," Gennady said. But he too lingered at the top of the steps, in the sunlight.

"I guess there's no point suggesting that we should keep in touch?" Daniel said, with some hope that there was.

But Gennady shook his head. "No, no. They would frown on it very much if I exchanged letters with a known American agent."

"Oh. Yes, I guess my government wouldn't like it if I wrote to a Soviet agent, either," Daniel admitted. He shoved his hands in his pockets. "I've never been good at goodbyes," he confessed. "The big goodbyes, when you might not see someone again..." His voice hitched. "At least for a long time. When I shipped out to Korea, I shouted 'See you later, alligator!' to my sister."

"See you later, alligator?" Gennady echoed, puzzled.

"It's from a song. The response is 'After a while, crocodile.'" It felt inappropriately light, just as it had when he called it out to Anna. "You'll look me up if you're ever in America again, won't you?"

"Yes, of course," Gennady said. And then, to Daniel's

surprise, he pulled Daniel into a bear hug, and held on until Daniel hesitantly hugged him back. "Not too tight, I'm wounded," Gennady reminded him, and Daniel laughed and gingerly patted his back. Gennady let go and kissed his cheeks in the Russian fashion. "That's how we leave for the wars in Russia," he said. "That's better, isn't it? And then we say *proshai*."

"*Proshai?*"

"Farewell."

Daniel's eyes misted, despite his best efforts. "*Proshai*, Gennady.*"

"*Proshai.*"

And then Gennady disappeared down the steps, into the darkness of the subway station.

Daniel had a different subway line to catch, and he walked to the station slowly, to give himself time to fight back the tears. He could cry later – that night, he promised himself, once he was safe in a hotel room somewhere. But he couldn't show up to see Mr. Gilman with bloodshot eyes. It would be ridiculous, a total waste of Gennady's generosity in warning Daniel about the honeytrap, if Mr. Gilman guessed that Daniel had fallen for his partner *again*, after Mr. Gilman had given him a second chance...

Maybe Daniel ought to quit.

It was this thought almost as much as Gennady's impending departure that had dogged Daniel's spirits for the last few days, much more than any concern that Gennady would tell. Gennady's attempt to soothe Daniel's nerves by giving him correspondingly juicy blackmail material had been so gallant that Daniel would never tell him that it had been unnecessary, but Daniel had already believed implicitly in Gennady's silence, based purely on the fact that Gennady had warned him about the honeytrap.

The honeytrap.

The Soviets had known enough about him to set a man as bait for a honeytrap. That meant he was a security risk.

But he loved his job; he had always dreamed of being an FBI agent. Probably he *ought* to quit, but he couldn't make up his mind to do it, and arrived at Mr. Gilman's office still in a state of indecision.

Mr. Gilman greeted him with a smile. "Agent Hawthorne," he said. "The man of the hour. I've read your report, but I want you to tell me all about the case."

And, for a wonder, Mr. Gilman actually sat at his desk to listen, instead of meandering around the room as usual. At the end he leaned back in his chair with a satisfied sigh, as if he had a long cool drink on a parching day.

"You've done well," he said. "I knew you could do it."

Daniel's cheeks grew hot. He hoped that if Mr. Gilman noticed, he would take it for pleasure, but it was mostly shame. "Thank you, sir."

"How did you get along with Lieutenant Matskevich?"

"Well, I didn't fall in love with him," Daniel said, so dryly that Mr. Gilman laughed. Daniel laughed too, and felt like a world-class fraud. "No, really, we got along all right. It was a little difficult at first – you warned me that the Russians can be hard to work with. Suspicious, stubborn. Unfriendly. But we had a good working partnership by the end."

Mr. Gilman had drifted across the room to his window. Daniel wondered if he briefed everyone while staring out at the lawn, or only Daniel. "And how did he like America?"

"Pretty well," Daniel said. "Once he let himself show that he was interested in it. I guess they told him not to seem too impressed by anything. But he admired the roads and the heating and the natural beauty of the country. The covered bridges. The girls," he added cravenly.

Mr. Gilman's eyes remained on the red dots of the early tulips on the lawn. "I imagine that's why it took you so long to solve the case," he said mildly. "His mind wasn't on his work."

That was a fair criticism. "I'm sorry, sir."

"But then," Mr. Gilman mused, "How can you blame him? This must have been a once-in-a-lifetime opportunity for him. The Soviets give their people so few chances to travel…"

His voice trailed off. He continued gazing at the lawn, and Daniel waited and shifted in his seat and finally burst out, "Mr. Gilman. Why did you give me a second chance?"

Mr. Gilman turned to look at him. Daniel dropped his eyes to one of the many knickknacks on Mr. Gilman's desk.

"You're a good agent," Mr. Gilman said. "I didn't want the Bureau to lose you."

"Yes, but..." The knickknack, Daniel discovered, was a Chinese puzzle ball. He might never lift his eyes again. Mr. Gilman trusted him, and if Gennady hadn't stopped him, Daniel would have thrown that away like yesterday's trash. "I don't want to be a security risk," Daniel said.

"Agent Hawthorne." Mr. Gilman came back over to the desk. "I know that your... peccadilloes, shall we say, may make you more vulnerable in certain respects than other agents. But... Daniel, look at me."

Daniel looked up. Mr. Gilman picked up the Chinese puzzle ball. "When I was in France during the last war," Mr. Gilman said, "one of the MI6 officers that I worked with became a very dear friend. A very dear friend," he repeated, with a meaningful look at Daniel. "You understand?"

Daniel nodded, mesmerized.

Mr. Gilman tossed the Chinese puzzle ball lightly in the air as he talked, as if it were a tennis ball and not an expensive piece of carved jade. "Of course, MI6 is just like that," he mused. "They all came up through the great English public schools – boarding schools, you understand – where young men have almost no contact with women, which has a, hmm, stunting effect on their development. But still, many of them are excellent agents."

The Chinese puzzle ball landed in his cupped palms and stayed there. "Well, no one was paying much attention during the war, so we never got in trouble. Then the war ended, I came back to the United States, and I got married. And here I am today." He set the puzzle ball down gently on its wooden base. "And here you are. And I imagine your story will work out much the same way. Agent Preston, on the other hand, seems rather... set in his ways... but after all, he does fine work too." He adjusted the puzzle ball minutely, then looked Daniel in the face. "Do you understand?"

Daniel nodded.

"Good." Mr. Gilman leaned back in his chair and picked up a small lacquered box. "Do you think Lieutenant Matskevich would be interested in defecting?"

Daniel started guiltily. "Sir?"

"A Soviet agent so enchanted by his American trip that he can't resist defection... It would be a real public relations coup.

Do you think he might?"

Daniel nearly blurted out everything Gennady had said about Khrushchev, and then veered too hard in the other direction. "No," Daniel said firmly, and then hedged. "Well, he might. We didn't discuss it, but…" Daniel's thoughts bumped up against the obvious problem. "But now that we've closed the case, Lieutenant Matskevich and I won't be working together anymore. I'm not going to have a chance to sound him out."

"Oh, right," Mr. Gilman said carelessly. He turned back toward Daniel. "Someone's been smuggling Baltic amber into the Boston. I realize is not your usual area, but the Soviets have some interest in continuing this unorthodox partnership in order to investigate the matter. Or so they claim. Mostly I think they're just interested in giving Lieutenant Matskevich the opportunity to gather more information on the United States, and as this case will take you mostly up through New England, I see no harm in it."

"As it's above the Mason-Dixon line," said Daniel. His heart thundered in his ears so that he could barely hear his own voice. A reprieve. More time with Gennady.

Mr. Gilman just laughed. "Enjoy your road trip," he said. "And do try to bring him to our side. It would be a real feather in our cap if he defects."

CHAPTER 20

After he parted from Daniel, Gennady crossed DC to see Stepan Pavlovich. "Good work," Stepan Pavlovich said, and even such mild praise from a GRU boss was like a twenty-one gun salute. "I've filled out the transfer paperwork to move you into my department. It all came through this morning, I already called up Arkady Anatolyevich to let him know."

Gennady kept his face smooth, although a horde of smiles fought to get out. "Very efficient."

"Yes. He wants you to come in, to say goodbye I suppose. Of course I told him you would go."

"A courtesy call," Gennady agreed.

"Yes." Stepan Pavlovich leaned back in his chair and lit a cigarette. "It's good that we found this Baltic amber case for you to work with the American," he mused. "Someone will shit everything up between our countries sooner or later and then it will all come to an end, but keep it up as long as you can. Your reports – it's like getting a new chapter of Ilf and Petrov every week."

Gennady blushed with pleasure.

He treated himself to an excellent lunch in celebration: steak, and bananas Foster, which he bought because he had never heard of it before. The waiter set the bananas alight by Gennady's table, and then poured the caramelized bananas and caramel sauce over ice cream, and Gennady ate it in bliss. Beautiful American custom, setting food on fire.

He got a bottle of champagne, too, and drank it all himself, the drink a perfect accompaniment to the golden bubbling happiness of his mood. Arkady must be furious – and he would be doubly so once Gennady told him the honeytrap failed. Gleefully he imagined the vein throbbing in Arkady's temple, his whole face turning red with rage, and all the time Gennady would hug to himself the knowledge that he *could* have carried it through if he wanted to.

He could have kissed Daniel back, standing in the moonlight on the grassy verge of the road, wrapped his arms around Daniel's neck or – no – kept his hands planted on Daniel's chest, pushed him down among the wildflowers (had there been wildflowers?), a tangle of arms and legs and mouths in sea of violets...

He could have done all of that and more, and still lied to Arkady about it, and sat smugly in the knowledge of this secret vengeance while Arkady danced with rage.

Gennady took a long walk after lunch: it would not do to show up at Arkady's office still tipsy from champagne. A cigar store caught his eye, and he nearly walked into traffic in his desire to go in at once. (Perhaps drinking the whole bottle had been a *little* too much.) He would buy a box of cigars for Sergeyich, who loved cigars – Sergeyich who had been his only friend in Arkady's office. A present to share his good fortune.

Perhaps he should buy Daniel a present too? Not cigars, of course, Daniel didn't smoke. And alcohol seemed out of the question, given Daniel's proclivities when he was drunk. (Gennady felt very tender for him at the thought: it must make life harder and life was so hard already.) A book perhaps?

But he could think about that later. For now Gennady focused on the wide selection of cigars, and finally settled on a handsome expensive box with a picture of a lightly clad lady. Sergeyich would like that.

Afterward, Gennady walked to the old office with a bounce in his step. The bounce didn't falter even when he found that the elevator was out of order – again! this was DC, not Moscow, what were they about? – and he had to climb three flights of stairs to the office.

Maksym Sergeyevich Bondar — Sergeyich to his friends — ran the front desk, a disorganized mess of forms and ashtrays and fossilized doughnuts. He was almost forty, with a long hollow face and long yellow teeth like a mule's — which explained, perhaps, why he remained so good-humored even though he had been in Arkady's office longer than anyone else: he was too old and ugly for Arkady.

Sergeyich sat more or less exactly as Gennady had left him four months ago, leaning back in his chair, his arms behind his head. Then, he had been watching the autumn leaves detach from the tree outside the window. Now he was gazing meditatively at a spider web.

But he swung around when Gennady arrived. "Ilyich!" he said, and came around the desk to pull Gennady into a bear hug and kiss his cheeks, ending with the traditional smack on the lips. "Back at Finland Station?"

"Only for a brief stop," said Gennady. "I've been transferred into Stepan Pavlovich's department."

"Comrade Matskevich!" Sergeyich slapped him on the back. "Congratulations!"

"I brought you a parting gift," Gennady said, and held up the box of cigars.

"Ah! Well, Ilyich, you ought to get transferred every day if it inspires such generosity as this." Sergeyich removed a cigar from the box, holding it under his nose and breathing in deeply. "Seriously, though, I'm glad for you, my friend. If I'd known your good news, I would have gotten you something, too. Let's see if I have anything in my desk drawers."

"No, I would rather not have a petrified doughnut, thank you," Gennady told him, but Sergeyich had already begun to disgorge the contents of his top desk drawer onto the desk, keeping a running commentary as he went.

"Paper napkins, Chinese take-out menu — have you had American Chinese food, Gennady? It's not bad. More paper napkins, *more* paper napkins... Well, they come with every takeout order, can you expect me to just throw them away? Ow! A tack. More paper napkins. A pen. Let's see, what's this?" He smoothed the crumpled sheet of paper and peered at it. "That might have been important," he said, and added it to a towering stack of papers.

"I see you'll attend to it right away," Gennady said.

"Naturally. I'm the soul of efficiency, as you know, the only reason this office runs at all."

"The mainspring of this well-oiled clock of espionage."

"Ah! That's nice. I like that. I shall say that to myself in the mirror tomorrow morning as I prepare for work. 'Maksym Sergeyich, you are the mainspring of this – ' Damn! Another tack." Sergeyich shunted the cigar to one side of his mouth and stuck the tip of his thumb in the other. He mumbled something unintelligible, and took his thumb from his mouth and said, "Perhaps I shouldn't go groping around in the drawer without being able to see what's in there."

"What? Are there more paper napkins blocking your view?"

Sergeyich gave him a bleak look. He put both hands in the drawer and removed two overflowing handfuls of napkins. Gennady shouted a laugh.

"Take them home and use them for toilet paper."

"A man only shits so much, Ilyich." Sergeyich's eyes moved behind Gennady, and he said, "Speaking of. Nikolai, what is it you want?"

"You're back," said Nikolai, with a stiff nod at Gennady.

"Would you like a cigar?" Gennady asked. It was an offer prompted by guilt: he had forgotten to get Nikolai anything.

Or no. Gennady had not so much forgotten Nikolai as drop-kicked his memory into the outer fringes of the solar system, somewhere out around Neptune. Nikolai had arrived in DC about a month after Gennady, and he had the bad fortune to be pretty: blonde hair, blue eyes, pale skin and fine bones and a delicate mouth. "He looks like a German doll," Sergeyich had commented upon his arrival.

"Do you think it ever bothered the Germans that we are so much more blue-eyed and blonde than they are?" Gennady asked.

"That's why they tried to get rid of us," Sergeyich said laconically. "Only if they killed us off would they be the blondest and bluest eyed of all."

It had been unpleasant to watch Arkady hang over Nikolai's chair, his hands on his shoulders or his hair; unpleasant to hear Arkady's shouts of "Nikolai!" ringing through the office. More unpleasant still when he called "Kolya!"

At least he had never called Gennady *Gosha*.

Unpleasant to think of Nikolai left behind in that stuffy office with Arkady always lurking, while Gennady larked around the United States listening to Elvis and trying out duckpin bowling. And so he had not thought about it.

But of course Nikolai was still here. He was not so pretty now: his eyes had the bruised pouchy look of someone who was not sleeping well. "You'll wake Arkady Anatolyevitch," he said.

This too Gennady had forgotten. Arkady took a nap in the afternoons, in his office, technically a secret though of course the whole office knew about it.

And, as if Nikolai's comment itself had wakened him, now Gennady heard the telltale squeak of Arkady's door. "Gennady!" Arkady roared. "Are you finally here? Stepan Pavlovich called hours ago."

Gennady rolled his eyes at Sergeyich, but he headed down the hall with alacrity. "I'm sorry, Arkady Anatolyevich," he said, falling instantly and without meaning to back into the old respectful tone. "I didn't mean to keep you waiting. Stepan Pavlovich sends his regards."

"Does he?" Arkady slammed his office door closed and gestured for Gennady to sit in the upright wooden chair in front of his desk. "Fucking bastard. He's sent you to gloat, has he? He's always stealing my best people."

Gennady sat gingerly. Arkady was not his boss anymore, he reminded himself, and attempted to relax. But he remained on the edge of the seat.

Arkady flung himself down in his own padded office chair. "Well, go ahead and make your report," he snapped. "Did you succeed?"

Gennady knew that he was asking about the honeytrap, but he answered as if Arkady was asking about his official mission. "Didn't Stepan Pavlovich tell you? We caught the villain who attempted to take our dear Nikita Sergeyevich's life."

"Naturally I was informed!" Arkady glared at Gennady, and Gennady tried to look innocent and stupid. "I meant your other mission, Gennady, the one I asked you to do for me. Have you honeytrapped the American agent?"

"No."

Arkady stared at him. Gennady looked back, wide-eyed,

trying to enjoy the reddening of Arkady's face. But he felt uncomfortably light-headed. He wished he had not drunk so much at lunch.

"No? No? What do you mean, no?"

"Well," said Gennady, "I tried, but..."

"Shut up! I don't need your excuses." Arkady shoved back his chair so hard that it slammed into the wall. There was a black streak on the paint, left by previous chair-slammings. "How could you let me down like this? Haven't I always been generous to you, Gennady, didn't I recommend you to Stepan Pavlovich when this job came up?"

Gennady doubted it. Stepan Pavlovich would have ignored any recommendation Arkady made on the assumption (quite accurate) that Arkady would only ever recommend an agent he wanted to get rid of. "I'm sorry, Arkady Anatolyevich..." Gennady began.

Arkady interrupted him. "How could you fail? Oh, I've seen the photograph in his dossier, I know you're not pretty enough for a man that good-looking, but still, if you get him drunk..."

"I did," Gennady protested. "But even when he's drunk, he's just repulsed by that sort of thing. I couldn't continue to pursue him without jeopardizing our partnership, and of course the most important thing was to find out who tried to kill our dear Nikita Sergeyevich."

Arkady's jaw clenched. "Of course," he said, through gritted teeth. Then he slammed a fist on his desk. "My God, Gennady! I don't ask much of you, do I? Was it too much to do this one thing for me? During the war we didn't accept excuses. 'Not one step backward,' we said, and if we were ordered to advance we found a way to do it or we died trying. We defended Stalingrad! We took Berlin! And you can't even seduce an American?"

"You said yourself it would be better if I were prettier," Gennady protested. "Or maybe he just likes them younger. Like you do."

Arkady's fist swung out too fast for Gennady to even try to duck. It caught Gennady on the cheek and flung him against the arm of the chair, right across the knife wound in his side. Gennady gagged and retched, unable to catch his breath.

When Arkady spoke again, his voice was quite different than it had been before. "You're injured."

"No," Gennady said. He meant the word as a denial, but it came out more like a plea, and when he heard that pleading note in his own voice his self-control snapped and he begged, "No, no, Arkady, please, no."

"Well, come on," Arkady said. "I'd better have a look at it, hadn't I? Come on!" he said, when Gennady didn't move. "Sit on the desk, take off your shirt. I can't send you out in the world to die, can I?"

Gennady unbuttoned his suit coat first, left it behind on the chair. He stood, and was afraid he might fall: his knees trembled and his head swam. He made his way around the desk and tried to hoist himself up, but his arms were too weak and his side hurt too much and he could not lift himself.

"Go on," Arkady said.

Gennady gave up on the desk for now and tried to undo his tie. His weak shaking fingers could not loosen the knot.

"Do you need help?" Arkady asked.

"I'm sorry, I'm sorry. I can do it."

But he couldn't, and at length Arkady knocked Gennady's hands aside and undid the tie himself. This was different, this was wrong, Arkady had never touched him before, usually he just looked.

But then, usually he was not so very angry.

"I'm sorry," Gennady said, his voice high and small. "*Prostitye,* Arkady Anatolyevich. I tried, I did, but lots of people don't like being pawed at by their colleagues, and Agent Hawthorne got more than enough of that from his previous partner, he was appalled when it seemed he had not escaped after all with this new assignment…"

Dirt rimmed Arkady's fingernails, dark against the white fabric as he undid the buttons on Gennady's shirt. He untucked the shirt, pushed it off Gennady's shoulders. The sleeves bound Gennady's arms and he could not seem to get the shirt off, and Gennady swallowed, close to tears, he *could not* cry in front of Arkady,

Arkady hit him again.

It knocked Gennady to the floor. He rolled, managed to stagger to his feet, stumbled back against the wall. He fully expected Arkady to follow him, pin him down, beat him up or rape him, Arkady never had before but then Gennady had never been stupid enough to get smart with him –

"Get out!" Arkady bellowed, and only then did Gennady realize that Arkady was on the other side of the room, almost hanging out the open window.

Gennady looked down. Blood bloomed like flowers on his undershirt.

The knife slash had reopened, and Arkady, veteran of Stalingrad, could not stand blood.

Gennady pulled his shirt back up on his shoulders. He redid the buttons swiftly, fingers shaking, and tucked his shirt in. "Out!" Arkady bellowed.

"I'm sorry." Gennady threw on his suit coat, though his wounded side screamed in protest at the movement. He grabbed up his tie and fled.

The hall outside Arkady's office was empty, thank God. Gennady retied his tie, and found his hands were shaking. Funny, there was no reason for it; he had escaped now, everything was all right. *Vsyo v paryodki*. Everything okay. His tie was uneven. Fine, fine.

His wound throbbed. He hoped the blood wouldn't spoil this nice new American suit. He had been a fool to wear it to see Arkady.

Sergeyich was leaning back in his chair, his big feet resting on top of a low filing cabinet, already smoking one of the Cuban cigars. He must have heard something – Arkady shouting "Get out!" if nothing else – but he seemed as serene as a summer cloud, thank God.

He blew a perfect smoke ring as Gennady approached. "Care for a cigar?"

"No, my friend." Gennady wanted a cigarette, but if he tried to light one, Sergeyich would see his hands shaking. "They're your present."

"Ah! Well, speaking of presents, I found one for you." Sergeyich lofted a peppermint wrapped in cellophane. "Remember the day we went to that Italian restaurant and filled our pockets with the peppermints at the cash register? Only to realize later that all American restaurants offer bowls of peppermints?"

Gennady nodded, although he wished Sergeyich would shut up and let him go.

"The best gifts are the ones that remind us of the good times in our lives," Sergeyich sighed sentimentally. He leaned across the desk and solemnly closed Gennady's hand around the peppermint. "Treasure it," he advised.

The kind touch steadied Gennady's hands. "I'll drill a hole through the center and wear it over my heart," Gennady promised. He unwrapped the crinkling cellophane and popped the peppermint into his mouth. The flavor exploded on his tongue, bright and intense and sweet.

"There we go. Good lad." Sergeyich tapped his cigar in an overflowing ashtray. "Ah, Nikolai, I see you hanging around back there again. Don't be shy. We don't bite, do we, Ilyich?"

"Only when cornered." Gennady laughed a little madly, and nearly choked on the peppermint.

Sergeyich pounded him on the back. Pain radiated from Gennady's side. "There," Sergeyich told Nikolai. "You see?"

"I was just wondering," Nikolai said, "if you had finished those forms Arkady Anatolyevich wanted."

"Oh, I'm sure they're around here somewhere." Sergeyich poked vaguely at the stacks of papers on his desk. "Oh, don't *look* for them, Nikolai, you'll only disturb my system. Tell him I have a system, Ilyich, won't you? He doesn't believe me."

Gennady coughed. "He's always told me that he has a system," he told Nikolai, "but I've never seen any sign of it."

Nikolai looked at him. His lip curled. "Comrade Matskevich," he said. "You've buttoned your shirt wrong."

Gennady froze like a rabbit. "Excuse me," he said, although he did not see how he could speak when there was no air in his lungs; and then he was not frozen after all, but pushed past Nikolai, down the hallway toward the bathroom.

He shut the lavatory door behind him and took hold of the sink in both hands and bent down, mouth gaping, as if he was going to vomit or scream.

He did neither, just grasped the cool porcelain and panted. Fuck Nikolai, fuck him, fuck him, this was the worst of it, not Arkady himself but the petty unkindness it bred. You might have thought there would be some solidarity among his underlings but you would have been wrong, they were all ashamed and it made them hate each other, Sergeyich was different only because he was well out of it. He was too old for Arkady, nearly forty, if he had been younger even his ugliness wouldn't have protected him.

Gennady wanted to rip off the shirt and tear it to shreds and stuff it in the rubbish bin. But that wouldn't help anything.

He redid the buttons, carefully this time, and tucked the shirt in very gently over his wounded side. He retied his tie three times, pausing between tries to kick the wall, nearly crying with frustration. He shouldn't have drunk so much at lunch. He could have dealt with his tie then, his own buttons, Arkady would not have touched him, none of this would have upset him so much if he were sober. They said alcohol dulled the pain but it didn't always, sometimes it just brought everything closer to the surface.

But he got the tie at last, and blew his nose and splashed his face and looked hopefully in the mirror. Perhaps he looked all right now.

There was a bruise coming up on his left cheek.

He would have to explain that to Daniel.

Daniel. *Fuck*.

He wanted to shrink to the size of a spider, a pinhead, a mote of dust on the air, very still and small and silent, too small to ever speak to anyone again.

But no, no, no. No. It would be all right. It could have come from a fight, that bruise. It might be an honorable battle scar. All he had to do was lie about it, and everything would be fine.

CHAPTER 21

"Oysters Rockefeller," Daniel told the bartender, "and a steak for me, and – you want a steak for that eye, Gennady?"

Gennady's hand stole upward as if to cover the bruise. "For my eye?" he echoed.

"Classic cure for a black eye," Daniel told him.

"Could just get you some ice for it," the bartender put in. "Cheaper'n steak."

Gennady shook his head. "A shot of vodka." He closed the menu. "Two shots. And a hamburger."

"Treat yourself, Gennady. Get something fancy," Daniel told him.

"I like hamburger," Gennady said, and there was enough of an edge to his voice that the bartender stepped away smartly. "Capitalist nonsense – a steak on a black eye."

"Probably," Daniel conceded. "Ma never actually got me a steak for any of my black eyes, mind, it was always a chip of ice off the block in the icebox. There was one year I got in a fight with Jeremy Wojcik practically every week, it felt like, for no reason I could see, until I found out later he had a crush on Helen…"

The bartender delivered Gennady's shots. Gennady kicked

them both back, and held up a finger for another.

"You want to wait on the oysters Rockefeller maybe?" Daniel suggested.

Gennady glanced at him disdainfully. Daniel fell silent with growing mortification. After their parting that morning, the bear hug, that *proshai*, Daniel had expected Gennady to be pleased that they could continue working together, but instead...

Well, of course Gennady didn't really want to keep working with the sloppy drunk who had kissed him.

But then Gennady smiled. In combination with the black eye, it gave Gennady's face a lopsided look that Daniel found strangely heart-breaking. "I'm being very rude," Gennady said. "This is a celebration, you're surprised I am not more happy. And I am happy, my friend. It's only..." He gestured at the black eye. "I got mugged this afternoon."

"Mugged!" Daniel said.

The bartender delivered a third shot, and Gennady drained it and smacked it on the counter and signaled for another. "Anything for you, sir?" the bartender asked Daniel.

"No, I'm not drinking tonight," Daniel told him, and then to Gennady: "Mugged?"

A shrug. "I was looking at the map, an easy mark, a tourist," Gennady said, "or so he thought. He ran when I put up a fight. But still, after all, to be interrupted by an attack, just when you are happy because of a promotion..."

"A *promotion*! I'd better have a beer after all," Daniel said, and smacked Gennady's back. Gennady looked startled, almost ill, and Daniel withdrew his hand hastily and said, "To toast, you know. Just one beer. Not enough to get drunk."

Gennady smiled again. "Yes, of course, a toast," he said.

He drank his fourth shot as soon as the bartender delivered it. It was his fifth shot that he clinked against Daniel's beer.

Once the oysters Rockefeller arrived, Gennady alternated oysters and shots. He was in the double digits by the time the bartender brought their food. "Don't you think you'd better slow down a little?" Daniel said, with the forced jocularity he used to use to try to cajole his frat brothers out of drinking themselves sick.

It had rarely worked then and did not work now. Gennady scowled at him. "It's hot," he said, and made to take off his suit jacket.

The movement exposed a cluster of rusty red dots on the side of his shirt. "So," Daniel said, trying to sound casual, "the fight with the mugger reopened your wound?"

Gennady froze. He jerked the suit jacket back on his shoulders. "It's fine."

It must have hurt like hell. *That* was probably why he was drinking so much. "You want me to look at it again?"

Gennady's look of fury nearly blasted Daniel from his barstool. "You Americans! You're all such babies about injuries and pain. When I was eight I broke my arm. Do you think they had painkillers to waste on a child? It was all needed at the front. You just accept the pain and you live with it until it is over."

Daniel essayed a pacifying smile. "I'm sorry."

"We're the ones who did all the real fighting in the war anyway," Gennady said, his voice far too loud. "Your troops didn't even make landfall in France until 1944, and the war was practically over by then. And now you swan around like you own the whole world when you didn't even conquer Berlin. We did! You didn't drive Hitler to his death. He killed himself to escape our Red Army! Your troops didn't even make it to Berlin until – "

A movement in the mirror above the bar caught Daniel's eye: a man with graying red hair was listening, his face turning red with fury. Daniel interrupted Gennady. "We're not going to discuss that here," he said and he got out his wallet and started counting twenties onto the bar.

"Why not?"

"Because I don't want to get in a bar fight, you moron," Daniel told Gennady.

But before Daniel could drag Gennady off his barstool, the red-haired man stormed over. "Commie bastard," he snarled.

Gennady spun himself off the barstool so fast he nearly fell, swinging his arm in a powerful poorly-aimed punch. He missed, and the red-haired man tried to swing back, but his two friends caught his arms. "Easy, Zeke. Easy."

Daniel grabbed Gennady by the arms and frog-marched him out of the bar. He couldn't have done it if Gennady were sober, but as it was Gennady didn't manage to free himself till they were outside in the cool night air. "Get off!" he shouted, and made as if to go back inside. Daniel leaped in front of the door.

"If you want to get beaten up that badly, *I'll* beat you up!" Daniel shouted.

Gennady's face blazed. For a moment Daniel thought Gennady would take him up on the offer. But then Gennady sagged, and staggered, and vomited into the gutter.

He ended up on his knees on the concrete, still retching, though there was nothing left to come up. At last he wiped his mouth on his sleeve. "I would have won," he insisted. "I could have beaten him into the floor."

"For God's sake," Daniel snapped. "Get up and get into the car."

The reek of booze and vomit filled the close confines of the car. Daniel drove in silence for a while, inwardly seething. At last his rage boiled over, and he snarled, "What the hell were you thinking, letting loose with a rant like that in an American bar?"

"You think too much of yourselves! You think you are so great, so amazing, you think everyone wants to be like you. And you have the audacity," Gennady said, his voice rising, "to show off your beautiful roads and restaurants and big shiny department stores as if they prove your country is better than mine, as if they are a result of capitalism, when really all they show is that you were never invaded. You were sitting pretty behind your two oceans while my country was burned and trampled to the ground by Nazi troops. We've had to rebuild from the ground up, and that's why we're behind you, but someday we will catch up, and then we'll bury you just as Comrade Khrushchev said."

"That's why you almost dragged us into a bar fight? What the hell is wrong with you?"

Gennady swore at him in Russian, furiously, steadily, a whole string of words that Daniel had never heard from the Polyakovs. Suddenly Gennady's voice cracked. He stopped, and tried to start swearing again, and choked.

Daniel felt a flicker of sympathy, and set his jaw against it. He had expected a nice night, a celebration, and he'd gotten barely two bites of his fucking steak, and he wanted to stay angry.

Gennady drew in a faint rattling wet breath. Daniel glanced over at him. Gennady had both hands pressed to his face, his shoulders drawn high, his whole body tense, and despite himself

Daniel felt sorry for him, after all. Gennady did not usually drink that way. Something must have upset him.

"Were you looking forward to going home?" Daniel asked.

Gennady shook his head.

Daniel's hands flexed on the steering wheel. It occurred to him that perhaps Gennady had not been as successful fighting off the mugger as he said. Losing a fight could leave anyone with bruised pride and a chip on his shoulder. But it wouldn't do any good to ask directly, so Daniel just said, "Bad day?"

Gennady gulped again.

Daniel extended an olive branch. "We *are* damn smug. Americans, I mean. And we've got nothing to be smug about, really. Did you know Mr. Gilman told me specifically not to take you below the Mason-Dixon line? 'Don't give them more fuel for their propaganda,'" he said, in his best Mr. Gilman imitation. "But it's not propaganda if it's true, is it?"

"You shouldn't say that to me."

"Why not?" Daniel said. "Mr. Gilman already knows what I think. It doesn't matter if you tell the KGB."

"I'm not a KGB agent." Gennady sounded tired.

Suddenly Daniel felt exhausted, and very lonely with the weight of the lies and the truths they couldn't speak. "Yes, fine. Whatever. I'm stopping at the next motel, all right?"

The next motel was small and dilapidated, and the room itself tiny and grimly Spartan. A single flickering low-watt lamp illuminated twin beds with threadbare blankets. At least the ashtray had been cleaned.

Gennady kicked his shoes off. He lay down on the floor between the beds.

"Gennady, what are you doing?"

"I thought the world would spin less down here." Gennady's mouth twisted. "If it were not so unpleasant to be drunk, no one would ever be sober."

Daniel massaged the bridge of his nose. Then he sat on the floor, too. The thin layer of carpet appeared to be lying directly on top of concrete. "You don't usually drink that much," Daniel said. "Why tonight?"

Gennady shrugged. He rested his cheek against the cold floor.

"Is it that bad having to keep working with me?" Daniel

asked. He tried to smile as he said it, as if it were a joke, but his voice came out wistful.

"No, no," Gennady said, and he sounded so surprised that Daniel believed him. "No. It was…"

But he didn't finish the sentence, and eventually Daniel prompted him. "Did you lose the fight with the mugger?"

"What?" Gennady sounded astonished.

And then Daniel realized: "There never was a mugger."

Gennady sighed. "No," he agreed.

He looked at Daniel, a transparently calculating look, and Daniel said, "Oh, just tell me the truth, why don't you? That's less trouble in the end."

Gennady let out a breath. He tucked his chin against his chest. "Arkady hit me."

"Who is Arkady?"

Gennady glanced at him. "My boss – my old boss. He was angry when he heard I have been promoted out of his department, and he punched me."

"Is he allowed to do that?"

"No. I know you think we are barbarians, but no. It's not allowed. But what is allowed in the rules and what a powerful person can do – these are two different things, you understand?"

"Yes," Daniel said. "It's like that here too." He thought suddenly, almost irrelevantly, of John, who had been so popular, the treasurer of the frat. "I'm sorry that happened, Gennady. That's awful."

Gennady shrugged. He picked at a hangnail. "I went to gloat," he said. "Naturally it made him angry."

"Well, sure it would," Daniel conceded. "But he still shouldn't have hit you, Gennady."

Gennady looked up at him briefly. "I was so happy," he said. "It was such a good day. I got a promotion, and my new boss was pleased with my work, and our road trip will continue. And then Arkady hit me, and then I felt…" He made a gesture with his hand, like a bomb falling, and a sound effect that must have been the Russian noise for an explosion. "It spoiled everything. And until then I had been so happy." Another glance at Daniel, even briefer this time. "Are you angry with me?"

"No. Not anymore."

Gennady's face twisted, like he really might cry. "I behaved so badly this evening…"

"It's all right," Daniel assured him. "I mean, you did behave badly, and for God's sake don't go getting us into any more bar fights. But I'm not mad."

He touched Gennady's hand. Gennady's head snapped up. Their eyes locked, Gennady's huge and gray and wet, and for a long moment neither of them could move; but then Daniel blinked, and Gennady flung himself toward him, his arms around Daniel's neck, his face pressed into his shoulder.

Daniel's arms closed around Gennady. "It's okay," he murmured, and got a mouthful of Gennady's hair. He tightened his grip, and felt a sort of relaxation in his chest, because here was Gennady, finally in his arms. "It's okay. It's okay."

Gennady was so close that Daniel could not only hear but actually feel his shaking breaths. He smelled like alcohol and faintly of vomit and it should have been repulsive, but Daniel just pulled him closer. Gennady tried to speak, and choked.

"It's okay, it's okay," Daniel soothed, and stroked Gennady's hair.

"It's not the pain," Gennady choked out. "The pain doesn't hurt. It's the indignity – the *indignity* – you understand?"

"Yes, of course," Daniel said, not really understanding but willing to sympathize anyway. "Of course."

Gennady's whole body tensed like a spring. A sob ripped out of him. "I'm sorry," he gasped.

"It's all right, it's all right," Daniel assured him, and kissed his hair, and then wished he hadn't, because what if Gennady took that the wrong way? But Gennady was still clinging to him, not shaking so badly now, but still trembling, and he didn't pull away.

"You must hate me," Gennady mumbled.

"Of course not. I'm used to this, Gennady, honest. Half the brothers in my fraternity came to cry on my shoulder when they were drunk."

Gennady made as if to speak, and then choked again and let out a whole string of sobs.

Eventually he stopped sobbing. The tension relaxed out of his body. He sagged against Daniel, and sniffed, and rubbed his face on his sleeve. "I'm sorry." His voice was hoarse.

"It's all right."

But Gennady was already slipping off Daniel's lap. He slid across the narrow space between the beds and drew his legs up to his chest like a shield. His voice was quiet when he spoke again. "You must think I'm pathetic," Gennady said, half-defiant.

"Gennady. Of course not."

Gennady twisted the end of his tie between his fingers. "It must seem so stupid to you," he insisted. "To be so upset over a single punch..."

"No, no. Even a single punch is terrible when it's someone you can't punch back."

Gennady's mouth dragged down at the corners. "What do you know about it? I bet your boss never hit you."

"No," Daniel admitted.

"Not even when he discovered you are a homosexual."

Daniel flinched. "I'm not."

"It is a little late in the day to be saying that, my friend."

"No, no, I'm not saying... I mean, I'm not homosexual because I'm not attracted only to men. I'm attracted to women too. It's called, um." His face was flushing, dammit, his shoulders bracing as if in expectation of a blow. "Kinsey calls it bisexuality," he said, as if Kinsey's imprimatur made it a real and respectable thing, although that certainly hadn't worked when he discussed it with Paul.

("That's not real," Paul had snapped. "There are gay men trying to deny their true nature, and oversexed straight men who will satisfy their base urges with a man if they can't find a woman."

"So which one am I?"

Paul's jaw had twitched. "Both.")

Damn Gennady anyway for prying when he had no right to ask. An equally prying question occurred to Daniel, and he cracked it out like a whip. "What about you?"

Gennady blinked at him. He looked genuinely confused. "What about me?"

"Well, they didn't choose you to honeytrap me because you're straight as an arrow, did they?" Daniel said. Gennady still looked puzzled, and Daniel snapped, "They must have had some reason to think you could seduce a man."

Gennady flushed. "I wasn't chosen for that," he said stiffly. "It was after I received the assignment – then Arkady had the idea for the honeytrap. He was angry they were taking one of his agents away, he wanted to turn it to his advantage, to secure a source for himself. But he would have sent someone else if he could. It would have been better to send someone younger and prettier..."

"So the honeytrap wasn't part of your official mission? It was a favor that your boss asked of you."

Gennady nodded.

In a way that was comforting. The whole KGB wasn't gunning to blackmail Daniel, after all, just one venal intelligence officer who wanted to snag his own private turncoat.

And yet Daniel was disappointed, too, in a strange stupid way. "So you've never been interested in men at all."

Gennady sighed. "So, so, so. I've fooled around sometimes when I'm drunk."

Time stopped. Daniel remembered, could almost taste, Gennady's lips under his, Gennady's hands on his chest, the little noise that he made as Daniel kissed him.

"But, after all, everyone does that," Gennady added.

"I don't think that's true," Daniel said.

"And how would you know?" Gennady was scornful. "You barely drink."

"Yeah, but my frat brothers drank like gangbusters. Don't you think I would've gotten in on the action if they were all fooling around? Kinsey says that thirty-seven percent – "

"Who is Kinsey?"

"A sexologist. He wrote a book, *Sexual Behavior in the Human Male*..."

"A *sexologist*," Gennady scoffed. "What does this Kinsey know, anyway? How does he study this?"

"Interviews..."

"With Americans? How can he say that this is the way that all people are if it's only Americans he has spoken to? Do you believe your country represents the whole human race? Things are different everywhere. We drink so much more in Russia, of course things are different."

Daniel wanted to argue. Kinsey's samples might not be totally representative of the whole entire human race, but it wasn't like there was any kind of scientific evidence behind Gennady's belief at all.

Kinsey said that thirty-seven percent of men had some homosexual experience. The number had seemed shockingly high to Daniel when he read it: he would have guessed one in a thousand, one in ten thousand even.

But thirty-seven percent was still a hell of a lot less than *everybody*.

Daniel bit his lip. What was the point? He wanted Gennady to admit that he was part of that thirty-seven percent, that he was attracted to men, that he was attracted to *Daniel* – and why?

To assuage his own vanity? That was a damn selfish reason to browbeat Gennady toward a realization that would only make his life more difficult.

Gennady's mind seemed to be moving on an eerily parallel path. "Life is so hard," he said, "there is no reason to make it even harder. Wouldn't you be happier if you still thought you were normal?"

It was as if a whisper in Daniel's subconscious had raised its head and spoken. He stood up and walked to the window, peering through the broken blinds. Neon lights blinked above the Laundromat across the street. "I'd be lying," Daniel said, "if I said I haven't asked myself that question. If I wouldn't have been better off if I married Helen right out of high school and settled down, instead of going to college and falling for one of my frat brothers and getting my face beaten in."

Gennady made a small sound. Daniel turned around, glaring preemptively. But Gennady's eyes were wide with compassion, and Daniel had to look away.

"It was the last day before Christmas break," Daniel told him. His face was hot. "John and I – that was his name, John. We were the only ones left in the frat house, and we were drinking schnapps in John's room. Peppermint schnapps. Festive, you know. Just passing the bottle back and forth and shooting the shit, and then he kissed me, and…"

Daniel laughed and gave the Venetian blinds a push that sent them clacking against the window. "I kissed him back. And he rammed my head sideways against the bed frame."

Daniel turned away from the window and smiled and shrugged, to show it was a long time ago and it didn't matter anymore. His heart was roaring in his ears. He had never told anyone this story.

"But why?" Gennady asked. "If he kissed you first…"

"Maybe he wanted to make sure I really was a faggot." Daniel turned away sharply as he said the word, and drew in a shaky breath, and shrugged and laughed again. "Never would have happened if I'd stuck with making out with girls," he said, and added, acid rising in his throat, "I never told anyone. He was so popular – not just in the frat. A big man on campus. No one would have believed me. Or if they had, they would have figured I deserved it."

"Daniel…"

The sympathy in Gennady's voice was unbearable. "I didn't go back to college after Christmas break. I signed up to go fight in Korea instead, just so I wouldn't have to go back. Everyone thought it was so brave and patriotic and really I was just running away."

"It's good to run away when you can." The vehemence in Gennady's voice startled Daniel. "When you are faced with a force so powerful that you can't fight it, of course you should run. What else could you do? Sit and endure? Save that for when you have no other choice."

"Do you really think so?" Daniel asked.

"Yes, of course. The only people who don't think that are the ones who want you to stay so they can keep hurting you."

This was so wildly divergent from everything Daniel had ever been taught – *a real man should stand and fight!* – that he didn't know what to do with it. He tried to speak, and choked on it. At last he said, "I'm taking a shower," and beat a retreat to the bathroom.

He spent a long time in the shower, although the water never got hotter than lukewarm. By the time he came back in the motel room, Gennady had fallen asleep on the carpet, and Daniel had a hell of a time waking him up enough to get him onto a bed.

CHAPTER 22

Gennady woke just before dawn, stiff and dry-mouthed and sticky, still fully dressed in yesterday's clothes.

He slipped out of the room and went behind the motel. There, hidden behind the dumpster, Gennady smoked a cigarette and gave himself a few minutes to collapse.

The alcohol had done its work. It had opened a gap in time, so that everything with Arkady seemed ages ago, a week at least, instead of a few hours. But it had left him with a throbbing head and an aching throat and burning eyes, even aside from the pains of his bruised face and wounded side, and he felt he had disgraced himself, crawling onto Daniel's lap and clinging to him like a baby monkey.

And Gennady remembered, only it wasn't so much a memory as a tactile sensation, Daniel's arms around him, holding Gennady tight against his chest, warm and strong.

Daniel must think less of him now. Americans were so judgmental. It was too bad their partnership could not have ended with the case. Then Gennady could have gotten drunk with Sergeyich, who knew everything, and would have fought in the bar brawl with him instead of cutting it short. And then there would have been no tears and no clinging, none of this, and no conversations about whether normal men fooled around with other men when they were drunk, as if Daniel who barely drank knew a damn thing about it.

The pink light of dawn stretched across the empty lot behind the motel. Gennady's cigarette burned down. He dropped it in a puddle on the asphalt, and ground it out with his heel, and went back to face the day.

***

Gennady felt terrible all day, all along the long road to Boston. The hangover and the pain from his various injuries made it impossible to overcome his poor spirits, and by the time they checked into a cheap hotel in Boston, he felt at odds with the whole world.

He sat down at the end of Daniel's bed, as he used to. He wanted Daniel to pay attention to him, to fuss over him, but Daniel ignored him and went right on reading *A Separate Peace*. Gennady felt, quite unfairly, and he knew it was unfair and nonetheless felt it, that Daniel hadn't cared a twig for him since he learned about the honeytrap. That had changed everything and they weren't even friends anymore. "Did you only ever like me because you thought we were going to fuck?"

"Gennady!" Daniel set down his book. He looked so aghast that it was a little funny. "Do you really think that?"

"No." Gennady thought about it. "Just because I feel bad."

"You drank a hell of a lot last night."

Gennady found the disapproving note in Daniel's voice unsympathetic. "I got stabbed," he reminded Daniel.

"You poor kid." Now Daniel was teasing him, but affectionately, which was better than disapproval. "You'd better lie down."

Gennady suspected that Daniel meant for him to go to his own bed, but he scooted up to lie next to Daniel instead. It hurt to lie on his stomach, so he rolled over to his back, which still hurt, but slightly less.

The spectacle of Gennady's awkward floundering awakened Daniel's sympathy after all. "I'll get you the amenities of the house," he offered. "Which aren't much, I'm afraid. I can get you an extra pillow..." He leaned over to the other bed to snag one, and fluffed the pillows so Gennady could prop himself up against them. "And a glass of water. And maybe some ice for that eye."

Propped against the pillows, a cup of water in his hand, a washcloth full of ice on his eye, Gennady did feel a little better. He would have liked Daniel to sit down again, and perhaps let Gennady lean his head against his shoulder, but Daniel moved restlessly around the room, finally kneeling to unpack his suitcase into the cheap chest of drawers. This would be a far less peripatetic investigation than their first: they would be at this motel a while.

Gennady's spirits flagged again. "It's just that you seem different now," he said.

"Of course I'm different. I'm not flirting with you anymore."

"Were you before? I thought you were just being friendly…"

"Well, I don't know. Of course some of it was just friendliness." Daniel levered himself to his feet. "I guess maybe I've gone too far in the other direction. I just didn't want to make you uncomfortable…"

"I'm not uncomfortable," Gennady objected.

"No, you're certainly not," Daniel said, so ruefully that Gennady knew that he was referring to Gennady crawling into his lap the night before.

Gennady shifted the ice to shield his furious flush, and insisted, "You're the one who's uncomfortable."

"Yes." Daniel admitted it with a sigh. "I'm just not used to… well, to anyone *knowing*."

"Paul must have known."

"Paul!" Daniel sounded startled, as if he had forgotten that he told Gennady about Paul.

But of course he had forgotten, he had been very drunk that night, and had not recognized Arkady's name when Gennady said it again.

Then Daniel blushed, as if realizing when he must have told Gennady about Paul. He said stiffly, "But that was different, Paul knowing. We were… well, he was in love with me."

Gennady mulled this over in silence. Of course men had sex with each other sometimes, but that was quite different than love; drunken and impulsive, not a matter of kisses and flowers…

And then it struck him that Daniel might really be in love with him. The idea took him aback. He felt like a cad, who had led Daniel on and then dropped him flat, and he wanted to apologize.

But it seemed presumptuous to say, *Sorry for making you fall in love with me* – when probably Daniel was not in love with him at all. Instead Gennady asked, awkwardly, "Did you love Paul?"

Daniel's mouth twisted. "I thought so. For a while, at least. But maybe I never did. 'Love is not love which alters if it alteration finds…'"

"Oh, how silly," Gennady said impatiently. "Everything in this world alters. If love is not love if it changes, then love can't exist."

"You can take that one up with Shakespeare, Gennady."

Gennady turned the cup of water around in his hands. "Was he good to you? Paul?"

"Yes," Daniel said, so definitely as to quash any other questions.

Gennady finished the water. He handed the glass to Daniel, who put it on the side table, and finally sat down beside Gennady, after all. Gennady leaned the unbruised side of his face against Daniel's shoulder.

"Do you feel better?" Daniel asked.

"I feel terrible."

"But do you feel less terrible than you did before?"

"Yes," Gennady conceded, although he wished Daniel would put an arm around him instead of sitting there with his hands clasped primly in his lap. "A little bit."

"Maybe we ought to take tomorrow off," Daniel said. "Let you rest."

"It's better to keep going. That's what they found in Leningrad, when the people were starving during the war, the ones who kept going lived longer…"

"I don't think that's exactly a parallel situation."

"Still." Gennady yawned. It was nice, it was warm and peaceful, leaning against Daniel. He would have liked to fall asleep like this. "It's better to keep going."

"Fine." Daniel pushed Gennady off his shoulder, very gently, and Gennady rolled on his side and curled up like a gray flannel pill bug. "If we're starting the investigation tomorrow, then I'm going to get a shower."

***

That conversation knocked a few things off their shelves in Gennady's head, and for the next few weeks he was picking them up and turning them over gingerly. The idea that a man could be in love with a man was new to him, but he could see how his own behavior fit this pattern: the giddy playfulness, the desire to pester Daniel and bask in his attention, that snowball fight that almost ended in a kiss. Hadn't he compared it in his own mind to his first kiss with Galya?

It felt like the world had expanded, like this was a new country that he could visit. In his mind he stood at the gates and looked in, and in imagination it was good.

And perhaps, probably, very likely it would have been good in reality, if he could have let Daniel kiss him that night by the roadside. But now, after that last meeting with Arkady, the thought of someone's hands on his skin, of someone looking at him – not just Daniel, anyone, even a pretty girl – it all made Gennady feel uneasy.

So he tried to think about other things. The case didn't strike him as particularly interesting: let the Americans have their Baltic amber if they wanted it, why not? But he began to like Boston, with the Old World tangle of its streets, and sites from American history as thick as plums in a pudding. Daniel got as giddy as a schoolboy when they stood at these historical places, and told Gennady their stories with a patriotic fervor that Gennady found funny and oddly touching.

Here was Boston Harbor where the colonists threw the tea overboard; here the Old North Church, where the patriots hung the lanterns that sent Paul Revere on his ride. Here, the site of the Boston Massacre, marked with a star in the pavement.

Gennady listened solemnly enough as Daniel told him the story, although privately he felt the five deaths wasn't much of a massacre. But he held his peace until a week later, in late April, when they took a Saturday off to walk on the Boston Common and found another memorial of the Massacre: a statue of Lady Liberty with an eagle preparing for flight at her side.

It seemed a pompous memorial for such a little event, and Gennady couldn't help scoffing. "What kind of massacre kills only five people? Thousands died in the massacres under the tsars, thousands."

"Only under the tsars?" Daniel said.

Dammit. Gennady had opened himself up to that one. He shrugged and turned away. "She loves blood, the Russian earth."

"You're going to blame the earth and not Stalin?"

"Well, so. Stalin too then." Gennady shrugged angrily. "I'm a Soviet citizen. What else can I say?"

"Have you ever thought of defecting?" Daniel asked.

Gennady felt like he'd fallen into a bucket of ice water. "No," he said.

"But you said when the tanks rolled into Hungary..."

"I expected things to change too fast. But when does anything ever change overnight? Just look at your newspapers. All these sit-ins, these marches, to fight this racial caste system that persists even though your Civil War ended nearly a hundred years ago."

"And how," Daniel muttered. "All right. All right."

They stood a while looking at the bronze lady trampling a crown beneath her foot. At last Gennady shook his head and walked on. "I wish I could take you to see our statues. There's no variety in yours, they're all Lady Libertys and men on horseback. If we could see the fountains at Petrodvorets..."

"Petrodvorets?"

"Your Polyakovs probably called it Peterhof. It was Peter the Great's show palace, his answer to Versailles."

Daniel's eyes brightened. "Where else would we go? If you were showing me around the Soviet Union?"

"Leningrad: our Boston, the place where our Revolution began. We would see the Finland Station, and the Smolny Institute, and Kronstadt..." Were Americans allowed to visit Kronstadt? Probably not, but then none of this could ever happen anyway, they would never let an FBI agent into the USSR. "And we would go to Moscow," Gennady continued, "to the Red Square and the Kremlin, and Lenin's Mausoleum and the Bolshoi..."

"St. Basil's Cathedral?"

Gennady had noticed this American obsession with St. Basil's cathedral before. Perhaps it was the onion domes. "Yes, if you wanted. I would take you all over Russia if I could, the way you have shown me America."

"And the Crimea?" Daniel said. "The Polyakovs always said

that the Black Sea was so beautiful."

"Yes, of course. It's wonderful there, a paradise. And we would ride the Transiberian Railway to see the beauty of Siberia – our great steppe, like your Great Plains – and get off in Vladivostok, and dip our hands in the Pacific Ocean. And when we returned to Moscow, I would take you to our dacha," Gennady added, carried away by his imaginings, "and teach you how to find good mushrooms. Can it be true that Americans never go mushroom hunting?"

Daniel confirmed this sad fact with a nod.

"We will sit in the garden under the sun and eat the tomatoes still warm from the vine, just sprinkled with salt, and make strong black tea in the old charcoal samovar. And in the night we will drink vodka and sing all the old songs around a fire."

"I wouldn't know any of your songs."

"Well, so, I'd teach you. Everyone has to learn sometime. Grandfather will play for us on the ukulele."

"The ukulele!"

"Yes! Did you think only Americans had ukuleles? They were very popular with us too, in the twenties. He stopped playing when my mother died, she was his oldest daughter, but, after all, perhaps after more time has passed…"

They walked on for a while. Small early leaves dotted the trees like a green mist.

"I didn't know your mother was dead," Daniel said.

"It wasn't in my dossier?" Gennady asked dryly.

"Well, no." Daniel glanced over at him. "I'm sorry."

Gennady shrugged. "It was two years ago."

They had reached a lake now. On the water floated a ferryboat with two sculptural swans at its stern. Gennady shoved his hands in his pockets. "She would have been interested in all of this," he said. "This trip. America. She kept all the old copies of *Ogonek* with Ilf and Petrov's photographs."

"*Ogonek*?"

"A magazine. It runs, how do you say, articles with many photographs."

"Photo essays. Like *Life*."

"Yes. She was always interested in that sort of thing, in faraway places." His throat hurt. He shrugged and moved on, and Daniel kept pace with him, mercifully silent.

The path was busy but not crowded: not so full that it was difficult to find a place to walk. A few cherry trees grew near the shore, their blossoms like pink clouds.

"I thought," Gennady said, "that it was Washington DC that had the cherry blossoms."

"Oh, there are cherry trees there too. They were a gift from Japan to celebrate friendship between nations."

"Was this after you dropped an atomic bomb on them?"

"Two atomic bombs," Daniel corrected, with a wince. "No. They gave us the cherry trees long before the war. And we only dropped the bombs after we had been at war with them for years," he added. "It wasn't a sneak-attack, like when they bombed Pearl Harbor."

"Behold friendship between nations."

"You're a cynic, you know that?" Daniel said. "You're probably right. But damn, you're depressing."

"Yes, perhaps."

They were walking more slowly now. A swirl of petals fluttered off the cherry tree, landing on the path and the water and their shoulders.

"Do you think that could ever really happen?" Daniel asked. "That I could visit you in the Soviet Union?"

Gennady burst into laughter. "Of course not," he said, and laughed some more. The idea was so ludicrous he just couldn't stop. "No, they would never let you in: a real American agent. Don't try to visit." He grew serious suddenly. "I suppose we'll never see each other again after I leave."

A stronger breeze blew a shower of petals from the trees. They landed like pink polka dots on Daniel's suit and his dark hair, and it struck Gennady as almost unbearably beautiful. He wanted to brush the petals off Daniel's shoulders and his hair, to kiss him perhaps, as if that would make this moment last forever, a reverse of *Sleeping Beauty*, a kiss that would freeze them both in time.

Only real life was not a fairy tale, and a kiss would not freeze time, and it would be inviting arrest to kiss Daniel out in public where anyone could see.

Gennady walked out of the shadow of the cherry tree into the warm sun.

Daniel fell in alongside him. "Well, that won't happen for a while," Daniel said, his voice light and false. "You'll be stuck in the US till we solve this case."

"Maybe." If relations between their countries remained good. *Behold friendship between nations*, Gennady thought, and felt cold despite the sunlight. "What else should I see in Boston?"

"Bunker Hill," Daniel said promptly. "And we ought to drive out to Lexington and Concord, too. And if you'd like to see Emily Dickinson's house…"

"Yes!" Gennady was delighted. "Her poems – I have been reading them in the book you gave me. *Because I could not stop for Death, he kindly stopped for me…* She is a little morbid, but it is a pleasant change from ordinary American optimism. Only sometimes I do not understand what her poems are about."

"Sometimes," Daniel said, "I'm not sure Emily herself knew what she was getting at. But the poems are beautiful anyway, aren't they? She lived in western Massachusetts. We could drive over some weekend."

"Yes," said Gennady. "Let's do that."

CHAPTER 23

RUSSIA REPORTS DOWNED U.S. PLANE. PILOT REMAINS ALIVE, TO BE TRIED AS SPY

That headline smacked Gennady in the face on Saturday, May 7th. They had driven out to Amherst and spent the day at Emily Dickinson's house, so he didn't see the papers until he stepped out to buy cigarettes in the evening.

He allowed himself three minutes to pretend that nothing had changed. He could buy his cigarettes and eat his dinner with Daniel and their partnership would go on forever.

Then he bought the newspaper, and chain-smoked as he read the article.

An American U-2 spy plane had been shot down over the Soviet Union. The Americans, thinking that the pilot had died, pretended it was just a weather research plane – but then Khrushchev gave a long speech in which he revealed that the pilot was still alive, then railed against American duplicity and spy craft.

Even the American newspaper cringed over being caught in such a lie. Gennady could well imagine how it was playing in *Pravda*.

He stopped at a pay phone and put through a call to Stepan Pavlovich's office.

***

Daniel was still sipping his coffee when Gennady slid into the booth. "Where've you been?" Daniel asked.

Gennady tossed the newspaper on the table, folded so the headline was prominent. "It's over," he said. "I'll be heading back to Moscow tomorrow."

"What? But – "

Gennady jammed his finger at the newspaper. Daniel picked it up. He winced as he read the article. "Are you sure?" he said. "We're so close to cracking the case! This could all blow over…"

Gennady shook his head. "I've already called in," he said. "They wanted me to take the train back tonight. I only put them off because there is nothing leaving until the morning."

"I could drive you back to DC," Daniel offered.

"No, no. Your boss wouldn't want you to abandon your case. And, anyway, they want me to take the train. My people never liked this partnership. It only happened at all because Chairman Khrushchev supported the idea."

"And what Khrushchev giveth, Khrushchev can taketh away. Damn it," Daniel said, and slapped the newspaper down. Then he looked embarrassed, and glanced over the back of the booth to see if any ladies had overheard his language. "I'll drive you to the train station tomorrow morning, at least. What time does the train leave?"

"At 6:15."

Daniel grimaced. "Well, that can't be helped. I'll drop you off and then head over to the Boston field office. They'll want me to call in too."

They lingered over their coffee, barely speaking. Gennady lit a cigarette, then tossed it half-smoked into the dregs of his coffee. "Let's go back to the motel."

"We could hit the town," Daniel offered. "I noticed a bar a couple blocks over."

"No, no. We will need to be up very early," Gennady said.

When they got to the motel, Daniel took over the bathroom to shave while Gennady collapsed in the armchair. It seemed a sad waste to spend his last evening in America staring at the paisley drapes. (Of course he would probably still be on American soil for a few days, but once he left Daniel behind it wouldn't count.) There was still so much he wanted to see, to do, to experience — all of it now out of his reach.

The Rocky Mountains. The California redwoods. New York City. The deserts of the southwest, which Ilf and Petrov said were so beautiful.

Really it was a miracle that Gennady and Daniel had been on the road so long. Ilf and Petrov only got ten weeks. It was silly to think, *oh, if only I had two more months, I could have seen the Fourth of July…*

He would have liked to watch the fireworks with Daniel, and tell him that Soviet May Day parades were better. And visit a county fair. And go to a drive-in movie theater…

Daniel came out of the bathroom, clean-shaven and tired-eyed. "It's all yours," he said, and flashed a smile.

He would have liked to kiss Daniel again.

Gennady fled into the bathroom to splash his burning cheeks. Of course he had thought about this before, but there had always been something theoretical about the idea: it was easy to put it off for later.

But now there was no later.

Do everything; try everything. Grab happiness when you find it. And he would never get another such good chance to try this. Daniel would almost certainly say yes, and he was good-looking and kind, and with him it wouldn't hurt any more than was unavoidable. If it went well, it would be a happy memory to take back.

And if it turned out not to be pleasant, after all, it wouldn't matter. He would never see Daniel again after tomorrow.

This thought hurt, and Gennady shook his head to rid himself of it. Then he smacked his cheeks lightly, trying to draw some color in them. Maybe this was why Arkady was always patting his cheeks. He bit his lips to redden them, and attempted a smile at the mirror. Daniel liked it when he smiled.

Gennady propelled himself back into the motel room. Daniel was reading in the armchair by the window, and Gennady walked over and drew the curtain and leaned against the wingback. His heartbeat pounded in his ears.

Daniel looked up at him over his reading glasses.

"Gennady?"

"I thought," Gennady started, and then stopped, and then started again. "Since this is the last night…"

"Is there some American experience you've managed to miss out on all these months?" Daniel asked amiably. "Baseball? Monopoly? Hula hooping? I draw the line at Monopoly, but I bet we could pick up hula hoops somewhere around here."

Gennady shook his head. He couldn't catch his breath. "I wondered," he said, and drew in his breath, and for a moment thought he would not be able to finish the sentence. "Do you still want to kiss me?"

Daniel stared at him. He set his book aside. "Have you decided that you've got to work the honeytrap, after all?"

CHAPTER 24

Gennady jerked backwards, eyes wide and mouth open with the kind of genuine surprise that was almost impossible to fake, and instantly Daniel was sorry he had said it. He had probably ruined their last evening together – perhaps cast a shadow over the memory of their whole partnership, just by bringing it up.

"I'm sorry," Daniel said. "I just – I had to ask, you know?"

"No, of course," Gennady said. The first flush had faded from his face, leaving his cheeks a dull mortified red. "I should not have brought it up. I thought – " He lifted his hands, as if to signify the uselessness of further words, and took a step back. "Perhaps I should go."

"No!"

The word exploded out of Daniel. Gennady stopped.

"I mean," Daniel said. He flushed too, and he wasn't sure if it was nerves or arousal singing in his blood. "You've already got more than enough material to blackmail me with, anyway."

Gennady's brow smoothed. He leaned against Daniel's chair again, and said, "I'm not going to blackmail you."

"No. Of course not," Daniel said, and hesitated, uncertain. "I just… I'm not sure why you asked if I wanted to kiss you."

He thought maybe he knew, actually. But he had thought Gennady wanted to kiss him before, at the roadside, and he did not want to be wrong again.

Gennady sighed. "How can I answer this? Why does anyone want to kiss anyone, Daniel?"

Daniel's heart beat so hard he felt light-headed. "Do you want to kiss me? Is that why you asked?"

Gennady hesitated. His tongue flickered over his lips, thoughtful rather than seductive. "I think so," Gennady said, and oddly Daniel found that more reassuring than an easy yes. "It was nice when you kissed me that night…"

So Gennady had responded to that kiss. Daniel hadn't been imagining things.

"But I've never kissed a man before – not sober." Gennady scuffed his foot. "I want to try it."

Daniel cracked a grin. "I'm a perfection salad?" he said.

Gennady's face was serious. "I hope perhaps better than perfection salad."

"One more American experience to try before you fly back to Moscow," Daniel said, still smiling, although the words hit him like a punch. Gennady was leaving. They wouldn't even be able to keep in touch.

He found himself studying Gennady's round face: high cheekbones, gray eyes under straight thoughtful brows. Gennady met Daniel's gaze, a faint flush rising in his cheeks under Daniel's scrutiny, till at last Gennady averted his eyes and bit his lip. "Go on," Gennady said.

Daniel stood up and cupped Gennady's face in both hands and kissed him.

It was not a long kiss; just long enough to ascertain that Gennady was not going to pull away. Then Daniel broke the kiss himself, and Gennady drew in a slow shaky breath and put a hand to his mouth.

"How was that?" Daniel asked.

Gennady's eyes brightened with mischief. He looked up at Daniel, his mouth half-obscured by his hand. "I don't know. Try it again."

Daniel took a step forward, then paused. "Maybe I ought to check you for hidden cameras."

It was mostly a joke, and Gennady kept smiling. But his voice was serious when he said, "Yes, do."

"Well, sit down," said Daniel. He pushed Gennady lightly to sit on the foot of the bed, and went down on one knee beside him. He cupped Gennady's left foot in both hands, and slid one hand up under his trousers to the inside of his knee. He kept his eyes on Gennady's lower leg, as if he really were looking for cameras, but mostly to give Gennady time to adjust to being touched.

He squeezed Gennady's calf just below the knee. Gennady drew in his breath, and Daniel still didn't let himself look up, but hooked his fingers over the top of Gennady's sock. He slipped the sock off and set it aside, and squeezed the ball of Gennady's foot.

"Are you going to take all my clothes off?" Gennady's voice was unsteady.

"No," Daniel said. He kissed the inside of Gennady's knee through his pants, and Gennady's leg gave a little kick. "Just the ones that are a pain to get off later. Your socks..." Daniel drew off the second sock. Then he put his hands on Gennady's knees, over his pants, and ran them right up his thighs. "And your belt," he said, suiting actions to words.

As he tossed the belt aside, he looked up at Gennady. He found Gennady wide-eyed, his shoulders tense, his fingers clenched on the bedspread, and Daniel was mortified. "Christ! All you said was *kiss*. And here I am ripping your clothes off..."

Gennady laughed. His fingers relaxed on the bedspread. "No, no, nothing is ripped. It's okay."

"Well, at least I'd better kiss you before we go any further. All right?"

"Yes, okay."

Daniel rose high on his knees to kiss him. First a small peck, almost to give Gennady a last chance to back out; and then, when Gennady did not pull away, a more lingering kiss, very gentle.

Daniel expected hesitancy. He had been very hesitant himself the first time Paul kissed him properly; had panicked and run out of the room halfway through.

But Gennady's hesitation lasted only a breath, and then Gennady was kissing him back, soft and questioning, perhaps a little shy. One hand brushed Daniel's cheek, moved away, then moved in again to cup Daniel's face. Gennady laughed just a little.

His mouth opened as he laughed, and Daniel touched Gennady's parted lips with his tongue. Gennady gasped, very softly, and he did draw back, but an inch or two, still so close that Daniel could feel Gennady's breath on his face.

"All right?" Daniel asked.

"Yes, okay," Gennady said. His lips and cheeks were flushed, and his eyes were bright. He leaned in to kiss Daniel again.

This time, it was Gennady who touched his tongue to Daniel's lips. Daniel let Gennady kiss him, gentle, tentative, and then growing bolder, more demanding, a little frustrated noise in his throat, and only then did Daniel open his mouth and kiss him back.

Gennady's hands were in Daniel's hair now, kneading the back of Daniel's neck. Daniel cupped Gennady's hips, and when he drew back to catch his breath, he found that he had pulled Gennady to the very edge of the bed. He tugged on Gennady, an invitation, and Gennady slid obligingly off the bed, so he was straddling Daniel's lap; and quite suddenly Daniel could feel just how hard Gennady was, and knew that Gennady could feel the same for him.

Gennady's cheeks flushed. He pushed himself off Daniel's lap, and drew his legs to his chest, and hid his reddened mouth against his knee. Then he began to laugh, and Daniel laughed too, giddy with delight, and wrapped a hand around Gennady's calf.

"All right?" Daniel asked, rubbing his hand up and down Gennady's leg.

"Yes, yes! It was just so sudden," Gennady said. His gaze flickered toward Daniel's groin, and then he hid his face behind his hands, although Daniel had already drawn up his legs to hide that telltale bulge. Gennady looked at Daniel through his splayed fingers, and Daniel laughed and kissed the back of Gennady's hand.

"If we had more time..." Daniel began.

"But we don't," interrupted Gennady. He lowered his hands. "We have only tonight. And I want to do everything."

"God, I love you," Daniel said, because it was just such a characteristic thing for him to say, so *Gennady* – and he kissed Gennady again, and although he had meant to say some other things, for a while he forgot it all entirely in the pleasure of Gennady's lips, and his tongue, and his hands on Daniel's face and neck, and the way that he shivered when Daniel kissed the place where his jaw met his ear.

"Is it all right if I take off my shirt?" Daniel asked.

"Yes, okay." Gennady was breathing hard. "Do you always ask so many times?"

Daniel fumbled a button. "I don't know." Did he? It was hard to remember now. "I just want to make sure you're comfortable."

"Yes, well, so," Gennady said. "I'll tell you if I'm not." His forehead furrowed. "Will it hurt?"

The matter-of-factness of the question gave Daniel a strange pain. "No, we won't do anything that would hurt," he said. "If..." *we had more time*, he almost said again.

But they didn't, and he didn't want to spoil their one and only night together by attempting something he didn't really know how to do: Paul had never let him top. ("The older partner tops," Paul had said. Those ancient Greeks again.) And there were plenty of things they could do that had no chance of hurting at all.

Daniel slipped his shirt off his shoulders and then stripped off his undershirt, slow, hollowing out his stomach as he pulled it over his head. Putting on a show.

All for nothing, it turned out. Gennady had politely averted his eyes, as if they were in a locker room. Daniel poked Gennady's stomach. "You can look, you know."

Gennady gave him a quick shy glance, and then a longer look; and then, third time's the charm, he looked Daniel over, starting at Daniel's waist and raking slowly up his chest, so that Daniel was blushing by the time Gennady met his eyes.

There was a tenderness in Gennady's eyes that startled Daniel, and Daniel kissed him again without thinking. Gennady kissed back, his mouth open and eager, his palms pressed firmly against the flat hard carpet. Daniel drew back, laughing a little, and told him, "You can touch me if you want."

He expected the same process as with the gaze: the quick light touch, then longer, more lingering. But Gennady launched himself forward, knocking Daniel flat on his back, and Daniel's legs curled around Gennady's waist as Gennady pressed against Daniel's chest, palms on his shoulders, kissing Daniel again.

Even with the layer of Gennady's clothes between them, it was burning hot. Daniel wanted more, skin on skin, he wanted

Gennady inside him, fuck the ancient Greeks anyway. Or maybe not, Gennady had probably never done it before and it was hard to get right, Paul had taken a few tries to master it, it was just – Christ, Daniel wanted *more*.

Daniel tugged Gennady's shirt out of his waistband, *Christ* he had such a little waist, those blocky Soviet suits hid it. The shirt came free, Daniel's hand grazed bare skin on Gennady's back, and Gennady hissed and bit him – "You don't like that?"

"Idiot! I do!"

Daniel pressed his hand against the small of Gennady's back, and Gennady gasped and bucked against him. "You like that?" Daniel teased, and pressed his hand against the same spot, rubbing, loving the way that it made Gennady wriggle against him, the way Gennady's mouth fell open, his lips wet against Daniel's neck.

"Yes, yes." The words came out as a gasp.

Daniel rolled them over, so now Gennady was lying on his back. He paused afterward, just in case Gennady didn't like that, but Gennady just looked up at him, so trusting, his chest rising and falling as he panted, a quarter inch of pale skin showing at his stomach where his shirt had been pushed up. His parted lips curved upward in a smile as Daniel stroked a knuckle along his cheek.

"Yes, yes, okay," Gennady prompted, and darted a kiss on Daniel's finger. Daniel laughed and kissed him again.

He wanted to take off all Gennady's clothes and kiss him all over, kiss right down Gennady's chest and take his cock in his mouth and suck it till Gennady came; or to hook Gennady's legs over his shoulders and push into him, feel Gennady all tight and hot around him, his heels digging into Daniel's back, toes curling, his mouth gaping open with pleasure.

But he had said they wouldn't do anything that might hurt. So Daniel put that second thought aside, and pushed Gennady's shirt up another couple of inches, and kissed the soft vulnerable skin of his stomach.

Gennady's hands tangled in Daniel's hair. This position put Daniel close enough to feel the little tremors under his skin, to smell his arousal. He breathed it in, and popped the button on Gennady's fly, and worked his pants down (thank God he'd dealt with the belt earlier) just enough to expose his navel. Daniel sank his teeth in very gently there, and Gennady's hands tightened on Daniel's hair. "Not so hard!" Daniel gasped, and Gennady let go, and Daniel sat up and ran a hand over his smarting scalp.

But he was glad that Gennady had yanked, because drawing back gave Daniel a good look at him, and God was it spectacular. Stomach hollowing, lips flushed and parted, a sweet little line between his eyes, *so* close. He'd come in a minute if Daniel let him.

Daniel rested a hand on Gennady's exposed stomach, hooking his thumb in his navel, and Gennady twisted his head and made the most wonderful wretched tiny noise. Daniel kissed the inside of his knee. "I want to suck you off," Daniel said, and Gennady blinked up at him, those big gray eyes, God.

"Okay, okay," Gennady said, and then: "What does that mean?"

Daniel blushed so hard that he couldn't speak. He lifted Gennady's hand and slid two fingers into his mouth, and sucked so hard that his cheeks hollowed.

This Gennady understood. His hips bucked; he blurted something in Russian, certainly not a word Daniel had learned from the Polyakovs. "Are you sure?" Gennady gasped. "Will it hurt you?"

"No," said Daniel, with a robust confidence borne mostly of desire. He'd never actually done this before. And, well, he figured Gennady wouldn't last thirty seconds once Daniel got his mouth on him, even though Daniel had no technique to speak of.

Gennady fumbled at his own zipper. He undid it on the second try, and pulled his pants down just far enough to expose his cock, and Daniel's mouth went dry. From this angle, so close up, Gennady's cock looked far too big to fit in Daniel's mouth, and briefly Daniel quailed.

But he rallied, and kissed him right at the tip, and then licked him all along his length. The line was back between Gennady's eyes, his stomach hollowing again, and Daniel put his hand around Gennady's cock and took just the head in his mouth, and he had only just begun to suck when Gennady came.

That left Daniel with a mouthful of stuff, and he felt a moment's confusion as to what precisely he ought to do with it. But Gennady was already pulling him back up, and Daniel swallowed almost automatically, and then Gennady was kissing him, his hands on Daniel's cheeks, murmuring, "Thank you, thank you."

Daniel nuzzled into Gennady's neck, and Gennady sighed, and relaxed, and to Daniel's secret vexation tucked his cock back into his pants. At least he did not pull his pants all the way back up: his navel remained exposed, and a sliver of pale stomach.

Once his breathing had softened again, Daniel ran his fingers over that soft exposed skin. Gennady's eyes opened, and then he smiled at Daniel, and rolled on his side, propping himself up on an elbow. "Your turn?" he said, and poked Daniel lightly in the stomach. "What would you like?"

"Well..." Daniel was not quite sure. It had startled him when Gennady came in his mouth. Not that it was bad, exactly, just not quite what he had expected, and some of the urgency had gone out of his arousal.

He slid his hand up under Gennady's shirt, feeling the ribs in his side, the muscles in his back. Gennady giggled when Daniel got high up on his side, near his armpit.

"Are you ticklish?" Daniel teased.

"Are you?" Gennady threatened.

Daniel took evasive action and pushed Gennady onto his back again. He looked gloriously disheveled, his hair kicked up in little devil horns, his shirt crumpled and twisted, his pants just low enough to show a smattering of pubic hair. Daniel kissed him there, and his navel, and his stomach again, and Gennady caught Daniel's face in his hands and lifted it so that Daniel looked up at him.

"But seriously," Gennady said. "Don't you want anything?"

"This is what I want." Daniel slid up along Gennady's body to kiss his mouth again, grinding his hips against Gennady's so Gennady could feel his arousal, and Gennady's cheeks turned pink and he laughed and put his hands lightly on Daniel's sides. "The small of my back," Daniel told him, "like I did for you," and Gennady dug the heel of one hand in just where Daniel said, and Daniel shuddered as pleasure flashed like lightning along his spine, up to his neck, down into his ass.

God. Maybe he *did* want Gennady to fuck him, after all. That'd take some working up to, though, he'd have to get Gennady hard again...

Which probably wouldn't be that difficult.

Gennady ran his hands up Daniel's back, pressing hard, the way Daniel liked it, and then he rolled them both over so he was straddling Daniel's hips. Daniel had to push him off. If Gennady stayed pressed against Daniel like that, Daniel was going to come in his pants.

Gennady let himself be pushed. He sprawled, lying on his side like a Roman senator at a banquet. His shirt had fallen back into place, covering his stomach, and Daniel looked at that and groaned and said, "Let's get your shirt off."

"What?" Gennady's eyes widened. Then he darted in to kiss Daniel again, and said, "Yes, okay…"

Daniel started at the top button. Gennady drew back slightly as Daniel's hands brushed his chin – gosh, he really must be ticklish – then went very still, except for the rise and fall of his chest, rapid enough that Daniel could feel it under his hands. His breath sounded harsh in the quiet room.

Daniel was on the third button when he looked up at Gennady, and found him biting his lip, his face averted and pale. A sense of unease settled on Daniel. "Everything okay?"

"Yes, yes, okay."

Gennady sounded flustered. Daniel let go of the button and lifted his hands to touch Gennady's cheeks lightly, and Gennady flinched so hard he slammed against the foot of the bed. "*Prostitye*," Gennady blurted. A tidal wave of scarlet flushed his face. He pushed Daniel's hands away and began to fumble at his own buttons. "I'm sorry, I'm sorry, I'll do it myself."

His fingers were shaking. Daniel stared. Gennady's fingers slipped off the button, and he gasped, a weird frightened sound.

"Stop!" Daniel said.

For a moment they stared at each other. Then Gennady leapt to his feet. Daniel snatched up his own discarded shirt and put it back on, although even after he'd done up all the buttons he felt as exposed as a worm under an upturned rock.

He expected to hear the door slam. But he didn't, and when he dared to look up, Daniel found Gennady sitting at the foot of the bed. He had taken off his shirt after all, although not his undershirt, which was worn so soft that it seemed molded directly to his body.

Daniel was too upset to find the sight arousing. "Gennady," he said.

Gennady's shoulders jerked. "I'm sorry."

Daniel wanted to go to him, but he thought Gennady might flee, so he stayed on the floor. "It's all right."

"I'm sorry," Gennady repeated. He raked one hand through his hair. "You must be thinking, what an asshole, he gets off and then he won't even take off his shirt for me. What is it that you Americans call it? Second base? It's nothing, not even enough to score a point."

"I'm not thinking that at all."

"American puff," Gennady snapped. "You say, 'It's all right, it's all right,' smiling all the time, when really you must want to punch me – "

"No!" Daniel said, forcefully enough that Gennady at least stopped talking. He glanced over at Daniel, quick and half-frightened, and Daniel softened his voice when he spoke again. "Listen, Gennady, I never thought I'd have the chance to kiss you at all. I'd be an idiot to be mad when I got to do so much more than that. And it's my fault, anyway, I pushed you too hard. I never thought we'd make it this far in the first place, so I got greedy. I mean, you've been told this is a perversion all your life, right? It's hard to set all that aside. All that ingrained shame can hit you unexpectedly…"

And so forth and so on, rattling on to give Gennady time to compose himself, repeating things that Paul had said to Daniel when Daniel panicked and fled after Paul kissed him. Guilt, shame, societal condemnation of homosexual love affairs, it could all crash down on you unexpectedly and send you heading for the hills. Paul had talked on and on as Daniel nodded like a bobble head doll, petrified that Paul might guess why Daniel had really run.

It occurred to him for the first time that probably Paul had known very well that it was a bad experience in his past that sent Daniel flying. In giving his long soothing talk about crushing religious guilt, he had done Daniel the very great kindness of allowing him to think he'd kept his secret.

Certainly that was why Daniel kept talking. He figured that someone had gotten rough with Gennady sometime, likely one of those drunk guys Gennady had fooled around with, and probably Gennady didn't want to talk about it any more than Daniel had wanted to tell Paul about John.

Some color had come back into Gennady's face. He drew his legs up onto the bed and sat cross-legged, and when Daniel finally stopped talking, Gennady said again, "I'm sorry."

Daniel rose to sit gingerly on the edge of the bed. "It really is all right," he said. "You don't have to apologize."

Gennady sighed. "What else can I say? I feel bad. You were so good to me, and I did nothing for you, and now you are so nice about it, pretending it's your fault, you pushed too hard, blah blah blah, when we both know it's my fault, you asked if it was okay and I lied."

Daniel thought about that. He drew his legs on the bed to sit cross-legged, too, mirroring Gennady's position. "Why did you do that?" he asked, trying through his tone to convey that it was a genuine question, not an accusation.

"I don't know." Gennady drew his knees up to his chin. "I asked what you wanted, and it was that, and I didn't want to say, no, this one thing you've asked for – I won't do that..."

His jaw clenched. His throat bobbed visibly as he swallowed. "And I thought you wouldn't notice. I wish you hadn't noticed," he added, and pressed his hands to the bed. "I could have finished it," he insisted, glaring at Daniel as if daring him to contradict.

"I'm sure you could have," Daniel began, "but..."

Gennady interrupted him. "Yes, I could have finished it, and then we could be falling asleep right now in each other's arms, together in the darkness like two cats."

The image opened a pit of longing in Daniel's stomach. He fell silent in the struggle not to let the longing show on his face – although Gennady had slid off the bed to turn off the reading lamp, and could not have seen it.

Even after Gennady turned off the lamp, the room was not quite dark: the dying light of the sunset seeped in above the curtain. But when Gennady returned, and sat cross-legged on the bed, the dimness made it easier for Daniel to complete his interrupted sentence. "But I didn't want you to finish it. Not like that. To force yourself through something you didn't want to do."

"It would have been all right," Gennady said carelessly. "After all, I like you."

"Gennady," Daniel said. Gennady smiled, and it struck

Daniel that Gennady was teasing him, and he grabbed a pillow and started thwacking Gennady, until Gennady, laughing, wrested the pillow from Daniel's hands and hugged it to his chest. "I'll never be able to ask you for anything ever again if I think you're going to say yes whether you want to or not," Daniel told him.

"I wouldn't." Gennady shifted the pillow to rest his chin on it. "It wasn't that I didn't want to. Do you understand? I did want to. To be looked at, to be touched by a lover... I wouldn't have tried so hard if I didn't want it. It was just..." He made a slight gesture with his hand, open-palmed. "I was afraid. You understand? Both things at once."

Daniel caught Gennady's hand and kissed it, and he turned Gennady's hand over and kissed his palm, too. "I understand," he said, and he looked up at Gennady, and found Gennady biting his lip, looking at him, gray eyes bright and shy and hopeful.

"Let me try again?" Gennady asked.

Daniel held onto his hand. "Do you want to?"

"Yes. I hate to go back to Moscow knowing that I chickened."

"Chickened out," Daniel corrected, and hesitated, uncertain.

Gennady kissed Daniel's hand. "You're very picky. That's not a good enough reason? To save myself from lifelong regret? You'll only say yes if I say, I want to taste your lips again, I want to lick your sweat from your skin, I want to feel you move against me?"

Arousal flushed through Daniel's body. "Do you want that?"

Gennady tossed the pillow back against the headboard. He scooted forward so they sat knee to knee. "Kiss me again and we'll see," he said; and, when Daniel still hesitated, Gennady leaned forward and kissed him.

Daniel's heart fluttered a little too fast, and not pleasantly. He knew that if they couldn't make this work he would have to be the one to call it, and he didn't particularly want to be responsible for inflicting Gennady with a lifelong regret.

But then Gennady put his hands on Daniel's waist and hitched himself forward, so he was straddling Daniel's lap, and Daniel gave a little gasp and fell back against the pillow, pulling Gennady with him, and relaxed under the warm heavy weight of his body.

It was different than before, slower, both of them careful with each other. Gennady stretched like a cat as Daniel ran his hands up and down his back, up his neck, touching the hollows behind his ears, messing up his hair.

Gennady drew back eventually, his lips full and red, his hair tousled. "Will you...?" Gennady asked, and touched Daniel's shirt buttons, asking without asking.

Daniel undid his shirt and tossed it aside. Gennady kissed his collarbones, then slid down to kiss his solar plexus, and Daniel wrapped his legs around him and pulled him close, and realized how hard he was only when he felt himself pushing against Gennady's stomach. "Oh," he gasped, aroused, half-apologetic, and Gennady laughed at him and began to grapple with Daniel's belt.

"I must be good at this," Gennady said, teasing, pleased with himself.

"I'm just easy," Daniel told him, and Gennady laughed again, and gave up on the belt, and simply shoved a hand under Daniel's waistband and wrapped it around Daniel's cock. "Jesus Christ!"

Gennady squeezed. "Too much?" he asked.

"No – Christ – " Daniel fumbled at his belt himself. "Let me get my pants off, Jesus," and then Gennady took his hand away and Daniel nearly whimpered, which would have been embarrassing if Gennady hadn't kissed him again. Daniel kissed him repeatedly, needy, breathless. "*This* is why I took your belt off earlier."

"Yes, you're very wise."

He nearly came just from the relief of pressure when the belt finally slid off. Then Gennady's hands were on his fly, unbuttoning, unzipping, and it all would have gone faster if Daniel had stopped moving, but his hips kept bucking at every bit of friction, until finally Gennady just shoved Daniel's clothes down to expose his cock and took him in hand.

"Kiss me?" Daniel said. Gennady's free hand found Daniel's neck, his mouth pressed against Daniel's mouth, his tongue thrust between Daniel's lips, and Daniel thrust against his gripping hand and came.

Afterward, they rested against each other, sweaty and sticky and sated. After a while Gennady took his undershirt off and used it to rub them both clean. Daniel roused himself to mumble, "Do you need...?"

"No, I'm all right." Gennady snuggled in beside him again, his head on Daniel's shoulder, and Daniel looped an arm around his bare back, trailing his fingers slowly over Gennady's skin.

He was almost asleep when his fingertips tripped over the nearly-healed wound on Gennady's side. Gennady shivered, his mouth opening against Daniel's collarbone, and Daniel's breath caught in his throat as Gennady got up. He caught briefly at Gennady's arm, then let go, and maybe Gennady didn't even notice that Daniel had tried to hold him.

The latches on Gennady's suitcase clicked; the bathroom door squeaked. Daniel closed his eyes, and reminded himself that he was, after all, lucky to have had all of this, and it was greedy to want Gennady share his bed all night, in the darkness, how had he put it? Together like two cats...

But then Gennady was back, dressed as he usually dressed for sleep, shorts and a clean undershirt. "Here," he said, and held out a cup of water. Daniel drank half of it in a greedy gulp.

Then Gennady sat on the edge of the bed, and Daniel drank more slowly, because Gennady was sure to get up and leave once the water was gone.

"Put on your pajamas," Gennady said. "Or at least take off your suit pants. They will wrinkle if you sleep in them."

"I'd better get a shower." Daniel drained the water and went.

He took a long shower, mostly because he started to cry. It hit him once again that Gennady was really leaving – that he was going back to Moscow, and this was the end.

But it was fine. It was okay. He was calm again and even managed a smile when he left the bathroom.

The room was almost dark; only a little light from the streetlamps seeped in over the curtains. Daniel found his way to the unused bed mostly by touch, and was pulling back the stiff cold sheets when Gennady said sleepily, "Daniil?"

Daniel looked over at him. Gennady pulled back the covers to welcome Daniel in.

Daniel's heart was in his throat. He slipped in bed with Gennady, and Gennady nestled in against him, tucking his face against Daniel's shoulder, slinging an arm over Daniel's chest. Daniel wrapped an arm tentatively around Gennady's back, and

Gennady gave a sleepy snuffle and snuggled closer.

"I'll miss you," Gennady murmured.

Daniel closed his eyes and kissed Gennady's hair. "Yes," he said. "I'm going to miss you too."

CHAPTER 25

"You don't have to go, you know," Daniel said.

It was the next morning, and Daniel was driving slowly in the pre-dawn dimness. Gennady was smoking a cigarette. He blew a stream of smoke out of the open car window. The sky flushed pink as the sun rose.

"Don't be ridiculous," Gennady said, not unkindly.

"I'm not being ridiculous," Daniel said. "You could stay. You could defect."

Gennady didn't answer. Daniel took his eyes off the road briefly to look at him. Gennady had turned his face toward the open window, so Daniel could only see the curve of his cheek and the tip of his cigarette.

"Keep your eyes on the road," Gennady said, and Daniel faced front again. The roads of New England didn't spool on straight forever like the roads in the Midwest. They wandered through the woods like something out of a fairy tale.

They had driven perhaps two miles before Gennady spoke again. "It wouldn't be the same," he said. "We would no longer be working together. Your FBI is not going to hire me."

Daniel drummed a hand on the wheel. "But at least you'd be here," he said. "You'd be safe."

"I'll be safe enough at home, Daniil." The Russian pronunciation of his name sounded particularly affectionate, but also firm. "Stalin's been dead for years now. They are not throwing people into the gulags for every little thing."

"And how long is that going to last? Who knows what the next guy after Khrushchev might be like?" Daniel argued.

Gennady didn't answer for some time. At last he said, "This is why Mr. Gilman agreed to let you continue to work with me. He hoped you could convince me to defect."

Daniel glanced at him. Gennady's face was unreadable. "He came up with the idea on his own," Daniel said. "I didn't tell him anything that you said about Khrushchev, or anything like that."

Some expression eased back into Gennady's face. "So what did you say to him? Did you tell him you thought I would?"

"I said you might," Daniel said, suddenly worried. "That won't get you into trouble, will it? I thought he might not let us keep working together if I didn't hold out some hope that you might defect. But I can tell him that you rejected the proposal in the strongest possible terms, if that will help. I can tell him you punched me."

Gennady's mouth twitched in a brief smile. "Don't overdo it. Just tell him that I said I love my Motherland, and I could never betray her."

Daniel's throat hurt. "Yes," he said. "I'll let Mr. Gilman know."

"Will it cause you trouble?"

"No," Daniel said. "He knew it was a long shot."

They reached the outskirts of town. Daniel followed a sign for the railroad station. At this early hour, the streets were almost empty.

"I'll be assigned a new partner, I guess," Daniel said, mostly because if he didn't talk he might cry.

"Ah, good. Someone new for you to fall in love with."

"I don't think I will, you know," Daniel said, his voice unsteady.

"No more falling in love with agents," Gennady agreed. "Get married, have children, have a happy life."

"And what about you?"

"I'm Russian, I was never going to have a happy life."

"Gennady," Daniel said, choked and unhappy.

"It's a joke, Daniel. I'll be fine," Gennady said, and smiled at him, and Daniel nearly broke down.

The train station was really nothing more than a platform. Daniel parked the car across the road and sat, clinging to the car wheel as if to a life preserver, while Gennady retrieved his luggage from the trunk.

Then Gennady leaned into the car through the open window. Daniel had gotten some control of himself by now. He managed a smile. "*Proshai*," he said.

"*Proshai*."

The train whistle sounded. Daniel couldn't see the train yet, but he could hear the rattle of its wheels. "You'd better run if you're going to catch it," he said, which was not strictly true, but he wasn't sure how long he could maintain this pose of nonchalance.

"Yes," said Gennady, and stepped back. But then he leaned in through the window again and said rapidly, "Daniel. Is there an address where I could write you? One that will not change for a long time."

"What? My mother's, maybe. I don't..."

Gennady interrupted him. "It will be impossible to write to you from the Soviet Union. And you mustn't try to write to me there. But if I am ever posted abroad again, then I'll write to you, I'll send instructions how you could write back. Would you write back?"

"Yes." Daniel ripped a page from his address book and wrote his mother's address. His fingers brushed Gennady's as he put the paper into his hand. "Gennady..."

The ground trembled as the train pulled into the station. "*Do svidanye*, my friend," Gennady said.

He lunged into the car and kissed Daniel so quickly that Daniel had barely registered the touch of his lips before Gennady was sliding out of the car again, snatching up his luggage from the pavement. "Goodbye!" Daniel shouted after him.

Gennady crossed the street and sprang up the steps to the platform. He paused briefly to speak to the conductor. It took less than a minute, and yet it seemed an agonizing eternity to Daniel: this long last look at Gennady standing in the early morning sunlight, almost painfully beautiful in that ill-fitting Soviet suit.

The train began to puff. The conductor swung Gennady's suitcase up the steps, and Gennady followed, taking the steep train steps with an easy swing of his legs. The door shut behind him, and the sunlight flashed across its window, so Daniel couldn't see if he had turned to wave or not.

And then the train was pulling out of the station, wheels clacking on the tracks. Through the train windows, Daniel caught one last glimpse of Gennady as he moved down the rows of seats looking for a place to sit. Then the train car passed out of sight, the train was picking up speed, it moved out of the station and rolled away into the forest.

Daniel stayed and watched until the train disappeared between the trees – until the rattle of its wheels had faded, and he could no longer hear its whistle. Then he turned the key in the ignition and drove away.

ASTER GLENN GRAY

Part Two
1975

ASTER GLENN GRAY

CHAPTER 1

When Daniel arrived home from his business trip, he found his wife Elizabeth clipping the hollyhocks in the dusk. She looked up at the creak of the porch steps, and Daniel leaned over the porch rail and asked, "Did you finish the hollyhock paintings?"

She set aside her clippers. "That's why I'm clipping them back," she said. "Did you walk all the way from the subway station? You could've called."

He set down his briefcase and leaned over the porch rail to kiss her. "I didn't want to wake the kids. How are they?"

"Emily learned the butterfly at swimming lessons this week and has decided she wants to be a mermaid. David still thinks he's too old to go to bed at eight o'clock – "

Daniel laughed. "I bet he fell asleep before his head hit the pillow."

"Of course he did. These swimming lessons are great for tiring them out." Elizabeth picked up her clippers again. "I left the last slice of pie for you on the kitchen counter."

"My lovely wife." Daniel kissed her again and picked up his briefcase.

It was blackberry pie; Elizabeth must have taken the kids up to the cabin to pick berries while he was gone. Daniel ate it out of the pie pan while he flipped through the stack of mail. Bill, bill, junk mail. A postcard from Sante Fe, sent by Anna and her second husband, Nate, who were always jetting off to somewhere for their joint career as travel writers. More junk mail.

A letter from Gennady.

It had been fifteen years since Daniel had seen him; six years since he'd seen that handwriting, when Gennady finished his last international posting in Zurich. Daniel dropped his fork on the pie tin and ripped the letter open.

My friend –
I have received a two-year assignment to Washington DC...

Daniel had to put the letter aside for a moment. Then he picked it up and read the rest of it greedily, not that there was much more: Gennady mentioned a post office where Daniel could send a reply, P.O. Box 675, under the same name he'd used for his Zurich letters. A time and a place they could meet for lunch. A week from now at a cafeteria. *Write and let me know if you will be there.*

Like all of Gennady's letters, it was short and unsigned.

He would discuss the letter with Elizabeth soon, but not right now. Instead, he went quietly up the dim stairs to their bedroom and got out a shoebox that he kept on an upper shelf, well out of reach of his children.

It was his box of keepsakes from past love affairs. By far most of the objects recalled his relationship with Helen: Daniel had been a sentimental high school student. Here was a pencil she had lent him before they began dating (how he had tried to transmute that simple pencil into a confession of love), notes she had left in his locker, ticket stubs from every movie they'd seen together...

Here also was the book of Whitman Paul had given him; tickets to a symphony he had attended with Janet.

And, of course, mementoes from Gennady.

The brief note Gennady left Daniel the morning after Daniel had kissed him. The little metal stagecoach from the Cracker Jack box. The photograph that Daniel's mother had taken Christmas morning, Gennady opening his Christmas present while Daniel leaned over the back of his armchair and smiled down at him.

The letters Gennady had written from Zurich.

Daniel was sitting on the bed by the window, rereading the old letters in the dying light, when Elizabeth came in. "You'll ruin your eyes," she told him.

"Yes, probably," he said. He set down the letter he was reading. "I got a letter from Gennady."

"Gennady?" Elizabeth had never met the man, so it took her a moment to place the name; but when she did, she smiled. "So he's been posted abroad again! How is he?"

"He's – well, he's in DC," Daniel said. He held the most recent letter out to her. She moved closer to the window to read it, and he leaned over and switched on a lamp.

"Will you meet him?" she asked.

Daniel hesitated. Of course he wanted to, but at the same time… "It's been fifteen years," he said at last. "People change."

Just look at Paul. Daniel had run into him six months earlier at Bureau cocktail party. Physically, Paul was just as handsome as Daniel remembered. Perhaps even handsomer: the addition of a few wrinkles and a little silver in the hair only made him look distinguished.

But it had been an awkward meeting. They exchanged only a little chitchat before Paul said, an edge to his voice, "I suppose you're married by now."

"Yes," Daniel said, and made for his wallet to show Paul the photograph of his wife and children.

"I thought you would be," Paul said, the edge even more cutting, and on second thought Daniel didn't take out his wallet after all.

Actually, the problem with Paul was that he hadn't changed at all.

In any case, Daniel knew from the Zurich letters that Gennady himself was married now. Her name was Alla.

"The worst thing that can happen is an awkward lunch, right?" Elizabeth said. "You should do it."

"Yes, you're right," Daniel agreed. He flipped back through the Zurich letters till he found the first one, and held it up for her to read. "I think he wanted me to come visit him in Switzerland."

Zurich, Gennady had written, was "clean and pretty and boring, but the mountains are very fine. They say the skiing is good in winter, but right now we hike, and admire the views and the wildflowers, and feast in the inns in the evenings."

Enclosed: a dry yellow wildflower, fragile after all these years.

"Why didn't you?"

"Well, I didn't realize at the time. And this was right after we bought the house... right after our honeymoon..." Daniel grimaced. "I'm pretty sure I wrote about our honeymoon in reply."

"Daniel!" Elizabeth laughed at him.

"He didn't go all tourist-brochure about Switzerland again," Daniel said ruefully.

"Have lunch with him, Daniel," Elizabeth said. "Invite him here for dinner. I'll make chicken Kiev." She lowered her voice, although the kids were safely asleep. "You can hardly decide if you want to sleep with him again without even seeing him."

Daniel began to gather up the letters again. "You wouldn't mind?" he asked, although he knew that answer would be –

"No, of course not."

She really meant it, too. He tried to mean it when he said that he did not mind about her lover Ronald Benson, but it wasn't always true.

Daniel evened up the edges of the letters and returned them to the box. "It's been fifteen years," Daniel reminded her. "He's married. And he may look like a Politburo member now."

***

Gennady did not look like a Politburo member.

An objective observer probably would have said that he hadn't aged as well as Paul. He looked tired, and his suit still didn't fit, but instead of giving him a boyish charm, now it just looked sloppy.

But when Daniel came into the cafeteria, Gennady sprang to his feet with his old youthful energy. "Put down your tray," he ordered, and as soon as Daniel did so Gennady gathered him into a bear hug, and even kissed him on both cheeks in the Russian manner. "Old friend! Old friend!" he said, holding Daniel at arm's length and smiling at him.

"It's good to see you," Daniel said, smiling back. He would have liked to return the cheek kisses, but he was too shy, and slid into the booth instead.

His shyness infected the conversation. For a little while they ate in silence, until Daniel blurted, "I told my superiors that I'd be meeting with you. I thought it would look funny to meet a Soviet spy without telling them. I hope you don't mind."

"Of course not," said Gennady. "I'm glad you've finally learned some wisdom and discretion, my friend. You wouldn't want to be executed like the Rosenbergs. Naturally I told my people too. Although, of course..." That tiny ironic smile that Daniel had nearly forgotten. "I'm not a spy. I'm a cultural attaché."

"Of course, of course. Careless of me. And how's it going spreading Soviet culture to the American masses?"

So they chatted about books and films. Gennady smiled with pleasure when Daniel mentioned that he had taken his children to see an American release of the Soviet film *The Wild Swans*. "Ah! How many children do you have?"

"Two; a boy and a girl. David and Emily." Daniel took a photo from his wallet. He had taken it in front of the cabin earlier that summer, Elizabeth and David and Emily all sitting in the dappled sunlight beneath the maple tree.

Gennady inspected the photo. "Very pretty, all of them."

"Do you have children?" Daniel asked.

Gennady gave the photograph back and shook his head. "Alla doesn't want them and, after all, she would be the one looking after them."

"I see women's lib hasn't made it to Moscow," Daniel said wryly.

"Nothing has made it to Moscow since 1965," Gennady replied.

His voice was flat. Daniel hesitated, then decided not to follow up on that comment. Instead he asked, "How is Alla liking DC?"

Gennady's face tensed. "She didn't come. She doesn't like to travel."

"Really?" Daniel said, startled. That was not the impression he'd gotten from the hiking and skiing and fondueing in the Zurich letters.

"You see, there is not much chance to travel abroad in the Soviet Union," Gennady said. "So she had never traveled before we got married, and then we were posted to Zurich, and..." He shrugged. "She found she didn't like it."

Daniel felt that he had been tactless, and cast around for something else to talk about. "How are you liking DC?"

Gennady's face relaxed. "It's very hot," he said. "Muggy. I learned this word last week," he added, and that characteristic pride in a piece of vocabulary acquisition struck Daniel with painful fondness. "Did you know you have a National Gallery? Of course it is not as fine as our Tretyakov Gallery..."

Daniel laughed. Gennady gave a quick sly grin.

"But some of the art is good," Gennady said generously. "And it is cool inside."

"Which is the most important thing in a DC summer," Daniel agreed. "Have you been to any of the Smithsonians? They're building an Air and Space Museum down on the Mall..."

Gennady looked rather cold. Daniel should have guessed the Apollo missions would be a sore topic.

But Gennady thawed again when Daniel began to talk about the restaurants in town. It transpired that Gennady had been to many of them – "Cultivating sources," he explained. "In the culture industry."

"So let me get this straight," Daniel teased. "You're taking other people to La Colline, but I only rate a cafeteria?"

He really was a little hurt: not about the cafeteria, but because it was clear Gennady had been in town at least a couple of months before he wrote to Daniel.

Gennady actually looked embarrassed. "I wasn't sure you would come."

"How could I say no? I've missed you, you know."

"I doubt it," Gennady scoffed, but Daniel could tell he was pleased. "You've been too busy to miss anyone. Traveling across the United States with your Elizabeth, living out of a camper and sleeping under the stars, skinny-dipping in the Colorado River..."

"Stop, stop, stop," Daniel begged. "My life isn't usually like that. That was just my honeymoon."

"You wrote six pages about it." Daniel hid his face in his hands, and Gennady added happily, "Many exclamation points. A great deal of capitalization."

"Shoot me now."

"It was sweet," Gennady said, slightly mocking. Then suddenly his voice became serious again, and he said, "I'm glad you are happy, my friend."

Daniel lowered his hands and looked at Gennady. "And how about you? Are you happy?"

Gennady shrugged. "I'm okay."

"Just okay?"

"You're so American. Okay isn't good enough for you?"

"I'd like you to be happy."

"I'm happy to be having lunch with you. And I will be happier still if you agree to do it again."

"Yes, of course," Daniel said. He couldn't help smiling. "I'll have to write a report about it, you know."

"Yes, of course. And so will I." Gennady finished his pot roast and switched his plates around to start in on his coconut cream pie. "Would your superiors prefer to hear that the Soviet agents in DC are industriously scouting for information, or that we are all too busy taking long lunches to do so?"

"I don't know that anyone would believe me," Daniel said, "if I tried to pass you off as *industrious*..."

Gennady laughed. Daniel grinned. "Why don't you come to my house for dinner?" Daniel suggested.

The coconut cream pie bulged as Gennady tried to cut it with his fork. "Yes, yes, that would be nice."

"Maybe sometime next week? Friday?"

Gennady paused, his fork mid-pie. "You're serious?"

"Yes. My wife suggested it," Daniel said, and added, "She's heard a lot about you."

The fork descended gently to Gennady's plate. "Has she?"

Daniel heard the question behind the words: *What exactly have you told her about me?*

He answered as directly as he could in a crowded cafeteria. "Yes. I tell her everything."

Gennady didn't reply. He took up his fork again and made inroads on the coconut pie. "This filling, it's falling apart, it's like soup," he muttered. Then, to Daniel: "What would the FBI think if they found out? A Soviet spy in your house?"

"I doubt they'd be happy," Daniel admitted. He poked at his stiff Jell-O. "You would be in more danger than I am," he said, without looking at Gennady. "Your government is far more likely to execute you for espionage than mine."

Gennady shrugged. "Yes, theoretically, but you understand my colleagues wish to complete their American tours with as many three-hour lunches and as little actual work as possible, so it is not in their best interests to notice anything."

Daniel dissected a cube of Jell-O. The noise of the cafeteria rose up around them: chattering voices, the clink of forks on plates and ice in glasses, the clatter of a pan on the serving line.

"Elizabeth's looking forward to meeting you," Daniel ventured. "She says she'll cook chicken Kiev."

"Real chicken Kiev with plenty of butter? Not one of your American low-fat creations?"

"Real chicken Kiev," Daniel promised.

"Well." Gennady capitulated. "For real chicken Kiev I would walk over broken glass."

CHAPTER 2

Gennady arrived for dinner at Daniel's house very early.

He left his apartment in Washington DC with time to spare, just in case he needed to shake off a tail. But the American intelligence community was almost insultingly uninterested in the doings of the Soviet agents in their capital: no one followed him.

And he gave himself a little extra time, too, because he had no directions but the sketchy map that Daniel had drawn on the back of a napkin. But in fact he had no difficulty finding Daniel's house. He got off at the last stop on the Metro line (the DC Metro was far less grand than the Moscow subway) and walked a pleasant two miles along a leafy suburban street.

Daniel had clearly done well for himself. The trees were stately, the houses spacious, and the air full of the pleasant scent of cut grass, the hum of lawnmowers, and the happy shrieks of children splashing in pools. Gennady walked slowly, but even so he ended up in front of Daniel's house more than an hour early.

He hesitated on the sidewalk, looking up at the two-story house so lushly planted with lilies that it seemed almost embowered. Perhaps he should take a turn around the block?

But then the front door of Daniel's house opened and Daniel's wife stepped out, instantly recognizable from the photograph with her dark gold hair and her smile.

In the photograph, her voluptuous figure hadn't been evident, but it certainly was now as she came down the porch steps, barefoot in slacks and a loose peasant blouse. "Gennady?" she said, the word half a question.

"Yes. And you must be Elizabeth?"

She held out her hand to shake. "Won't you come in?" she asked. "I'm afraid Daniel isn't back yet, but I could grab you some lemonade."

"All right."

The front hall seemed dim after the brightness of the sunshine. Gennady slipped off his shoes and padded down the hallway into large, light, spacious room, its walls covered with paintings.

Two of the paintings extended from floor to ceiling. Another, horizontal, stretched six feet across the wall, and beneath it hung a series of tall thin paintings of hollyhocks, three feet high and less than a foot wide.

The hollyhocks Gennady recognized on sight. The painting above seemed more abstract, but upon further consideration he saw that it was not abstract after all, but a landscape, a lake, unrecognizable at first glance because one did not expect to see a lake in soft orange and sunshine yellow, shadowed with deep purple trees.

"Do you like it?"

Gennady had grown so absorbed in the picture that he didn't notice Elizabeth's return until she spoke. She looked almost like a painting herself: Socialist Realism, the pretty lady of the house in her embroidered blouse, holding a silver tray bearing a blue glass pitcher already weeping condensation.

"They're beautiful," he said. Then he remembered a comment in one of Daniel's Zurich letters: *Elizabeth is a painter.* "They're yours, aren't they?"

He had envisioned sweet little pictures: pretty little flowers, perhaps. Not towering bold hollyhocks.

She laughed. "Yes! I suppose I can't hope for an objective comment on them now. You can hardly tell your hostess that you hate her paintings, can you?"

"No," he agreed. "But I like them," he added. "They are so alive."

She laughed again. "Thank you. Come down into the

conversation pit, why don't you? We'll have our lemonade there."

The conversation pit proved to be an actual sunken space in the floor. Three steps led down to a pit lined with couches, with a glass coffee table in the center and a fireplace at the far side. "It's like a Roman..." Gennady didn't know the word in English. "A Roman room for eating, with the couches."

"A triclinium! Yes, it is, isn't it?" She set down the tray and poured two glasses of lemonade. "I'm afraid I'll have to stand in for the Gaulish slave girl at present."

"You are French?"

"On my mother's side. She came to the United States as a war bride after World War I. And *wasn't* she proud of it! She used to tell us that she modeled for Renoir."

Yes: Elizabeth looked very much like one of Renoir's women. "This is how you became interested in art?"

"How does anyone become interested in anything? I just always liked to draw." She was on her feet again. "Do you want something to eat? I made cheese straws."

"Yes, thank you," he said. She left, and he collapsed back into the colorful pillows on the couch.

The truth was that he had not expected to like Elizabeth. He had conceived a slight antipathy toward her when he read Daniel's six-page letter about his honeymoon. Daniel and Elizabeth had driven across the United States in a camper, sleeping under the stars, fleeing a grizzly bear in Yellowstone, walking on the beaches in California, where Elizabeth set up her easel and painted as the sun set. (And then, Gennady had thought sourly, expanding upon Daniel's gentlemanly ellipses, Daniel and Elizabeth fucked on the beach.) They skinny-dipped in the Colorado River: "She rose out of the water with a snake over her shoulder, like some ancient river goddess, and she didn't even scream when she saw it – only let it slide back into the river and then ran like hell for the bank."

Until Gennady had received that letter, somehow he had envisioned Daniel frozen in amber, still pining away by the roadside. Of course it was not so: Daniel had moved on, just as Gennady had. But it was unpleasant to receive such a lengthy letter about Daniel's wedded bliss right when Gennady's own marriage to Alla was beginning to come apart.

They had been drawn together, Alla and Gennady, by a shared interest in *za granitsa*: abroad. They met standing in line for tickets to foreign films at the Moscow House of Cinema: this pretty dark-haired girl with thick dark brows, whose wide dark eyes kept catching on Gennady's, until one day at last they found themselves next to each other in line.

These lines generally lasted for hours, and they spent those hours talking together, and when at the end they really did get tickets to Fellini's *8 ½*, it seemed like a sign from fate. At the end of the movie they kissed, and left the theater hand in hand, and walked the streets of Moscow where the sun shone on the wet pavement after rain.

Within three months they were married. Alla had never been abroad and wanted very much to go, and so Gennady began to push for a posting. Not only for Alla's sake, of course; Gennady wanted to go abroad too, had dreamed of travel since he was eight years old, had chosen his profession because it was one of the few in the Soviet Union that offered the opportunity to pass the borders.

When at last they were posted to Zurich, they toasted each other with a bottle of champagne. There was the flurry of packing, tearful goodbyes, finally a plane ride, and at last their dream came true, and they were abroad together, in the sunny mountains of Switzerland.

And Alla hated it. Not just Zurich itself, but the whole experience of being a stranger in a strange land. Never mind that her German was good, better than Gennady's, and so what if a few mean people laughed at her accent? It was the nature of humans to laugh at each other, you couldn't take it too seriously. Wouldn't she like to come see Lenin's Zurich home on the Spiegelgasse? To go to the opera? (In Moscow, Alla loved the opera.) To hike or ski in the Alps? To leave their apartment for any reason at all, please?

And so Gennady had conceived a dislike for the Elizabeth of Daniel's besotted letters, this woman so fearless that she did not scream even when a snake wrapped itself around her shoulders. But in the face of the actual woman this dislike evaporated: he even forgave Daniel the tactlessness of writing six whole pages, and felt only a faint ruefulness because, of course, when he had such a charming wife, Daniel could hardly have an interest in

Gennady anymore.

Well, that had never been very likely. Gennady washed his disappointment down with a gulp of lemonade. Probably it was better this way. Certainly an affair would have been dangerous, and anyway it was still possible that Alla might change her mind about the divorce.

Elizabeth returned, plate of cheese straws in hand. She refilled Gennady's lemonade glass. "Was it a very hot walk?"

"Yes, but not unpleasant," he told her. "I've never been in a room like this before."

"It's not very homey, is it?" she said. "This front room is mostly for cocktail parties. We have a few every year, people from the art world mostly. It's easier than transporting these monsters to a gallery, and I've sold more paintings than you might expect that way. They think it's hilarious coming out to the suburbs."

A smile flashed across her face as she spoke, good-natured mockery of the conceit of art buyers. Gennady gulped his lemonade and blurted, "Where is Daniel?"

"He's dropping the children off to stay with my parents for the weekend," she said. "I would have thought he'd be back by now. He's been so looking forward to your visit." She touched his arm lightly and added, "He's told me a lot about you."

Gennady had the feeling that *a lot* meant *everything* – really everything – and now she was either warning him off or...

Well, perhaps giving her blessing; but this thought made him intensely uncomfortable. He fiddled with one of the colorful crocheted blankets on the couch. "Perhaps you will show me the house? No, the garden," he said, relieved at the idea. It seemed like a good idea to get out into the fresh air and the sunshine.

But a rumbling noise intervened. "That's the garage door," Elizabeth said, rising to her feet with a smile. "Daniel must be home."

***

They had dinner out on the patio: a big tossed salad, straw potatoes, the promised chicken Kiev oozing with butter. They drank wine and lingered over cups of coffee, chatting, until Daniel heaved himself from the chair and began to gather the plates. "Gennady, would you like to see our cabin?"

"Your cabin?"

"It's just a little place up in the mountains. No electricity, no indoor toilets, just a pump over the sink."

"A dacha." Gennady was enchanted. "You have a dacha?"

Daniel looked bemused. "Well – I guess so."

"Do you grow tomatoes? Are there mushrooms in the woods?"

Daniel and Elizabeth looked at each other. "There are wild raspberries," Elizabeth offered. "And blackberries. We go up in the summer to pick them."

Most Americans wouldn't recognize a morel if it bit them. "Take me there sometime and I will look for mushrooms for you," Gennady promised. "Next spring perhaps, when it is the season for – oh, I don't know the English word – for *smorchok*, a queen among mushrooms, you cook it in butter and it's the best thing you've ever tasted."

"Well, send some back if you find them," Elizabeth said with a smile. "I'll get the dishes this once, Daniel. You'd better get going if you're going to make it before dark. The roads are pretty winding in the mountains," she added to Gennady. "It's a bad place to drive at night."

Gennady was startled. "Tonight?"

Daniel had piled the plates on his arms like a waiter. "Unless you need to get back to the city?"

"No..."

"Don't forget the picnic basket," Elizabeth told Daniel.

Gennady felt flustered and breathless. He had come here with the idea of seducing Daniel, but he had expected it to take months at least, if it ever came to anything, and really he had not thought it likely that it would. It unnerved him to find things moving so quickly. He had thought there would be more time to prepare.

Unless of course Americans often invited their former lovers to their dachas overnight for completely normal friendship purposes.

But even as his mind whirled, Gennady was following Daniel into the kitchen, where they left the dishes on the kitchen counter; and following him out to the garage (two cars! A bourgeois extravagance); and climbing into the car, and Daniel was backing down the driveway, and driving down the quiet street beneath the rustling trees.

And then Daniel said, almost casually, "I could drop you off at the subway stop if you want. There's no reason to drive all the way out to the cabin unless you... unless you're interested in... Oh, Christ." He ran a hand over his face. "Listen, Gennady. I know that you're married, so stomp on me if this is out of line, but I thought I might as well ask. Do you want to sleep with me again?"

Gennady nearly choked. "Are Americans always so blunt?"

"No," Daniel said, "but I thought it was better to be blunt than to pussyfoot around it till the last night before they recall you to Moscow."

"There were good reasons why we did nothing before then," Gennady protested. "It wasn't just 'pussyfooting'."

"Yes, I know. And – as I said – Alla..."

It annoyed Gennady to hear Daniel say her name. "She's very angry that I continued to apply for foreign assignments after Zurich, after it was clear she did not want to go abroad again," Gennady said. "We argued a great deal, we discussed divorce, and perhaps we will and perhaps we won't, but she told me she will not sit in Moscow faithfully waiting while I am gone, and if she does not consider herself bound then certainly I don't."

"Gennady. I'm so sorry." Daniel's voice had gone soft with sympathy.

Gennady flushed. His voice came out rough when he said, "But of course there is *your* wife. What about Elizabeth?"

"Elizabeth's fine with it. I think she's kind of into it, now that she's seen how cute you are." He glanced at Gennady, saw perhaps Gennady's incredulous look (*cute*?), and added, "She was practically shooing us out the door, Gennady. With a picnic basket."

"Why?" Gennady demanded. At the end of the day, after all, a Russian could beat an American at bluntness every time. "Why would she encourage this?"

"I suppose swinging hasn't made it to Moscow, either."

"You should read about our Silver Age poets," Gennady snapped. "America is not on the forefront of everything."

"I know that, Gennady," Daniel protested. "There's no need to pick a fight. Just tell me to drop you off at the Metro and I will. It's been fifteen years, I understand if you're not interested anymore."

"It's not that," Gennady said, because it was not. It was just that it was all happening so fast, he felt off-balance, and he did not know how to slow it down without putting a stop to it altogether. "It's just... You have so much to lose. Your wife, your children. Your nice house. Your happy life."

"I promise you, I promise you, Elizabeth really doesn't mind. We can do whatever you want," Daniel said. "Or nothing at all, if that's what you want. No harm no foul." He turned off the end of the tree-lined avenue and pulled up outside the Metro station: bright lights and graffiti, the pavement littered in cigarette butts. "Do you want to meet at the cafeteria again? Same time next Thursday?"

Gennady thought about the dark Metro tunnels, the stench of cigarettes and old sweat in the swaying cars. His empty apartment, silent and dark.

He twisted the seatbelt around his wrist. He could not look at Daniel. "I want," Gennady began, and felt a catch in his stomach, as if he had tripped over a crack in the pavement, and fallen. "I want to see your dacha."

After all, if you didn't grab happiness when it was offered, it might never come again.

***

Daniel's dacha sat in a clearing among the trees at the end of a winding gravel drive. The car's headlights illuminated the little log cabin briefly as Daniel parked; then Daniel turned off the car, and the clearing plunged into darkness.

"Should've gotten an earlier start," Daniel said.

"Yes," Gennady agreed, gripping the edges of the seat.

Daniel led the way up the porch steps with a flashlight. Once they were inside he lit a lantern, which revealed a sink with a long-handled pump, a little Primus stove, a heavy wooden table where Daniel set the picnic basket. Shadows gathered in the corners of the little room, swung across the wall as Gennady worked the pump handle. Cold water spurted out, and he splashed his face. "Is this water safe to drink?"

"Yes. Here, have a cup." Daniel fetched an old jam jar and

then leaned over to open the dark square of a kitchen window, letting in a breeze that ruffled the lantern light. Gennady filled the jar and drank the water off in slow nervous gulps as Daniel went to open the other windows.

When Gennady had toyed in his mind with the possibility of this affair, he had thought of the good things. The sweetness of Daniel's mouth. The pleasure of waking up in his arms – for Gennady had woken again and again the night that they spent together, afraid of missing his train, and each time he had snuggled in against Daniel's chest and listened to his heartbeat, happy in the knowledge that he did not have to get up just yet.

But now that things had come down out of the realm of golden possibility and into real life, the memory that gripped him was his panic when Daniel had tried to unbutton his shirt; the ghost of Arkady's dirty fingers on his buttons.

And of course it had been fine, fine, Daniel had been patient and kind; but that was fifteen years ago and he had been in love with Gennady then.

Daniel returned. Gennady gulped the last of his water so hastily that a little spilled over his chin. He wiped it away, embarrassed.

Daniel hoisted the lantern. "Come on," he said. "Let me show you the place."

There was only one other room downstairs, a living room with a comfortably shabby couch and a wood stove, dark and cool right now. "Do you cook on that?" Gennady asked. His voice sounded compressed and breathless.

"In the spring or fall. In the summer we use a camping stove in the kitchen, because it heats up the house less."

Between the two rooms a narrow dark staircase rose to the attic, stuffy in the summer heat. Daniel flashed the lantern over the two slant-roofed attic rooms in turn. The first held twin camping cots; the other, a double bed covered in a quilt with a spiral pattern, the colors rich in the lantern light. Gennady saw Elizabeth's hand in its selection, and his nerves pulsed as if touched by an electrical wire. "It's so hot up here."

"Let's go downstairs," Daniel agreed. He plunged back down the stairs and disappeared briefly into the kitchen, the lantern light receding. Gennady's heart thumped as he followed down the steep dark steps.

Daniel reappeared just as Gennady reached the bottom of the stairs. They bumped into each other, and Gennady leaped like a startled cat.

Daniel stepped back. "Am I going too fast?" he asked. "We don't have to do anything tonight, you know."

"You drove me out to your dacha! Of course we have to do something!"

His voice sounded too loud, panicky. Gennady felt naked suddenly, pinned and inspected like an insect and found wanting. Daniel would go home to Elizabeth and they would laugh about him. *I drove him all the way to the dacha and he chickened out. Can you believe it?*

"I'm sorry," Gennady gasped.

"It's all right."

"No, I'm sorry, I'm sorry. It's just that it has been so long…"

"Listen, Gennady, it's all right. I know you haven't had a lot of experience with men…"

"No," Gennady agreed. He felt he could not breathe, it seemed impossible that he should be able to talk without any air in his lungs, but he blurted, "Only you and Arkady."

"Arkady?" Daniel echoed, as if he didn't recognize the name. But saying the name aloud seemed to connect some circuit in his mind, and his eyes widened. "*Arkady?*"

"I need a cigarette," Gennady said, and fled to the front porch.

It was very dark outside, only a sliver of moon, a hundred million stars. His lighter flared garishly bright as he fumbled to light his cigarette. He could see the future rolling out before him like a rug. The long sleepless night – or no, Daniel would not want to wait till morning; they would leave tonight, they would risk the winding road in the darkness. The long endless drive back, the awkward silence in the car. That false American cheerfulness at the end. "See you again soon!" Daniel would say, when really they would never see each other again, and this night would spoil even the memory of their friendship that Gennady had treasured in a small lacquer box in the back of his mind.

Just as Gennady managed to light his cigarette, the door creaked open. Light spilled on the porch. "Do you mind if I come out here?" Daniel asked.

"It's your own dacha."

"Yes, but..."

"Oh, sit," Gennady said, and gestured at the porch steps with his cigarette. "Unless you've come to drive me back."

"No," said Daniel, and then choked, visibly gagging, as if on a bad oyster. "Yes, of course I'll drive you back if that's what you want. I'm sorry. I've been inexcusably pushy all evening; of course you want to get out of here. Let me get the house closed up..."

"No!" Gennady said, and Daniel stopped in the threshold. "I only meant – perhaps you want to get rid of me."

"No," said Daniel. "Of course not. It's been fifteen years since I've last saw you, the last thing I want to do is get rid of you."

A knot loosened in Gennady's chest. "Well – sit, then."

Daniel moved to sit on the steps. The door clanged shut, blocking out the lamplight, and the lost dazzle left them both blind in the dark.

"So," Daniel said, and Gennady's nerves thrilled painfully. "Arkady."

"Arkady," Gennady agreed, and could not go on, his throat swelled so it choked him.

"Your boss?" Daniel prompted. "The one who hit you?"

"He only hit me once." Well, twice, but both the same day, together it counted as one time. "And I was very insolent that day. Oh, he was not as bad as you are thinking. He was just... he was handy."

"Handsy," Daniel corrected automatically.

"Handsy. Yes. Like a man who chases his secretary around the desk but thinks he is a gentleman because he never fucks her." Gennady took a long drag on his cigarette. "How do you think he came up with the honeytrap idea? Doubtless he thought, if he couldn't keep his hands off me..." Gennady flushed painfully, and was glad that the shadows hid his face. "He was one of those people for whom the whole world is a reflection of himself. Anything he wants, anyone else will want too."

"And I did." Daniel's voice was nearly toneless, but Gennady heard the guilt in it.

"And I wanted you," Gennady shot back fiercely. "That was why I came to you on the last night, that's why I'm here now. Don't you understand? Even though I like you, even though I trust you, I thought that would be enough to wash over all that, and it isn't." His voice had gone hoarse by the end. He swallowed. "I need a drink."

The porch creaked as Daniel rose. "I'll get you a glass of water."

"Daniel! Vodka, brandy?"

"Oh." Daniel sounded aghast. "We don't have any alcohol at the cabin. I'm so sorry."

Gennady thought darkly of the antifreeze in the car. But he was not Alyosha, he hadn't sunk that far, even if he felt tears rising in his throat. "Oh, I never should have told you. It was nothing, and it's not even true anyway, you were not the only two, there was Alyosha also, he is the one I messed around with when I was drunk." He took another drag on his cigarette, and to his horror the tears stung his eyes. He glanced at Daniel, uselessly of course, he couldn't see Daniel's face in the darkness. "Daniel…"

"Gennady?"

But Gennady could not bring himself to say, *Do you despise me now?*

The porch creaked again as Daniel sat back down. Gennady tried to blow a smoke ring, but he was not good at them at the best of times, and now his hands were shaking too badly. His cigarette was burning down anyway, he lit a second off the butt of the first, and ground the first out in a knothole.

"He died seven years ago," Gennady said. "So there is no point in telling your FBI that you have a prime piece of blackmail material about one Arkady Anatolyevich."

"*Gennady!*"

"Your FBI would want to know," Gennady insisted.

Daniel didn't reply at once. "Is that why you didn't tell me back then? Because of the FBI?"

Gennady shook his head. "No. I never even thought of telling you. Impossible." Gennady pressed his hand against the porch step, feeling the grain of the wood under his fingertips. "I never told anyone."

"Not even Alla?"

"Of course not." How could he have done that to her? "Did you tell Elizabeth about John?"

There was a brief pause. "I tell Elizabeth everything," Daniel said.

"Yes. Well." Gennady's throat felt hot and tight. "I suppose you will tell her all about this, too."

"No," Daniel said. "I told her everything about me. I'm not going to tell her your secrets."

"No, tell her if you want to," Gennady said. Suddenly he didn't care anymore. He felt as if he had fallen from a great height and every single part of his body was sore.

Daniel did not speak for a while. The wood creaked as he shifted his weight. Gennady kicked a heel against the edge of the steps.

"You were the first person I ever told about John," Daniel said.

That surprised Gennady. "You didn't tell Paul?"

"Oh. Well. He was so pleased to be the first man I kissed..."

Gennady snorted.

"Oh, shut up," Daniel said.

Gennady smiled. He took a drag on his cigarette and risked a glance at Daniel. His eyes had adjusted to the darkness: he could see Daniel's face now, even met Daniel's eyes briefly. But he couldn't hold the eye contract, and looked away across the clearing, the tall grass touched in silver by the moonlight, and asked, "Are you angry with me?"

He asked only because he knew Daniel was not, but still it was a relief to hear the surprise in Daniel's voice when he said, "No. Of course not."

"You must be disappointed," Gennady insisted. "After you drove me all the way to your dacha... And I wanted so much for this to go well. To make up for behaving so badly all those years ago."

"What do you mean?"

"The last night... You know. The buttons on my shirt. Well, at least now you know why. Probably you have been wondering."

"Oh. Well, I always figured... I mean, I never guessed it was Arkady. But I figured someone had been rough with you."

Gennady's eyes pricked. It depressed him that this had been so obvious, that he had hidden nothing at all, when he had tried so hard.

"And I wouldn't say that you behaved badly," Daniel added.

"I did," Gennady insisted. "I made things very awkward for you, when I should have just said no." A brief silence, his heart swelling in his throat; and then he said, "I never said no to Arkady." That was the worst of it, that he had not tried to stop Arkady; it would have been useless, he might have gotten fired, but it shamed him that he had not tried. "Except the last time. There was no point, worse than pointless, it made things worse."

His voice withered into nothingness at the end. He drew in his breath, and held it, and felt he might explode; and when Daniel touched his elbow, Gennady did explode off the step, he nearly ran into the darkness, he stood panting as if he had already run a marathon. He stood a long moment, shivering, and then collapsed back down on the warm steps. He could not speak, he put a hand on Daniel's arm; and then he felt Daniel's arms around him, and he put his arms around Daniel and clung to him.

"It was nothing," Gennady mumbled into Daniel's shoulder, "nothing. He did not even touch me usually, he just looked."

"Fuck him," Daniel said fiercely. "Fuck him. *Fuck him.*"

He rubbed Gennady's back, and cupped a hand over the nape of his neck, and Gennady let out a shuddering sigh and pulled himself close to the warmth of Daniel's body and the strong solid beat of Daniel's heart.

Daniel held him for a long time, until Gennady's heart rate slowed and his breath smoothed. Gennady felt very shy and small and childish, and rather too warm in Daniel's arms; but comfortable, too, he did not want to let go. But then Daniel shifted, as if he were getting stiff, and Gennady wriggled free so that Daniel would not have to push him away.

"We should go inside," Gennady said, and stood. He felt stiff himself, and chilly, although the night was warm. "I'm tired."

"Yes, of course." Daniel got up too. "Let's fold out the couch. The back goes down to turn it into a bed."

Gennady followed him inside. He made no move to help Daniel lower the back of the couch till Daniel said, "C'mon, Gennady, grab the far corner, will you?"

Gennady did it with ill grace. He did not want to be banished to sleep on the couch, and he watched with his arms folded as Daniel spread sheets, and fluffed a couple of pillows, and sat on the edge of the couch-bed to take off his shoes.

It was only when Daniel made to remove his polo shirt that

Gennady began to understand. "Are you sleeping down here?"

"I thought..." Daniel said. His half-removed shirt hid his face, but Gennady could hear his embarrassment. "I thought it would be nice to sleep together. Just to sleep," Daniel clarified hastily, jerking his shirt back down. "No hanky-panky."

"Hanky-panky," Gennady echoed. The silly word pleased him, and that made it easier to say, stumbling, "Do you still want...? Not tonight. I'm so tired. But do you still..."

He could not finish his sentence: it seemed so unlikely that Daniel could still want him, after all of this. But Daniel touched Gennady's forearm, and Gennady raised his eyes, and Daniel squeezed Gennady's forearm and smiled at him. "You know I'm crazy about you, Gennady," Daniel said.

Gennady could not speak. He smiled at the floor, and gently kicked the side of the couch.

"But if you'd rather..." Daniel began. He let go of Gennady's arm and cleared his throat, and it struck Gennady that Daniel was not quite sure himself either. "If you'd feel more comfortable," Daniel said. "I can sleep upstairs if you'd rather sleep alone."

"No, no, no," Gennady said. "No. Stay."

But Gennady still felt shy, and did not undress until Daniel had blown out the lantern. He lay down gingerly atop the sheets in boxers and undershirt, prickling with the awareness of Daniel lying beside him.

For a long time they just lay quietly, and slowly Gennady relaxed. A soft breeze blew in through the open windows, and it felt good on his hot skin. "Do you remember," Gennady said softly, "the time we had to share a bed in that motel room up in Minnesota?"

"When the power went out?" Daniel said. "And you snuggled right up against me and started stroking my stomach like a little creep?"

Gennady smiled. "Only till you told me to stop," he protested. He rolled onto his side, peering into Daniel's face in the moonlight. "Did you already like me then?"

"I was trying not to. I think what really tripped me over the edge," Daniel said, "was the time that you compared me to a British warrior daubed in woad." Gennady laughed again, and Daniel added, rather wistfully, "Was that real, or just for the honeytrap?"

"Both, maybe." Gennady yawned. "If it hadn't been for the honeytrap, we could have been making good use of those motel rooms – oh, starting soon after Christmas, perhaps."

"Would you have insisted on getting drunk every time?"

"Probably at first." Gennady yawned again. "But you see, you can convince yourself you are drunk on two shots, if that's what you need to believe."

Daniel touched Gennady's arm lightly, right where his sleeve met skin. Gennady scooted a little closer, even though it was so warm. Daniel draped an arm around him, and so they fell asleep.

CHAPTER 3

When Daniel woke the next morning, he found Gennady still asleep beside him, lying on his stomach with one arm hanging over the side of the couch. He must have gotten hot in the night, because he had taken off his shirt, and Daniel lay there and gazed at his bare skin and felt that here, finally, was the sweet sleepy morning that the fates had denied them fifteen years ago.

On the day Gennady went back to Moscow, Daniel had awakened in the pre-dawn darkness to find Gennady already out of bed, tying his tie: "Get up, let's go, I have to catch the train." There had not even been time for a final cup of coffee.

But today, they did not have to go anywhere, and the morning light lay softly on Gennady's skin. It felt like a miracle, after so much time had passed, and when Daniel had come so close to fucking everything up last night, too. That moment when Gennady said, *Only you and Arkady...*

He hoped in the end Gennady would be glad he had told, just as in the end Daniel had been glad he had told Gennady about John. It had hurt in the telling, but a lot of the pain had gone out of the memory after. Like slashing open a blister to let out the pus.

Still. Daniel should have backed off when Gennady was so hesitant to go up to the cabin in the first place.

"Are you sorry you didn't get this chance fifteen years ago?"

Caught out, Daniel tore his gaze from Gennady's back. Gennady was looking at Daniel, his gray eyes bright with amusement.

"Yes," Daniel said. "I always felt that we got cheated. We should have had a long leisurely morning in bed, and instead..."

Gennady cocked his head, then nodded. "Ah. Because I had to catch the early train." He poked Daniel in the stomach. "I meant, are you sorry you didn't see me without my shirt," Gennady said, "when I was young and beautiful."

"Don't fish for compliments," Daniel told him.

Gennady laughed. "Did you miss me after I was gone?"

"Yes, of course." Daniel had been miserable. But he didn't want to talk about that now. Instead he poked Gennady in the side, and teased, "I bet you didn't miss me, though."

"You understand," Gennady said, and he sounded almost apologetic, "once I was back in Moscow, it was like everything in America was a dream." His brow puckered, like he was afraid this might hurt Daniel's feelings.

It did, just a little. Not that Daniel had wanted Gennady to be miserable, but it would have been nice if he'd said that he'd pined just a little.

But then Gennady kissed him, light as a butterfly, and suddenly Daniel didn't mind about anything anymore. "Every year on American Christmas," Gennady said, "you understand we do not celebrate this in the USSR..."

"Because you're all godless heathens," Daniel said, smiling.

"Yes, exactly. Godless heathens. But nonetheless, on your Christmas, I get out the book that you gave me, the volume of Emily Dickinson, and I read it."

Daniel was too pleased to speak. He put his hand on Gennady's, and Gennady lifted Daniel's hand and kissed it. He tugged Daniel's hand gently, and Daniel allowed himself to be pulled in, and Gennady caught Daniel's face between his hands and kissed him, more deeply this time, his hands tangled in Daniel's hair. "I like your hair like this."

Daniel wore his hair longer now; not long like a hippie's, but long enough that it would have given Hoover an aneurysm if he'd been alive to see it on an FBI agent. Daniel fingered Gennady's hair. "You should grow yours out."

"None of my colleagues would approve."

"To hell with them," Daniel said, and kissed him.

For a long time there was nothing but their mouths, lips and tongue and teeth, Gennady's hands in Daniel's hair. Daniel touched Gennady's shoulders, his shoulder blades, the line of his spine. The morning was quiet except for the crickets in the grass, the sound of lips on lips.

Daniel's fingers stumbled over the rough skin of a scar on Gennady's side: legacy of Peter Abbott's knife. Gennady broke the kiss.

"Does it hurt?" Daniel asked.

"No," Gennady said.

But Daniel had the feeling Gennady was not comfortable having it touched. He moved his hand back up Gennady's side, and Gennady caught Daniel's hands in his own and rolled them both over till he pinned Daniel lightly, pressing Daniel's hands against the couch.

Daniel smiled up at him. He wanted to touch Gennady, caress his collarbones, his taut nipples, and he tried to pull his hands free. But Gennady's grip tightened, and the pressure sent a jolt of desire through Daniel's body.

"What are you going to do with me now?" Daniel asked, breathless.

"I don't know," Gennady said. His tongue flickered over his lips. "Kiss you again, I think."

He lay down on top of Daniel as he kissed him, and Daniel rocked up against him, thrilling as he felt the hard heat of Gennady's erection through his boxers. "Let me touch you," Daniel begged. Gennady let go of Daniel's wrists, and Daniel ran his hands down Gennady's sides, pressing the small of his back just where he had liked it all those years ago.

Gennady bit his shoulder. Daniel yelped, hips bucking against Gennady's, and Gennady asked, "Did I hurt you?"

"No," Daniel panted. "You could slap me right now and I'd love it."

"I can if you want," Gennady said, and Daniel laughed, giddy, because he did want it and he didn't. He wasn't sure what he wanted: to kiss Gennady all over, to fuck or be fucked, anything to be closer, skin against skin.

Daniel shimmied out of his boxer shorts. Gennady's hands slid down Daniel's back, over the curve of his ass, and Daniel's hips rose in the hope of Gennady's fingers sliding between his buttocks, the burn in his thighs as Gennady hooked Daniel's legs over his shoulders and pushed inside, the heat, the stretch, the rhythm as Gennady rocked inside him...

But Gennady's hands slid on down Daniel's thighs, instead. Daniel shivered. "Your *shorts*, Gennady," he gasped, and at last Gennady took his shorts off, and his naked body pressed all along Daniel's, all hot slick skin, his mouth open and wet against Daniel's as Daniel wrapped his hand around their cocks and jerked them both off together.

Afterward, Gennady smiled at him sleepily, and kissed the place where he'd bitten Daniel's shoulder, and cuddled in close as Daniel ran his hands over Gennady's sides and back. Daniel stroked him, and rested, and felt the lassitude of satisfaction settling over his limbs; but desire till simmered under his skin, the fire banked but burning, the honeymoon yearning to make love again and again.

Gennady's mouth moved against Daniel's shoulder. "We ought to have breakfast," he murmured.

"Yes!" Daniel thought with pleasure of the good coffee in the picnic basket: much nicer than anything they could have gotten at a diner in 1960. "It's just coffee and toast and preserves," he said, and wished he had brought something fancier, although he had spent all week telling himself to keep the breakfast menu casual. It would have been silly to pack something fancy when Gennady might not even come to the cabin. "I'll bring you breakfast in bed."

"Capitalist nonsense," Gennady scoffed.

But he remained lying on his stomach in the welter of sheets as Daniel put on his boxers and headed for the kitchen. Halfway there, Daniel looked back. Gennady's face brightened into a soft smile when he caught Daniel looking; and Daniel felt a tenderness for him so intense that it was painful, and nearly went back to kiss him again.

He went on to the kitchen instead, and busied himself making breakfast. He was just spreading the cherry preserves over the freshly toasted bread when Gennady came in, yawning, half dressed in boxers and undershirt. "I told you to stay," Daniel scolded.

Gennady came up beside Daniel and leaned his cheek against

Daniel's shoulder. "And get crumbs in the bed?"

Daniel kissed the top of his head, then shook him off to ferry the toast plates to the table, next to the tin camping mugs of rich dark coffee. "Your timing is perfect," Daniel allowed. "The coffee ought to be just cool enough to drink."

Daniel almost couldn't eat his own breakfast for the pleasure of watching Gennady: the crunch of the crusty bread between his teeth, his lips stained red with the cherry preserves, the contented-cat narrowness to his eyes as he sipped the good coffee. Gennady leaned back in his chair and gazed out the kitchen window, sipping his coffee as if he had all the time in the world, and Daniel asked, "How long can you stay today?"

Gennady tilted his head, and smiled, and said, "Oh, a while, I think."

Daniel was smiling too. "I'd better wash the dishes."

Gennady watched Daniel as he worked the pump handle, his gaze almost like a touch. Without meaning to Daniel stretched, preening, showing off as he dragged the pump handle up and down, as if it were very heavy. He bent over and pumped cool water over his head, and it gushed over his shoulders, trickling down the line of his spine and beading on his chest hair.

Gennady let out a breath. Daniel turned around to look at him, and leaned back against the counter. "Do I look like a British warrior now?"

"No," Gennady said. "Now in the sunlight you look like one of the gilded statues at Petrodvorets."

Daniel shouted with laughter, although he could feel himself blushing. "I doubt the statues have chest hair."

He was much hairier now than he had been fifteen years ago. Paul had always taken such pleasure in the near-smoothness of Daniel's chest.

"It's pretty," Gennady told him. Daniel laughed again. "Why are you laughing?"

"I've never heard anyone describe chest hair as *pretty* before."

"What word would you use then?"

"Oh, I don't know. I'm glad you like it."

Gennady looked at Daniel, bright-eyed, his chin lifted as if daring Daniel to kiss him. It would take only two steps to cross the kitchen. But the pleasure of anticipation kept Daneil at the sink, washing the dishes, his blood thrumming under his skin.

He was pumping the handle, sending gushes of cool water over the dishes, when Gennady's hands touched his waist.

Daniel went still. Then he gently released the pump handle. Despite the warm morning Gennady's hands were cool as they slid over Daniel's stomach, and Daniel's skin quivered at the touch. Gennady pulled himself in against Daniel's back, and rubbed his face against Daniel's shoulder, and kissed the nape of his neck.

Daniel turned around, leaning back against the counter so it dug into his ass. He looped his arms around Gennady's neck and kissed Gennady again. His mouth still tasted sweet from the preserves. "You're insatiable," Daniel told him.

"Hmm? What is this word?"

That made Daniel laugh.

"Hmm?" Gennady pressed.

"Insatiable. It means you can't get enough," Daniel said.

"You are describing yourself, I think," Gennady scoffed, grinning.

Daniel didn't even try to protest. He rolled his hips against Gennady's. "Just bend me over the counter and fuck me."

He meant it to sound light and flirtatious. But it came out with a hint of a growl, clearly a serious request, and Gennady blushed and paled and grew tense. "Okay."

"No, no, or don't, it's fine," Daniel said.

"No, I want to," Gennady insisted, flushing again. "I want to," he said, and he let go of Daniel, "it's only..." He backed up till he bumped against the table. "I don't know how to do that."

"That's all?" Daniel was relieved. "Oh, that's all right. I can talk you through it."

"Do *you* know how to do it?"

Now Daniel tensed. He had never told Gennady that Paul never let Daniel fuck him, and it embarrassed him that Gennady must have guessed. "Yes," Daniel said stiffly. "Before I met Elizabeth, I had another lover..."

"Ah! Your next FBI partner?"

"*Gennady!*"

Gennady laughed. Suddenly the tension fell away, and Daniel laughed too. "You'll be happy to know," Daniel told Gennady, "I haven't slept with any more agents at all."

"Yes, good," Gennady said. "I told you that you should stop. But then," he said, cocking his head in mock puzzlement, "how did you find this new lover, if the FBI did not assign him to you?"

Daniel rolled his eyes. "Taylor was a friend of Anna's," he said. "A photographer. No, not *that* kind of photographer," he said, because Gennady looked worried. "And even if he were, I wouldn't have let him photograph me. Christ." He shuddered at the thought of erotic photographs getting back to the FBI. "No, Taylor was a wildlife photographer. And he... Well, we... Anyway, yes, I do know how to top now."

Gennady nodded. He started to speak, and stopped, and then he said, "It's just that what you've asked me – I've never done it before, and I don't want to fuck it up, when I was so troublesome last night."

"You weren't – " Daniel protested.

"You're so American," Gennady scoffed. "Always putting a smiling face on everything, it's horrible. You brought me up here to fuck, not to be burdened with this story about Arkady, what is that if not trouble?"

An entire childhood of Midwestern manners training nearly impelled Daniel to finish his interrupted sentence: *You weren't any trouble*. He drew in a deep breath instead, and let it out slowly, and said, "Gennady. You're worth any amount of trouble."

He thought for a moment this was a mistake. Gennady stood frozen, mouth open, eyes unfocused. But then Gennady crossed the space between them, and crushed himself against Daniel's chest. "And it's *not* a burden," Daniel said, speaking into Gennady's hair. "I'm glad you told me. It explained a lot of things. Not," he added hastily, "that you owed me an explanation..."

"It's not about *owing*," Gennady said. He stepped back to look into Daniel's face. "That's so American; everything is debts and spending for you. It's not about *owing*, it's about what is necessary to move forward, like a roadway that comes to a river and you need a bridge or a ferry to cross. And if there is no bridge, no ferry, there's nowhere left to go."

"Yes," said Daniel. He would have liked to say something else, something even half as eloquent; but then Gennady was kissing him, and Daniel had to kiss him back, and when Gennady pulled back to catch his breath, there seemed to be nothing worth saying except, "Why don't we go back to bed?"

"Yes," said Gennady. He let out a brief laugh, shy and joyful, and he added all in a rush, "And if you still want me to fuck you, if you're sure I won't hurt you, I would like to fuck you, I would like at least to try."

Daniel was momentarily too dizzy with desire to respond. "Oh, thank God," he said, and kissed Gennady; and it was only with some difficulty that he removed his hands from Gennady to snag the lube out of the picnic basket.

Gennady led him back into the living room, and they fell on the tangled sheets. Gennady rolled on top of Daniel, as he had that morning; but this time he did not pin Daniel's wrists, and Daniel stroked his hands over Gennady's shoulders and arms, kissing him with long sweet kisses, till Gennady murmured, "Daniil…"

Daniel paused to admire him: flushed lips, flushed cheeks, those big eyes. He slid a hand under Gennady's undershirt and stroked the small of his back. Gennady, to Daniel's delight, shucked his shirt and pulled Daniel close, bare skin to bare skin.

"I wish," Daniel gasped, "there was an American version of your name."

Gennady kissed along the line of Daniel's jaw. "You used to call me *tovarisch*."

"That's *not* American. And you always complained that I didn't pronounce it correctly."

"Well, so." Gennady laughed, and Daniel kissed him again, and kept kissing him till Gennady was rocking against him, breathing in ragged little gasps. "Yes, go on," Gennady prompted. "So I'm going to fuck you, what do I do next?"

Daniel thrust against Gennady's thigh. It pressed him right up against Gennady, the heat of Gennady's erection like a brand through his boxers, and it made Daniel crazy, he wanted to touch it and put his mouth on it and feel it naked against his skin. He sucked in a breath and held it and gasped out, "I'll take care of the prep work today."

"Shouldn't I learn how to do it?"

"Next time," Daniel said, and ground against Gennady, so Gennady could feel exactly why Daniel didn't have the patience right now.

It had been a long time since Daniel did this, but his muscle memory unlocked as he slid his slick fingers inside himself. He clenched around his fingers, the feeling deliciously, shockingly good; and the goodness redoubled when he found the sweet spot inside him, and he closed his eyes and stroked himself and shivered with pleasure, aware even with his eyes closed of Gennady watching him.

"It feels good?" said Gennady. He sounded surprised, as if he really hadn't expected that, and Daniel understood suddenly that Gennady had hesitated to fuck him partly because he did not expect Daniel to enjoy it.

"Did you think I asked you to fuck me over the sink because I'm a glutton for punishment?" Daniel asked.

"Well, I know from the past, you are a very generous lover…"

"Not to the point of self-sacrifice," Daniel told him. He crooked his fingers again, right where it felt good, and gasped, "*Christ*, you don't know how much I've wanted you to fuck me. This morning, God, when you put your hands on my ass, I wanted you to just push right up inside me. Even the first time we made love, do you remember…"

"So long ago?"

"Yes. God, I wish I'd asked," said Daniel. They had both been in their twenties then, Gennady could have fucked him all night.

"No, no, perhaps it's good you didn't. I would have been too shy."

Daniel wrapped his free hand around the nape of Gennady's neck and pulled him down to kiss, hot and open-mouthed and dirty. He broke the kiss to murmur, "Your *shorts*, Gennady," and obediently Gennady took them off; and Daniel looked at his cock and moaned. "*Christ*, I want to put my mouth on it," he said, which made Gennady laugh, a little shocked perhaps, but delighted too. "I'm much better than I was last time," Daniel confided, and Gennady laughed some more.

"I thought you were very good," Gennady told him.

"Well, I'm even better, then," Daniel retorted, and went on, the kind of dirty talk that he could never manage when he wasn't turned on out of his mind. "I just want to take you in my mouth and suck you wet and dirty and let you fuck me just like that," he said, "just my spit on your cock, I've been fucked like that before, but…" And here he moaned again, with frustration as well as desire, "I think that'd be tough for your first time. I should go easy on you. I'm sort of reverse-deflowering you…"

"*Deflowering*," said Gennady, as if he knew just from the sound of it that this was a silly and old-fashioned word, and they both laughed. "All right, all right, make it easy for me. What should I do?"

"Slick your cock up," Daniel said, and tossed the lube to him. "I want to see you touch yourself."

Gennady fumbled the catch. He blushed, and Daniel remembered suddenly what he had said the night before, *he just looked*. "On second thought," Daniel said. He tackled Gennady playfully, and Gennady was laughing again, wriggling underneath him, "God, at least let me get my hands on you, I'm dying over here."

He couldn't resist kissing Gennady's cock, just at the tip, and then he had to nose at his balls, too. Then he planted a kiss at the base of Gennady's cock, just where it rose from his rough pubic hair, and licked up right along it and took the head of Gennady's cock in his mouth, loving it with his tongue, while Gennady's hips rose in little infinitesimal thrusts and his breath burst out in gasps; and then Gennady's hands were on Daniel's cheeks and he was gasping, "Daniel, Daniel," and pulling him off.

Daniel was breathing too hard to speak. At last he gasped out, "What?"

Gennady's chest was heaving. "If you want me to fuck you," he managed, "you had better let me do that first."

At the moment all Daniel really wanted to do was put his mouth back on Gennady's cock and suck him till his jaw ached. He rested his head against Gennady's thigh and panted. "I told you my blowjobs had gotten better," Daniel said, so smug that Gennady swatted him.

"Yes, yes, you are very wonderful," Gennady said, and Daniel laughed and pulled himself up alongside Gennady so they lay nose to nose. He fumbled through the sheets for the lube. It was cool on his hand, and normally Daniel would have rubbed his hands together to warm it up before he put it on Gennady's cock, but he figured it wouldn't hurt to cool Gennady off a little just then; and Gennady stretched and sighed as Daniel stroked his cock.

"How do you want me?" Daniel murmured. "Ass up, head down? On my back?" Gennady's eyes widened, and Daniel added, "Ass up is classic." He would've preferred to be on his back, mostly so he could watch Gennady fuck him, but, well. Later maybe. "Why don't we try that?"

"Yes, all right." Gennady kissed Daniel swiftly, and Daniel kissed him back, just enough to sweeten him up; and then he rolled over onto his hands and knees, his knees spread apart to give Gennady access. "Oh..." Gennady said, and then Daniel felt Gennady's hands on his hips, the touch so light that Daniel nearly moaned with frustration.

"Just take hold and fuck me, Gennady, *Jesus*."

"Just like that?"

Daniel would certainly have taken more time to prep if their positions were reversed, stroked Gennady's stomach and his sides and the insides of his thighs; and the image got him even hotter, so he was rocking his hips and Gennady wasn't even inside him yet, though he could feel the heat of Gennady's cock touching his buttocks. "Gennady," he begged.

"Will it fit?" Gennady asked.

"Yes," Daniel snapped. "Don't flatter yourself."

Gennady laughed. His hands tightened on Daniel's hips, more businesslike, and he pushed inside, not as fast as Daniel might have liked, but steady, hot, that exquisite stretch, close enough to pain that Daniel was chewing his lips.

Daniel's first moan was partly for show: he wanted Gennady to feel good about what he was doing, not to worry about any clumsiness, because he was a little clumsy, at first. Gennady laughed, his laughter breathless, almost soundless, mostly a vibration between their two bodies.

"Rock your hips," Daniel told him, and rocked his hips to show Gennady how it was done. He stopped mostly because he did not want to make Gennady come too fast. He wanted Gennady inside him forever, Gennady's hands sliding up and down his thighs, Gennady's lips dotting kisses on the backs of his shoulders. "You feel so good inside me," Daniel said, and Gennady made a little choked noise, and Daniel flushed all though his body. He clenched down around Gennady, and moaned at the rush of heat as Gennady came.

He kept Gennady inside him after, and stroked his own cock almost lazily. Eventually Gennady pulled out, and Daniel rolled over so they lay face to face. Gennady lay all flushed and damp with sweat, Daniel leaned forward and kissed his mouth. "You have a nice time?" he murmured.

"Yes," said Gennady. He touched Daniel's cheek. "You?"

"Yes," said Daniel, and crowded a little closer, so Gennady could feel his still-hard cock. Gennady's hand dropped, as it were almost by accident, so his fingers brushed Daniel's cock; and he wrapped his hand around it, and caught Daniel's mouth against his lips, his kiss sleepy and sloppy and sweet, and Daniel was so lost in his kisses that it was almost a surprise when he came.

Gennady put his hands on Daniel's face afterward, very lightly, cradling his cheeks. Daniel kissed Gennady's temple. "Same time next week?" Daniel asked, half-teasing.

Gennady smiled and shook his head. "It would be a bad idea to come here so often. A Soviet and an American agent meeting so often in private, what could they be doing?"

"I guess so," Daniel sighed.

He felt that this should bother him; but he felt too good to be bothered by anything right then. He smiled at Gennady, and Gennady smiled back at him, and Daniel closed his eyes and spread his limbs and let the breeze through the window cool his heated body; and all felt right with the world.

CHAPTER 4

Gennady's life seemed to divide into two after that.

Outwardly, nothing was going well. Work was dull; his colleagues were dull. He would have given a lot for a Sergeyich in the office.

But Sergeyich was long gone. He had disappeared in 1960, defected presumably, and his defection had accomplished what nothing else would have done: Sergeyich had been in Arkady's office, defected on Arkady's watch, and so Arkady had been demoted.

The news from home was mostly bad. Gennady's cousin Oksana wrote that Grandfather was ill, Aunt Lilya was ill, Oksana's husband Alyosha was going on bender after bender because his mother was ill as well... Oh, but one bright spot: Oksana's daughter Dasha had joined the Young Pioneers, and she looked cute as a button with her little red scarf.

And Alla barely wrote. She would divorce him as soon as he got back to Moscow, and the prospect of living there without her, all alone, never mind all the problems they had, pressed on his chest like a paralyzing weight as he lay on the empty bed in his empty apartment. Sometimes when the nights were bad Gennady imagined Daniel holding him, and the tension in his chest relaxed, although it made him cry.

After all, it was silly for a man of forty to feel this way, for a relationship that had no future. In the end Gennady would go back to the Soviet Union, and Daniel would stay in America with his wife and his children in his beautiful house on the tree-lined street.

Gennady did not begrudge him that: Daniel deserved all the nice things in the world. But it created an asymmetry in their relationship that sometimes hurt himl. Daniel had so many things in his life to make him happy, inevitably this affair must mean more to Gennady than it did to Daniel, and he was a little afraid that Daniel would notice.

But sometimes, none of this seemed to matter. Gennady had conceived a silly schoolboy infatuation for Daniel, so that even a stray thought of him gave Gennady a happy expansive feeling in his chest. Their weekly lunches were an exquisite torture, to sit so close to Daniel and talk to him and yet be unable to touch, except perhaps for a handshake at the beginning and end; their infrequent visits to the dacha, like a glimpse of paradise.

By their fourth visit, Gennady nearly vibrated with longing as they drove up to the dacha. The autumn leaves glowed orange and gold, and there was such a fire in Gennady's blood that he wanted not only to rip off his clothes but even almost his skin itself, as if it was only another barrier between them and without it he and Daniel could melt together.

By the time they reached the cabin the desire to touch and be touched was so intense that it nearly paralyzed him. He sat on the kitchen table – this had become his habit somehow, to sit on the table as Daniel brought in the picnic lunch. Daniel touched a hand to the back of Gennady's neck as he went back out to the car to fetch a blanket, and Gennady shivered all down his spine, and when Daniel finally came back and kissed him, Gennady nearly ripped the buttons off Daniel's shirt.

"What do you want?" Daniel said, and Gennady replied, "I don't know, I don't know," sitting on the kitchen table with his legs around Daniel's waist and his arms around his neck and his hands tangled in his hair, kissing him with an open urgent mouth, wanting Daniel to fall to his knees and suck him off and yet somehow not stop kissing him, or drag off his pants and fuck him right there on the table, raw, even though he was not at all sure that would feel good, as a fantasy it sounded perfect but as a physical sensation it might just hurt.

The table legs scraped across the concrete floor as Daniel climbed on the table and pinned Gennady to the wooden surface. "Is the table strong enough for this?" Gennady panted.

"I sure hope so." Daniel held Gennady's face as he kissed him, and Gennady let go of Daniel's neck and began to undo the buttons on Daniel's shirt, running his hands over the bared skin, touching him and yet also holding Daniel a little bit away. He wanted him so much that he felt as if he might catch fire if they got any closer.

When Gennady undid the last button, Daniel tossed his shirt aside. Gennady made another noise, desire and frustration, and propelled Daniel off the table and across the room, till he had him pinned against the sink, kissing his mouth and running his hands over the long smooth muscles in his back. He thrust one leg between Daniel's and banged his knee painfully on the pipes, and almost didn't feel it.

"What do you want, Gennady?"

"Everything, I don't know."

"I want you to fuck me," Daniel said roughly, and Gennady turned him around and bent him over the sink and pulled his trousers down. Gennady put his hand around Daniel's cock and squeezed, and Daniel cried out; and then Gennady took off his own shirt and pressed his chest against Daniel's back and kissed the sweat from his shoulders. "In my pocket," Daniel told him, gasping, and Gennady slicked his fingers and thrust them inside Daniel. It felt good, Daniel clenching tight and hot around his fingers, "Come on, come on, fuck me, please," and actually crying out with pleasure when Gennady pushed inside him. His gasps turned into greedy moans as Gennady rocked inside him, *more, harder, faster.*

"Am I going to hurt you?"

"No."

Daniel came almost as soon as Gennady wrapped his hand around his cock.

Gennady fucked Daniel more slowly after that. Daniel's breath came out in soft pants. Gennady ran his hands along Daniel's thighs, which quivered with tension, and pressed inside him to that spot he particularly liked. "Do you want me to stop?" he asked, kissing Daniel's shoulders.

"No – no." Daniel's voice trembled on the cusp between

pleasure and distress.

Gennady wrapped his arm around Daniel's chest. He pressed his mouth against Daniel's shoulder and pressed close inside him, and the pressure built in Gennady till he felt like a corked teakettle on the verge of boiling. "All right, all right," Daniel said, and Gennady thrust inside him and came.

Gennady stayed inside Daniel for a little while after, his breath slowing to match Daniel's, their hearts beating together. He felt hot and sleepy, and he slid out of Daniel and pulled his pants back into place and lay down on the cold concrete floor. It felt good on his sweaty skin.

Daniel slid to the floor too, and kissed Gennady's collarbone repeatedly. He ran a hand over Gennady's chest, his nipples, his ribs, his stomach, sliding into his pants to briefly cup his spent cock. "You are so good at that," Daniel murmured.

Gennady rolled over on his stomach, blushing with pleasure, pressing his hot face to the floor. He pressed his cheek against the cool concrete, and smiled at Daniel, and Daniel put his arms around him and held him close.

***

If they had still been in their twenties, probably they could have fucked all day. But as it was they didn't have the stamina, and throughout the summer and on into the fall Gennady dragged Daniel off into the woods to forage: late raspberries, blackberries, wild grapes, hickory nuts.

On that October trip, Gennady found a great haul of chanterelles. He gloated as he picked them, filling an entire basket as Daniel sat on a fallen log and watched. "Take these home to Elizabeth and fry them in butter," Gennady instructed. "They are a prince among mushrooms, my friend."

Daniel eyed the chanterelles dubiously, which Gennady found almost insulting even though he had read that all Americans were afraid of wild mushrooms. "We'll never get through this many mushrooms, Gennady," Daniel protested. "Why don't you take some?"

"No. How could I explain where I found them? And all my colleagues would want to know. They will chase this as if it is the secret for a new nuclear bomb, only even more, because from this they stand to gain personally."

Daniel's mouth curved into an almost reluctant smile. "Well, at least let's cook some for lunch, then."

"Watch how I do it so you can show Elizabeth," Gennady told him.

"Come back and show her yourself," Daniel said. "She wants you to come to dinner again."

Gennady doubted that very much, and it made him uneasy to hear Daniel say it. "Now that you know you have chanterelles on your property, you can pick them all season long, they will come up always after it rains. You can serve them at your cocktail parties, and your guests will buy a thousand pictures just so they will be invited again next year."

Daniel laughed. "Elizabeth doesn't need mushrooms for that," he said fondly.

"Of course, of course," said Gennady. "But still it's nice to have good food."

The fondness in Daniel's voice puzzled him a little. Not that Daniel should love Elizabeth – that was understandable. But that he should love her, and yet nonetheless be here with Gennady. How Elizabeth felt about it all.

Of course, she was an artist, and everyone knew that artists had unusual love lives. But nonetheless it made Gennady uneasy, and so in the woods he gathered these propitiatory offerings. Perhaps it was odd that Gennady's growing love for Daniel made him worry more about hurting Daniel's marriage, but it was so, and as he gathered the mushrooms, that fear tightened around his chest like a metal band, till it hurt to breathe.

He breathed out slowly, and imagined the Hawthornes serving these chanterelles he had found for them at their cocktail parties for years to come, long after Gennady himself had gone back to Moscow. He liked to imagine Daniel biting into a piece of toast topped with buttery mushrooms, and the taste flooding his mouth with the memory of Gennady; and he liked too this vision of their marriage continuing on, not only uninjured by his brief intrusion but in this small way enriched by it.

CHAPTER 5

In early November, Daniel went to Copley University on the outskirts of DC to give a career talk. It was crowded – a big change from even a few years ago, when lots of students wouldn't be caught dead at a talk about joining the FBI – and he spent some time afterward chatting with a young woman about the FBI's recent initiative to recruit female agents.

After she left, laden with pamphlets, a paunchy middle-aged man ambled up to the lectern. "Yes?" Daniel said with a smile, straightening his leftover pamphlets to put them into his briefcase.

"Agent Hawthorne," the man said. "You probably don't remember me…"

The pamphlets tumbled to the floor. Daniel hadn't recognized the face, but the voice he knew. "John."

"I'm sorry for thrusting myself on your notice like this," John said. "But I saw the flyers about your talk and I thought it must be you. You used to talk about joining the FBI, after all…"

Daniel was struggling to catch his breath. He felt as if a grizzly bear had sauntered up to the podium. "Excuse me," he said, and snatched up his briefcase, never mind about the pamphlets on the floor. "I'm afraid I'm late for my train…"

"I came to apologize," John said, all in a rush.

Daniel stared at him. John bent down, his knees creaking, and began to gather up the dropped pamphlets. He held them up to Daniel without getting to his feet again. "I signed up to fight in Korea because I never wanted to see you again," Daniel said, and added, brutally, "My tour of duty fucked me up less than you did."

John took the words with a bowed head. "I'm sorry."

Daniel nearly walked out. To leave John kneeling on the floor, pamphlets still in hand, apology utterly rejected: that would be a good vengeance.

But that idea was the last flare of Daniel's old anger: almost as soon as he thought it, the old rage burned away into nothing. It was all so long ago. "Of course," Daniel said, with a sigh, "I wasn't on the front lines in Korea."

John looked up. Daniel held out a hand, and helped heave the man back to his feet.

"Have a beer with me?" John said. "I'll buy."

"Yes," Daniel said, a little amazed to hear himself say it. "Why not?"

***

They went to the campus bar. It was almost empty this early in the evening, and John selected a booth at the far end of the room, the wood scarred with generations of carved initials. Daniel settled his beer carefully on a heart bearing the legend *E.L + D.G, 1953.*

It felt surreal to sit in a bar with John, as if they were old friends catching up. "How are you doing these days?" John asked, his voice falsely hearty.

"I'm good," Daniel told him. "I'm working at the FBI... Well, you probably heard all about that at my talk. And I'm married now," he added. He got out his wallet to show the photograph. "That's Elizabeth and Emily," he said, indicating his wife and daughter, who were both giggling for the camera as they posed in the dappled sunlight beneath a maple tree. "And that's David. I would have liked to get one where he's laughing too, but he's a serious little fellow. We were lucky to get the smile."

"You always had a way with the ladies," John said, and raised his eyes to Daniel, half-questioningly: *Are you happy? Or did you just get married to appease the straights?*

"Elizabeth's a painter," Daniel said. "She was one of my sister's friends, actually – Anna invited me to see one of Elizabeth's shows, practically had to drag me along, and then I met Elizabeth and... I don't really believe in love at first sight," he said. "But we went out to an all-night café after the show and we talked until dawn, and I knew by the end of the night that this was the girl I wanted to marry."

John was smiling. Daniel had forgotten – well, everything about him, really, except for that horrible last night. He had forgotten the way that John listened with his whole attention, and entered into other people's happiness as fully as if it were his own.

Daniel used to love this quality, but now it made him uneasy. "So how about you?" Daniel asked. "What have you been up to?"

"I'm a professor here. Art history," John said, "focusing on the Italian Renaissance and Italian film. We're working to start a film history department. Do you still like movies?"

"Everyone likes movies, John."

John laughed. "Fair point. The film history classes are always popular – at least at intro level. A lot of people are disappointed when they realize the class isn't just watching movies."

"I'll bet."

"We've been trying to raise money for a campus cinema," John said. "Some of the students are organizing to bring independent films to campus. French New Wave, Agnes Varda's 'Black Panthers.' Queer films. I'm also," he said, twisting his beer on its coaster, "the faculty sponsor for the Copley University Gay Club."

He slipped the last sentence in so casually that it took a moment for Daniel to parse it. "*Are* you?" Daniel said. "That's a thing that exists?"

"Do you want to see the yearbook picture?"

"An official club? In the *yearbook*?"

John got the Copley University yearbook out of his briefcase. He opened to a marked page with a photograph of a baker's dozen of students smiled at the camera, long-haired boys and short-haired girls, all touchingly, terrifyingly young. They had even listed their names under the photo.

"Are they going to be all right?" Daniel asked. "A yearbook photo is… well, that's pretty permanent."

"The world's changed a lot since we were young," John said.

"Has it?" Daniel said. He paused, reflecting. Civil Rights, women's lib. Vietnam War protests. Free love… But only for heterosexual couples. "No, it hasn't. Not about this."

"It's beginning to change," John corrected himself. "They want to be a part of it."

"That's… idealistic," Daniel said, because it seemed more polite than saying it was irresponsible of John to let these poor sweet kids announce their sexual orientations to the world (in the yearbook! With their real names!) without warning them about all the doors it would slam shut.

He checked the photo again, just in case the girl he'd spoken to that evening was in it. She'd never get into the FBI with that kind of club on her record.

Daniel's voice was cool when he spoke again. "How'd they rope you into it? Is this some form of atonement?"

"Well." John hesitated. "Self-acceptance."

"Oh." This felt incredibly obvious now that John had said it. "So you did kiss me first," Daniel blurted, and suddenly he felt angry again.

John drew away. "Yes."

"I always thought that was unfair," Daniel said. "You kissed me first, and then you smashed my face because – why exactly?"

"I felt so bad for kissing you – for wanting to kiss you…" John's face scrunched up as if in physical pain. "I'm so sorry. I can't say how sorry I am."

"I – " Daniel began, and then bit his lip. He was not going to say *I nearly shot myself*.

A painful silence ensued. Across the room, two young men set up the pool table.

"I've got a photo too," John said. "Of me with my boyfriend." His voice bobbled before the word *boyfriend*, and he finished almost apologetically, "If you'd like to see?"

"Sure."

Daniel had never before seen a happy couple photograph of two men. At first it looked very strange to him, but as he looked at it a little longer it became almost painfully touching. Daniel knew, precisely because he had no intention of doing it, the kind of bravery it would require to be so publicly out of the closet.

Daniel felt a sudden horrible urge to tell John about Gennady. *Oh, by the way, I'm seeing a Russian spy on the side. A male one. You're right, every single part of that is 100% not allowed in the FBI handbook.* Instead he said, "This is why you sponsored the club, isn't it?"

It was a vague way of putting it, but John understood. "To help these kids feel comfortable with who they are," he said.

"You've warned that things like the yearbook photo could have consequences, right? It might haunt them once they're out of school," Daniel said.

"Daniel," John said. "They already know how tough the world is out there. I'm just trying to help them suffer a little less than we did."

Daniel was so fascinated by the photograph that he actually missed that *we*. Who had taken it? It looked professionally done, like a wedding photo. Was there an underground gay photographer who took couples pictures?

Then John said, "A couple of the kids in the club are bisexual."

That was too much. "Really?" Daniel said, his voice bright and hard and quelling.

John took the hint. They talked about movies until it was time for Daniel to go.

***

"That's crazy," Gennady said. "You always say Russians are crazy, but that's *crazy*, Daniel."

They were lying on the cabin floor by the lighted wood stove. The gray November rain splashed against the windows. "That's what I thought too," Daniel began, "but…"

"What will their families think?" Gennady interrupted. "Will they pay for their sons' education if they know that it will be useless now that they have joined this club? Who will hire the boys now that they have publicly declared themselves to be deviants?"

"There were girls, too," Daniel said.

"Oh, yes! Because parents certainly approve of sexual impropriety in their daughters! I really can't believe that this man, this professor, encouraged these children in this foolishness," Gennady said. He rolled over on his stomach. "This is illegal in your country, isn't it? There are laws against public indecency, against sodomy. Why is he encouraging them to publicly declare themselves as criminals?"

"Dissidents in your country do practically the same thing," Daniel objected. "Just for free speech instead of free love."

"Yes, and the rest of us know that they're *crazy*," Gennady returned. "Just live your life quietly and try to get as much happiness out of it as you can. If you rock the boat, it will sink."

Daniel didn't answer. He had shared Gennady's reservations, after all, but he had been so won over by John's description of the club, and Gennady's response left him deflated and confused.

"Perhaps it is different in your country," Gennady mused. "There is a tradition of ordinary people winning rights for themselves, Civil Rights and women's liberation. In my country, there is a tradition of people sticking their heads up and getting them cut off." Daniel winced. "Even if the Party decided to reform, after all, this will only last until the next wave of hardliners take over. Then it will be taken away."

"Doesn't that bother you?"

Gennady shrugged. "There's nothing I can do about it."

Daniel rolled over on his stomach too. "You could defect," he said.

"This again." Gennady sighed. "No, I couldn't do this. If one person leaves, the rest of the family suffers for it. They've all suffered enough already. And anyway," he added, "that's not doing anything about it. Nothing will change for anyone else if I defect. Not for the better, anyway."

CHAPTER 6

Gennady had no intention of telling Daniel about it, but Daniel was not the first to speak to Gennady of defection this trip.

A few weeks before, fairly early in the morning, Gennady woke at the sound of a knock on his door. He was still blinking sleep from his eyes when he opened it, and then the sight on his doorstep knocked sleep out of his mind, because there was Maksym Sergeyevich Bondar. Sergeyich.

"Maksym!" said Gennady, because Sergeyich seemed too informal when they had not seen each other for fifteen years.

A good Soviet citizen ought to slam the door in a defector's face, perhaps even inform the embassy of his whereabouts. Gennady had no intention of doing the second, hesitated a moment on the cusp of doing the first, then gave Sergeyich a good Russian bear hug and kissed both his cheeks.

"Let's go out for coffee," Gennady said. He did not think his apartment was bugged, but it was better to be safe. "A good American breakfast. Yes?"

They ended up at a café a couple of blocks from Gennady's apartment. Sergeyich ordered a massive meal, of course: bacon, sausage, orange juice, a fruit cup, three blueberry buttermilk pancakes swimming in maple syrup, and a "granola parfait," although neither of them were sure what that could be. "I'll have one too," Gennady decided.

"Really, is that all you're having for breakfast, Gosha? The Americans are paying, so you might as well get more."

"Do they think they can buy me with breakfast food?"

"Well, hope springs eternal – " this phrase Sergeyich said in English, and Gennady laughed, because his accent was nearly as bad as ever. "Yes, I know," Sergeyich said, with a sigh. "But eat more, Gennady, eat more. You're too thin."

So Gennady ordered bacon and eggs and a cinnamon roll, and teased Sergeyich, "Perhaps this will make me as fat as you."

Sergeyich smiled and patted his belly. "My wife feeds me well."

"Ah! So you convinced some poor girl to marry you?"

"Yes, yes! An American girl. Polish heritage," Sergeyich added, "so she cooks well."

There was a slight hesitancy in his voice as he spoke Russian, as if he did not speak it often. Probably the American government had settled him somewhere far away from other Russians. Still, Sergeyich looked happy. His face retained its natural hollowness, but it no longer gave him the look of a saint suffering in an icon, and he smiled easily, just like an American.

But of course, the Americans must have asked him to look happy when they sent him here.

The food arrived. The parfaits came in tall glasses, layers of granola and yogurt and those out-of-season American strawberries that had no taste. Gennady tried one and made a face and pushed it aside in favor of the cinnamon roll.

They did not speak about why Sergeyich had come until they were done eating. Then Gennady said, "You cannot imagine the turmoil on the dock when you did not show up."

"Oh, I think I can," Sergeyich returned, with relish. "Arkady storming up and down, red as a tomato, tearing at his hair? Perhaps in actual fact ripping some of it out of his head? I have seen him do that – before your time, I think."

"Yes, yes, all of that," said Gennady, although with considerably less relish. It might be a pleasant scene to imagine, but it had not been pleasant when Arkady stormed across the dock, his lips flecked with spit, and screamed in Gennady's face, "Bondar's your friend! Where is he, that son of a whore?"

The waitress refilled Gennady's coffee cup (wonderful American service: he hadn't even asked). Gennady took a sip of the fresh hot coffee. "He's dead now," he told Sergeyich. "Heart attack."

"He had a heart?"

"I know. A surprise for everyone," Gennady said, and rolled his shoulders and sat back in the booth. "So? Is that why you defected? To make Arkady angry? They demoted him, you know."

"Oh, well! I'm glad to hear that. But no, that wasn't my plan: as usual I was thinking of myself." Sergeyich spread his hands. "Look around you, Gosha! The cars, the clothes, the girls!"

"There are girls in Russia."

"But do they swoon over a Russian accent? No. Everyone has a Russian accent there. Here, though..." Sergeyich bunched his fingertips and kissed them.

Gennady couldn't help laughing. He slung an arm along the back of the booth. "I'm married."

"Well, so, she can stay here too," Sergeyich said. "She probably wants to already. The supermarkets! The children in American schools! Suggest it to her and see if she doesn't kiss your hands."

Gennady's arm slipped back down to his lap. "No, she stayed in Moscow. She didn't want to come."

"Oh." Sergeyich paused. "Well, so. If you defect she'll divorce you, and then you can marry an American girl."

"Your Polish-American girl has a sister?" Gennady teased. "I will marry her, live right down the street, in the evenings we will all get together and play Durak?"

"Wouldn't that be the life?" For a moment Sergeyich looked wistful. "No, of course, we couldn't see each other. All defectors have to go into witness protection." *Witness protection* he also said in English.

"And never see my family again? My Alla, little Dasha?" Dasha was his cousin Oksana's daughter, not Gennady's, but in his heart she was almost his own. "No, no. Listen, Sergeyich, I'm glad to have seen you, and it seems that this life agrees with you, but it's not for me. I hope the Americans don't begrudge you the cost of the cinnamon roll when you tell them that."

Sergeyich shrugged and smiled. "Oh well," he said. "It was worth a try, no?"

HONEYTRAP

***

In mid-December, the winter cold chased Daniel and Gennady out of the dacha. They went one last time to close it up for the winter: close the shutters, check the cupboards, pack the soft furnishings and take them into town until spring came again.

"You seem quiet," Daniel observed. They were upstairs, both of them in their coats because of the cold. They folded away the two camp cots, and now they were folding up the down comforter on the double bed.

"It's *toska*," Gennady told him. "Did the Polyakovs teach you this word?"

"They used it when they talked about Piter," Daniel said. "Old St. Petersburg, as it was before the Revolution. I thought it meant something like homesickness?"

"Yes – no. Not exactly. If you can be homesick for a home that doesn't exist, that has never existed and could not exist... *Toska* is a little like that."

Daniel smiled, one of those funny American smiles that expressed sadness. "Are you going to miss this place?" he asked. "We'll open it up again in April. March if we're lucky."

"Only three months." A yawning pit in time. They finished folding the comforter, and began to fold the quilt, and Gennady said, "It's not only that. Alla had said she might visit this winter, and of course I always knew this was unlikely, but now it is certain that she is not going to come..."

He hadn't meant to tell Daniel. It seemed impolite to talk about his wife to his lover, unfair to both of them. But there was no one else to tell, and when Daniel said, "I'm sorry. That must be so disappointing," his sympathy undid Gennady, and Gennady sat on the edge of the bed and pressed his hands to his face.

Daniel came and sat beside him and put an arm around his shoulders.

"We're going to get divorced," Gennady said. "Which I already knew, I already told you, but I suppose in my heart I still hoped we would reconcile. I hoped," Gennady confessed, and then shook his head, "No, I didn't hope, I knew this wouldn't happen, but I dreamed that she would come to the United States and find that she liked it and stay, and our marriage would continue the way we both dreamed it would, back in the beginning."

Daniel's face took on that funny smile again. "And how did I fit in this plan?"

"Well, you didn't, but then it wasn't a plan. Even if she had come to visit, she would not have stayed. It was a daydream," Gennady said, "an impossible daydream..." He felt he had erred in telling Daniel. Naturally it must be unpleasant to Daniel to hear about a vision of Gennady's life in which he played no part. "I have such daydreams about you too," he said, and swung his foot sideways to nudge Daniel's foot.

Daniel smiled. "Oh yeah?"

"Yes." Gennady smiled down at his hands. "We come here to this cabin and stay for a week, a month, forever, in endless summer, and the berries are always ripe and the good mushrooms always growing, and the sunsets linger on for hours. But of course," he added, because he didn't want Daniel to misunderstand him, "this also is a daydream that wouldn't be so pleasant if it came true. It would get boring to be a hermit and never go anywhere. You would miss your wife and children. Murderers would roam free without Special Agent Daniel Hawthorne to catch them."

The last sentence made Daniel laugh. He leaned back on the bed, propped on his elbows, his eyes dreamy. "It would have been nice, though," he said. "To have a week."

"But impossible," Gennady reminded him. He stood up. Daniel caught hold of his hand and tried to pull him on the bed, but Gennady won the tug of war and pulled Daniel to his feet, instead. "We should finish packing up the house."

They folded up the quilt and the sheets and carried it all downstairs. But they didn't leave yet: the wood stove had finally warmed the living room, and so they spread the down comforter on the floor and took off their coats and lay on their stomachs in front of the fire.

Gennady still felt a little uncomfortable, in spirit rather than body. "You understand," he told Daniel, "what I told you about Alla, this is not a reflection about my feelings about you. I love her, but of course I love you too..."

A smile lit Daniel's face. "Do you love me?"

"Of course," Gennady said, a little irritably. "Why else would

I take such risks to see you?"

"It's nice to hear you say it," Daniel said. He leaned over and kissed the top of Gennady's head. "I love you too."

Gennady blushed like a schoolboy and hid his face in his folded arms.

The fire crackled. Daniel ran his hand down Gennady's spine, to the small of his back, and insinuated his hand beneath the layers of sweater, and shirt, and undershirt. A little cold air seeped in with his warm hand, and the contrast made Gennady shiver.

"What are we going to do until March?" Daniel murmured.

Gennady did not feel like thinking about that now. He rolled over onto his back, and tugged his layers of shirts back into place, and pulled Daniel's arm around him. "We'll still have lunches."

"That's not the same."

Well, it wasn't, but Gennady had no intention of suggesting a sordid motel rendezvous. That *might* make some spy agency sit up and pay attention. It was too bad Daniel couldn't come to Gennady's apartment... Gennady thought with horror of the unwashed sheets on his bed and the mildew on the shower curtain and the dishes piling up in his sink, and mentally cleared them all away... But it didn't matter anyway. Daniel couldn't come; Gennady lived too close to his colleagues, someone might notice.

"You could come to my house," Daniel said.

"Daniel," Gennady scolded.

"Not for sex, idiot," Daniel said, and his ears turned red. "Just... I like having you around."

Gennady was almost painfully touched. But. "Will your wife like having me around?"

"Didn't she like you when you met?"

"That was different," Gennady protested. True, she had sent them up to the dacha with a picnic basket, and after all she *was* an artist, and French too, but – well, it was different to send someone to a dacha than to have that person right under her nose.

"I wish I could ask you to come to Christmas," Daniel said, "but we'll be celebrating with Elizabeth's family, and it would be hard to explain..."

"No, no," Gennady said. He could hardly inflict himself on

Elizabeth at Christmas. "We don't celebrate Christmas anyway." He snuggled into the comforter. "We had a fine Christmas at your mother's house," he mused, "all those years ago. How is she, your mother?"

Daniel hesitated just a moment. "She died a few years ago. A car accident..."

Gennady had only met Mrs. Hawthorne the one time, for just a few days, and yet the words struck him as though he had lost a dear old friend. "I'm sorry," he said. "She was a wonderful woman."

"Yes, she was," Daniel said, and they lay for a minute in sorrow. The fire crackled in the stove.

At length Gennady asked, "And your sister? Is she well?"

"Oh, yes. Anna's great. She and Joseph divorced... Christ, it must be nearly fifteen years ago now. She showed up for Christmas – this was the year after you visited us – and she told us, 'My Christmas present to myself was a divorce.'"

Gennady laughed.

Daniel grinned at him. "She remarried. Anna and Nate – that's her husband's name, Nate – they write travel articles together. Anna does the photography and Nate writes the articles to go with her photos."

Gennady felt a tiny lance of envy in his heart. This sounded like an ideal life: to make your living traveling with someone you loved. "Lucky them," he said lightly.

"Yes," Daniel said. "It all worked out well in the end." He glanced over at Gennady. "But it was pretty hard for her for a while. I think the end of a marriage is always hard."

Gennady found the compassion in his face painful. He rolled over on his stomach again. "Do you think I did the wrong thing in coming to the United States?" Gennady asked.

Daniel looked taken aback. "I'm probably the wrong person to ask. I'm too glad that you're here to think it was wrong for you to come."

Gennady sighed. He took up a stick from the wood box and poked at the fire. A log collapsed in a shower of sparks. "Pretend I was sent somewhere else then, Australia perhaps. I will not say that your presence was not an extra incentive to take this assignment, but it was not the deciding factor, if they had assigned me to go to the land of kangaroos I still would have gone."

"What did your family think about it?" Daniel asked. "Your Aunt Lilya and..." He paused. "The others," he added apologetically, as if he should have remembered their names, although Gennady had not ever talked about them much with Daniel.

Gennady poked at the fire some more. "Aunt Lilya said that of course I must go where the Soviet Union sends me. But of course she would say that: she flew fighter planes during the war." Gennady plucked at a bit of fluff on the comforter. "And Oksana said that I have always wanted to travel, ever since I was seven years old and we played Three Musketeers and I said someday I would go to Paris. If I did not go I would resent Alla for keeping me, and Alla would resent that resentment, and it would ruin our marriage more surely than if I went, so I might as well go."

"Of course I'm biased," Daniel said, "but I think that's wise." Gennady sighed, and Daniel added, "I think that there are some things you can't sacrifice for another person, even if you want to, no matter how much you love them. Like Anna trying to set aside her love of art to be the model wife that Joseph wanted."

Gennady did not think this was exactly parallel. Alla was unhappy, and felt bad for wanting him to stay just as much as he felt bad for leaving. But in the end it did not matter that they felt bad, they both still wanted what they wanted.

Suddenly he did not want to talk about it anymore. It was like Tyutchev said, a thought once uttered is untrue. To say anything, to try to reduce this complexity of feelings to words, inevitably simplified it so much that it became almost a lie.

Daniel kissed the side of Gennady's head. "I'm glad you're here," he said again.

Which did not really solve anything. But still it was pleasant to hear.

CHAPTER 7

It was nearly the end of January before Gennady actually came to Daniel's house. Daniel was lying on a couch in the conversation pit, trying to read but really checking his watch every other minute or so.

Not that Gennady was late. Daniel was just impatient.

In fact Gennady arrived about five minutes early. He looked like an Abominable Snowman, his scarf and his hat both encrusted with snow, and Daniel laughed at him. "I could have picked you up at the station."

Gennady shook his head. He was stomping the snow off his boots and unwrapping his scarf at the same time, and when cold air touched his face, he began to cough thickly.

Daniel shut the door hastily to keep out the cold air. "Are you sick, Gennady?"

Gennady waved a deprecating hand. "A cold, it's nothing."

"And you walked all the way from the station! You shouldn't have come."

"I might infect the children," Gennady agreed, and made as if to wrap his scarf up again. "I'll go."

"No, no! I didn't mean it that way. It's just the walk from the station in this cold... I really could have picked you up, you know, you could have called me from the pay phone."

Gennady sat heavily to take off his boots. "I don't know your number."

"It's in the phone book. There ought to be one in the phone booth."

"The phone book?"

"Don't you have phone books in Moscow?"

"They are always out of date." Gennady hung his coat over the coat rack.

"Well, let me write my number down for you." Daniel checked his pockets for a pen, and then Gennady started to cough again, deep frightening chest coughs. "Oh, Christ. No, let's get you warm first. C'mon, I've got the fire going in the conversation pit."

"It's ridiculous that you have a pit in your house."

"It absolutely is. Emily knocked out two of her baby teeth falling over the side when she was three. Bounced off the couch and knocked into the coffee table... Here, take this afghan. There. Elizabeth's mother crochets them. How long have you been like this?"

The purple afghan rose as Gennady shrugged. "Since yesterday."

"You should have let me know."

"And what? You will show up at my office with soup?" Gennady scoffed.

This was impossible on so many levels that Daniel could only smile weakly in reply. He checked Gennady's forehead for a fever, but his skin still felt chilly from his long walk in the cold. "Stay here for a few days," Daniel urged.

"Impossible." Another series of deep chest coughs.

Daniel stroked Gennady's hair. "It's not impossible. We'll put you up in the guest room."

But Gennady shook Daniel's hand away. "And what will I say when I call into work? 'I'm ill, but don't come check on me, I am staying at my American friend's house?'"

"Well..." Daniel's voice dwindled. A terrible feeling of helplessness clawed at his throat.

Gennady patted his hand. "It's okay, Daniil."

"I'm going to have to send you back into the cold to die of pneumonia, and that's okay?"

"I don't have pneumonia. And, after all, there are a few hours before I have to go anywhere. Stop worrying and get me a cup of tea."

"We've only got chamomile."

"Chamo..." The unfamiliar word defeated him. "Yes, fine. As long as it's hot."

Daniel kissed his cold cheek and went to brew the tea.

When Daniel returned with a steaming mug, he found that Gennady had drawn another afghan around him, this one vibrant green. Daniel sat down beside him as he sipped, and touched his fingers to Gennady's neck to see if he could get a better read on his temperature now. He felt warm, but not fever-hot.

"At least stay the night," Daniel coaxed.

"I don't want to infect you, my friend. And what would be the point? You can't stay with me anyway."

"Elizabeth won't mind," Daniel insisted.

Gennady was incredulous. "You're going to stay with me in your guest room? With your children here?"

This was a compelling point. Certainly Daniel would have balked if Elizabeth had wanted Ronald Benson to spend a night under their roof.

"I could sit up with you," Daniel suggested at length. "We could put sheets on this sofa here and I could sit up in one of the chairs..."

"Oh, Daniel." Gennady started to laugh, and the laughter turned into more coughing. "I'm not dying. You always think I'm dying," he complained, "and I have never once been dying in all the time you've known me."

"It's true," Daniel admitted. "It's just you, too. I don't worry nearly as much about anyone else that I know dying. But then," he mused, "you're the only one who got stabbed on my watch. And the only one who lives in a totalitarian dictatorship."

Gennady sighed. "I do not."

"Gennady."

"Stalin is dead. We haven't had totalitarianism since Stalin died." He began to cough again, wretchedly, and when the coughing fit was over Daniel held out his arms to him, and Gennady burrowed in against Daniel's sweater. "Your family won't walk in?"

"Elizabeth's gone out with her camera in search of inspiration. She loves snow scenes. And the kids are sledding over at Slater Hill. Emily's in seventh heaven because she got to go along with the big kids."

He could feel Gennady smiling against his chest. "And the big kids? They are glad to have a tagalong?"

"I wouldn't say *glad,* but David's tolerating it, at least. He's much more patient with Emily than I was with Anna at that age."

"Mmm. Yes, my cousin Oksana and I used to fight like – what is the American expression?"

"Cats and dogs?"

"Yes." Gennady yawned. "During the war Oksana lived with us and she was a little hellion. I suppose she missed her mother." A cough, softer this time. "Sometimes Oksana's little daughter Dasha stays with Alla and me. She sings all day until we all want earplugs, but we love her very much."

Daniel smiled down at him, and then kissed the top of his head. Gennady mumbled something that might have been Russian but might equally have been the unintelligible gibberish of sleepy protest.

"Daniil," Gennady mumbled.

"Hmm?"

Gennady resettled himself against Daniel's chest. Daniel stroked his hair, and smiled as Gennady's breath evened out, and Gennady fell asleep in his arms. For once in his life he might get to hold Gennady as long as he wanted.

In between the warmth of the fire and Gennady and the afghans, Daniel fell into a doze too, and woke only at the sound of the back door opening.

It was Elizabeth; Daniel recognized her footsteps. He was still blinking sleep out of his eyes when she came into the living room, extremely pretty with her hair still flecked with snow and her cheeks flushed from her walk.

She paused when she saw Gennady burrowed against Daniel's chest. She smiled, raising an inquiring eyebrow at Daniel, and Daniel nodded and touched his finger to his lips, *shhhh.* Elizabeth slipped back into the kitchen.

Daniel gave Gennady a little shake. Gennady woke and looked around with confused eyes. "Gennady," Daniel said. Gennady's eyes fastened on Daniel, and Daniel smiled. "Elizabeth's here."

Gennady blanched and propelled himself out of Daniel's arms. "I should go."

"Gennady. It's so cold. You should stay here and rest."

"It's disrespectful," Gennady insisted hoarsely. He tried to rise, but fell to the couch when Daniel tugged the afghan.

"Gennady, please. Elizabeth's been looking forward to your visit, so just stick around for a little while, okay? If you still want to leave later, I'll drive you to your apartment."

"To the station. You mustn't be seen at my apartment."

"*Christ!* Fine. I'll drive you to the station and you can infect all the other passengers. Happy? Just give it a few minutes, okay? Elizabeth was planning to make hot chocolate, and she's going to be so disappointed if you're not here to have some."

Gennady looked incredulous, but he didn't have time to protest, because at that moment Elizabeth appeared from the kitchen, balancing a tray on one hand as she came down the two steps into the conversation pit.

"These servings are small, but they've very rich," Elizabeth said, smiling at Gennady as she slid the tray onto the coffee table. "I make my hot chocolate just the way my mother did. Chopped chocolate melted directly into the milk... How much whipped cream would you like?"

Gennady looked at her, mute and miserable. Daniel told Elizabeth, "Emily's going to be devastated if she finds out we had hot chocolate without her."

"Oh, I'll make some when they get back from sledding. The whipped cream would go to waste otherwise, anyway, the recipe makes so much..." Elizabeth dolloped whipped cream on Daniel's hot chocolate, and also her own. "Gennady?" she said kindly.

"Yes, whipped cream, please," Gennady managed.

His embarrassment filled the room like a fog. Daniel wanted to put an arm around him, but he suspected that would drive Gennady right out of the house, so instead he cleared his throat and said, "The kids are in for a rude awakening when they figure out the rest of America makes hot chocolate using a powdered mix."

"Oh, I'm pretty sure they've already been awakened. Mrs. Hancock brought along a Thermos last time the kids went sledding, and David told her that was *not* hot chocolate..." Elizabeth said it in such a perfect imitation of David's very definite voice that Daniel had to laugh. "Mrs. Hancock was taken aback. I was a little surprised that she offered to take the children sledding again, honestly."

Her eyes were on Gennady, who hunched under the afghans, looking as if he wanted to shrink away into nothing. Elizabeth glanced over at Daniel, and Daniel spread his hands in a small gesture of bafflement.

Elizabeth set aside her hot chocolate and came to sit on the hearth beside Gennady. "Is there anything I can do to make you more comfortable?" she asked. "I think maybe you're feeling guilty, and you have nothing to feel guilty about, you know. I know about you and Daniel, and I don't mind a bit."

Gennady stared at her as if she were speaking Martian. "I know that artists have bohemian views about these things," he said, "and the French too. But still I think it is not expected in France that the wife should pour hot chocolate for the mistress and make polite small talk…"

"Did you think I was only putting up with you because I could pretend you didn't exist?" Elizabeth asked. Gennady opened his mouth, and then closed it again, and coughed softly. "We all had a wonderful time at dinner last summer, didn't we?" Elizabeth added.

"Daniel and I weren't fucking yet."

Daniel winced at this bluntness. Gennady himself blushed, and even Elizabeth looked a little taken aback.

Then she put a hand on Gennady's arm. "Listen," she said. "I appreciate that you're concerned about my feelings. But please believe me when I say that I'm not jealous. I think," she said, and paused, "I think that people just have different natural levels of jealousy, and mine happen to be pretty low. Of course," she said, and suddenly her brow creased, "I understand that a lot of people aren't like this. Maybe you've only been able to put up with me because you could pretend *I* don't exist?"

"No!" Gennady protested, his voice so vehement that it set off a series of coughs. He soothed his throat with a sip of hot chocolate, and said, "No, of course not. Daniel, you have brought her the things, the mushrooms and berries and…"

"Yes, of course," Daniel said.

"Those mushrooms were the talk of our last cocktail party," Elizabeth added.

Gennady nodded fervently. "Yes, they're very fine, a gold

mine. It was a gift – all these things were gifts for you. I can see that you and Daniel are so happy together, and a happy marriage is a beautiful thing, and I have worried so much about damaging that."

Elizabeth looked chagrined. "Maybe we should have talked about things last summer instead of proceeding on an unspoken understanding."

"No; how would that help? The picnic basket spoke well enough. It's just that this was six months ago, your feelings might have changed in this time."

"That's why I kept asking you to come to our house again," Daniel told him. "So you could see that everything really was all right."

"I thought perhaps... American courtesy," Gennady said, with a vague sketchy wave of his hand. "You make invitations you don't mean."

"Well, it's true, Americans do," Elizabeth admitted. "But this is a real invitation. We had such a pleasant evening last time that you came to dinner."

Gennady managed a smile. "Of course it's my pleasure to come to your dinners," he told Elizabeth. "You are a wonderful cook."

"Oh, well, that's my French mother. It certainly didn't come from the American side."

"Hey!" Daniel protested. Both Gennady and Elizabeth laughed, and then looked at each other and laughed some more.

"Really, it's been very selfish of Daniel to keep you all to himself," Elizabeth said.

"Hey!" Daniel protested again, but it was entirely pro forma: really he was pleased.

Gennady's laughter turned into coughs. Elizabeth rose from the hearth and put a hand briefly on his shoulder. "Drink your hot chocolate," Elizabeth told him. "It will coat your throat. Then you'd better try to rest. Daniel, you'll look after him? I want to get some work done on that spider web painting before the kids get home."

"Yes, of course," Daniel said.

She left. For a while Daniel and Gennady remained at opposite ends of the couch, sipping their hot chocolate. At last Daniel finished his cup, and set it back on the tray, and scooted down the couch to put an arm around Gennady. "Did you think I was lying to you when I said it was all right?"

"No, I knew you believed it. But of course that does not mean it is the truth."

Daniel leaned his cheek against Gennady's hair. "But you believe me now?"

"No," Gennady said. He drew the green afghan around him. "I believe Elizabeth."

"Yes," Daniel agreed, after a moment's thought. "I suppose that's wise."

CHAPTER 8

They moved from the conversation pit in the living room to the den, a little room upstairs with a door that shut. Gennady shuddered at his own carelessness in falling asleep in Daniel's arms in that living room with a whole wall of windows. "You can't see into the conversation pit through the windows," Daniel pointed out.

"Yes, well, so." Gennady rubbed his cheek against Daniel's scratchy sweater and breathed in the warm woolen scent. He coughed again and said, "I'm sorry," because that was less embarrassing than saying, *thank you*.

"Don't worry about it. You know it's the dream of my life to hold you for hours."

Gennady's laugh very quickly turned into another coughing fit.

"I mean it, you know," Daniel said. His chest rumbled under Gennady's cheek. Gennady turned his face against Daniel's chest, and Daniel kissed his hair.

Daniel stayed for a couple of hours, until the children arrived back from their sledding party. Then he plumped up some pillows and tucked Gennady in firmly under yet another one of those crocheted blankets, and Gennady fell asleep again.

He woke up to see a large pair of eyes peering at him, perhaps half a foot from his face.

When Gennady sat up, the eyes moved respectfully away. They were attached, he saw, to a little blonde girl, dressed in corduroy pants and a sweater, who stood with her hands clasped behind her back. This must be Daniel's daughter Emily.

"Hello," she said. "Are you one of Mommy's friends?"

"No." Gennady's throat was clogged with phlegm. He cleared it. "One of your father's friends."

"Oh." She sounded surprised, then shrugged, and smiled winsomely up at him. "We can play checkers if you want."

He almost laughed. "Yes, all right," he said, and she was off like a shot.

Gennady had not been telling the truth exactly when he told Daniel that Alla didn't want children. Alla loved children, and an evening at her brother's apartment toting around her little niece always brought back to her some of the sparkle and joy that had left her in Zurich.

After one such evening, as Gennady and Alla walked home late in the frosty night, Alla began to cry. She cried so hard that they had to stop walking and sat on a bench in the cold, while Gennady held both her hands.

When it seemed that she might be able to talk, Gennady squeezed her hands and said, "What is it, Alla?"

"I want to have children," she gasped out.

"Well, after all, why not?" Gennady said, relieved almost, because he was fond of children, and this at least was a wish that could come true.

But Alla shook her head and kept on crying, until finally she managed to gasp out, "I don't want to have children *here*."

Here. In Moscow, in Soviet Russia.

Perhaps she had cherished dreams that they might defect and have their children elsewhere, and those dreams had died when she had realized that she could not cope with the difficulties of being a stranger in a strange land.

He put an arm around her shoulders and they sat together until she calmed down, or perhaps simply grew too cold to cry; and then they walked home in the icy Moscow night.

But if that conversation had ended differently, Gennady might have had a little daughter about Emily's age. Dark-haired instead of blonde, probably (Alla was dark; her mother was Armenian), but like Emily, she might have set up a checkerboard with her tongue poking out of her mouth in concentration, and played her checkers with exactly that intensity of interest. Perhaps her eyes too would have filled with tears when she lost the game; perhaps she also would have rubbed her nose and given a big sniff and managed to say, "Do you know how to play fox and geese?"

"No."

Emily cheered up instantly. "Well, I'll show you then."

They were on their second game when Daniel poked his head around the open door. "Emily! Didn't I tell you not to wake Gennady up?"

"He woke up on his own, Daddy," Emily protested.

"Yes," Gennady confirmed. "Emily has been entertaining me. She taught me to play fox and geese."

"Of course she has." Daniel looked fond and exasperated. "Well, you'll have to finish the game later, Em. Your mother wants you to set the table."

Emily got up with a great show of reluctance and sidled toward the door. She paused by her father and tugged his hand. "Is he going to stay for dinner?" she asked her father, in a stage whisper that could have carried to the back of a theater.

Daniel lifted his eyebrows at Gennady, echoing the question.

"Yes, *myshka*," Gennady told Emily. "I am staying for dinner. Now go. Your mother is waiting for you."

***

Gennady returned the next weekend. It was careless to go two weekends in a row, but he was still sick and miserable, and the lure of having someone to fuss over him proved irresistible.

It was this desire that prompted him to walk from the station to the house, and sure enough, Daniel scolded him for it. "Gennady! Did you walk all the way here again?"

"No, I rode a goose like Nils Holgersson."

Gennady said this so seriously that Daniel looked at him for a moment in half-belief before he laughed. "Well, your sense of humor is recovering at least," Daniel said. "Come in. I'm afraid the house is a mess; we had a cocktail party yesterday, and by the time the guests left we were too tired to clean up…"

Gennady was taking off his boots, but now he paused.

"Perhaps I should not have come?"

"No, no!" Daniel said. "I'm so glad you came, Gennady. I worried about you all week."

This seemed excessive for what was after all just a cold, but Gennady's heart warmed anyway. "If I nap in the den, perhaps that will keep me out of the way."

"You're not *in* the way," Daniel said. "But yes, the den would be a quiet place to nap."

Daniel sat on the couch in the den with him. He kept reaching down and resting his hand on Gennady's forehead as if checking for a fever, and then smoothing his hand back through Gennady's hair before he took up his pen again and began scratching away on whatever he was working on – "Taxes," he muttered, when Gennady asked.

Gennady fell asleep eventually. Daniel must have slipped out of the room, because when Gennady woke he was alone, and the air smelled like vanilla and chocolate.

He followed the smell down the stairs into the kitchen. Daniel's children sat the kitchen table, eating cookies with tall glasses of milk. When Emily saw him, she catapulted herself from her chair and ran over to him, grabbing his hand. "No one said you were *here*," she cried, outraged.

"I'm sorry, *myshka*. I've been sleeping."

She looked up at him, still clutching his hand. "Are you still sick?"

"Yes."

She pressed both her small hands on either side of his large one, and looked intensely up into his face. "What are you doing?" he asked.

"Making you better," she said, and he couldn't help smiling.

"I think it's working, *myshka*. Keep doing it."

CHAPTER 9

After Gennady's illness, he began to come to the house more often. Daniel would have had him down every weekend, but Gennady refused: "The neighbors will talk."

"I don't think they're that interested in what we do," Daniel told him.

"People love to talk about each other, my friend. It is the favorite human pastime. And, after all, you don't know which one of them might be talking to the FBI."

"The FBI doesn't have a network of informants spying on its agents," Daniel protested.

Gennady shook his head like he couldn't be bothered to argue any further. But he must have believed Daniel at least somewhat, because he continued to visit once or twice a month, generally with a bakery box in tow: a cake or a dozen doughnuts or half a dozen éclairs, which delighted Emily so much that afterward he always brought an éclair just for her.

"You don't have to play checkers with her every time you visit," Daniel told Gennady one evening. It had been a soggy March day, and Emily – cooped up inside by the cold rain – had made a bit of a pest of herself.

But now Emily and David were in bed and Gennady lay on the couch in Daniel's den, with his head in Daniel's lap, and Daniel was stroking Gennady's hair and squashing his desire to ask Gennady to spend the night.

"No, I don't mind," Gennady said. "And, after all, perhaps it will give you and Elizabeth a break from endless checkers."

"As if! The moment you're out of the house, she starts carrying around the checkerboard trying to get someone to play with her for practice. She's determined to beat you fair and square someday."

Gennady smiled. "She will," he said. "Someday. She's a clever child."

The fondness in his face struck Daniel. He rested a hand against Gennady's cheek. "Maybe it's not such a bad thing if you and Alla get divorced," Daniel said. "You could marry again. Find a woman who wants children."

"No, I'm too old."

"You're forty, Gennady, not decrepit."

But Gennady was shaking his head. "No, no, I'm too old," he said again. "We age faster in Russia than you do in the States." He pulled Daniel down and kissed him, and swung his legs off the couch to stand up. "I need to get going. The last subway leaves soon."

And he kissed Daniel again, and wouldn't stay any longer.

There were only a few stolen kisses that winter. "I don't want your children to see anything, I don't want them to have to keep our secrets," Gennady said, adamant. "Children should be carefree, they shouldn't have to worry about grown-up things," and Daniel thought about Gennady's childhood, when the Germans were dropping bombs on Moscow and Stalin was tossing people in jail for telling jokes, and agreed.

Daniel loved having Gennady in the house. He loved to see him sitting at the kitchen table in the evening, with the snow falling past the windows – it could not really have snowed that much that year, but that was how Daniel always remembered it later – chatting with Elizabeth over coffee while Daniel did the dishes. Once the dishes were done Daniel joined them, dropping a kiss on Elizabeth's head as he passed her chair.

He would have liked to kiss Gennady too, and perhaps it was because this scene was otherwise so peaceful and contented that this longing sometimes caused him physical pain, a literal ache in his heart. The quiet evenings at the kitchen table seemed like a glimpse of an alternate reality where Gennady lived right down the street and could drop by every evening, and it would be all right if Daniel kissed him right in front of the open curtains where anyone could see.

In the real world, all of this was impossible, and Daniel contented himself with a brief hand on Gennady's shoulder before he took his own chair, and they all talked until Gennady had to leave to catch the last train home.

"It's too bad he can't stay the night," Elizabeth said one evening. It was an unseasonably warm late March, and they had the kitchen window open.

"I wish he could stay," Daniel agreed. He was silent a moment, staring out the window into the darkness. "I wish," he began, and then he stood and closed the window, not that anyone would be standing outside listening – but just in case. "I wish he would defect and stay here. But he'll never defect, he's loyal to the USSR, and it drives me crazy that he's so loyal to a country that would toss him in the gulag on suspicion of espionage if they found out he was eating dinner at an FBI agent's house."

"The FBI would fire you if they knew you were sleeping with Gennady," Elizabeth pointed out. "And not just because he's a Soviet. They'd fire you just the same if you were sleeping with an American man."

"Yes. But there isn't a country on earth where that wouldn't be true."

This bleak truth silenced them both. Daniel gathered up Gennady's abandoned coffee cup and set it on the drain board. Elizabeth stood with a sigh. "How long will he be in the US?" she asked.

"About another year, I think. Give or take."

"Well then," she said, and kissed the side of his head. "*Carpe annum.*"

***

It was a beautiful spring.

Daniel had expected that once it was warm enough to go to the cabin again, Gennady would never come to Daniel's house anymore. In one sense, of course, Daniel had looked forward to going back to the cabin, but in another sense he was sorry. He liked to see Gennady bending seriously over a checkerboard with

Emily, or helping Elizabeth maneuver a new big painting into the living room, and then spending the next hour changing all the paintings around so that the light would show each to the best advantage. He hated to lose this feeling that Gennady was one of the family.

But, as it turned out, he didn't. Oh, they did start going up to the cabin again, but Elizabeth pressed Gennady so warmly to keep coming round for dinner (enthusiastically seconded by Emily, who had recently augmented her passion for checkers with an interest in cards) that Gennady came to the house almost every other week.

Easter fell in mid-April that year – American Easter, anyway; the Russian Easter was later, and so Gennady was free to come to Daniel's house on Easter Sunday. "My sister Anna will be there," Daniel warned him. "And her husband Nate."

"The travel writer?"

"Yes. He's sort of quiet, but he's a great guy. And you've met Anna before; you liked her," Daniel added, because he really wanted Gennady to come. It pained him that Gennady had no public presence in his life, not even as much as Ronald had in Elizabeth's. Of course most people didn't realize the true nature of Ronald and Elizabeth's relationship, but at least he could come to their cocktail parties, everyone knew they were friends.

Daniel could hardly invite a Soviet agent to a cocktail party.

He expected Gennady to say no to Easter, too. But Gennady smiled suddenly, looking almost surprised, and he said, "Okay. Why not?"

When Gennady arrived for Easter, Anna and Elizabeth were already deep in the process of decorating eggs. (Anna's husband Nate, fulfilling his part of Easter tradition, had taken Emily and David to the park.)

"Do you remember Gennady?" Daniel asked Anna. "He came to Christmas one year…"

"Of course!" Anna said. "The year before Joseph and I divorced."

Gennady smiled at her. "You're looking very well."

"Yes; getting out of a bad marriage will do that for you." Anna laughed. She held out her hand, then drew it back. "I'd shake your hand, only I think I'd get black dye all over your fingers."

"Why are you painting the eggs black?" Gennady asked.

"Well, we had to use brown eggs, because Elizabeth forgot to — "

"I didn't *forget* to buy white eggs," Elizabeth protested, laughing, "it was all part of my cunning plan – "

" – to force us to paint the eggs to look like ancient Greek red figure pottery," Anna finished. "What do you think, Gennady?"

Gennady came over to inspect the eggs. He picked one up, and looked surprised to find it so heavy. "You didn't blow out the insides?" he asked.

"Every year I tell them to do that," Daniel told him, "and every year they decorate hard-boiled eggs."

"Oh, but they're so much more beautiful when they last only a few hours," Anna objected. "And decorated eggs make the best deviled eggs, too. All the care and affection that goes into the decoration makes them taste better: I'm sure of it."

***

"But really," Gennady said, as he and Daniel walked to the subway stop that evening, "it's too bad they did not hollow out the eggs." He lifted the clear plastic bag, admiring the eggs in the slanting sunlight that deepened the rich brown of their shells. "These would be worth keeping."

"I'll tell them you said so. Maybe next year they'll take it under advisement."

"Yes, do." Gennady shifted the bag from one hand to the other. "Although it will do no good for me: I'll be back in Moscow by then," Gennady said, and Daniel felt a disagreeable sensation in his throat. He had almost forgotten – he had refused to remember – that Gennady would not be here forever.

"Perhaps it is just as well," Gennady mused. "Hollow eggs are very delicate. It would be very difficult to carry them home without breaking them."

CHAPTER 10

It all came to an end quite suddenly in early May.

Gennady took the subway down just as usual. He had brought along a book, but once the subway had emerged from the tunnel he stopped reading, and instead watched the rain splash against the windows.

The road would be too muddy to drive up to the cabin that day, which was disappointing in a way, and yet Gennady wasn't unhappy. Emily would be running around the house carrying her red rain boots of which she was so proud, wanting someone to help her put them on so she could go outside and stomp in puddles, while David drew quietly at the kitchen table and complained that his sister was too loud.

The prospect of éclairs might cheer them both up – and here Gennady smiled down at the bakery box on his lap. Daniel and Elizabeth would like them too. Elizabeth might make hot chocolate, and if she did not, certainly there would be coffee; and perhaps they would light the fire.

Indeed, a fire already crackled in the fireplace when Elizabeth let him in. She took the box of éclairs with an exclamation of pleasure. "Maybe this will cheer Daniel up," she said. "He's in some sort of funk and he won't tell me why. He's barely left the den since yesterday."

She didn't sound too worried, though, and so Gennady didn't

worry either. He slipped off his rain boots and hung up his raincoat and headed to the den. The door was closed, so he knocked. "Daniel."

"Gennady. Come in."

The door squeaked on its hinges. Daniel sat at his desk, watching the rain beat on the window.

Gennady couldn't see his face, but his sharp voice and slouched posture suggested that he was indeed in a sulk. "Why are you hiding away like a bear in his den?" Gennady asked. "Come downstairs and splash in the puddles with Emily. That should cheer you up."

Daniel swiveled his chair, and Gennady fell silent at the expression on his face. "Here," Daniel said. He picked up a letter from his desk. "Read this."

It was quality stationary, heavy paper with a navy blue monogram at the top of the page: *Paul Everard Preston.*

Gennady glanced at Daniel. "Paul..." he began. Daniel gestured impatiently for him to go on reading. The handwriting was visibly imprinted into the page, as if the writer had pressed hard on his pen.

Dear Daniel:

By the time this reaches you, you'll probably already have heard about my suicide. I've tried to set it up to look like drugs drove me to it, but I wanted you to know the truth. I'm being blackmailed. The Soviets –

Gennady felt as if the floor had dropped away from under his feet.

Arkady. He had mentioned Paul to Arkady. *His previous partner kept pawing at him,* something like that. Gennady could not recall if he had said Paul's name, but it didn't matter, Arkady could have found it easily enough in Daniel's dossier.

The Soviets have pictures. That's my fault: I brought it on myself by going to sordid places.

Of course I'd rather die than betray my country, so I'm going to shoot myself as soon as I've mailed this letter. All my affairs are in order. I've enclosed the cufflinks you gave me. I hope you'll keep them.

HONEYTRAP

Burn this letter once you read it.

Paul.

Gennady read the letter a second time. He didn't need to: the letter had burned itself into his soul. He was just buying himself time before he had to look at Daniel's face.

But finally he lowered the letter and force himself to meet Daniel's eyes. "Did you tell them?" Daniel asked. "About Paul."

"Yes." Gennady heard himself as if someone else was speaking.

"When?"

"Fifteen years ago. When you first told me."

Daniel turned away. "They've been patient."

"They must have been waiting for photographic proof."

"I suppose you had a hand in that, too?" Daniel's tone was snide.

"No." Gennady could hear the tonelessness of his own voice. "Pictures aren't my line."

"No," Daniel agreed. "I didn't really mean that."

They fell silent. Daniel put the letter on his desk and pressed his hands against his knees, clenching his fists in the fabric.

"Say something," Daniel said abruptly.

"I'm a Soviet agent," Gennady said. "You've always known this."

"Yes." Daniel stood up abruptly, and crossed the small room, picking up one of the decorative decoy ducks off his shelf. "It's my own fault. You told me that I shouldn't trust you."

Gennady stirred. "I should go," he said.

Daniel regarded the wooden duck. "Yes."

Gennady hesitated, just a moment. "I never told them about you."

It felt important that he should say it. But Daniel's eyes bulged and his skin stretched over his bones so he looked like a death's head, and his voice when he spoke was barely above a whisper. "Get out."

Gennady went.

Emily caught him while he was still putting on his boots. "Uncle Gennady!" she cried, gleeful as only a small child can be. "Are you going for a walk? Can I come with?"

"Not today, *myshka*," Gennady said, and he managed an apologetic smile. "I've got to go back to the city."

"But you just *got* here."

"I know. I know."

"But when will you be back?" Emily pressed.

When Gennady was just a little older than Emily, so many adults had disappeared from his life, swept away by the war that had sucked everyone up like a vacuum cleaner. His father had gone without even a proper goodbye – said *do svidanye* like he was going to another day at work, and then disappeared forever.

Gennady went down on one knee to look Emily in the eye. "I won't be back, *myshka*. I'm sorry."

He understood then why his father left like he had. He hadn't wanted to see Gennady cry.

"I'm sorry, I'm sorry, Emily," Gennady said. He took her by the shoulders and kissed her forehead. "Go find your mother, *myshka*, all right? Tell her your father needs to talk to her."

She ran off. He swung his raincoat on and left without buttoning it, and didn't stop to do so until he had reached the end of the block, beyond the line of sight from the den window.

He lingered longer than was necessary. He was hoping that the door would open again: that Elizabeth would come running after him, to attempt a reconciliation, or at least say that she would talk to Daniel. To her, perhaps, he might be able to say, *I'm sorry*.

But the door remained closed. The cold rain was falling faster now, and he had left his umbrella inside.

Well, he couldn't go back. He held his raincoat closed over his throat and trudged to the Metro station, and sat on the cold bench in the wind to wait for the next train. They didn't run often on Saturdays. He tried to light a cigarette, but his hands were shaking too badly, and in the end he threw it away.

CHAPTER 11

Elizabeth grew very pale as she read Paul's letter. At the end, she set the letter down and looked at Daniel, unspeaking.

"This is my fault," Daniel said. "I told Gennady about Paul. Years ago."

"And he told them? You're sure?"

"I asked him today," Daniel said. "Yes. Of course he did."

"Oh, Daniel." Elizabeth put her arms around him. Daniel felt this would be a good moment to break down, to bury his face in his wife's shoulder and cry, but he felt stiff and frozen.

"I keep thinking," Daniel said. "I keep trying to remember what else I might have told him. Who else might be in danger. Thank God," he said, and laughed briefly, "Thank God I never told him about Mr. Gilman's wartime lover. *That* would have been a plum to take to the KGB. But I told him about John…"

"But Daniel," Elizabeth said. She put her hands on his cheeks. "John's safe, he's already out. Everyone already knows he's gay, so the Soviets can't blackmail him."

Daniel let out a shaking breath. "Thank God," he said, and he pressed his face into her hands. "If only Paul…"

But that was impossible. John's university might be willing to employ an openly gay professor, but Paul was an FBI agent, and the FBI still fired people for that.

"The Soviets never would have been able to blackmail him if

the FBI weren't so prejudiced," Daniel said. He couldn't hold still any longer; Elizabeth let go of him, and he began to pace. "The FBI – hell! American society! If people weren't so goddamn prejudiced, then it wouldn't have mattered..."

That Daniel had told Gennady.

But they were – and Daniel had – and it did. And now Paul was dead.

"Paul would still be alive right now if I weren't so stupid. If I'd never got drunk and kissed Gennady and told him everything – everything about Paul. I can't imagine what I was thinking. I was so drunk I barely even remember the conversation." Daniel pressed a hand over his mouth. "God alone knows what I said. Elizabeth," he said, and he went down on his knees and took both of her hands, "promise me, promise me, if things get bad, I want you to take the children and get out of here."

"What do you mean?"

"If Gennady... if the Soviets try to blackmail me."

"Do you really think he'd do that?"

"I don't know." Daniel tried to collect his thoughts, but they refused to settle. In the end he just shook his head. "I don't know. After the way things ended today..." Christ, he should have thought this through. "He might be angry. He might tell someone about me, and if he does, if they blackmail me... Elizabeth, I don't want you dragged into it. Divorce me."

She knelt beside him, holding his hands tightly. "I absolutely will not," she said. "If it comes to that, I'll send the children to stay with my parents, but I'm not going to let you face it alone. *If* it comes to that," she added, with extra emphasis. "I can't imagine Gennady would do that, Daniel. He loves you."

"Or this has all been one big honeytrap. Or – or maybe he's just been stringing me along hoping I'd let slip some more pieces of intelligence."

"Do you really think that?"

Daniel's hands dropped from hers. He pressed his palms to the floor. "I don't know. I've always been an idiot about him. I didn't just mention Paul once, Elizabeth. I've talked about him with..." He could not bring himself to say Gennady's name. "We've had whole conversations about Paul, and it didn't even occur to me..." He pressed a hand over his face. "It didn't even occur to me that I was compromising Paul. I got him killed, I practically threw him on the grenade in my place. I've been so cavalier about the risks of – God, *dating a Soviet agent*, how stupid could I be? I wish he'd gone ahead with the honeytrap," Daniel said savagely. "At least then I wouldn't have told him about Paul. Or maybe I would have," he said, and his head sunk into his hands. "That's the point of blackmail, after all. I doubt *I* would have had the guts to kill myself."

Elizabeth took his head between her hands, and stroked his hair. "I love you, Daniel," she said gently.

"Why?"

"You're not going to believe any of the reasons I give right now," she said. "Just know that I love you. We're going to get through this."

***

Four months passed. No blackmail threats arrived, no packets of incriminating photographs, and although Daniel hadn't exactly expected them – a part of him still couldn't distrust Gennady – another part of him could not let his guard down.

They'd waited fifteen years for Paul, after all. They'd wait for Daniel, too.

So when Mr. Gilman stopped by his desk and said, "Agent Hawthorne, if you'll step into my office, please?", Daniel was certain that the ax had finally fallen, and in a way he was relieved. At least now he didn't have to wait any longer.

Daniel went into Mr. Gilman's office, and shut the door, and sat down in the chair that Mr. Gilman indicated. Mr. Gilman settled in a chair himself and began to roll a paperweight in his palm. "You've been moping ever since Agent Preston's death, Agent Hawthorne."

Daniel felt a sort of shock, although it wasn't so surprising that Mr. Gilman had noticed. He saw quite a lot for a man who seemed to spend most of his time peering absentmindedly at paperweights. "I was shocked to hear about his suicide," Daniel said. "We haven't been close for years, but when something like that happens... You always wonder if you could have done something to prevent it. If it was your fault." His throat clogged. He felt he should stop talking, but against his will he kept going. "He must have felt very alone."

"What do you know about the circumstances of his death?"

Daniel tried to remember what rumors were current in the Bureau, and couldn't. "Just rumors," he said vaguely.

Mr. Gilman considered Daniel with much the same benign gaze he had bestowed on his paperweight. "You understand," he said, "that what I tell you next is not something that I want contributed to the rumor mill."

Daniel nodded.

Mr. Gilman took a folder from his desk and slid it over to Daniel. "Agent Preston was being blackmailed by the Soviets," he said. "We found these in his mailbox on the day of his death. I suppose the Soviets were trying to tighten the screws."

Daniel already had some idea what was in them, given the contents of Paul's last letter. But naturally Mr. Gilman didn't know about that, so he tried to prepare himself to look shocked.

But the photos really did shock him. They had been taken through a window, which gave an obscenely voyeuristic tinge even to the first photograph, even though it only showed two men, fully dressed, sitting on the end of a bed. Paul and a younger man, dark-haired, handsome.

Daniel could envision, vividly, horribly, similar photographs of himself and Gennady. That imaginary vision was so intense that he actually flinched when he flipped to the next photo and found Paul and the dark-haired man kissing and shirtless.

The rest of the photographs were practically a gay Kama Sutra. (Daniel noticed irritably, and was disgusted with himself for his irritation, that apparently *now* Paul was willing to be the passive partner. No, not just willing. *Thrilled*.)

It wasn't till the last photograph that Daniel paused. The Kama Sutra had ended. Paul and his young man had fallen asleep, spooned together, Paul's arm slung around his partner's chest and his face resting in the man's thick shoulder-length curls.

Daniel felt like his heart was going to claw its way out of its chest. For a moment it was jealousy: Paul had never held him like that. Then the jealousy was gone, and it was only grief, because here was Paul relaxed and happy and loving and this was what he got for it. Blackmail and a bullet in his head.

"Naturally the young man was a honeytrap set by the Soviets," Mr. Gilman said.

"A honeytrap," Daniel echoed, his voice a whisper.

Paul truly had fallen on the grenade meant for Daniel.

"Yes. I realize that many people would find this an even more sordid cause of death than any of the rumors. But I thought it might help you to know that he died a hero, protecting the secrets of the United States."

Daniel knew that was exactly how Paul must have seen it, and he felt disloyal because it made him feel sick instead. "He died heroically protecting the Bureau," Daniel said, "which would have fired him the instant it had any proof of his homosexuality."

Mr. Gilman fell silent at the bitterness in his voice. After a pause, he said, "You know perfectly well that's not true. If it was, Agent Preston would have been fired sixteen – hmm, seventeen years ago, is it?"

"You had no proof," Daniel shot back, "just suspicions, and that was enough to get us both demoted. And Paul's career never really recovered, did it? Mine only got back on track because I got married."

"Agent Preston could have gotten married too."

"No, he couldn't. He's not like you and me."

Mr. Gilman frowned, very slightly. He took off his glasses and rubbed the little indentations that they left on either side of his nose. "He knew that when he joined the Bureau."

"He died heroically protecting the Bureau whose policies made him feel he had no choice but to commit suicide. He loved the Bureau, and the Bureau would have thrown him out like yesterday's trash – "

"Don't shout at me, Agent Hawthorne. I have no desire to put you on administrative leave."

Daniel caught his breath. He swallowed and pressed his sweaty hands against his thighs.

Mr. Gilman resettled his glasses on his nose. He picked up his smallest millefiori paperweight. "I hadn't realized you and Paul were still so close."

Daniel felt tired suddenly. He almost wanted to fling himself on that sword: *Yes, we're so close, we've been carrying on in secret for years, please fire me.*

"No. It's just that... Well, he sent me a suicide note," Daniel confessed. "Maybe he had no one else to tell..."

"I don't suppose you kept the note?"

"No. He asked me to burn it," said Daniel. "He didn't want anyone to know." He probably ought to destroy the volume of Whitman that Paul had given him, too, the one with all the Calamus poems marked. "You ought to destroy these," Daniel added, nodding at the photographs. "Paul would never have wanted anyone to see them."

"You're not in a position to tell me what to do with a piece of evidence, Agent Hawthorne."

"Evidence of what? Paul is dead. There's nothing you can prove against him."

"Evidence that might help us locate ongoing Soviet spy operations on our shores."

"How the hell are these photos going to do that?" Daniel's hands were shaking.

"You never know," Mr. Gilman said, "which piece of evidence might crack a case."

Daniel took up the photographs and tapped them against the desk to straighten them. Then he ripped them down the middle.

Mr. Gilman set the paperweight down sharply. He and Daniel faced each other over the desk.

"I believe you ought to take that administrative leave, Agent Hawthorne. Six months, perhaps?"

"No," said Daniel. "I'm quitting."

He jammed the torn photographs into his briefcase. Mr. Gilman didn't try to stop him — which probably meant that these were just copies of the originals.

But when Daniel stood, Mr. Gilman stood too. "Agent Hawthorne," he said. "Reconsider. You're a good agent. The Bureau — "

"The Bureau won't even notice I'm gone," Daniel said. Blood rushed to his face and rushed out again. "I'm sorry. I can't do this anymore."

He left before Mr. Gilman could wheedle any further. He was not at all sure that he could remain firm for much longer.

Financially they would be fine. They had saved up, there was money in the bank, Elizabeth's paintings would tide them over till he got another job. But he had always dreamed of being an FBI agent, and he felt he might be sick as he walked away.

In his car, before he even left the parking lot, Daniel set the photos on fire with the car's cigarette lighter. They shriveled up to nothing in the ashtray.

He kept only one, the last: the photo of Paul and the young man curled up together, asleep. That sweetness was empty and false, a honeytrap, but he couldn't bring himself to set it on fire.

When he got home, he put the picture in his shoebox. He hadn't touched the box since he'd sent Gennady away, and when he opened the box, the old Christmas photo of Gennady hit him like a punch in the chest. Gennady glowing with pleasure as he unwrapped his unexpected present, and Daniel leaning against the back of the chair and smiling down at him.

Daniel settled the picture of Paul on top and closed the lid gently, and then sat a long time in the dark bedroom with the box on his lap.

A week later he wrote a letter to Gennady.

***

They met nearly a month after that, when the leaves were turning yellow, in the very early morning at an all-night diner. Bleary-eyed truck-drivers sat in the booths; nurses swung past the counter to grab a cup of coffee on their way into the hospital.

"We could have met later, you know," Daniel told Gennady.

Gennady cast weary eyes up at him. Daniel suspected that Gennady had suggested this early hour because he hoped Daniel would refuse. "Why are we meeting?" Gennady asked.

"I wanted..." Daniel played his coffee cup between his hands. "I wanted to see you again before you go back to the Soviet Union."

"Why?"

"I wanted..." Daniel tried to sip his coffee. It was scalding hot. "I wanted to apologize."

"What do you have to apologize for? – Thank you," Gennady added, his sharp voice softening as the waitress put down their plates of food: eggs and toast for Daniel, a single enormous pancake for Gennady. But then she left, and Gennady continued, his voice lower but still razor sharp. "I ought to be the one apologizing. I'm the one who got your friend killed."

"The FBI got Paul killed," Daniel said. "American society got Paul killed by being so goddamn prejudiced. I... well, here."

He took a folder from his briefcase and slid it across the table. Gennady looked for a long time at the photograph Daniel had saved. Daniel had taped it back together.

Then he flipped the folder shut and looked back at Daniel. His face was still hard and cold. "So? I told Arkady about Paul fifteen years ago. So it took them a long time to get photographic evidence to blackmail him, that's all."

Daniel couldn't meet his gaze. He poked at the yolk of his sunnyside up egg. "Gennady, fifteen years is a long time. For all we know, the KGB found out about Paul on their own more recently. And even if that's not the case," Daniel added hastily, because he could see Gennady was about to object, "even if the KGB did look into him because of some note in an old file, it was my fault for mentioning him to you. I blamed you for it because I couldn't bear…"

He couldn't finish the sentence. Gennady's stone face softened. "You were very drunk when you told me, Daniel."

"And you were just doing your job. You always said I should have been more careful what I told you, and you were right."

Gennady sighed. "Say it was both of our faults, then," he said. "This association was always going to hurt someone in the end."

The diner was getting busy now. The waitresses and the cooks shouted cheerfully at each other. Gennady cut long straight lines through his pancake, then sliced crossways to make squares, and ate the squares methodically. Daniel had never seen him eat anything with so little relish.

Halfway through the pancake Gennady set down his fork. "Daniel," Gennady said. "Do you remember when I told you that we couldn't be friends?"

"No."

Gennady sighed. "Of course you don't. You were *very* drunk."

Then a stray wisp of memory wriggled. "That was the time when…" Daniel's voice dwindled and his face warmed.

When he had gotten drunk and kissed Gennady. When he had told Gennady all about Paul.

"This is what I meant," Gennady said. "This was always going to happen, or something like this. We were both assigned to report on each other from the start, Daniil. And we both tried to…" He paused, and took up his fork and swabbed a square of pancake in the maple syrup. "To craft those reports in such a way that we would protect each other. I think that's true, isn't it?"

Daniel nodded.

"But still, in the end this giving of reports is a betrayal of the trust that there should be in friendship. We should have accepted that it was impossible to be friends and remained friendly colleagues who never told each other anything important."

In light of Paul's death, Daniel had no counterargument. He felt like he was suffocating. "Did you come here just to tell me that?"

Gennady drew his fork through the maple syrup, leaving behind raked lines that the syrup slowly filled. "I came here because you asked me to," he said.

Daniel toyed with a burnt piece of toast. Across the room, a young waitress dropped a plate of scrambled eggs, and stood petrified among the wreckage.

"I was the one who understood it couldn't work," Gennady said, "so I should have acted to keep more distance between us. But…" He shrugged. "Well, it was a beautiful dream, wasn't it? The power of friendship bridges East and West, capitalist and communist, overpowers even the power of the state. Love is stronger than fear. When you want something to be true it is hard to believe that it isn't."

"But it still isn't."

Gennady didn't answer right away. "Maybe it is for a while," he said finally. "But not in the end. No."

They were silent. The diner clattered around them.

Gennady pushed the folder gently across the table. "Keep that," he said gently. "Remember him happy. It's best not to think about how people die."

Daniel slid the folder back into his briefcase. "This is the end, isn't it?" he said. "For us."

"Unless the world changes," Gennady said steadily, "which it won't. Yes."

Daniel clipped his briefcase shut. But he didn't make a move to leave, and neither did Gennady. Gennady sipped his coffee. Daniel continued to shred his toast.

At last Gennady said, "I have to get to work." He stood, but remained by the table. "Daniel, you ought to eat that."

"I'm not hungry."

"You will be later," Gennady urged. "You should always eat when you have the chance."

Daniel put a piece of toast in his mouth. Gennady raised a hand, as if to touch Daniel's shoulder or shake hands, then let it drop again. "*Proshai*," he said.

"*Proshai*," Daniel said.

Gennady crossed the crowded diner, slipping neatly past a waitress with a laden tray. A group of burly truckers came in, and Gennady disappeared behind them; and then he was gone.

Part Three
1992

CHAPTER 1

"It's a nice apartment," Gennady said.

He was leaning against the stainless steel island in Daniel's kitchen, munching one of the apples out of the wooden fruit bowl. Daniel had bought both the bowl and the fruit in preparation for Gennady's visit, in the somewhat forlorn hope of making the studio apartment look like a home rather than a room where he crashed when the janitors finally prodded him out of the office for the night.

"A nice view," added Gennady, nodding at the window, which did indeed have a pleasant view of the nearby skyscrapers, currently glowing orange in the February sunset. "Your letters didn't do it justice."

Daniel had sent the first letter four years before, in 1988. One of his old frat brothers had become a diplomat to Moscow, and Daniel sent the letter through him, if he should happen to find a way to get it to one Gennady Matskevich. "Don't send it if you think it might put him in danger," Daniel told him. "The newspapers keep going on about Gorbachev's *glasnost*, but I don't know if that actually means much on the ground."

But it must have seemed safe enough, because a few months later Daniel received a reply from Gennady, guarded but friendly – and possessed of a return address.

And now it was 1992 and Gennady was in Daniel's apartment, crunching an apple at the kitchen island. "What brought you to the United States this time?" Daniel asked. "Is the KGB still sending spies? Does the KGB even still exist?"

"The KGB will always exist," Gennady said, "although perhaps they'll change its name now. But I am not a KGB agent." A slight smile curved his mouth. "I never was. I was a GRU operative. Military intelligence."

"Really! So you really were a lieutenant in the Red Army when I met you?"

"In a manner of speaking. But no longer. I quit."

"Really?" Daniel said. "Good for you."

Gennady shrugged. "Everyone is getting out who can – like rats from a sinking ship. And I've always wanted to travel, and after all I'm not getting any younger..." He shrugged. "And there are so many parts of the United States I would still like to see. The Rocky Mountains, the Grand Canyon, the sequoia trees. And New York City."

"And you just happen to have a friend in New York City," Daniel said, smiling, although he was wondering how Gennady intended to pay for this trip now that he didn't have an expense account. The papers said that the post-Soviet economy was in shambles.

But he could hardly ask, so he said instead, "How long are you going to be in New York?"

"Oh – a few days perhaps. As long as it takes to see the major tourist sights. The Statue of Liberty, the Empire State Building, the World Trade Center. The Metropolitan Museum of Art. Central Park."

"Want a tour guide?" Daniel asked lightly. "I pretty much did the circuit when my kids visited last summer, so I could easily show you around."

Gennady's eyelids flickered. "If you've seen these sights already, I don't want to make you see them again."

Daniel couldn't tell if Gennady's demurral was genuine or merely polite. "I've barely scratched the surface on the Met and Central Park. They're both huge. I'd be happy to spend more time there."

"Then I would be happy to see them with you," Gennady said.

Daniel's heart squeezed in his chest. The truth was that he wasn't sure why Gennady was here: if it was just a courtesy call, a brief stop to see an old friend, or if, like Daniel, he hoped that they might rekindle what they once had.

Well, what they'd never had, really. There never had been any possibility for Gennady to stay before. But now that the Soviet Union was gone...

The oven timer rang. Daniel hurried to get out the lasagna.

They discussed Gennady's travel plans over dinner. He meant to go south first, to see Florida "while it is still not too hot," and then to head west. "Ilf and Petrov said the deserts in America are very beautiful," Gennady said, and Daniel couldn't repress a smile.

"I finally read Ilf and Petrov's *Little Golden America* a few years ago," he told Gennady.

"*Little Golden America*! Is that how they translated the title in English?" Gennady scoffed.

"What's the title in Russian?"

"Oh – it would translate to *One-Story America*, something like that. Because the belief in the Soviet Union, certainly in the thirties and perhaps now..." Gennady faltered. The Soviet Union had fallen less than two months before. "The belief in Russia," he corrected himself, "is that all of America is New York City, all skyscrapers."

A brief silence followed. Daniel wanted to say something, but *Sorry about your country* seemed inadequate.

"How are your children?" Gennady asked.

"Oh, great," said Daniel, with an enthusiasm that was mostly genuine but partly just relief at this change in topic. "David's got a job up in Boston working for an engineering firm, and Emily's going to graduate from Georgetown this spring. Here, I've actually got a photo of them both from just last summer, Emily gave me a framed copy as a Christmas present..."

Gennady set aside his fork to take the picture in both hands. The photograph showed Daniel with his two children on the ferry out to Ellis Island. David stood taller than Daniel; Emily had a wide purple streak in her blonde-brown hair, tucked neatly behind her ear in the photograph.

"Emily is all grown up," Gennady observed.

"Yes. That shocks me too, sometimes."

"Does she still play checkers?"

"No. It's all D&D these days – Dungeons and Dragons. I

don't pretend to understand it myself, but it seems to make her happy."

"Well, that's the important thing." Gennady handed the photograph back and Daniel went to set it on the bookcase again. "And you? Are you happy?"

If the question had come from almost anyone else, Daniel would have answered with a hearty and insincere "Yes." But he couldn't bring himself to lie to Gennady.

He also couldn't bring himself to tell the truth, so instead he temporized. "I've been better," he said, and added, "Elizabeth and I are divorced. Well, you know that already, I mentioned it in a letter."

"Yes, you did, but I don't understand it," Gennady said. "You loved each other so much."

Daniel stared down at the last few bites of his lasagna. "Oh, well. She fell in love with someone else. Another artist. They met at the opening of one her shows..."

Daniel had come to that show, although he had arrived late. The caterers were packing up, only a few hors d'oeuvres left, and he had snagged a stuffed mushroom as he scanned the room for Elizabeth.

He heard the swell of her laughter first, as unrestrained as an ocean wave, and then he saw her. She was talking with a tall thin man in a corner, the two of them leaning toward each other. In retrospect Daniel felt that he had known in that moment that he had lost her, although he must not have seen it really: they had been together for two more years before Daniel asked for a divorce.

"But I love you," Elizabeth had protested.

"I know," Daniel had said, and tucked a strand of her hair behind her ear. "But Julian's the one you're in love with, and I can't stand playing second fiddle for the rest of my life, Elizabeth, so please just let me go."

"Daniel?" Gennady's voice brought him back to the present, and Daniel realized that he was staring blankly at his lasagna.

Christ. That probably undermined his concerted efforts to look like he had it all together: the fruit bowl, the fruit. An actual home-cooked lasagna instead of take-out.

Daniel cleared his throat. "Do you have a place to stay lined up? The hotels in New York are so expensive."

Gennady waved that away. "Money is no problem."

"Really? I guess it's none of my business. But didn't the ruble just tank?"

"Well," said Gennady. "When I was posted to Zurich, I opened a Swiss bank account. And once I had opened one for myself, I began to help intelligence officers who wished to have a hard currency account, for a small fee of course..."

"Of course."

"And in the course of time other opportunities arose..."

"Oh no."

"You should be proud of my capitalist instincts, my friend. In America perhaps I could have been a successful businessman. But it was not possible to do these things legally in the Soviet Union," Gennady said, "so perhaps I had better not tell you more."

"No, I think we'd better stop there," Daniel agreed. He hesitated, then added, "But still, if you want to stay with me... Just for the night. Or for a few days, as long as you're in New York City. Or not," he said, wilting with embarrassment, because Gennady was staring at him, and clearly Daniel in his hope (desperation?) had misread the situation.

"Where would I sleep?" Gennady asked.

"The couch," Daniel said, and managed not to say, *Or the bed's big enough for two if you don't mind sharing...*

Gennady cocked his head. He peered into Daniel's face as if trying to read his thoughts.

"I bought cannoli for dessert," Daniel added, and winced as he said it. He felt like a small child. *I'll give you a tootsie roll if you'll be my friend.*

But Gennady said, "I have never had cannoli." He was not smiling, but there was something conciliatory in his voice. "Yes, I'll stay on your couch. It's been a long day, why not?"

***

They went to Central Park the next morning, for about an hour. Then Daniel conceded that he was too cold to wander the park any longer, and they headed for the Metropolitan Museum of Art. "You still haven't bought a real coat?" Gennady scoffed. "Americans."

"We're perfecting the manly art of freezing to death," Daniel protested, pleased beyond measure to find Gennady teasing him, just like old times.

Of course, in those old times they'd never been to an art museum together, so that was something new. Daniel was not an art aficionado (really he couldn't blame Elizabeth for wanting a partner who shared her interests), but Gennady was clearly enjoying himself. In fact it reminded Daniel a little of going to an art museum with Elizabeth, and the parallel felt like a spar in his throat, but fortunately Gennady was absorbed in Georgia Keeffe's *Cow's Skull: Red, White, and Blue*, and didn't notice.

"They could have brought this to Moscow as a propaganda piece," Gennady mused. "The cow's skull over the colors of the American flag."

"Are you surprised to see it in an American museum?"

"Nothing you people do surprises me anymore."

They stopped in one of the Met's cafes before they went back into the cold. Gennady sat, chin on his hand, gazing down at his coffee. "Your nation was founded on blood and terror," he commented. "Slavery. The slaughter of your Indians. There has always been a skull on the red, white, and blue."

Daniel couldn't quite read his tone. "Yes," he said cautiously.

"I've been reading your papers since I came here," Gennady said, "and they have been crowing about the fall of the Soviet Union. Well, the victors always crow once they have won the war."

"Have you been in the United States a while, then?"

Gennady shrugged. "A couple of weeks perhaps."

Clearly visiting Daniel hadn't been high on his priority list.

"Some of your newspaper writers seem to believe the Soviet Union was always destined to fall because it was founded in blood," Gennady said. "But your nation was founded in blood too." He rubbed his face. "Were we so much worse than you? You committed the worst of your crimes longer ago, that's all. And yet already your writers are writing as if the Soviet Union was only ever a mistake."

Daniel felt a sudden painful wave of compassion. Of course Daniel wasn't Gennady's top priority right now. If their positions were reversed – if it had been the United States that collapsed...

Daniel doubted he could have carried himself with as much

composure as Gennady displayed.

"A lot of Americans have always thought the Soviet Union was only ever a mistake, Gennady," Daniel reminded him gently.

"Yes, I know. And when we had shot a rocket into space and you couldn't get one to launch, it was easy to laugh at those people. But now how can I argue with them? So much misery, so much death, and it's all come to nothing in the end." He toyed with his coffee cup. "But then that's the way of all empires. The empires of Egypt, and Greece, and Rome, and Great Britain, all fell in the end. And yours will too, someday."

"I guess that's logical," Daniel said reluctantly.

"But you don't believe it," Gennady said. "It will not seem possible to you until it actually falls."

Daniel stirred his own coffee (decaf; he could no longer drink the real stuff after lunchtime). "It's a little like imagining my own death," he admitted finally. "Of course, in either case the world would go on afterward, but trying to imagine what it would be like if the star-spangled banner no longer waved..."

His voice trailed off. Just saying it gave him an unpleasant feeling, as if someone had stepped on his grave.

"Ask me in two years and maybe I will understand it well enough to tell you what it might be like for you," Gennady told him.

"So you'll be back in two years, then?" Daniel asked, raising his eyebrows.

Gennady leaned back in his chair. "Why not? After all there is always more of New York to see. Would you let me stay again?"

"Yes, of course," Daniel said. "Any time you want to come visit, just let me know."

***

Despite their busy day, Daniel didn't sleep well that night. This had begun to happen frequently as he grew older, particularly since the divorce, and usually he turned on the light to read till he felt sleepy again.

Only once the light was on did Daniel remember that it might wake Gennady. Daniel switched the light back off – the twist knob on the lamp sounded horribly loud – but Gennady was already sitting up. "Are you awake?" Gennady asked softly.

"No. I turned the lamp on in my sleep."

Gennady laughed at him. Daniel waited for Gennady to lie back down again, but Gennady remained sitting, and so Daniel sat too, both of them sitting in the dimness and waiting for the other to speak.

"I'm glad you came to visit," Daniel said, at length. "That you're staying with me."

"I was surprised when you wrote to me," Gennady said. "I thought I would never hear from you again. After the way we parted."

"We parted because we realized that it was too likely that someone else might get hurt if we kept seeing each other," Daniel said. "'Until the world changes,' you said. And then the world changed, so... I wrote to you."

Gennady plumped his pillow. "The world has changed, but not in that way. FBI would still fire you if you had a male lover."

"Oh." And Daniel realized that he'd never told Gennady. "I quit the FBI."

"Oh. Well, you are of an age to retire, I suppose."

"No. I mean, I left after Paul... died."

"Oh." Now Gennady sounded truly shocked. "Why? It was not the FBI's fault."

"Well, it was, sort of. I mean, if the FBI wouldn't have fired him for being gay, no one could have blackmailed him about it. But really I quit because... I felt guilty, I guess. I never should have told you about Paul, and even if that's not how the KGB found out about him – well, I guess it couldn't have led the KGB to him, unless the KGB and the GRU get along a lot better than the FBI and the CIA..."

Gennady snorted.

"I figured," Daniel said. "Nations come and go, but interagency squabbles are eternal. But even so..." He twisted the comforter in his hand. "I guess I felt like I shouldn't be working for the FBI if I couldn't keep my mouth shut. I mean, sure, I told you by accident, but accidents get people killed. And if Paul..." Daniel closed his eyes. "If Paul had known that I told a Soviet agent about him, he would have broken my jaw. And that would have been better than I deserved, given how that worked out for him."

The mattress dipped. Gennady sat down on the bed beside him. "Daniel," he said.

"Sorry. If you'll pass me those tissues..."

Gennady passed Daniel the tissue box. Daniel blew his nose.

"Sorry," Daniel said again.

"No, I'm sorry. Maybe I should not have come here. Perhaps I have only made you feel bad again."

Daniel shook his head. "No, no. I'm glad you're here. I've wanted to see you again for a long time. I'll probably always feel guilty about Paul, but throwing away my last chance with you wouldn't bring him back. And with everything that's happened, the Soviet Union falling, for the first time we really do have a chance to build a life together..." He folded over the tissue in his hands. "If you have any interest in doing that."

There was a long pause. Daniel bit his lip. He wanted so badly to make a joke, to say anything to undercut the seriousness of the moment, because he felt like more of an idiot with every second that Gennady didn't answer. Probably thinking of a gentle way to let Daniel down. Undoubtedly Gennady had moved on.

At last Gennady said, "I don't know. It's not that I'm angry about anything that happened," he added. "Of course you were appalled by Paul's death, naturally the only course was to break things off, what else could you do? But still it was painful, and once you have been burned it is hard to put your hand on the stove again. Do you understand?"

Daniel nodded.

"I hoped when I visited you that perhaps you would be old and ugly and covered in warts," Gennady told him. "Or old and boring and talking about nothing but golf. Then I could dust my hands of you, and that would be the end of it. But of course you're an American, you've barely aged at all." He sighed, and rubbed his face, and then perked up and added hopefully, "I have, though. I don't even have all my teeth anymore. You see?" He hooked a finger in the left corner of his lips display a gap of three or four missing teeth in the side of his mouth. Daniel leaned in to peer at it.

"What happened?"

"Bar fight."

"Of course," Daniel said. He fell back against the pillows. "I like your face," he told Gennady, and Gennady sighed again. "C'mon. You don't have to sound sad about it," Daniel told him.

"It would have been easier if it had just died naturally. I could have eaten your lasagna and left and that would have been the end of it."

"Do you really want that?"

Another sigh. "Well, I'm here, so no, clearly I don't."

A long silence followed. Daniel wanted very much to put his hand on Gennady's, or put an arm around him and pull him close. But when he moved as if to do it, Gennady drew back, and Daniel fell still again.

When Gennady spoke again, he didn't look at Daniel. "I thought I would visit Paul's grave."

For a long moment Daniel couldn't speak. Then he said, "You don't have to."

"No, of course not. But I think it would be a good thing to do." There was another silence, and then Gennady said, "I went to DC first when I came to the United States. To your old house, to ask Elizabeth where he was buried. But of course she didn't know, why should she?"

"She could have called me and asked."

"She offered. I asked her not to." Another pause. "I don't know, I wasn't ready to see you yet." He glanced at Daniel. His eyes looked liquid in the refracted gleam of the streetlights. "I was so in love with you in 1976," he told Daniel. "Everything else in my life was so terrible and there you were. A refuge. Safe harbor."

A lump rose in Daniel's throat. "I didn't realize…"

"No, of course you didn't know. I didn't want you to know, it would have been very painful for me if you did, and after all everything would have been just the same, in the end. I'm only telling you now because…" He looked down at his hands. "Well, so you will understand how it hurt me the way that things ended. More painful because, after all, I could not even comfort myself that it was unfair, or that you were cruel, because what else could you have done? And so it's hard to say, oh yes, let's try again."

"You don't have to decide right away," Daniel told him. "I know you're headed out on a trip, anyway, I don't want to get in the way of your travel plans. I just… I wanted you to know it was an option. Just to let you know that you can always come back here to me if you want to."

Gennady smoothed one hand over the coverlet. "I think that would be hard on you," he said. "To leave things so uncertain."

"Well, I'm hoping eventually you'll make up your mind," Daniel admitted. "But now that I'm old and boring and warty, I'm a little more patient, too."

Gennady laughed at him. "You know very well you're not boring or warty."

"Patient, though. More patient than I used to be."

He smiled at Gennady, and at last Gennady smiled back.

"If you'll make room," Gennady said suddenly, "perhaps I could sleep here? The bed is very wide, plenty of room for two, and the couch, you understand…"

"God, of course." Daniel was already scooting over, his heart beating with happiness. "That couch must be hell on your back."

***

Gennady stayed three more days. Daniel took the time off work. "My boss is delighted," he explained to Gennady. "She thinks I work too much."

"Your boss is a woman?"

"The world is always changing," Daniel told him. "She's nice when she's not trying to set me up with her friends."

"She's wise," Gennady said. "It's not good for you to be alone."

"I'm fine," Daniel protested.

"You're not fine. You're one of those people who always needs to be in love with someone," Gennady told him.

"I got a crush on my boss for a while," Daniel admitted, which made Gennady crow with laughter. "Oh, shut up," Daniel said, and Gennady grinned and leaned against the boat rail, the salt spray spitting on his face as they crossed the water to the Statue of Liberty.

"What is it that you do now, anyway?" Gennady asked.

"Oh," said Daniel. "I'm a counselor. After I left the FBI, I got a master's degree and… yeah."

"Really?" Gennady turned away from the sea to look at him. Then he nodded. "Yes, I can see that. You always listened well."

They hit all the major tourist sights: the Empire State

Building, the World Trade Center, Times Square and Broadway. They stood in the cold under the marquee lights and discussed seeing a show, until Gennady admitted, "I've never cared for musicals. It was always Alla who liked them."

"Alla," Daniel echoed. "Did you end up getting divorced?"

He thought they probably had, but he had never known for sure.

"Oh yes. She met another man while I was in America." Gennady shrugged. "A guitar player. He lived on the floor below us, and the sound of the guitar carried up through the floor... and one day she went down to see who played so beautifully. And so."

"I'm sorry."

Another shrug. "It was a long time ago."

They walked on under the garish glaring lights. "What have you been up to since then?" Daniel asked.

"Do you mean, am I married again? No. Two relationships fell apart in a row," Gennady said, and waved a hand, "no, maybe I am just not meant for romance."

"Oh," said Daniel, and felt terrible, although it wasn't like he'd dated much since his divorce, either. He'd only really felt ready to try again within the last few months. And then Gennady's letter had arrived, saying that he was coming to New York, and Daniel had decided to wait for that. To see.

"Oh, you sound so sad, it's not that important. There are other things in life," Gennady said.

"Black marketeering?"

Gennady laughed. "No, no. Well, yes, but not only that. I bought a car, have I told you that? And on summer days we all pile in, Aunt Lilya and my cousin Oksana and her daughter Dasha, and we drive out to the dacha, where we eat tomatoes from the vine and raspberries off their canes, and Dasha tries to find Voice of America on the radio and complains that they play too much news and not enough music..." He sighed. "Well, of course, no longer. Dasha lives in Berlin now – Berlin! She got herself stranded there when the wall fell, with her rock band, and we were so worried... But of course with everything that has happened, probably she is safer there than if she stayed in Moscow."

Daniel had gotten stuck earlier in the sentence. "Rock band?"

"Yes! You think we have no rock? You haven't heard of Aquarium, Kino, Viktor Tsoi...? Dasha went into mourning when he died. Of course her band is not so famous," Gennady said, "perhaps they are not very good, what do I know about music, after all? But still they are playing in Berlin."

His words might be deprecatory, but his tone was full of pride. Daniel was touched, not only because it was clear that Dasha was like a daughter to Gennady, but because Gennady had never spoken so openly or at such length about his family before.

"It's asking a lot to ask you to stay here, isn't it?" Daniel said.

"Not as much as it was when you kept saying *defect, defect*," Gennady said.

Daniel winced. "You must have thought I was such an asshole."

"No, no. The FBI wanted you to say this, didn't they? They sent Sergeyich too, my old friend who had defected. I suppose they liked to win defectors; it was a..." He paused, searching for a phrase.

"A feather in their cap."

"Yes. A feather in their cap. But pointless for me: it is not like they would have let me live near you, you know. But now the borders are open, I can stay here, go back, back and forth, whatever."

Gennady fell into a thoughtful silence. Daniel didn't speak either, for fear of bursting the soap bubble of hope that had risen in his heart.

It wasn't till they were back on the subway car, rattling through the dark tunnels toward home, that Gennady spoke again. "I should start looking for a car," he said.

"Oh," Daniel said, and slouched in his seat, and tried to sound cheerful. "Of course. You want to be getting on with your trip. Where will you go first?"

"South," Gennady reminded him. "Where it's warm. I will drive to Florida and drink fresh orange juice from a stand by the side of the road. Are there still oranges in Florida in February?"

"I've got no idea." The conversation depressed Daniel. "You don't need to look for a car. You can borrow mine."

Gennady looked startled. "I can't take your car, Daniil."

"Why not? I never use it. It's faster to take public transport than try to find parking in the city."

Gennady was silent. Then a smile quirked his lips. "You want me to have to come back at the end of the trip," he said. "To return the car."

Daniel had thought that at sixty he was beyond blushing, but his face reddened. "I guess so."

Gennady's smile had turned playful. "Yes, all right," he said, and he slapped Daniel's shoulder. "I'll take your car. I'll look forward to seeing you again," he said, "at the end of the trip."

CHAPTER 2

Gennady drove to Washington D.C. first, to the cemetery where Paul was buried. It took him some time to find the grave, and when he found it he stopped a while and looked at the clean neat headstone and the manicured grass, and found that he was not sure why he had come here after all.

It was strange to see Paul's full name carved in the granite: *Paul Everard Preston*. Strange to realize that he had no face to match to the name. Strange that he had destroyed this stranger's life, almost by accident, a sentence that he dropped while half-drunk on champagne and fear.

The Communist Party line was that there was no afterlife, just as there was no God. But sometimes Gennady doubted this, and thought they would all be called to account some day for the evil they had done on earth, and then he would meet Paul face to face.

Gennady took off his glove and put one bare hand on the cold granite headstone. "Until then," he said, and stopped, embarrassed. His materialism reasserted itself. What was he doing, talking to a rock in a field full of rocks? The dead were dead. Paul couldn't hear anything, and there was no way to make amends.

Gennady patted the rock. "I'm sorry," he said.

Then he walked back through the graveyard, his breath

making white puffs in the air and his hands in the pockets of his heavy coat. He got back in his car and continued southward on I-95.

He intended to drive to Florida: all the way to Key West, perhaps, to see Ernest Hemingway's six-toed cats.

***

The American interstate system, still in its infancy when Daniel and Gennady crossed the US in the winter of 1959 and 1960, now covered the country like a cobweb. It made travel fast, you had to give it that, but boring, boring, with the same restaurants at every exit: McDonalds, Pizza Hut, Taco Bell.

Of course in 1959, all the drugstores and diners had sold essentially the same food, with perhaps some regional difference in pie fillings. But they were at least not five thousand carbon copies of the very same restaurant.

That earlier trip was much on his mind as he drove – or rather, Daniel in general was much on his mind. When Gennady had gone to New York, he had almost hoped to find that their former connection was now only a ghost of the past, and they had nothing in common anymore. Then the thing would be over and he could lay it to rest.

For a long time, the abrupt terrible ending of his relationship with Daniel had overshadowed everything else about it. He had put the whole thing in a box, not a fine lacquer box this time but battered cardboard tied viciously with twine, and tossed it to the back of his mind. And there it was quickly buried, because it turned out to be only the first in a series of calamities that swallowed up the next two years.

First Gennady and Alla divorced, an event no less devastating for being expected. Then Grandfather died, and Aunt Lilya had a heart attack, and for some time they thought she would die too. Gennady sat at her bedside in the hospital, more sober than he had been for some time, and cursed himself for taking that assignment in America. Perhaps if he had stayed, he and Alla would not have divorced. Certainly he would have had more time with Grandfather and Aunt Lilya.

And just when Aunt Lilya began to mend, and it seemed things might get better, Oksana's husband Alyosha stumbled, dead drunk, into the path of a truck.

This, too, was almost expected. Drunks often died like that. But Oksana collapsed, and barely got out of bed for a month, and Gennady had to stop drinking quite so much, because someone needed to look after Dasha.

Someday perhaps Gennady would tell Daniel about it all, but he saw no point in doing it now. And anyway, things had gotten better after that. By 1980 Aunt Lilya and Oksana were both back on their feet, and Gennady got the green Zhiguli, which Dasha named the Frog. In the summertime they drove out to the dacha and drank raspberry-infused vodka in the evenings as Dasha taught herself to play her great-grandfather's ukulele.

"I'll be a female Vysotsky," she said, with all the confidence of her fourteen years. "I'll write songs that speak to the soul of the people." She stopped to write something in the notebook that she carried with her everywhere that year. "The real people as they actually are. Not like in anything official." And she wrinkled her nose.

"You're going to sing about vodka?" Aunt Lilya scoffed.

"On a ukulele?" Gennady teased.

He got Dasha a guitar, and Alla's new husband agreed to give Dasha lessons for cheap. They all still lived in the same apartment building, and Alla often came up to drink tea with Oksana and Gennady, and oddly they were all great friends again.

A few years later Gennady bailed Dasha out when she got arrested playing in an illegal rock club. He scolded her all the way home: "Don't you have exams? Don't you have Komsomol meetings? Do you want to get expelled, do you want to lose your future? Did they at least let you play one of your songs, Dasha, you didn't get arrested playing nothing but other people's music, did you?"

She blinked, startled, and then said shyly, "Yes. We played 'Fossils.'"

"Ah. So you were singing about the Politburo." Gennady considered the matter. "So if I knew a source of blank cassette tapes," he said, "and, oh, let's say tape recorders..."

"Uncle Gennady, are you kidding?"

"Not at all. Unless you object to becoming a black marketeer? Such a good Komsomolka you are, with such great respect for the Soviet law..."

"Uncle Gennady!"

And then Gorbachev swept into power, and the rock clubs were allowed to reopen, and if Dasha didn't become a female Vysotsky, well, at least she and Gennady made a killing selling blank cassettes and tape recorders, because the official Soviet manufacturers couldn't come close to meeting the demand.

It was about this time that Daniel's letter arrived. The sight of his handwriting opened up the box Gennady had tossed to the back of his mind, and he found to his surprise that time had taken most of the sting from the memories. He was no longer sorry he had gone to America in 1975. Alla was happier with her new husband, who shared her dream of a quiet life, and Aunt Lilya had not died, after all. And Paul...

Well, Gennady had told Arkady about Paul in 1960; and it was also possible that some other Soviet agents had learned of Paul's proclivities on their own. (Those *sordid places* Paul mentioned in his suicide note, after all.) Either way, Paul would have died even if Gennady stayed in Moscow in 1975.

And it was so like Daniel to take the trouble to write to Gennady now that the political atmosphere made it possible.

At the dacha that summer, Gennady told Dasha and Oksana and Aunt Lilya about Daniel. Not the whole story, of course. An expurgated version, his picaresque adventures with his American friend, which he had not told them before because it was officially secret. "Isn't it still a secret?" Aunt Lilya said, querulous with the echo of Stalinist era paranoia.

"Which of you is going to tell the KGB?" Gennady asked.

"Anyone could tell the KGB once that girl's done writing a song about it!" Aunt Lilya said, gesturing at Dasha, who strummed with seeming aimlessness on her guitar and grinned. And Gennady lay back in the grass and smiled at the sky, and Daniel became a fond memory, something fine and beautiful and far distant that had happened long ago.

But then the Soviet Union fell, and the gangsters took over the black market, and they'd shoot you as soon as look at you. There was no reason to stay in Russia anymore, and, as Oksana reminded him, "You always wanted to travel, Gosha." And he remembered that he had never seen New York, or the Great Lakes, or the deserts that Ilf and Petrov had considered so fine;

and so he wrote to Daniel that he was coming to America.

He had no misgivings about it till he actually got off the plane at Washington Dulles, and contemplated the fact that he would soon see Daniel face to face, which was a very different thing from making peace with a Daniel who existed as a memory and a few words on the page. And the thought struck him, for the first time, that if he wanted, if there was still anything between himself and Daniel, which there couldn't be after all this time and pain, but if there was –

He wouldn't have to defect in order to stay. He might be able to be with Daniel without throwing everything else in his life away.

Perhaps he had hoped visiting Paul's grave would bring clarity. As if Paul would rise from the grave and give him a sign.

Any sign from Paul would undoubtedly say, *Fuck you*. And that was only fair.

On the third day of his trip, just a little north of the Florida state line, Gennady took an exit. He stopped in the shade to pull out his map and plotted a course on the old highway system instead of the interstate. This would take him through all the little towns, like the roads he and Daniel had traveled all those years ago.

But the little towns seemed to have died in the years since 1959. The downtowns were empty, the drugstores and diners and department stores closed, their windows covered over in fading newspaper. Only the government buildings clung on, courthouses and Carnegie libraries, lone tired outposts on the empty streets.

He wished he could take some pleasure in it: see how capitalism has hollowed out America! But capitalism was coming for Russia now, too. Not that socialism had done so well for it (what kind of country created a booming market for black market cassette tapes, after all?), but there had to be another way. Dasha made Germany sound idyllic – *Germany* of all places. Couldn't Russia have copied that instead of the Wild West, complete with gunslingers?

Gennady took a detour for the sea.

He found a quiet beach, almost empty on this rainy Tuesday in late February. The waves lapped at the sand and the seagulls called, and the water stretched away toward a vast distant horizon. Gennady walked along the edge of the waves so the warm water sometimes washed over his feet.

He had come to America because he remembered being happy here. He thought it would make him happy again, that he could recreate one of the happiest times in his life, rolling down the endless American roads, as if the road had been the most important thing and not Daniel in the seat by his side.

He looked out at the sea, and watched the waves roll up the beach, and let out a breath and drew it all in.

Then he went back to his car, and headed north.

***

It was late when Gennady arrived at Daniel's apartment, 7:30, but Daniel still wasn't home. He didn't arrive for another half hour, when he tromped down the hall with his head hanging low, a bag of takeout in his hand. He didn't notice Gennady until Gennady stood up.

Daniel dropped the takeout. "Gennady! Did the car break down?"

"No, no. The car is fine. I came back because..." He didn't want to have this conversation in the hall. "Let's go inside first."

"Yes, of course," Daniel said.

He unloaded cartons of Chinese food on the kitchen island, but he kept glancing at Gennady. The hopeful smile on his face should have made things easier, but nonetheless Gennady was not sure where to start, and he began to talk almost at random.

"Your interstates are very boring," Gennady said. "I left them to take the highways, but those are boring now too, Daniel, all the downtowns are dying, it's like the streets themselves have caught the Dutch Elm disease that once infected the trees. Of course all the downtowns were always very much alike, every American town very much like all the others, it was not perhaps any inherent interest about them that made our trip together such a pleasure, but the fact that I took it with you."

He caught his breath, and stopped talking, and felt a sting nearly like tears in his eyes. "I came back because I hoped..." Gennady had to catch his breath. "Will you come with me?"

He raised his eyes to Daniel only as he spoke the last sentence, and found Daniel staring at him. Then Daniel crossed the space between them, and crushed Gennady in a bear hug, and kissed both his cheeks like a Russian. "Yes, yes," Daniel said, and Gennady put both hands on Daniel's face and went up on his toes to kiss him on the lips.

They kissed a long time, until Gennady said, "Your food will get cold."

"To hell with it," Daniel said. "That's what microwaves are for."

But he let go of Gennady, and tore two paper towels off the roll to use as napkins, and filled two glasses with water. "I may not be able to leave right away," Daniel said. "I've got a lot of vacation time saved up, but I've got to get it approved before I can go anywhere. You don't mind waiting a little while, do you?"

"It's been thirty-two years. What are a few more weeks?"

Daniel swooped in and kissed him again. "Do you like fried rice?"

"Yes, probably. Nothing fried can be too bad."

Daniel popped the lids off two of the plastic containers and used them as plates, naming the dishes as he loaded them on: vegetable fried rice, orange chicken, General Tsao's chicken, moo shu pork.

"You bought all this food for yourself?"

"I like to have leftovers. It's easier than going out every day."

Once Daniel set the last carton aside he didn't sit down to eat, but caught Gennady by the shoulders and kissed him again. "After the trip," Daniel said. "Will you stay?"

Gennady moistened his lips. "There will be so many issues with immigration, with my visa, it will be so complicated..."

"Gennady, Gennady, Gennady." Daniel kissed him until Gennady shut up. "Gennady, I know it won't be simple, I know it might be hard as hell. But what was it you always said: you should grab happiness when it's on offer? And for the first time you can actually stay, the Soviet Union can't suck you back in like a black hole."

"The Soviet Union wasn't a black hole," Gennady protested. "All my family lived there, all my friends, everyone who meant anything in the world to me, except you. I wish that you could meet them, Daniel, I wish that you could see..."

And then a new vista seemed to open up before him. The

Soviet Union had fallen. The borders had been opened. "You could come visit," Gennady said. "You could come to see Russia with me."

Daniel's lips parted. Gennady lifted a finger to Daniel's mouth before he could speak. "We will have to wait till the situation stabilizes," he warned Daniel. "It may be some time. And certainly it would take some time for them to give you a visa to visit, a former FBI agent, it may move very very slowly."

Daniel kissed Gennady's finger. "Do you remember that day on the Boston Common, when the cherry trees were in bloom?" he said. "And we talked about visiting Moscow and Leningrad…"

"They are calling it St. Petersburg now."

"The Polyakovs must be so pleased." Daniel kissed Gennady again.

"You could meet my Aunt Lilya," Gennady said. "She flew fighter planes during World War II. And my cousin Oksana, who has been like a sister to me, and her daughter Dasha, if we can convince her to visit from Berlin…"

Daniel was looking at him, his face tender. "Would you like me to meet them?" he asked.

"Why else would I invite you, my friend?"

Daniel smiled. "Then of course I'd like to go."

HONEYTRAP

ABOUT THE AUTHOR

Aster Glenn Gray writes historical romance, romances with a fantastic twist, and fantasies with a romantic twist. (And maybe other things too. She is still a work in progress.) When she is not writing, she spends her time haunting libraries, taking long walks, and drinking copious amounts of hot chocolate. Her other books include *Briarley* and *The Threefold Tie*.

Made in the USA
Middletown, DE
28 January 2023